Smoke

and

Mirrors

A Forever Inked Novel

Sabrina Wagner

Stay Connected!

**Want to be the first to learn book news, updates and more?
Sign up for my Newsletter.**

https://www.subscribepage.com/sabrinawagnernewsletter

**Want to know about my new releases and upcoming sales?
Stay connected on:**

Facebook~Instagram~Twitter~TikTok
Goodreads~BookBub~Amazon

**I'd love to hear from you.
Visit my website to connect with me.**

www.SabrinaWagnerAuthor.com

Books by Sabrina Wagner

Hearts Trilogy
Hearts on Fire
Shattered Hearts
Reviving my Heart

Wild Hearts Trilogy
Wild Hearts
Secrets of the Heart
Eternal Hearts

Forever Inked Novels
Tattooed Hearts: Tattooed Duet #1
Tattooed Souls: Tattooed Duet #2
Smoke and Mirrors
Regret and Redemption
Sin and Salvation

Vegas Love Series
What Happens in Vegas
Billionaire Bachelor in Vegas
Behaving Badly in Vegas
Technically Yours in Vegas

Table of Contents

"911. What's your emergency?"

"I think he's going to kill me," I whispered. I was crammed back into the closet, hidden behind my skirts for work.

"What's your name ma'am?"

His heavy footsteps pounded on the hardwood floors getting closer by the second. "He's going to find me. Please help me."

"Where are you? What's your address?" the operator asked calmly.

"445 Willow Way Drive. Please hurry."

The closet doors flew open, and I scrunched back into the corner as far as I could go, praying he wouldn't see me. My breath hitched as the clothes parted, and his shoes and pants came into view.

"There you are, you little bitch!" he roared.

I dropped my phone to the ground. "Please…"

"Please what? Fuck you, you little slut!" He spied my phone on the floor and I scrambled to pick it up. "Did you call the fucking cops, you bitch?" His heel came down and smashed my phone and hand in one swift motion. I clutched my hand to my chest, sure the bones were broken. "You called the cops on me?" he roared. He grabbed me by my hair and yanked me forward, forcing me to my knees.

"Please don't hurt me. I'll do whatever you want." The tears streamed down my face. I was shaking with fear. This wasn't the first time he'd gotten physical with me, but it was the worst. Things had gotten progressively worse over the past few months, as had his drinking and cocaine use. His jealousy and paranoia had climbed to epic proportions.

It started with a backhand across the face when I didn't have dinner ready on time. He'd apologized and promised it wouldn't happen again, blaming it on his stressful day at work. The next time was when I left the bed unmade as I rushed off to work. A shove into the wall had my nose bleeding like a faucet. Again, he told me how much he loved me, promised me it was the last time. It was all a lie. I became an expert at covering my bruises and making excuses.

"Don't hurt you? What about me? Do you know how much you've hurt me? Embarrassed me? You need to be taught a lesson," he hissed in my ear.

He pulled me to my feet and pressed me back into the wall, his hand wrapped around my throat. I heard the click of the blade before I saw it. He ran it down my cheek and over my jaw until the sharp edge rested against my neck. His whiskey laden breath made me cringe, letting me know there would be no reasoning with him tonight. The blade pressed into my throat. "Why were you late tonight? Who is he? Did he fuck you good?"

"There's no one else, I swear! It's only you, baby."

"So, if I fuck you right now you'll be tight? You won't be wet from having his cock come inside you?"

"No, baby. There's no one else!" It was the truth. I'd always been faithful, even after the abuse started. I'd been foolish to think I could fix this. Fix us.

"We'll see about that," he sneered.

The knife slid down my throat to the buttons on my blouse. One by one he plucked them open and slid the knife down my body, the blade pressing into my skin. The sting of the blade barely registered in my mind. All I could think was *He's going to kill me.* "Please stop," I begged through my tears. "Don't do this. I love you." That was a lie. I couldn't love him anymore. He was a monster. Something found in my nightmares that had come to life.

His hand pawed at the button and zipper of my pants. He yanked them down in one swift motion and threw me onto the bed. I tried to crawl away, but he was faster. I was pinned to the bed by the weight of his body. One hand held my arms above my head while the other thrust inside me. "You fucking, lying bitch!" he screamed. "I can fucking smell him on you!"

"I swear I didn't do anything! I had a meeting, that's why I was late," I cried. "Liar!"

The sound of his belt unbuckling made me cringe. I knew what was going to happen and I was powerless to stop it. "Please don't," I cried, "not like this."

"What? My dicks not good enough for you anymore? Fuck you!" He thrust inside of me, my body shaking, wishing I could make this stop. "I'll be the last one to ever fuck you! You hear me bitch?"

He was relentless. He thrust in and out of me. Harder and harder. I closed my eyes, trying to pretend it wasn't happening. And I wondered if he had ever loved me at all.

He shuddered and roared out with his release. His body collapsed on mine, crushing me with his weight. Tears streamed from my eyes. I laid there lifeless, hoping it was over.

He crawled off and relief filled me.

I wasn't prepared for the fist that plowed into the side of my face. My head snapped to the side as the bones in my cheek shattered. The coppery taste of blood filled my mouth. I was yanked to the floor by my ankles, my back smashing onto the hard surface. He dragged me into the hallway and began kicking me. I curled up in a fetal position, desperate to save the life inside me.

"Get the fuck out!" he screamed. One more kick and I tumbled downward. My head smashed into something hard. Every part of my body was being battered, as I continued to free fall down the stairs.

Then the stabbing began, the pain searing me to the core. I couldn't see him, but I felt the knife piercing my back. I prayed for death. It had to be better than the torture I was enduring.

"Never again, you fucking bitch!"

Everything started to go numb, and darkness closed in. I barely felt the pain anymore. This was the end. I was sure of it. *I'm so sorry I disappointed you, daddy.* No parent should have to find their daughter like this. I should have been stronger. I should have been smarter. My mom and dad had raised me to be better than this.

The faint sound of sirens penetrated my foggy mind. I was fading fast. Struggling for breath, I gasped for air.

I rolled to my stomach and clawed my way toward the door, summoning up every ounce of energy left. "Help me," my voice strained, pleading to anyone who could hear me.

The door flew open, and an angel framed in glowing light leaned over my mangled body, "Who did this to you?"

I wanted God to send my attacker to hell for what he'd done to me. My body begin to drift away into nothingness.

It was two words. That was all. I forced them from my throat before darkness took over. "My husband."

3

Chapter 1
Layla

Dangerous.

That's the first word that came to mind when I set my eyes upon my new co-worker.

Beautiful.

That's the next word my mind conjured up. I'd never thought of a man as beautiful before. Handsome? *Yes.* Cute? *Sure.* Freakin' hot? *Absolutely.* Beautiful? *Never.*

Draven was beautiful. Six foot-three, maybe four, with defined cheekbones that looked like they'd been sculpted from stone, long dark hair tied up in a knot at the back of his head, and those eyes... amber with flecks of green. I felt like they were piercing my soul, trying to penetrate the deepest parts of me. My eyes roamed him from head to toe, taking in the perfection of his body. He had muscles on top of his muscles. His black T-shirt hugged tight across his wide chest. Black ink covered his arms in intricate designs.

I clenched my thighs together. I was sure I could come just from staring at him.

Draven was dangerously beautiful.

I blinked, realizing our handshake had lingered too long. I quickly pulled my hand back and wiped my sweaty palm on my jeans. "Welcome to Forever Inked."

My voice was raspy and breathless to my own ears. I cursed myself for letting him have this effect on me. He was here to work, and I was going to be his boss for all intents and purposes. Zack, our owner, was leaving for California with his wife, Rissa, for a month and he'd entrusted his beloved tattoo parlor to me in his absence.

"I'm happy to help. I owe Zack, so when he called, I couldn't say no."

The rough timbre of his voice vibrated through me from my head to my toes. I took a step back.

Straightening my spine, I led him to the empty studio that would be his. "This is your workspace. You can go ahead and get settled. I don't have you on the schedule until tomorrow, so there's no rush. If you need anything, my studio is right across from yours. I have an appointment in ten, so I need to get prepped. Are you good?" I asked, taking another step back.

He gave me a chin jerk. "I'm good." He eyed me up and down, "Are you good?"

I swallowed down the lump in my throat. "Perfect. Let me know if you need anything." I turned on my heel and strode through the door of my own studio, closing it behind me. I sagged against the door, counting down from five in my head. *Five, four, three, two... one.* I slowly let out the breath I was holding.

Dangerous. God help me.

I stopped dealing with dangerous men years ago. I'd gone to extremes to avoid them. I'd created a new life for myself. I was happy. Perhaps a little lonely, but safe. I'd take lonely over a dangerous man any day, no matter how beautiful he was.

I was perfectly happy. Some would say I was running, but I was living, and I'd come to appreciate that more than a normal person should.

I just didn't know how I was going to avoid Draven since I had to work with him every day. Not even God was going to be able to help me with this one.

Chapter 2
Draven

I chuckled to myself as her door shut. That was interesting.

As a matter of fact, I knew my time here was going to be very interesting. My new "boss" was curvy as hell, all tits and ass wrapped in tight jeans and a t-shirt that showed just a hint of cleavage. Layla's inky black hair fell halfway down her back and begged to have my hand wrapped around it as she screamed out my name. I didn't miss the way her perfectly drawn, dark-lined cat eyes had roamed over my body or the way she had clenched her thighs together.

I wouldn't be here long, but Layla could entertain me while I was.

Why Zack had moved to this tiny town when he could have gone anywhere, was beyond me. Utica, Michigan was nothing like New York. The only thing it provided for me was a reprieve from my family, something Zack and I had in common. But Michigan? For Christ's sake, he could have chosen something a little more enticing. Miami? New Orleans? Los Angeles? Nope. Utica. I'd never even heard of it before he called. I came anyway because I owed him and needed an escape.

A knock sounded on my doorframe and Chase, one of my other new co-workers, stuck his head in. "You all unpacked?"

"Getting there," I answered. "What's up?"

"We're all heading over to The Locker around eight. Rissa's doing her last show before she becomes famous. It's sort of a good luck and bon voyage thing."

"That's Zack's girl, right?" I hadn't met the new Mrs. Kincaid yet, but she was the whole reason I was here. Apparently, Rissa was going to LA to record her first album.

Chase shook his head. "Zack stole her from me. I was this close," he said holding up his fingers, "from sealing the deal with her."

Zack appeared out of nowhere and clapped Chase on the shoulder. "You never stood a chance, asshole. But keep dreaming." He then turned to me. "You should come. I'll introduce you to some people and it'll give you chance to bond with Layla and Chase. I want you to feel comfortable here."

I had no desire to go out but couldn't turn down the invitation without looking like an asshole. "Yeah, I'll be there."

"Cool," Zack said. "I need to know you guys are okay before I leave. I've never left for more than a week before and it's putting me a little on edge."

Chase crossed his arms over his chest. "Despite you stealing the beautiful Rissa from me, I've still got you covered. You know we won't let anything happen to your business while you're gone. All you need to do is soak up the sun and take care of my girl," he smirked.

"*My* girl," Zack growled.

Chase waved him off. "Same difference."

"*Not* the same difference. Not even close," Zack retorted.

"Now, now boys, play nice." I checked out the blond walking toward us holding a baby in her arms. She tucked one hand under the bundle and extended her other to me. "You must be Draven. I'm Rissa and this little girl is Alexandria."

I shook her hand. "Nice to meet you." I knew instantly why Chase teased Zack. "How do you always find the hottest chick around?" I asked him.

Zack wrapped his arm around Rissa's waist and kissed her on the head. "I'd say it was luck, but with this one I'm pretty sure it was destiny."

I'd forgotten how smooth he was. Zack had always been a ladies' man. He'd hit the jackpot with Rissa.

"Are you coming to my show tonight?" Rissa asked. "A lot of our clients will be there, and it will be good for them to put a face with a name."

"Yeah, I'm coming. What time should I be there? I want to get some unpacking done upstairs." I turned to Zack. "Thanks for the apartment, man. It's pretty cool that all I have to do is go up the stairs and I'm home."

Zack rubbed the back of his neck. "Moving out was bittersweet, I loved that apartment. But once Alexandria was born, it wasn't really practical for us anymore. On the upside, we've got a huge house to fill with kids."

Rissa rolled her eyes. "Let's get used to having one first, then we'll talk about more." Rissa handed Zack their daughter and leaned in to give me a hug. "We're glad you're here. Meet us around eight or so. The Locker is just down the street. You can't miss it."

After putting most of my things away in the apartment and setting up my studio, I was ready for a stiff drink. Chase and Layla had already left, so I locked the shop and headed down the street. There was a line outside the door, and I walked right to the front of it. Zack assured me I was on the list and wouldn't have to wait. Sure enough, once I gave him my name, I was ushered right in.

I went to the bar and ordered a vodka straight up. I wasn't sure I was going to fit in here. I'd stay the required month, no longer. Everyone had been nice so far, but it wasn't New York.

Zack clapped me on the shoulder. "You're here. We've got a table up front."

He led me to a table with Chase and Layla. She was busy texting on her phone. Layla let out a huff and set her phone down. "Oh, hey," she acknowledged me and pushed back from the table. "I need a drink. Anybody want anything?"

"Have Lou put it on my tab," Zack told her.

She squinted at him with her hands on her hips. "You think I won't take you up on that, but I will."

He laughed. "I know you will. Go get your drink on."

"Damn right, I will." She winked, turned on her high heels and strode off to the bar.

"She's feisty. What's her story?" I asked.

"She's a lot of bark, not a whole lot of bite," Chase answered. "She's more like a kitten than a pit bull. Unless you piss her off, then all bets are off. I'd stay on her good side if I were you," he advised.

I nodded my understanding. I hoped her good side was on her back, because that's where I planned to have her. I'd have her purring in no time. "She have a boyfriend?"

Chase and Zack gave each other a knowing look. "Don't go wading in those waters man, it's not safe," Chase answered.

"I've known Layla for almost five years and I've never seen her with anyone serious," Zack admitted. "She keeps her personal life very private."

"So, no boyfriend?"

Zack shook his head. "Not for lack of guys trying. She gets hit on all the time, but ninety-nine percent of the time, she goes home alone. Actually," he mused, "I've got no fucking idea what she does."

"Same," Chase confirmed. "She's an enigma."

Just then, Layla returned with her drink. "Don't go using big words you can't spell."

"I can spell it," Chase retorted. "I-N... I-N-I-G-A... fuck! Who cares if I can spell it? I know what it means."

Layla threw her head back and laughed. "Sure, you do." She reached over and ruffled his hair.

Chase swatted her hand away. "Enough with the hair. It takes a lot of work to look this good."

She rolled her eyes. "Yeah. You've got that *I just rolled out of bed and don't give a fuck* look mastered."

"Welcome to my life," Zack sighed. "I swear these two were brother and sister in a past life."

"I can handle it. Got one of each, it ain't nothing new," I assured him.

Layla flipped me off across the table. Feisty... and I loved it! I wanted nothing more than to grab that finger and suck it into my mouth, if for no other reason than to see how she reacted. I was *that* guy. A total asshole that pushed limits and crossed boundaries. All for my own entertainment.

"Jesus Christ, Layla! Can you at least pretend to be on your best behavior on Draven's first day here?"

She held her hand to her ample chest. "My bad! I promise I'll be on my best behavior while you're gone, Zack. I don't want you to worry. I'll be a total professional. Cross my heart."

I put my hand on his shoulder. "Don't sweat it, man. I don't get offended that easily. I have a feeling Layla and I are going to get along just fine. No worries."

Layla gave me a hard stare across the table. I didn't know what her problem was, but I was pretty sure if she could shoot flames from those green eyes, I'd be toast by now. Little did she know that she'd already started a fire within me. A curiosity. I wouldn't be happy until I solved the puzzle that was her.

Returning her stare, I refused to back down, "Isn't that right, Layla? Zack's got nothing to worry about."

"Absolutely nothing," she deadpanned. Then her face broke into a huge smile and she focused back on Zack. "I can't believe you guys are going to be gone for a month, but I'm sure you'll be so busy that it'll fly by. Rissa's got to be crazy full of nerves."

Pride filled Zack's face. "She is. This is her dream come true. I'm just glad I get to be by her side for it. Every song slated for the first album, she wrote herself."

As if it were her cue, Rissa stepped on the stage and the bar went crazy.

Chapter 3
Layla

I banged on the door, impatiently tapping my foot. The lock clicked, and the door swung open. I didn't wait for an invitation before pushing inside. "Where were you?" I demanded. "You didn't answer my texts."

"Hello to you too." Brian had been my neighbor across the hall for the last two years. My very built, very attractive, very sexy, very gay neighbor. Once we'd gotten past the embarrassing way I'd first flirted with him, we'd become fast friends.

I didn't have a lot of friends. To be someone's friend, you had to trust them. Trust was not my strong suit. I could count my friends on one hand, and I worked with two of them, Zack and Chase.

Brian was my very best friend. The only one who knew the real me. The only one I could let my guard down with.

I plopped down on his couch in an exaggerated manner, dropping my head into my hands. He shut the door. "What's wrong, baby girl?"

"Nothing. Everything. I don't know." I finally glanced up at him. He wasn't wearing a shirt and the top button of his jeans was popped open. Guilt washed over me. "Are you on a date?" I stole a quick look toward the bedroom. "Do you have company?"

He sat down next to me. "No one that can't wait." He gently ran his hand through my hair. "What's got your panties all in a twist?"

I wiped my hands on my black jeans. "Forget it. It can wait." Blowing out a breath, I stood and headed for the door. With my hand on the knob I asked, "Is he cute?"

Brian quirked his eyebrow at me.

"I know, I know. You only date hot guys. How is this even fair? Just one little peek, please?"

Brian shook his head and kissed me on the cheek. "You sure you're okay?"

I attempted a smile. "Of course. I'll see you tomorrow. Have fun and don't forget to wrap it before you tap it."

"Always." He opened the door for me, and I slipped across the hall. My key slid into the lock, my eyes cast downward. "Layla, you sure?'" Concern laced his voice.

"Always." I turned the knob. "Good night, Brian."

"Good night, Layla."

Shutting the door behind me, I went through my ritual of securing the three locks that kept me protected. Even those locks didn't make me feel safe tonight. Nothing could.

Draven Constantine had me tied up in knots. The way he looked at me and his subtle innuendos, tore at something deep inside. I slid down the door and dropped my head to my knees.

It shouldn't have bothered me. I'd been dealing with guys like him since I started tattooing. Arrogant assholes who thought that I would turn into a puddle at their feet and do anything to spend the night with them. I'd coated myself with Teflon years ago. It was a requirement of the job. I'd tatted a ton of guys who'd come on to me. Each one of them searching for something I couldn't give.

But Draven, he was a temptation that'd be hard to resist.

I pushed to my feet and stumbled to my bedroom. I yanked open the nightstand drawer and pulled out the framed photo that served as a reminder.

The girl that stared back at me looked so happy. Her honey-colored hair was pulled up in a mass of curls on top of her head. Her wedding dress hugged her curves in all the right places, showing off the flawless skin that covered her shoulders and arms. The handsome man with his arm around her waist looked at her with pure love and adoration. Their faces held the promises of happily ever after.

It was all a lie.

There was no happily ever after for her.

She'd learned that monsters didn't have fangs and claws. They looked just like the man in the picture.

I closed my eyes and remembered the words he'd said. *I promise to love and cherish you, 'til death do us part. You're the best thing that ever happened to me, Jenna. I'm never letting you go.*

Lies.

All of it had been lies. Smoke and mirrors.

I shoved the picture back in the drawer and slammed it shut before more memories could seep out. I'd been searching for a reminder, not a walk down memory lane. The past needed to stay locked in that drawer where it couldn't hurt me anymore.

I stripped out of my clothes and threw on an old t-shirt and sleep shorts. I scrubbed my face clean of the makeup that served as my mask. I'd put it back on tomorrow, but here in my apartment it wasn't necessary.

Sleep evaded me. I tossed and turned as the ache between my legs intensified. It hadn't been this bad in a very long time. Giving up, I reached into the nightstand drawer and pulled out my very expensive battery-operated boyfriend. It was a good one, with rabbit ears that tickled me in all the right places.

Damn Draven! He had me wanting things I shouldn't want.

I slipped my sleep shorts off under the sheets and turned the vibrator to its highest setting. Slipping it inside me, I succumbed to the feelings of pleasure. In and out, in and out. Slow at first, savoring the feeling. I let my mind wander to images of his face and body, and the fantasy of him inside me, his breath on my neck as he kissed me, the power of his thrusts as I let him have me, his mouth sucking on my breasts. My hand moved faster and faster. The orgasm continued to build in intensity, cresting to the point that it was almost painful. Finally, it broke, bringing me the release and pleasure I'd been denying myself.

I panted as my body came down from the high. Then the self-loathing took over. He shouldn't have this much control over me. Not after one day. Or two. Or three. Fuck… not ever! I was better than that. Stronger.

Tomorrow was a new day. A new start. I'd reinforce my walls. Make them impenetrable. No way would Draven Constantine get inside my heart or mind, and definitely not my body.

I woke to the rhythmic knocking on my door. Brian. He tapped out the secret code that told me it was him. Stumbling to the door, still half asleep, I checked the peephole just to be sure.

I undid the three locks and swung the door open. Brian strode in carrying coffee and a brown paper bag that smelled delicious. "Good morning, sunshine."

He handed me my coffee and pulled two chocolate chip muffins from the bag. "Someone had a good night." I took my coffee and plopped down on the couch.

"And someone obviously didn't. Want to talk about it?" He sat next to me, pushing a muffin into my hand.

I shrugged my shoulders sadly. "Just work stuff. The new guy started yesterday."

"And?"

"I don't trust him." I picked at the top of my muffin, tearing off a small piece and popping it in my mouth.

Brian wrapped his arm around my shoulder, and I sank into him. "You don't trust anyone, Layla."

I looked up at him with doe eyes. "I trust you. Sure I can't persuade you to change teams? I mean, you're like the perfect guy. We could be really happy together."

He kissed the top of my head. "Sorry, baby girl, not happening. But if I dug chicks, I'd be all over you."

"Awww. That's the sweetest thing anyone's ever said to me," I drawled sarcastically. I pulled another piece of muffin off and savored the goodness.

"So, what's wrong with this guy? Is he a troll or something? Third eye? Gnarly teeth?"

I laughed. "Definitely not. He's actually kind of... beautiful."

"Beautiful?"

"Yeah." I sighed.

"So, what's the problem? Was he mean to you? Cuz I can kick his ass if you need me to."

I waved him off. "I appreciate the offer, but he wasn't mean to me. Just the opposite. I think he wants to get in my pants."

Brian's face broke out into a shit-eating grin. "You gonna let him?"

I nearly choked on my muffin. "No!"

"Why not? He's beautiful and I assume there's a hot body to go along with that. Why not explore it?"

I gave him a stern glare. "You know why."

He sighed. "How long has it been since you've had sex, baby girl?"

"Last night." I sat up proudly.

"With someone besides yourself. Vibrators don't count," he clarified.

I deflated. "It's been a while."

"How long is a while?"

I picked at the polish on my black nails. I was the queen of avoidance. "So, who was the guy last night? Is it serious?" Getting Brian to talk about his conquests was usually effective.

He squinted at me. "Not going to work this time, baby girl. How long?"

I buried my face in my hands. "Five years."

"Five years! How is that possible?" he asked incredulously.

"Lots of batteries." Admitting this to him was a low point. I was twenty-eight and well on my way to becoming a crazy cat lady. If I only had a cat.

"God girl, aren't you dying for some dick? Nothing since…?"

I shook my head. "Nothing. I'm not even sure I'd know what to do with a dick anymore."

"That's so sad. I can give you some pointers, you know, in case you change your mind," he offered.

"Awww. Again, with the sweetness. Why do all the good guys have to be gay?"

Brian pulled me in for a hug. "There are good guys out there, Layla. You just have to give them a chance. You owe it to yourself."

"Maybe someday." Today was not that day and neither was tomorrow. But maybe one day, just not any day soon.

I went into work with a new attitude. Total professionalism, just like I'd promised Zack. I could do this. I even showed up early. Yay me!

I straightened and cleaned the waiting area, wiping down the table and arranging the photo albums on top of it. Then I checked the appointments for the day. It was unnecessary. I already knew them by heart.

Draven's first appointment was at ten, which meant he'd be showing up in the next twenty minutes.

As if on cue, the hairs on the back of my neck stood on end. "Morning, *pisoi.*"

I spun around, trying to reel in my confusion at the foreign word. "Excuse me?"

He winked at me. "I said, good morning."

"Good morning," I mumbled back. "You've got an appointment in twenty. Do you need anything? Anything I can help you with?"

"Not at this moment but check back with me later." He winked again.

I wasn't sure what that meant but dismissed it. "How's the apartment?" I tried to remain professional. I could do this. My status here depended upon it.

"It's great. Better than expected," he admitted. "The bed's big. Plenty of room."

I turned my back on him, not feeding into his innuendos. "Zack wanted you to be comfortable. He and Rissa bought all new furniture."

"So, what's the story with them?" he asked. "I gotta be honest, I'm shocked he got married."

"Don't be. They were like two magnets drawn to each other. They both fought it, but in the end, you can't fight what's meant to be. He pushed, she pulled. They couldn't stay away from each other. I've never seen two people more in love than those two. Nothing could have kept them apart." I was a hopeless romantic. Even if I didn't believe it would happen to me, some people were meant to be happy. Zack and Rissa were destined from day one. It was obvious from the first time I saw them together.

I swallowed down the lump in my throat. I knew I wasn't ever destined for that kind of love. BOB was my best chance at happiness. So sad, but true. He had been my longest standing relationship.

Draven reached over me, brushing against my arm, to grab the appointment book. Heat flushed my face, and I took a step to the side.

He chuckled. "I'm not going to bite, you know." Then he leaned down close to my ear. "Not unless you want me to." He purposely rubbed his arm against mine again.

A shiver ran up my spine. I hated reacting to him that way. It made me weak, and I wasn't weak. I wasn't *that* girl anymore. "Definitely not."

He cocked his head to the side. "Suit yourself." Draven stepped back and examined the appointment book. "I only have two appointments today?"

"We get a ton of walk-ins. Trust me, you'll be busy most of the day. I already put the paperwork in your studio." I took two steps back.

Draven took two steps forward. "Do I make you uncomfortable, Layla?"

I swallowed down the lump in my throat. Hell yes, he made me uncomfortable. There was no way I'd tell him that.

The bell over the door jingled and Chase walked in. "What's up, peeps?"

I breathed out a sigh of relief. *Saved by the bell.* Chase's carefree manner instantly broke the spell I was under. "Hey, Chase. Coffee's on in the break room."

"Thank God. I hardly got any sleep last night."

"Late night?" I asked.

"Becca." Nothing else needed to be said. Chase was a manwhore. He and Becca had been on again and off again for the last several months. In between, he hadn't been lonely.

Even though Chase could be a bit of an idiot, he seemed to do well with the ladies. He had boyish good looks and a heart of gold. He was sweet, even if I would never admit it. I saw him more as a baby brother. There was never a thought about the two of us hooking up and I found comfort in that. We worked well together, and the sexual tension was nonexistent. He was a friend. End of story.

Draven had disappeared into his studio and for that I was thankful. I couldn't stand having him so close to me. If we were going to work together, distance was essential.

Chapter 4
Draven

I picked up the paperwork and threw it back on the counter. Fucking A. I moved here for this? Two appointments?

I knew it wasn't Layla's fault, but fucking hell. I would have done better staying in New York dealing with my old man's shit.

He wanted me to be part of the *family business*. I left, much to his dismay, but for what? The apartment was great, but I needed to make money if I wanted to live any kind of life.

What my father offered me, was way better than this. Shady as hell, but cash in hand was worth something. I'd tried my whole life to escape who my father was, but as I got older it got harder. I took this job to get away from him for a while. I couldn't help but wonder if it was all a mistake.

Fuck! I'd give it a month. That was all I'd committed to. Then I'd go home and grovel at my father's feet for forgiveness. No doubt he'd make me suffer for leaving. I'd start at the bottom again, as a low-level soldier for The Organization.

As the oldest of his children and being the best at what I did, I'd rise quickly back to the top, but I would be punished. I hated that life, but none of it really mattered. When you were the son of a Romanian mob boss, you towed the line. My being here was a gift. I knew that. He was letting me get my rebellious streak out of my system. I was a fool to think that my father would ever willingly let me walk away for good.

I tried it once and it nearly got me killed. I thought the Marines would be my chance to form my own identity. And I did to a certain point. I got tougher. I became a man. I thought I was invincible.

Until I wasn't.

My team was scouting the perimeter of our camp, checking for hostiles. The vehicle in front of ours hit an IED and exploded, rocking the Earth and catapulting debris into the air all around us. The power of the blast flipped our Humvee, sending it careening head over ass. The last thing I remembered was being tossed like a ragdoll inside the truck.

From what I was told, Zack was the first one out of the wreckage. He pulled my lifeless body and two others from the Humvee. The gas tank cracked, and fuel poured out, covering the ground. Zack had just gotten the last of us to safety before everything went up in flames. I owed him my life.

During my recovery, I spent a lot of time with Zack. I watched and learned as he tattooed the other guys in our unit. Turned out all the doodling I did as a kid was more than the *stupid waste of time* my father said it was. I actually had a talent that had been suppressed. Zack trained me and soon we became a highly demanded team.

So yeah, now I was here. I owed Zack everything. My life not being the least of it.

I sucked in a deep breath and stole a glance at Layla. A month. Plenty of time to get that raven-haired firecracker in my bed. She was playing hard to get, but she had no idea how tenacious I could be. For better or worse, I got that trait from my father.

When Layla said I would be busy all day, she wasn't fucking kidding. We'd been nonstop, crazy busy.

Today was Zack's last day before he left. He leaned against the door of my studio. "It won't always be this hectic."

I shook my head. "Busy is good. Makes the day go by fast."

"I just wanted to thank you again for being here. I know you only committed to a month, but I'm hoping you'll stay."

I finished wiping off the counter and threw everything into the trash. "I'm not making any promises."

"Understood. I know this place is worlds away from New York but if you give it a chance you might just like it. It's not a bad place to settle down."

"Settling down isn't exactly on my radar." I laughed. "Besides, you know I have commitments back home. My father…"

Zack held his hand up. "I know all about family commitments. I also know that separation can make things a lot fucking clearer. You're not the only one with a dysfunctional family. This shop… we're our own family. It's a little like the Island of Misfit Toys, but make no mistake, there isn't anything I wouldn't do for any one of them. We've all got our issues, but here," he pointed to the ground, "this is our safe place. We've got each other's backs."

"I'll think about it." It was an empty promise he needed to hear. I didn't want him to worry about the time he would be spending in California with his wife and daughter.

He clasped my hand. "It's nice to know I have someone I can trust."

"Absolutely."

Chapter 5
Layla

I stood in Zack's office as he looked over the books one more time. "Stop worrying. I got this."

"You know I trust you. It's just…" Zack sighed.

"It's a long time to be gone," I finished, plopping down in the chair across from his desk.

He scrubbed a hand over his face. "Yeah. Do you need me to go over the books again?"

I held up a hand. "Stop. I've got a college education. I can do this." Zack and I had never talked about my past. I hadn't talked about it with anyone but Brian. What happened to me was no one's business.

Zack cocked his head to the side. "You went to college? I didn't know that. How come you've never said anything?"

I shrugged my shoulders. "I guess it never came up." I raised my fists above my head in a proud gesture. "Graduated summa cum laude from Oregon State. Was a cheerleader too." I smiled for the first time in days at the memory.

Zack rubbed the scruff on his chin and tried to suppress a laugh. "No shit. You were a cheerleader?"

I nodded. "Don't laugh. I was good at it. I was a flyer, you know, the girls you see getting thrown up in the air." I pointed at my chest. "That was me."

He rested his arms on the desk. "I'm sorry. I just wouldn't have guessed. You'd think I'd know more about you for how long I've known you. What's your degree in?"

He would know more about me if I had wanted him to. It all came back to trust. It was my biggest hurdle in life. I swallowed down my discomfort. Sharing this little piece of myself wouldn't hurt. Zack was a safe place.

"I got my degree in elementary education and art. I was an art teacher for a year," I confessed.

"What made you stop? How'd you end up here?"

"Circumstances," I said vaguely. "I just needed a change."

I saw the look of shock Zack tried to hide when I told him I was a teacher, and he didn't buy my line of bullshit on why I quit. But he didn't press me for details.

"You know what? Chase was right about you, Layla Roberts. You are an enigma." I could tell he was teasing, but his words held some truth.

I rolled my eyes. "A girl's got to have some secrets. What would be the fun if there was no mystery?"

Zack tapped his fingers on his desk. "Secrets have a way of biting you in the ass. Ask Rissa if you don't believe me."

I knew what he was referring to. Rissa had been engaged to Zack's brother. When he died, she found out she was pregnant. Zack and Rissa became friends when he went to New York for the funeral. They began dating and Rissa hid her pregnancy. It all worked out in the end, but it was hell for the two of them for a long time. Zack was actually Alexandria's uncle, but he was raising her as his daughter. She was one lucky baby.

My secrets really didn't have an impact on anyone here. The only one they haunted was me. Oregon was a long way away and so was my past.

I quickly changed the subject. "I can't believe you're taking my best girlfriend to California for a whole month. I'm going to miss the two of you."

He laughed. "Technically she's taking me to California, but I'd gladly follow her anywhere. Rissa's my heart."

I smiled at him. "I know. Don't worry. The shop will be fine."

"I know it will be, but what about you? Will you be fine?" Deep lines furrowed his brow.

"Always am."

He didn't look convinced. "I'll only be a phone call away and I can be back here in a few hours if you need anything." He stood from behind his desk and came around to give me a tight hug. "And I mean it. Anything, Layla."

I fought to keep the tears out of my eyes while I hugged him back. "I know. I love ya, Zack."

"Love ya too."

Wiping the tears that threatened to fall, I pushed him back. "Enough with all the mushy stuff. Get home to your wife and go make her a star."

"That's the plan," he couldn't keep the smile from his face. You could tell from just looking at him how much he loved Rissa.

I used to know that feeling and a bit of jealousy wound its way inside of me. Some people were destined for love. Others were damned to a life of loneliness.

I laid awake in bed last night, feeling alone and unsure. I didn't know if it was Zack leaving, he'd been a constant in my life for so long, or the fact that I was going to see Draven again.

Do I make you uncomfortable, Layla?

Yes. Very uncomfortable. I wouldn't let it show though.

I sat in my studio drawing up a sketch for a rose tattoo. My client had been specific. I sat back and looked at what I had drawn. It was a symbol of my own fucked up life. A beautiful flower that had started to wilt and die. The petals falling off and crumbling.

That was my life.

"Hey." Draven poked his head into my studio. "I just wanted to let you know I was here."

"Okay," I said without looking up.

"What are you working on?" He stepped inside and leaned over my shoulder. My skin began to prickle with his closeness. I smelled his cologne and took a deep breath. Why did everything about him have to affect me? And why did he have to smell so good?

"It's a mock-up for one of my clients." I tried not to breathe. I didn't want to smell him.

"It's good. Really good," he complimented. "May I?" He held out his hand for the pencil I was holding.

I pushed my stool back and handed over my pencil. "Knock yourself out."

He quickly added some extra lines and shading. I hated to admit it, but it was better. "I wasn't finished," I snapped.

He dropped the pencil and backed up. "Sorry. I was just trying to help."

"I don't need your goddamn help. I know what the fuck I'm doing." I don't know why I lashed out at him. He didn't deserve it, but a need gnawed inside of me to do it. A need to keep a distance between us. If I pissed him off enough, maybe he'd leave me the fuck alone. The last thing I wanted was to feel any gratitude toward him.

23

"Didn't say you didn't. What the fuck ever." Draven leaned against the wall with no intention of leaving. "Is this the way it's going to be for the next month?"

I glared at him, trying not to let on that I was checking him out. Men should not be that sexy. Not straight ones at least. "What are you talking about?" I snapped again.

"Me trying to be nice and you barking down my throat for no reason."

I let out a self-depreciating laugh. "I've got my reasons."

His jaw twitched. "Which have nothing to do with me."

He was right, but admitting it was not on my agenda. He didn't have a clue what my reasons were, and I had no intention of telling him. "You're standing in my studio uninvited. That's reason enough."

He shook his head in disgust. "God, you're a bitch."

That stung. I tried to not let his words sink into my skin. "Then maybe you should leave." My voice hitched betraying the façade I tried to portray.

My bitchiness was a way to keep people away. And most of the time it worked. That didn't mean it didn't hurt when someone called me out on it.

I hadn't always been this way. It was born out of necessity. Being sweet and nice made people think they could walk all over you. I wasn't that girl anymore.

Draven continued to stare at me and when I said nothing else, he left. I stood from my stool and shut the door. A tear rolled down my cheek and I quickly wiped it away. I wasn't weak. No way in hell I'd let him know he'd gotten to me.

Why him calling me a bitch bothered me so much I didn't know. I'd gotten what I wanted, him leaving, and that was all I should have cared about. But for some reason, it didn't feel as good as it should have.

Draven and I pretended as if the other didn't exist the rest of the morning. He did his job, and I did mine. That's why I was here. To do a job, not be distracted by a pretty face. Or his ridiculous god-like body. Nope. He wasn't a distraction at all.

Chapter 6
Draven

I saw the hurt flash through Layla's eyes when I called her a bitch, but then it was gone. I'd hit a nerve and it wasn't my proudest moment. Day three was off to a great start. Twenty-seven more to go.

At lunchtime I went out back to call my old man. Lighting a cigarette, I let the smoke fill my lungs. I hardly ever smoked anymore. It was a habit I picked up in the military and never fully shook. Talking to my father required a cigarette. I never knew what to expect with him.

"Draven. It's about fucking time."

"I've been busy. I got your message. What do you want?"

"Cut the attitude. Don't forget you're only there because I let you go. Don't mistake my generosity for something else." His accent was thick, something he'd never lost from the old country. In reality, I think he chose to keep it as a measure of intimidation. Which worked most of the time.

I rolled my eyes. He didn't intimidate me, but it pissed me off that he tried. "My apologies. What did you need, *tată?*" *Father.* My Romanian wasn't as fluent as he would have liked, but it was passable. My mother was American. She died when I was twelve. Or maybe she was murdered. I'd never know.

Since she'd been gone, my father had many mistresses, but never settled down again. A string of sleazy women had been paraded in and out of my life. It was probably the reason I'd never had a girlfriend. My father treated women as disposable, something that had rubbed off on me over the years.

Women were complications and a vulnerability. In the *family business*, if you pissed off the wrong person, chances were they'd come for those you cared about before coming for you. I'd seen it too many times to count. My rule had been simple: no vulnerabilities.

That didn't mean I didn't get my dick wet on a regular basis. I had my own parade of sleazy women for that.

My father's voice brought me back to my original question. "I might have a job for you."

Dread filled my chest. "Fuck. What kind of job?" It could have been anything from a delivery to a disposal.

"I'll let you know when the time comes. Be available."

"You've got connections here?" I asked.

He let out a chuckle. "I have connections everywhere. You're in Detroit. You think shit doesn't happen there?"

"I'm not *in* Detroit. I'm *by* Detroit."

"Close enough. Sit tight and wait for my instructions."

"That's not why I'm here," I insisted.

"You're there because I let you be. Make yourself useful and don't be such a pussy."

The line went dead. I stared at the phone. He was a cold fucking bastard. I should have known this wasn't going to be a month-long vacation. I was an idiot for being so naïve.

The back door pushed open, and Chase poked his head out. "There you are, man. Your next appointment's here."

"Yeah, all right." I stubbed out my cigarette and followed Chase inside. The blond in the waiting area was a knockout. Big tits covered by a tank top that could barely be called a shirt and long, tanned legs with cut-off jean shorts.

She scanned me with narrowed eyes. "You're not Zack." Then her lips curled into a wicked smile. "But you'll do."

Her reaction wasn't foreign to me. I knew what I looked like, and I'd never had a problem attracting women. I quirked an eyebrow at her. "What's your name, darling?"

She twirled the ends of her hair around a finger. "Sydney."

I reached forward and took her hand. "I'm Draven. Come on back, darling. Let's see if we can make you a happy woman today."

Her cheeks blushed crimson. "I have no doubt you can make me very happy," she said coyly.

This was too fucking easy.

My thoughts drifted back to Layla and our interaction this morning. That woman was already making me insane. She acted like I had the damn plague. Every time I got close to her, she moved away. Judging by the way this blond was following me, Layla was the one with the problem, not me.

Once inside my studio, Sydney shut the door behind her. "You're new here," she stated the obvious.

I leaned back against the counter. "Don't worry. I know what I'm doing." I winked and flashed her my panty dropping smile just to see her blush again.

She straddled the chair and leaned back. "I'm sure you do."

I pushed off the counter and straddled the chair in front of her. "What are we doing for you today? What is it you want?"

Sydney tapped a manicured finger against her lips. "Well, I was thinking I want a cross," her finger ran down between her breasts and tapped on the right side of her hip, "right here."

"I think I can do that." Standing from between her legs I grabbed my portfolio and turned to the pages with crosses. "Pick out something you like. If you can't find anything, I'll draw something else." I handed her the book.

She carefully contemplated her choices. Her finger tapped on a page. "This one."

Leaning over her shoulder, I looked at the cross she picked, but not before I checked out her ample cleavage. "That's cool. Where exactly do you want it?"

Sydney started to unbutton her shorts and pulled them to the side. "Right here."

I pulled the picture from the book. "You'll have to slide your shorts down. Just leave your panties on."

She giggled. "I'm not wearing any panties."

Fuck me!

Temptation stirred in my cock. I rubbed a hand over my jaw. "Seems we have a situation."

She started to remove her shorts. "I'm not shy. It doesn't bother me if it doesn't bother you."

I reached a hand out to keep her shorts in place. "How about this? I'll go make the transfer, you take your shorts off and cover yourself with this." I handed her a large, black swatch of material to drape over herself.

"It's not necessary," she insisted.

"If I want to keep my job, it is. Otherwise, I can't promise I'll keep my hands to myself."

Her fingers danced across my chest. "What if I don't want you to?"

She was bold. I'd give her that. It'd been a while since I'd dipped my dick into something as perfect as her and what she was offering was hard to turn down. "Tattoo first. We can discuss anything else after that."

Before I could change my mind, I headed to the back to make the transfer. As tempting as Sydney was, I couldn't get Layla out of my mind. I'd hurt her feelings this morning. She'd never admit it, but I knew I did. What was killing me was the guilt that it made me feel. It wasn't a familiar feeling. I rarely felt guilty about anything.

Like Sydney. I wasn't going to fuck her today. If it hurt her feelings, I wouldn't give a shit. Girls like her were a dime a dozen.

But my boss... there was something different about her. She had a tough exterior, but I had a feeling underneath she was just as Chase had said... a kitten. A *pisoi*. I shook the idea out of my head and returned to my studio.

Lost in my own head, I rushed around the corner and crashed right into Layla. She bounced off my chest and I grabbed her hip to steady her. She looked up at me with big green eyes. "I'm sorry," she said breathlessly, as her demeanor softened.

"Me too." My apology wasn't about our crash, but our earlier interaction. I still had my hand on her hip and backed away holding up the transfer. "Just prepping for my client."

I opened the door to my studio and Layla's eyes glanced through the opening, narrowing. "Wouldn't want you to keep her waiting." She stormed off, the niceties we'd just shared gone.

"Damn it," I mumbled and continued into my studio, only to see what Layla was so pissed about.

Sydney was barely covered. Her hip and side of her ass there for me to see, as well as a sliver of her bare pussy. I choked back my reaction, shut the door, and stepped to the counter, preparing my tools.

"Is this okay?" she asked.

I pushed down all the attraction I felt toward her and adjusted the drape, covering more of her. "That's better."

Although there was a sexual attraction, I felt nothing else toward Sydney. She frowned. "Yeah. That's great."

I put on my glasses and got to work. Once I got in the zone, that was it. The inking and swiping became a monotonous routine. I wasn't even thinking about Sydney's pussy. Mostly. Instead, I concentrated on my job. The cross I inked on Sydney's hip was stellar. First class. A work of art. I wiped the last of the blood and ink off her hip. "All done," I declared.

Sydney glanced down at the work I had done. "It's amazing." Before I knew what was happening, she whipped the drape off herself, showing me everything she had to offer. She stood naked from the waist down in front of the mirror on the back of the door. She swayed her hips from side to side. "What do you think?"

I looked away from her perfect ass. "If you're happy, then I've done my job."

She spun around. "I don't think you're quite done. I could be a lot happier. We both could be. I could make you very happy."

I didn't know why I was turning down this gift that was being presented to me on a silver platter, but it didn't feel right. I picked up her shorts from the floor and threw them at her. "As much as I'd love to take you up on that, I'll have to pass. Your hip needs time to heal, so maybe some other time." I pointed to the chair. "Lay back and I'll bandage you up."

Sydney laid back on the chair, so I could finish the job, then she shimmied her shorts up over her gorgeous ass. I internally groaned. I was an idiot for passing that up.

I walked Sydney to the front and settled her bill. Taking a Sharpie out of the cup of pens on the counter, she scrawled her name and number across my forearm in some girly script. "Call me."

Speechless, I stared at my arm as she exited the shop. Damn, I thought New York chicks were ballsy, but they had nothing on Sydney.

"Making nice with the ladies already?" Chase asked as he clapped me on the shoulder.

"Is that shit normal?"

He nodded. "Not a bad gig, huh? Zack used to get hit on all the time until he started dating Rissa. Soon as the chicks realized he was off the market, it just left more for me." Chase picked up the appointment book and scanned over the evening schedule. "Don't snake my girls or we're going to have a problem," he teased.

"Sydney yours?"

"Naw. That's all you, man."

Layla appeared out of nowhere. "You're not allowed to fuck the customers."

I crossed my arms over my chest. "I didn't fuck her." Then just for my own amusement, I tapped on my arm with her number. "Yet."

"Yeah, well, when it goes bad, we lose a client. Keep your dick in your pants."

I laughed. "Trust me, it won't go bad. As a matter of fact, we'll probably get a lot of repeat business."

She waved her hand in an unimpressed gesture. "If you say so. Just don't fuck them in your studio. I don't want to hear that shit."

"Why? Would it make you jealous? Make you wonder what you're missing?"

Chase leaned back against the counter waiting for her answer. "This is amusing."

She glared at him, "Don't you have something to do, like clean the bathroom or something?"

"Nope. Already done. Got nothing to do but enjoy the show."

Layla looked between Chase and me, irritation evident on her pretty face. I dug her cat-eyes drawn in black. The dark lines made her green eyes stand out and I found I couldn't look away from her. "Do whatever you want. I don't give a fuck." She stormed off again. Something I was getting used to.

"She always that fiery?" I asked.

"Nope. You seem to bring out the best in her."

"If that's the best, I'd hate to see the worst."

Chapter 7
Layla

I locked myself in Zack's office and dropped my head to the desk. I had no doubt I could run this business, but I was already failing. Snapping at Draven every two seconds was not productive.

Give me inventory lists, profit and loss sheets, appointment books, and I was a champ.

Give me people, and I sucked. And not like a little. Like on my knees, down my throat, sucked.

I groaned. I hadn't even given a blow job in years. Maybe I didn't suck. Maybe there was a whole other word for how bad my people skills were.

I wasn't always this way. I shut myself off from people before I moved from Oregon. I didn't want to hear the way they talked about me. I knew I'd made mistakes, but I didn't need to be reminded of them time and time again. Most people were gracious enough to talk behind my back, but some petted me like a lost puppy. Pretty soon I disengaged from people all together.

When my college roommate, also an art major, called and offered me a way out, I was on the first plane to Chicago. She worked in a tattoo parlor and I became her apprentice. I changed my look. I changed my attitude. And I got tougher.

It didn't take long to realize that Chicago wasn't a good fit for me. As a major tourist city, I ran into more than one person from my hometown. They may not have recognized me, but I recognized them, and I knew it was time to move again. It wouldn't be long before someone put the pieces together. I didn't want to be found.

I scoured the internet for jobs. When I saw Zack's ad for Forever Inked, I jumped on it. I moved to Utica, Michigan without hesitation. This time I didn't just change my look and my attitude. I changed my whole identity. Better to be safe than sorry.

Zack welcomed me with open arms, and I'd been here ever since. Zack gave me a home and a safe haven. Although he had no idea how much he'd helped, I'd be forever in his debt. Making his business run smoothly while he was gone was the least I could do to repay him.

I had to get my shit together. There was only one person I could count on to help me. Who always made me feel better.

Pulling out my phone, I FaceTimed my brother, James. His image popped up on the screen and I instantly smiled. Something I hadn't done very often in the last few days.

"Hey, sis. Long time no talk. I was just thinking about you. Must be that twin thing." Even though we were fraternal twins, we'd always had an eerie connection. Growing up we were connected at the hip.

"I miss you," I choked out. My eyes filled with unexpected tears and I wiped them away. We used to be so close, and I hadn't seen him in person in years.

"Hey, hey. What's got you so upset?" His green eyes that mirrored mine stared back at me with concern.

"Homesick, maybe." I shrugged, "I don't know."

"What if you came home for a visit? Mom and dad would love to see you. We all miss you so much."

I hadn't been home in five years. Once I left, I never looked back. "You know I can't do that."

"No one would even have to know you were here. You could meet Wendy. She was crushed when you wouldn't come to the wedding."

Guilt pressed down on me. I'd missed so much since I'd been gone. "You know I would have been there if I could. It wasn't that I didn't want to, I just couldn't."

"I know, sis. It's just that I feel like you're missing everything." He got a little smirk on his face. "Wendy's pregnant. You're going to be an aunt."

I covered my mouth with my hand in surprise. That could have been my life if I had made better choices. Now I wasn't sure if it would ever be in the cards for me. "That's so great! How far along is she?"

"Only six weeks. We haven't even told mom and dad yet. You're the first to know."

"I'm honored. I'm so happy for you guys. I really am." I tried to hide my regret, but my brother knew me too well.

"You can still have a baby. The doctors said…"

I cut him off. "I know what the doctors said, but… I'd have to find someone I can trust. I haven't even had a relationship in five years."

He sighed. "Jenna…"

I froze and instinctually looked around to see if anyone had heard, even though I knew I was alone. "That's not my name anymore."

Realizing his mistake, he apologized, "I'm sorry, but you'll always be Jenna to me. You're my sister. I won't forget who you were. Who you are. Underneath the hair and the makeup and the tattoos, you're still my baby sister."

I laughed. "By five minutes."

"Like I said, baby sister. I miss you, Jenna." He scrubbed his hand over his chin. "What would you think about me coming to visit you?"

"Are you serious?" My eyes welled with tears. "That would be... amazing. I miss you so much!"

"Then I'm coming. And when I get there, we're going to talk about what's really bothering you. No bullshitting. Honest talk. You and me. We can even build a fort out of blankets and make shadow puppets on the wall. We'll do whatever it takes to get you smiling again."

"Thanks. I love you, James."

"Love you too, Jenna. It'll be just like when we were kids... Wonder Twin powers activate." He held his fist up to the screen.

I touched his fist with my own. "Shape of an eagle."

He smiled. "Form of water. We're going to dump that bucket of water on whatever has got you down. Together we're unstoppable."

"I can't wait for you to get here." We made a plan before ending the call and I felt better. James always had the power to lift me up. As far as brothers went, mine was the very best.

I finished going over the instructions Zack had left me. After an hour of being locked in the office, I was ready to face Draven again.

When I walked back up front, his studio door was closed. I wondered if he had another bimbo in there with him. Why I cared, was beyond me.

The bells over the front door jingled and Kyla stepped in. She worked for Forever Inked as a freelance artist. She had amazing talent, but never the urge to tattoo. Zack had tried to hire her on the spot when he got a glimpse of the first design she'd done for herself. She'd turned him down but agreed to draw and design on the side.

I liked Kyla, but she reminded me a little too much of who I used to be. She was blond and bubbly. Kyla had been a cheerleader and ended up marrying the captain of the football team.

I knew that she'd had some bumps in the road, but I didn't know the whole story. She showed up here one day and started getting inked. A lot of ink. A girl like her didn't do that unless she was hiding something. It was a story I knew well. The similarities between us hit too close to home.

The difference was that her Prince Charming ended up being real. They were happily married with a set of twins almost a year old.

"Hey, girl."

"Hey, Layla. I promised Zack I have these to him by the end of the week." She said placing an envelope on the counter. "What's new around here?"

"Nothing. Same old crap." I took the drawings out of the envelope and inspected them. There was a variety of butterflies, flowers and birds. The last one caught my eye, "I love this." It was a Phoenix in flight. Beautifully colored feathers adorned its outstretched wings and long feathers trailed from its tail curling in several directions. The bird was clearly feminine but had a hooked beak and razor-sharp talons. The dichotomy entranced me.

"I call that one *Beautiful, Yet Fierce,*" she said proudly.

"I want it." I pulled the drawing from the pile and set it aside. "I can't believe you still name all your drawings."

Kyla shrugged. "It makes it more personal to me. I love that one too. I might get it on my thigh when Zack gets back."

"Not if I beat you to it. Unless you want to be matchy-matchy," I teased.

"I don't care. It's a great piece. Why shouldn't we both have it? I'm waiting 'til Zack gets back though. No offense, but he's my guy."

"None taken. I know you and Zack have a tight bond. But just so you know, if you change your mind either Chase or I could do it justice."

"I could do it," Draven's deep voice interrupted us.

Kyla quirked up her eye. "And you are?"

He reached his arm around me and took Kyla's hand. "I'm Draven. I'm filling in while Zack's gone."

I pushed Draven back. "One, no one asked you. Two, Kyla is Zack's client. And three, she's married, so you're not getting in her pants."

He looked her up and down. "Damn shame. You're a pretty woman, Kyla."

Kyla blushed. "Umm, thanks."

"And her husband is a professional football player. So, unless you want your ass kicked, keep your hands off," I added.

Draven held his hands up in surrender. "Message received. Can't fault a guy for noticing though." He backed away into his studio.

Kyla leaned in close to me. "I thought you said there was nothing new around here? Damn girl, he's delicious."

"Oh God, not you too!"

"Not for myself, of course, but for you."

"Oh, please. I do not need that type of complication in my life." I headed back toward Zack's office to get her check. Kyla followed behind me.

Once in his office, she shut the door. "Why not?"

I threw my arms in the air. "Because. That's why!"

She tapped her finger on her chin. "I've known you for two years and you've never had a boyfriend. You know what you need? A girls' night. You need to come out with Tori and me."

I shook my head. "Yeah, I don't think so."

"You're doing it. I'm not taking no for an answer. What? We're not cool enough for you?" she glared.

"I didn't say that."

"Then it's a date. Neither Tori nor I are pregnant right now, so the timing is perfect. I'll even get the guys to drive us. We can all get trashed."

The image of Kyla trashed was somewhat amusing and I had to admit, curiosity got the best of me. "Fine."

"Good. Tomorrow night. Text me your address and we'll pick you up at eight."

I had no idea what I had just agreed to or why I had agreed to it, but she was right. With Rissa gone, I was surrounded with testosterone. Maybe time with some other girls would be just what I needed.

God, help me.

Chapter 8
Draven

Pent up frustration permeated my entire body. After everyone left for the night, I changed into shorts and hit the gym in the basement. I found some tape, wrapped my hands, then slid on the gloves that had been sitting on the shelf.

The heavy bag taunted me. A quick right jab got it swinging. It did nothing to ease the tension inside. Another jab, a left, right, left. I kept at it until sweat dripped down my head and chest. Using my forearm to wipe my face, Sydney's number stared up at me.

I should just call her.

I shook the thought away. She was trouble with a capital T. I'd bet everything on it.

She wasn't what had me tied up anyway. Sydney might have taken the edge off, but she wouldn't cure what ailed me. Only one woman could do that, and she wanted nothing to do with me.

I hit the weight bench next, then the treadmill. The entire time Layla consumed my mind.

She'd taken up residence there and wasn't leaving anytime soon. She was tiny, maybe five-three without her ever-present heels on. Although she was tiny, she had amazing curves. I'd only gotten a hint of the ink that covered her. She had a flowery black bracelet tatted on her wrist, both wrists actually. Brightly colored flowers swirled down her arm, along with a hummingbird. I suspected her ink continued up under her sleeve and over her shoulder. I was dying to find out just how much of her body was artfully decorated.

If I kept acting like an asshole I'd never find out.

Acting like a man who was only interested in getting laid was not the answer. Layla obviously was not enticed by the prospect of getting laid by me. Not that I was easily deterred.

We could be perfect together. And after our time expired in a month, we would go our separate ways. No hard feelings. No attachments.

I turned off the lights in the basement and trudged my weary body up the stairs to my apartment. When I got to the door, I noticed the access to the roof was open. Zack had given me the key and I sure as hell didn't leave it open.

I quickly ascended the last flight of stairs and stepped out onto the roof. It was dark and quiet. I scanned the area for intruders.

I saw a shadow sitting on the ledge. I crept up behind the unknown figure. It didn't take long to realize that it was Layla sitting there with earbuds in, swinging her legs over the edge. I'd recognize her killer curves anywhere.

Not wanting to scare her, I placed a solid hand on her shoulder and sat down next to her.

She jumped a little, but my hand held her in place. She pulled out one of her earbuds and gasped at my presence. "I'm sorry. I saw the door open and came to investigate. I didn't mean to scare you."

"My bad," she said. "Since Zack moved out, I've gotten used to coming up here. I should have told you. It's your apartment now. I can go."

She pulled her legs up to stand. I put a hand on her thigh. "It's fine. You can stay. This place is more yours than mine." She let her leg back down. "Do you mind if I join you?"

"I guess not." She stared out into the night.

The lights from the bars and minor league stadium down the street illuminated her face. She was a beautiful woman. "What are you doing up here?" I asked. Afraid of scaring her off, I kept things light.

"Thinking," she answered.

"About?"

"Everything."

I let out a low laugh. "That's vague."

She shrugged. "I just want to do a good job while Zack's away. I owe him a lot. I don't want to let him down."

I dropped my head to my chest. "I can relate. I owe him a lot too."

Layla rolled her eyes. "Like what? Did he loan you money or something?"

I stared off into the distance. "I wish it were that simple. He saved my life," I admitted. "That's why I'm here."

Layla sucked in a breath. "Me too."

Her admission took me by surprise. This was my opening to start something with her. "Wanna talk about it?"

She furrowed her eyebrows. "Not really. He doesn't even know. I'm certainly not going to tell you."

Shot down, I huffed out a breath. "Fair enough." The walls around Layla were tall. She was hiding something, I just didn't know what. I accepted it. It wasn't like I was going to tell her my life story either. I mean, how did you tell someone that your father was a cold-blooded killer? And so was I.

We sat in silence for a while, staring out into the starry sky.

Layla cracked the silence first. "I'm sorry I've been such a bitch. I haven't been fair to you."

Regret filled my chest. "I shouldn't have said that."

"Why? It was true. You were just calling me out on my bullshit."

I tilted my head back and forth in contemplation. "Maybe, but I still shouldn't have said it."

She laughed. "No, you shouldn't have, but it was honest." She reached her hands behind her and leaned back. "I appreciate honesty."

I stared at her arched back and her tits pointed upward. "I'm not going to sleep with Sydney," I blurted.

She cringed then focused on my eyes. Her stare burned me from the inside out. "It's not my business."

I took a deep breath. "Maybe not, but I thought you should know."

She pulled her feet underneath her and balanced on the ledge on the building. We were easily thirty feet above the sidewalk. She walked along the edge like a balance beam, making me nervous. "You can fuck whoever you like." She held her arms out from her shoulders to keep her balance as she traversed the ledge. "She's pretty. I'd fuck her if I were into girls."

She made it to the corner, then did some intricate spin on her toe and headed back toward me. I wanted to tell her to get the hell down. I had a natural inclination to protect her. Instead, I sat frozen. Mesmerized by her body.

She wobbled once, leaning over the edge toward the street below. Not able to stop myself, I reached out and grabbed her arm, pulling her to the safety of the rooftop. "Are you drunk?" I asked.

"I wish. Do I make you uncomfortable, Draven?" she asked, throwing my own question back at me.

"Uncomfortable? No. Confused? Yes. I don't think you're really a bitch, even if you want everyone to believe it."

"Pfft. You don't know anything about me."

"I know you're talented. I know you're determined. I know you wish I weren't here, and I know that you hate me."

She picked at her black nail polish. "I don't hate you. I don't particularly like you, but I don't hate you."

I laughed out loud. "You could have fooled me."

"It's complicated."

"Uncomplicate it."

"I can't."

That was not the answer I wanted. I stood from the ledge and faced her. "How about this? We start over." I reached out my hand to her. "Hi. I'm Draven Constantine. I'll be here for a month."

She tentatively reached her hand out to mine and shook it. My large hand engulfed her small one. "I'm Layla Roberts. I'm your new boss and you're not getting in my pants."

I gave her hand a little tug and pulled her to my chest, my other arm wrapped around her waist. "We'll see about that. I too can be very determined. When I see what I want, I go after it."

She didn't back away. I felt her shiver and her eyes got wide. "Trust me. You don't want me."

I held her tighter, pulling her soft tits tight against me. My dick came to life and pressed against her stomach. "That's where you're wrong."

She squirmed in my arms. "I'm not like Sydney. I'm not an easy lay."

"Oh, I know that. Which will only make it sweeter when it happens. And it will happen. It's not a matter of if, but when."

"You sound awfully sure of yourself, Mr. Constantine."

"You can fight it all you want, Miss Roberts. But you can't tell me you don't feel it."

She swallowed down the lump in her throat. "Feel what?"

I rubbed my dick into her. "The electricity between us."

Layla put her hands on my chest and looked up at me. "I can feel something between us, but I'm not so sure it's electricity. It feels a lot more like your cock."

"Yeah, that too. How does it feel?"

"Big," she blurted. Then she pushed herself away from me and buried her head in her hands. "Oh my God, I can't believe I just said that. I need to go." She rushed to the door and frantically turned in a circle looking for her purse.

I grabbed it from where we had been sitting and held it out to her. "It is."

She reached for her bag. "I don't want to know."

I pulled it back just out of her reach. "I think deep down you do want to know, Layla Roberts. Lucky for you, I'm more than willing to prove it to you."

She lunged for her purse and snatched it from my hands. "Not happening!" She ran for the door and barreled down the steps.

I leaned over the rail of the stairway, watching her escape. "See you tomorrow, boss!"

I moved the rock that held the door open and headed down to my apartment. *Well, that went well.* I had intended to make amends with Layla. For her to see me as more than a sex-crazed deviant. It had started well, and then I let my dick take over. *Brilliant!*

As soon as I held her hand, I felt a spark shoot up my arm. It must have short-circuited my brain and sent all the blood rushing to my other head. In that moment, I had to feel her. And she felt amazing in my arms, pressed up against my body.

The only thing that made me feel any better about what had happened, was knowing that she was affected too. I felt her heart racing. I saw the way she looked at me. I heard the hunger in her voice. Layla Roberts could deny it all she wanted… she was into me.

It would happen. It was only a matter of time. I tried to imagine what sex with Layla would be like. Would she be wild and untamed, or would she be shy and reserved? Didn't really matter to me. Either way, one thing was certain, my dick was going to be buried deep inside her before my time here was done.

I stripped off my sweaty clothes and turned on the shower. The water pressure was spectacular. It massaged my sore muscles and the heat relaxed me. Everything but the raging hard-on I was still sporting.

Squirting some shampoo in one hand, I leaned the other against the wall and fisted my cock imagining it was her pussy wrapped around me. God, she felt amazing. I saw her tits pushed out while she braced herself against the wall, her ass tilted up as I pounded into her from behind. My hand moved faster, gripping myself harder. She was so wet, so slippery, so perfect. A couple more jerks of my cock and my balls tightened. It sent a jolt up my spine when I released and shot my load all over the wall.

I wasn't a big fan of jerking off. There usually wasn't a need. If I wanted to get laid all it took was a phone call or a quick trip to the bar. I could have opted for calling Sydney tonight, but instead I decided to fly solo. The only pussy I wanted was Layla's. And as great as my fantasy was, the real thing was going to be so much better.

Chapter 9
Layla

"And instead of saying something clever or witty, I told him how big his cock felt." I threw myself back into the couch and covered my face with my hands. "I'm so bad at this!"

Brian laughed. "Aww, baby girl, it couldn't have been that bad."

I glared at him. "It was. And then I got so flustered I bolted."

"Soooo, was it big?" he asked, clearly entertained by my humiliation.

I threw my hands into the air. "How the hell would I know? It's not like I've had a lot to compare it to recently."

Brian rolled his eyes. "It not like you've never had cock before, you're just out of practice." He took my hand and placed it on his crotch. "Did it feel like this?"

I gripped him through his basketball shorts, taking advantage of his offer. After indulging my groping, he removed my hand. "Well?"

"I'm not sure. Maybe I should test it out fully, so that if it does happen, I have something to compare it to." I reached for him again and he grabbed my wrist.

"Layla, my cock isn't going into your vagina. Ever."

"Please. We don't have to cuddle after, and I won't be upset when you kick me out."

Brian shook his head. "You do know I'm gay, right?"

I waved him off. "Technicalities. One vagina won't kill you. Take one for the team."

He wrapped me in tight hug. "God, I love you." Then he took me by the shoulders and gave me a stern look. "But the answer is still no."

I slumped. "Ugh! You're no fun."

"Oh, I'm plenty of fun. You just have the wrong equipment." He smirked.

"Bragger. This is so unfair." I went to my cupboard, pulled out a bottle of Jack and held it up. "You want one?"

"Yeah, sure. Why not?"

I brought the bottle to the couch, along with two glasses. Pouring us each a healthy measure, I sat back next to him and leaned into his side. He clinked his glass with mine. "To getting good cock."

"At least one of us is," I groaned.

"Baby girl, you could have as much cock as you wanted. You choose not to."

I stared into my drink. "I'm afraid."

He lifted my chin. "I know you are. Not all guys are like your ex."

"I know that logically, but my brain hasn't gotten the message. What if I let him in and he hurts me?"

"That's a chance you have to take. Living like you have, isn't healthy."

I jumped off the couch and paced in front of it. "You think I don't know that? You think I don't know I'm fucked up?" I pointed at my chest. "I know I'm fucked up! And I hate myself for it! I hate that I let him destroy me! I hate that I let him have this control over me." The tears rolled down my face. "Five Years! Five years and I can still feel everything he did to me. Everything he took from me! I'll never let someone do that to me again!" I sank to the floor and cried into my knees.

Warm arms wrapped around me. "I'm so sorry, baby girl. Let it out."

Brian rocked me until my sobs subsided. I wiped my eyes, smearing my eyeliner across my cheek. "Thank you. Thank you for letting me have my moment. I didn't realize how much I've been holding in."

He cupped my face in his strong hands. "Hey, that's what friends are for. Let's get you to bed. Everything will be better in the morning."

Brian walked me to my room. I slipped off my jeans and pulled on a pair of shorts. "Will you stay with me tonight?"

"Of course."

I pulled back the covers and got into bed. Brian took off his jeans and crawled in behind me. He pulled my back to his chest and I felt safe. "Sleep, baby girl."

When I woke in the morning, Brian was gone but the coffee was made. There was a note leaning against my mug, *You got this!* And that was why I loved him.

Picking up my phone I shot him a quick text. ***You're the best! Sorry about last night.***

His response was immediate. ***No worries. I got your back!***

He always did. Even if I never convinced him to sleep with me, I wouldn't trade Brian's friendship for anything. Last night was the first time I'd ever had a meltdown in front of him and I was slightly embarrassed. However, if I knew Brian, he wouldn't bring it up again if I didn't.

Ignore and avoid. It was my specialty.

And that included Draven. I pulled on a black Ed Hardy tank top, jean shorts, and combat boots. I finished the look with a flannel tied around my waist. I painted on my mask and slicked my dark hair back in a high ponytail.

No matter what Draven said to me about last night, I'd push forward. Maybe I would have sex with him, maybe I wouldn't. I had to do a risk analysis before deciding.

On the pro side was possibly having the best sex of my life. I had a feeling Draven knew what he was doing in bed… or against a wall or on a kitchen counter.

On the con side was risking my heart and my body. What if I fell in love with him and he was only in it for the sex. Or worse yet, what if he had a temper and he physically hurt me.

But God, the way my body reacted to him was like nothing I'd ever felt before. When he pulled my body against his chest, my nipples hardened. I could feel his heart beating against mine. The thumping vibrated my chest, and the sound filled my ears.

And then there was the little matter of his cock, which wasn't so little, pushing into my stomach. The asshole had to rub it on me, which made me want to climb him like a spider monkey. My panties were soaked.

Then I opened my big mouth. Way to play it cool. The worst part was that he found the whole incident humorous. I played right into his hand without even realizing it.

Well, it was game on today. The tank I was wearing left little to the imagination. It was cut low in the front and showed off my ample cleavage. I hoped he enjoyed walking around with a hard-on all day, because two could play this game.

When I walked into work, Chase let out a wolf-whistle. "Looking hot today, boss!"

I pulled out the ends of my flannel shirt like a skirt and gave him a little curtsy, "Why thank you, Chase. I can't keep letting you boys get all the attention around here."

He winked at me. "I don't think that will be a problem today. Try smiling too."

I gave him a big fake smile with lots of teeth.

He let out a loud belly laugh. "On second thought, the scowl is sexier."

I flipped him off and headed to my studio. I checked my schedule. Sid was my first appointment. He owned the pawn shop a couple of blocks over and he always asked me out.

Tapping on my chin, an evil plan took shape. A little competition never hurt anyone. Maybe if Draven thought I was interested in Sid, I'd be able to gage his true intentions.

The bell over the door jingled and my opportunity walked in. I put a little extra sway in my walk as I approached the front counter. "Good morning, Sid."

"Good morning, sugar." His nickname for me made me cringe internally even though I knew it wasn't special for me. I wondered how many girls it actually worked on.

Sid wasn't a bad looking guy. He spent a lot of time at the gym, and it showed. He was a typical muscle head. If only his brain was as big as his biceps. Sadly, it wasn't. He ran a successful business, but preying on desperate people wanting to sell their stuff wasn't at the top of my list of honorable professions.

Not that I was using my degree to its highest extent, but it was still art related. And it took talent. Transitioning into tattooing wasn't easy for me at first. When I finally got the hang of it, my skills were up there with the best. So even though it wasn't what I originally intended, I was proud of what I'd become.

I leaned over the counter to show off a little more cleavage. "What are we doing for you today?"

His eyes glanced down at my boobs and slowly slid back to my eyes. "I saw a cool Polynesian design last time I was here. I want it down the middle of my back."

I gave him a sassy smile, "Oooooh! I get to see you shirtless. It must be my lucky day."

"Sugar, you can see me shirtless or pantless anytime you want. All you have to do is ask." He winked at me for extra emphasis.

I played along. "You're a sweet talker, Sid. Show me what tattoo you want, and we'll get started." I walked him over to the photo albums and he flipped through the pages.

Sid pointed to the one he wanted. "This one. Right down the middle of my back."

Draven walked up just as I hooked my arm with Sid's. "Come on back. You get undressed and I'll prep the transfer." I led him to my studio and watched as he took his shirt off.

Draven's eyebrows shot up. "Morning, boss."

I turned to face him, crossing my arms under my breasts and pushing them up. "It's a very good morning. Sleep well last night?"

He mimicked my stance. "A hot shower helped. You?"

I shrugged. "For me it was a glass of wine and a hot bath. Nothing like a jacuzzi tub to release all my built-up tension. But I'm good now." I winked at him. "Those water jets always seem to do the trick."

He groaned.

"Did you need something?" I hiked my thumb over my shoulder toward Sid. "I have a client waiting." Sid was relaxed back in the chair sans shirt.

"No. Nothing. Just checking in."

"Cool. I'm going to make this transfer and then get started. If you need anything, make sure you knock first. I'll be busy for a while." And with that, I sauntered to the back room. I gave myself a little fist pump. Score one for me.

I endured two hours with Sid in the chair talking about ridiculous shit I had no interest in. Pretending to care was exhausting. But I flirted and giggled, making sure Draven could hear every word.

When we were finished, I walked Sid to the front. "Come back and see me real soon."

Sid leaned on the counter. "You have my number. Give me a call."

"For sure." I smiled at him.

He left the shop and I held back the impulse to gag.

Draven appeared out of thin air, his cologne invading my senses. "I thought we weren't supposed to fuck the clients."

I turned and smirked at him. "I'm the boss. I can do whatever I want. Besides, Sid isn't just a client. He's one of my regulars."

Draven's scruff-covered jaw ticked, and I knew my little charade was getting to him. He reached up and ran his hand over his hair and gave the knot on top of his head a little tug. What I wouldn't give to run my hands through his hair and pull the elastic from that knot. I wanted to know what he would look like with his dark hair down around his shoulders. To feel the stubble on his face between my thighs. He was gorgeous. Even more so when he was worked up. His eyes turned darker, and he sucked his cheeks in, making his face look like it was sculpted from stone.

I turned back to the desk and grabbed the appointment book. "I saw your schedule was clear, so I took the liberty of booking your next appointment." I looked at the clock over the door. "Kelly should be here shortly."

He grumbled as he turned around and headed to his studio. "I hope she's hot."

I barely contained the giggle from escaping my lips.

Chapter 10
Draven

It looked like I had sheared a goddamn sheep by the time I was finished shaving Kelly's back. Three hundred pounds of sweaty man laid on his stomach in my chair. She was so going to pay for this. When Layla said Kelly was coming in, the last thing I expected was some biker dude with a back that could pass as a sweater. Why he was getting his back tatted was a mystery. When all that hair grew back no one would see it anyway.

I could just see Layla now, sitting in Zack's office laughing it up. She knew exactly what she was doing when she scheduled this appointment.

"I wanted Layla to do my tat," Kelly said as I wiped the last of the hair from his back. "She said she was booked, but that you would do a great job."

"Did she now?"

"Yeah, said she was too busy to squeeze me in."

"She's busy all right." This was payback for last night. I knew it.

When I'd gone to make the transfer, I saw her lounged back in Zack's chair with her feet on his desk. I glared at her as she took a bite of her sandwich. "How's your client?" she asked between bites.

"Cute, Layla. Real cute," I said sarcastically.

She scrunched up her nose. "Not my type, but I'm glad you think so. This all worked out. You needed more clients and I needed time to go over the receipts."

Even though I was pissed, I couldn't help but ogle her toned legs and her tits. Fuck, she looked good today. The ponytail sitting high on her head made me want to wrap it around my fist, pull her back and kiss the shit out of her.

Three hours later, Kelly's tat was done, and I was sanitizing everything. I wiped the chair down. Twice. I'd never seen someone sweat so much in my life. Fucking disgusting.

I turned on the fan to air my studio out. Big mistake! The hair on the floor swirled around and blew everywhere. "Son of a bitch!" I tripped over my own feet lunging for the fan. When I finally got it off, hair covered my pants, stuck to the chair, and clung to the walls.

Layla stood in my doorway, hands on her hips. "Whoa! Did you shave Chewbacca in here?"

"Very funny." I grabbed a broom and started sweeping up the mess. "That was your friend, Kelly."

"Ummm, he's your client now." I scowled at her. "You're welcome for that by the way."

Layla disappeared, and I grumbled.

She returned quickly with a hand-held vacuum. "Next time sweep before you turn on the fan."

"Thanks for the tip." I continued to brush the hair off the chair and onto the floor where I swept it into a rather large pile.

Layla turned the vacuum on and sucked up the pile. Then she ran it over my legs and up to my crotch. I pushed her hand away. "What the fuck are you doing?"

She shrugged. "You've got hair all over your pants. I was trying to help."

"Fuck that!" I toed my boots off and undid my jeans, pushing them down my legs. I wadded them up and pushed them into her hands.

She stared at me standing there in a t-shirt and boxer briefs. "What am I supposed to do with these?"

"Go shake them out somewhere. You're not going to fucking suck my dick."

She pushed them back at me. "I wasn't sucking your dick. I was trying to help. Handle your own fucking pants."

"I'm in my underwear," I growled.

"I don't give a fuck! You made the mess! You clean it up!"

I snatched my pants back, "Fine!" I stormed to the back door in my underwear and slammed it open. I shook my pants out and stepped back into them. Did she seriously just stick a vacuum on my dick?

I overreacted; I know. But shit, she was on her knees, giving me an eyeful of her tits when I looked down. Next thing I knew, she was working her way up my legs and to my crotch. I didn't need her to know I had a hard-on from staring at her tits. But since I stripped my pants off, I'm sure it was more than obvious.

I lit a cigarette and took a deep breath. That woman was making me crazy. And who the hell was the guy who came in this morning? She smiled and flirted with him but pushed me away every chance she got.

I didn't understand it. I knew what I felt last night was real. Her body reacted, even if she tried to hide it.

I stubbed out my cigarette and headed back inside since my dick was back under control. Chase and Layla were bantering up front.

"You sucked his dick?" He laughed.

"I didn't suck his dick. This did." She held up the vacuum. "I was trying to help him."

"You don't have to lie about it. I know what I heard. You messed up his pants," he insisted, laughing again.

I clapped him on the shoulder. "Trust me, she couldn't make me come that fast. She wouldn't even know what to do with me if she tried. I'm thinking it's been a while."

Layla's eyebrows shot up and her face turned to stone. She took a deep breath through her nose, spun on her heel, and stormed off to her studio. The door slamming made both Chase and me jump.

"Smooth, man. Real smooth."

"What? She started it."

Chase shook his head. "You don't know anything about her, do you? Layla's not the kind of girl you can fuck with like that."

He was right. I didn't know anything about her, but I'd obviously just hit a nerve.

Chase backed away. "Just be careful with her. She's like a sister to me."

I kept fucking up when it came to Layla. The last thing I wanted to do was hurt her. It wasn't like me to care, but with her I did.

I was about to knock on her door to apologize when a tall guy walked in looking like he had stepped right off the pages of *GQ*. "Is Layla here?"

I stepped to the counter and placed my hands on it. "What can I do for you?"

He cocked his head to the side. "You can go get Layla and tell her I'm here."

"And you are?"

He lifted his aviators to the top of his head. "None of your business."

I heard Layla's door open. "Brian? What are you doing here?" She practically ran into his arms. He wrapped them around her protectively.

"Hey, baby girl." He kissed the top of her head and whispered something in her ear.

It pissed me off more than it should have. I should have walked away and let it be, but I couldn't. I was entranced by her show of affection toward this guy.

50

Something niggled inside me. It wasn't a familiar feeling, but it felt a little bit like jealousy. I had no right to feel it, but it was there just the same.

She took him by the hand and led him to the front door. "I'm going on a break. I'll be back in a half hour." Then she disappeared.

Fuck that! I couldn't let her get under my skin, but she was already creeping in. I stomped over to Chase's studio with more irritation than I should have felt. "What are you doing tonight?"

He looked up from the drawing he was working on. "Nothing yet. I might hook up with Becca, but nothing solid."

I pointed between the two of us. "We got a date. I need to get drunk and laid."

Chase chuckled. "You're a good-looking motherfucker, but I'm into tits and pussy."

"Yeah? So am I. I need you to take me to a club or something. You do have those here, don't you?"

"Yeah, we've got clubs. What are you looking for?"

Good question. "I have no idea. But something other than the sexy contradiction that works here."

Chase smirked at me. "You like her." It wasn't a question.

"I don't know her."

"But you like her. Like *like* her, like her."

"What are you, twelve? She doesn't like me, so it doesn't really matter."

Chase held up his hands. "I'm just saying." He quirked an eyebrow at me. "What makes you think she doesn't like you? Besides the fact that you've been a total dick to her?"

I pointed at my chest. "I've been a dick? She's the one who's been impossible."

He waved his hand in the air. "That's part of the charm that's Layla."

Looking up at the ceiling, I let out a sigh. "Haven't seen the charming side of her. All I've gotten is the cold shoulder."

"Give her time. She'll come around."

I wasn't counting on that. Tonight, I just wanted to forget about her.

Chapter 11
Layla

"You're looking sexy today." Brian motioned to the front of my shirt where my cleavage showed. "Very nice."

"I'm trying. To do what? I'm not sure," I sipped my coffee across the table from him. He was dressed in tailored pants and a crisp white shirt. The top two buttons were undone, and his sleeves were rolled up his forearms. He looked like sex on a stick. No wonder he never had a problem finding dates. "What are you doing slumming it today?"

He pulled back. "Hey, I take offense to that. I've been to your shop before." He pulled up his sleeve to show me the bottom tip of the tribal ink I'd put there.

"You didn't come in for a tattoo, Brian. Were you checking up on me?"

He shrugged his shoulders. "I just wanted to make sure you were okay."

I smiled at him. "Thank you. I don't know what happened last night, but my armor is back in place. I'm good."

Brian reached for my hand across the table. "It's okay if you're not, you know. You don't always have to be strong. It's all right to feel it. To let the fear and the pain in."

I dropped my head. "I had a weak moment. That's not who I am anymore. I don't want to be afraid. I want to live again."

"I want that for you too. You're a sexy woman who spends way too many nights alone. I'll always be there if you need me, but I want to see you happy. You deserve it."

I lifted my shoulders with an exaggerated pout. "I'm not sure I believe that. I was happy once and look where it got me."

"You need to leave the past behind. It's time." He tapped his fingers on the table. "Sooo… was that him? The guy who's got you all twisted up inside?"

I leaned back and sighed. "Yeah. He's beautiful in a dark seductive way. He's everything I shouldn't want."

Brian gave me a crooked smile, his dimples showing. "You sure he's straight?"

I reached over the table to slap his arm. "Hands off! Besides, I'm a hundred percent sure he's straight." I looked down at my chest. "I caught him checking out the girls."

"And…" Brian rolled his hand, motioning for me to continue.

"I don't know yet, but I'm not ruling it out."

"That's a start."

I checked myself one more time in the mirror. I looked exactly the way I wanted.

Sexy.

Dangerous.

Bold.

Unafraid.

I hadn't been out to a club in a long time. Tonight, I was going to test the waters. See if I could pull off the confidence that I showed on the outside but lacked on the inside.

I checked the buckles of my four-inch black strappy heels one more time. I tugged at the short, black leather skirt and made sure the girls were tucked into the black corset I wore.

I told Kyla she didn't have to pick me up. Instead, I ordered an Uber. One more look in the mirror assured me that my makeup was perfect and my hair tamed.

I knocked on Brian's door. When he opened, I turned in a tight circle. "Well?"

His eyes took me in from head to toe. "Baby girl, you look amazing."

"It's not too much?"

"Hell no." He grabbed me by the shoulders and kissed my forehead. "Get out there and have some fun."

"That's the plan… return to the world of the living."

Brian looked down on me. "It's a good plan."

I slid into the back of the Uber and started second guessing myself. What if I couldn't do this? What if it turned out that I couldn't escape the fear? What if I couldn't shake the scared girl who was afraid of her own husband, let alone a stranger?

I put up a good front, making everyone think I was fearless. That I was a bitch through and through. And yeah, some of that was true now. Being bitchy was the only way to let guys know I was off-limits.

But underneath it all I just wanted to be normal again.

To live life without looking over my shoulder.

To quit running and hiding.

To let my guard down enough to let someone else in.

To fall in love again and believe he would keep me safe.

To believe I was worth something more than to be someone's property.

I shook my hopes and dreams from my head. Tonight, wasn't about any of that. Tonight, was about being a girl having fun with other girls. I didn't really have any girlfriends except Rissa. Most girls were put off by my shitty attitude.

When I met Rissa, I thought she was about the purest, sweetest thing I'd ever met. But I'd quickly learned she had her own demons she was fighting. A past that wasn't all sunshine and rainbows.

I was a shitty friend because she'd bared her soul to me, and never once did I let her into my world. Nope. I kept that shit locked up tight.

I knew Kyla had a story too. I just didn't know what it was.

I wasn't planning on revealing my past tonight. But maybe, just maybe, I could forget about it for one night. And maybe one night would lead to two. And maybe two would help me move forward.

The Uber pulled up in front of Xtreme. It wasn't surprising Kyla had chosen this club. Her husband had done the start up for it. When he made it as a professional football player, he'd left it behind to pursue his real passion.

I tentatively climbed from the back of the car and pulled my skirt down. Taking a deep breath, the pulsing music pulled me forward. Once inside, my name was called, and I moved toward it. Kyla and Tori were seated at a high-top table, drinks already in front of them.

Kyla was shorter than me, which was saying something. At five-three, I depended on my heels to make me stand taller. She slid off her stool and wrapped me in a hug. We weren't really friends, so the gesture took me by surprise. I loosely hugged her back. "I thought you were going to bail on us."

"Don't think it didn't cross my mind."

She hopped back up into her seat. "Well, I'm glad you didn't. You look hot, by the way. Love the outfit."

"Thanks." I hiked myself up into the chair. "Hey, Tori," I acknowledged Kyla's best friend. Both girls were gorgeous without even trying. "So… girls' night. I haven't been to many of these. What are we doing?" I hadn't gone out with girlfriends since college.

Tori held up her drink. "Get wasted, gossip, dance and take in all the eye candy."

"I can do that." I nodded. "First, I need a drink."

Kyla motioned to the waitress. She and Tori ordered their seconds and a round of tequila, while I got a Jack and Coke. When the waitress returned with our tequila, all three of us licked our hands, sprinkled on the salt, threw back the shots and sucked on our limes. I scrunched up my face in disgust. "One more," I shouted. If I was going to do this, I was going to do it right.

After tossing back our second shots, Kyla started with the inquisition. "So, Draven's hot. How long is he here for?"

I felt the warmth of the liquor flowing through me and my lips loosened a bit. "He may be hot, but he's an asshole."

"But he's hot?" Tori questioned.

"Like off the charts," Kyla confirmed. "Why do you think he's an asshole?"

I sucked on the straw in my Jack and Coke. "He's arrogant, cocky, and thinks he's going to get me in bed."

Tori smirked. "Hell, if he's that hot, screw the bed. Fuck him against the wall."

I dropped my head, unable to stop the giggle that escaped my lips. I hadn't giggled in years, but it felt good. "Oh, dear God. I can't do that."

"Sure, you can," she said. "Just wrap your legs around his waist and hold on tight."

Kyla gave her a scathing look.

Tori threw up her hands. "What? Chris is strong. He's got no problem lifting my fat ass up. Layla's tiny. It shouldn't be an issue."

"Oh, I've got no doubt he could lift me up. I'm just not sure I want to let him," I admitted.

"Why not? He's single. You're single. What's the problem?" Kyla asked.

Now that was the million-dollar question, wasn't it? I scrambled to find a reasonable answer. "For one, we work together. I don't want it to be awkward."

Tori waved me off. "It'll only be awkward if the sex is bad. If he's as hot as you say, my bet is he's a stud in the sack."

"True," Kyla agreed.

"He's only here for a month. What's the point?" I argued further.

Tori raised her eyebrows at me. "The point is freaky good sex, girl. It's one of the non-negotiables in life. Every woman deserves it."

I tipped back the rest of my drink. "Easy for you two to say. You've both been with the same guys forever. You know them. You trust them. I don't know Draven. And I sure as hell don't trust him."

"I wasn't always with Tyler," Kyla piped up. "When we broke up, I dated, and it wasn't great. Actually, it was awful." She rubbed at the heart shaped tat on her chest. "But I knew it from the beginning and ignored it. Trust your gut. You'll know if he's a good guy, just listen to your instincts."

I huffed out a laugh. "My instincts aren't very good. I already fell for the wrong guy once." Crap. The alcohol had me spewing truths I didn't want to share. I put an end to it as quickly as possible. "Enough talk. Let's dance."

I hopped down off my stool and led the girls to the dance floor. My body swayed to the music and my hips had a mind of their own. All the fun I had back in college came rushing back. The music thumped and vibrated in my chest. My feet moved without thought.

The three of us attracted the attention of the bar. Next thing I knew, Tyler grabbed Kyla's hips from behind and turned her into his chest. Chris was behind Tori rocking his hips into hers. That left me flying solo. I leaned into Chris's ear, raising my voice so he could hear me over the music. "What? You don't trust your wife?"

He leaned down to me. "I trust her plenty. It's these other assholes I don't trust. Not when you three are the hottest chicks in here."

I threw back my head and laughed. I continued to dance and didn't freak when a hard chest pressed against my back. I looked over my shoulder at the blond-haired cutie and gave him a smile. He leaned down to kiss my neck and whispered in my ear, "You're beautiful."

I giggled again. Clearly the alcohol had gone straight to my head. I leaned back into him. His hands went to my bare shoulders and skimmed down my arms. He held my hips and rocked his body with mine. The way he caressed me felt good.

Until it didn't.

One arm wrapped around my waist and under my top, rubbing against my stomach. The other wrapped around my chest. His fingers danced along the top of my breasts. I felt trapped. I tried to wiggle away without making a scene, but his arms tightened around me. Pulled me closer. He was backing us off the dance floor. "Let go," I shouted. But no one could hear me above the thumping music.

"You're not going anywhere, baby. You know you want it. Look at you," he said into my ear as he kept stepping me backwards.

One of my arms was pinned at my side and my other hand went up to claw at the arm around my chest.

Tears filled my eyes. "Please!" I struggled to get out of his arms.

At the edge of the dance floor, I saw my salvation in the form of Chris and Tyler headed my way, fists clenched and eyes on fire. But before they reached me, I was released and stumbled forward. I turned to see Draven had my dancing partner by the neck. The look on his face was murderous. I saw something in his eyes I had never seen before. Anger and rage.

Tyler and Chris went right for the guy Draven had by the neck. Tori and Kyla were behind them, pulling me into the safety of their arms. I was shaking. "Let them handle it," Tori soothed.

"I don't know what happened," I cried. "One minute we were dancing, the next he wouldn't let me go."

"You're okay," Kyla assured as we walked back to our table. Tori went to the bar and returned with three waters.

I looked toward the front door where the guys had gone. "What do you think is happening?"

"Tyler still has a lot invested in this place. His uncle owns it. I'm sure whoever that guy was, he won't be setting foot in here again," Kyla said.

"Here they come. Who's the guy with them?" Tori quirked her eyebrow.

I swung my head their direction. "That's Draven." My mind swirled to figure out where he had come from. How he had ended up here out of all the bars in the area.

Tori licked her lips. "Ummm. Delicious."

Chapter 12
Draven

When Chase and I got to the club we went right to the bar and grabbed a couple of stools. I ordered a Kamikaze for myself and a beer for Chase.

"Thanks, man. You think you can find what you're looking for here?"

I scanned the club. It was the right age group and there were a ton of hot chicks. "Yeah, I think this will do."

"Cool. Mind if I call Becca? I kind of blew her off tonight, but if I'm lucky she'll still blow me later." Chase wiggled his eyebrows.

I threw my head back and laughed. "Call your girl, I'm good. You're cramping my style anyways."

Chase flipped me off and started texting.

The tall lanky blond across the bar swayed back and forth, smiling at me over her glass. She pulled the olive out of her drink and pulled it off the skewer with her lips in a seductive way. That's what I was talking about. She was a sure thing.

I jerked my head to the side, motioning for her to come my way. She was the total opposite of Layla. Where Layla was tiny, full of attitude, and dangerous looking, this girl was tall, blond and ready to fuck. She was exactly what I needed to scrub the image of Layla from my mind.

I watched her walk around the bar to stand next to me. "Hey."

I grabbed her around the hips and moved her between my legs. "Hey, yourself. You here alone tonight?"

"Came with a couple of girlfriends." She set her drink on the bar. "I'm just looking for some fun."

I took a lock of her long blond hair and twisted it around my finger. "What a coincidence. I'm just looking for some fun, too." Translation… I was looking to get my dick wet. I took in her dark makeup and shimmery pink dress. She was trying too hard.

Layla never had to try. She was sexy without even knowing it. Her tank top and shorts today shouldn't have turned me on, but they did. I wanted to pull her into my arms the moment I saw her this morning.

I shook the thoughts of Layla from my head. I was here to forget about her for one night. The blond in front of me would do the trick. "What's your name, darling?"

"Carrie." She giggled. "Want to buy me another drink?"

"If you'll keep me company, I'll buy you whatever you want." I motioned to the bartender.

Carrie placed her glass on the bar, "I'll take another strawberry martini." She pointed at me. "He's paying."

I gave the bartender a chin up, accepting the drink on my tab. It was a small price to pay for what she was going to give me later.

"So, where are you from? I haven't seen you here before."

I lifted my drink to my lips. "I'm from New York. I'll only be in town for a few weeks."

"Oooooh, I love New York," she exclaimed. "They have the best shopping."

"Yeah, well I'm from Brooklyn and I'm not much into shopping. It ain't Manhattan and it sure as hell isn't Fifth Avenue. I'm from a little seedier part of town."

"So, you're a bad boy? I bet you have a motorcycle."

This chick was looking for someone to piss her daddy off. I didn't give a shit, 'cuz I was never gonna meet her daddy. "Got a Harley. We can go back to my place and I'll give you a ride."

She tapped her fingers against my chest. "I might be persuaded to do that, but I need a sample of the goods first."

Fuck, this was easy. I lifted an eyebrow at her. "Come a little closer and I'll give you that sample."

She stepped in closer. My hand ran up her thigh and under her skirt, palming her ass. She gasped and rested her head on my shoulder.

That's when I was brought back to reality. Looking over her shoulder. There was my girl. She was dressed to kill in a black mini-skirt and a black corset. Some blond-haired douchebag was rocking up against her. Carrie nibbled on my neck, but I barely felt it. All I could focus on was Layla and the guy who held her hips, swaying to the music.

I couldn't get away from her for one fucking night. She was everywhere. Jealousy burned inside of me. I wanted to pummel the guy she was with. I watched them closely, ignoring the lips that nipped at my neck.

"Let's go out to your car," Carrie whispered.

I barely heard her. The only thing that registered with me was the way that guy had Layla wrapped in his arms. I couldn't take my eyes off the two of them.

Layla stumbled in her heels and her one hand came up to pull at the arm around her chest. I couldn't see her face, but something was off.

I pushed Carrie off me. "Some other time. Something just came up."

Carrie took two steps back. "Asshole," she hissed.

I didn't give a shit. All I cared about was the scene playing out in front of me. Nobody was going to touch my girl that way. Okay, so she wasn't my girl yet, but I cared about her and this shit wasn't cool.

I watched him move Layla further and further from the center of the dance floor. Everyone around her was oblivious to the struggle. She squirmed in his arms. She twisted, and I saw the fear in her eyes.

That fucker was a dead man. I stormed forward, pushing bodies out of my way. I only had one destination, and that was Layla.

I wrapped my hand around the back of the douchebag's neck and squeezed my fingers into the sides of his throat. He released Layla and she stumbled forward into her friends' arms. The relief on her face was palpable.

Two big guys flanked me. Fuck them. I'd take them on too.

But they weren't coming for me. Each one of the guys grabbed an arm of the guy I had in my grip. I released my hand and followed as they escorted him out of the bar.

"We don't put up with that shit here, asshole," one of them said.

"What the fuck is wrong with you?" the Italian guy asked.

"She was down for it! Did you see the way she was dressed?" Douchebag tried to defend himself.

My fists clenched and unclenched at my sides as we exited the bar. I wanted one shot. Just one. "Hold him up," I ordered, not knowing if they would. To my surprise, they didn't let him go. I cocked my arm back and let my fist fly into his face.

The two guys dropped him, and he fell to the ground, blood running out of his mouth.

I squatted down and hissed in his ear, "You don't treat women like that, fucker. Learn some goddamn manners."

"Bruno, take care of this piece of shit. I don't ever want to see him here again."

The bouncer, who I hadn't even noticed, gave a chin up. "Sure thing, Ty. He won't be a problem here again."

"Well, that was fun. I was hoping he wasn't such a pussy, so I could get a shot in myself. It's been a while."

Ty held his hand out to me. "I'm Tyler and this is Chris," he said, jerking his head toward the Italian guy. "My wife is a friend of Layla's."

I shook both of their hands. "Draven. I work with Layla."

"I've never seen you there." Ty crossed his arms over his wide chest, clearly not trusting me.

"I'm filling in for Zack while he's in California," I clarified.

He seemed satisfied. "Cool. Let's go check on the girls. Layla's got to be rattled."

I followed them in and over to a table where Layla was sitting with two other chicks. I pointed to the blond. "I know you. You're the chick that brought in all those drawings yesterday."

She smiled. "That's me. I'm Kyla and this is Tori."

The dark-haired girl, Tori, held up her hand across the table. "You must be Draven."

I took her hand loosely in mine. "I am."

Layla glared at me. "Are you fucking following me?"

I shook my head at her accusation. "I'm not following you. I came here with Chase. You're welcome, by the way."

The fear I had seen before was gone and her steely attitude was back. "I was fine. Tyler and Chris had it handled. I didn't need your help."

This woman was impossible. "Well, a guy puts his hands on you like that and you're getting my help whether you want it or not."

Chris and Tyler had pulled up chairs to the table. I grabbed my own and sat down next to Layla. She huffed at me. "What are you doing?"

I smirked at her. "Having a drink with my new friends." I motioned to everyone at the table.

"They're my friends," she said between clenched teeth.

61

"And now they're mine too." I rubbed my hand along her bare shoulders. The flower tattoo that started on her arm ran over her shoulder and down her back, disappearing under her top. "What's wrong, *pisoi*? Don't you want to share?"

"Quit calling me that. I don't even know what it means." She turned to Tyler and Chris. "What did you do with him?"

Chris spoke up first. "We just drug him out, but Draven made sure he won't be bothering you again. Gave him a good right hook."

Layla glared at me. She should have been appreciative, but instead she looked pissed.

Then Tyler piped up, "I'm sorry, Layla. We should have been paying closer attention."

She dropped her head. The fight left her eyes. "I don't know what happened. One minute we were dancing, the next he was dragging me away. I should have just stayed home tonight. It's not anyone's fault but my own."

Kyla took her hand. "It's not your fault. Some guys are just assholes."

She looked down at her outfit. "Yeah, well, I should have worn jeans and a t-shirt. I know better."

"Stop," Tori commanded. "You don't get to blame yourself. You look hot tonight, but that doesn't give any guy an excuse to touch you. No means no."

"Listen to my wife, Layla. She's right. Guys like that make us all look like assholes," Chris added.

I leaned in close to her ear. "You look beautiful."

Layla picked up her phone. "I think I'm gonna go."

Nope. Not happening. "Don't go." I took her hand in mine. "Come dance with me."

"I think I've had enough dancing for the night."

"Come on, you owe me one dance. I mean, I did save you tonight. It's the least you could do."

She rolled her eyes. "Oh, please."

I gave her a pleading look. "Just one dance. If you still want to leave after that, you can go."

"You should dance with him," Tori said with a wink.

"You should," Kyla agreed.

I was starting to really like Layla's friends, although she didn't seem as amused.

"Fine," she huffed. "One dance and then I'm leaving."

I led her to the dance floor, stopping by the DJ first.

"What did you just request?" she asked curiously.

I shrugged my shoulders. "You'll see." We made our way to the middle of the floor and a small smile started to make its way onto her face. The song changed, and "Rock Your Body" started playing.

A full smile took over her face. "I never pegged you for a Justin Timberlake fan."

"It fit," I defended. "You wanted to walk away, I wanted you to stay and dance."

"You're ridiculous," she laughed.

My hands went to her hips. "Hey, it worked. You're smiling and we're dancing."

She slung one arm over my shoulder and swayed her hips with me. "One dance."

She was so tiny. Even in her heels, she only came up to my chest. I felt the need to protect her. To keep her safe. I wanted her to trust me to do that for her.

Layla turned in my hands and leaned her back against my chest. My cock pressed into her back as we swayed together. She took a small step away and lifted her arms above her head. She closed her eyes, but I couldn't take mine off her. The way she moved mesmerized me. In this moment, she was someone different than the hard-edged woman she was at work. She was free. She let the music consume her and carry her away. She looked happy and I made a silent vow to put that look on her face over and over again.

When the song ended, I turned her toward me. "Was that so bad?"

She smiled at me shyly. "Not at all." The song slowed to Ed Sheeran's "Thinking Out Loud". "I love this song."

"Then dance with me one more time." I didn't care what the song was, I just wanted to hold her a little longer.

"Okay."

I wrapped an arm around her waist and took one of her hands in mine, holding it to my chest between us. She wrapped her other arm around my neck. "This is nice. I wasn't lying, you do look beautiful tonight."

"Thank you." She blushed. "And thank you for helping me tonight, but I don't need you to save me. I've been taking care of myself for a long, long time."

"How long?"

I could see her closing up again. "It doesn't matter." She shook her head. "What does it mean? That word you call me?

"*Pisoi?*"

"Yeah, that. What does it mean?"

I ran my hand through the long ends of her ponytail. "It's Romanian. It means kitten."

She scoffed. "Why would you call me that? I'm nothing like a kitten."

Smiling softly at her, I traced the dark liner that formed her cat eyes. "At first, it was this. But then it became more. I think underneath this harsh exterior is a scared little kitten. What you see is not really who you are."

Layla choked down the lump in her throat. "You don't know anything about me," she whispered.

"You can try to hide, but I see you."

She took a step back. "I need to go home." She let go of me and hightailed it back to the table. I quickly followed behind, refusing to let her escape. She grabbed her purse and phone from the table. Tapping on the screen, Layla let out an exasperated sigh. "It's going to take 45 minutes to get an Uber."

"We can take you home," Chris volunteered.

"We were planning on it. It's not a problem," Tyler added.

"I got her," I insisted, wrapping my arm around Layla's waist. "I probably live the closest anyway." Even though I had no idea where she lived, I assumed she lived close to work.

"You don't have to drive me," Layla protested.

"I do. We haven't finished talking."

"Fine. I just want to get home." She stepped to Kyla and Tori giving them each a hug. "We should do this again. Next time, minus the drama."

I gave everyone a wave. "I'll catch up with you guys soon. Maybe we can grab a beer sometime."

Chris held out his fist. "For sure, man. Thanks for your help tonight."

I bumped him back. "Anytime."

I led Layla to my blacked-out Hummer and opened the door for her. She hesitated. "How the hell am I supposed to get up in there dressed like this?"

"Easily." I lifted her around the waist and placed her into the seat.

Layla scowled at me. "Really?"

"Really." I closed the door and hopped into the driver's seat. "Where to?"

She crossed her arms over her ample breasts. "Take a right."

We drove in silence for a while. "Draven." "Layla." We both said at the same time.

She waved her hand at my face. "You first."

"What did I do to make you hate me so much?"

She sighed. "I told you I don't hate you."

"Well, you sure as hell don't like me."

"It's not you per say. It's what guys like you represent. You flash that panty dropping smile and expect girls to fall to their knees. I don't have time for games and I'm not into one-night stands."

She wasn't wrong, but hell if I'd admit it. "You don't know shit about me."

She huffed and let out a sarcastic laugh. "So, you don't want to fuck me? Cuz I know you sure as hell don't want to marry me."

"So that's it? Fuck you or marry you?"

Layla shrugged her shoulders. "Doesn't really matter because you're shit out of luck either way. I'm not going to fuck you and chances of me getting married are slim to none." She pointed out the windshield. "Take a left at the next light."

I put on my blinker and merged into the left turn lane. "You know there are things in between. What? Are you saving yourself for marriage?" The possibility that she was a virgin was almost inconceivable.

"I'm not a virgin. I just don't sleep around. And if you think I'm going to let myself become the property of any man, you're sorely mistaken."

My instincts told me she'd been hurt before. It made total sense. The bitchy attitude and cold demeanor. It was all a way to keep men away. I wasn't that easily deterred. "Maybe you just haven't found the right man."

"And you're him? Highly unlikely," she huffed. "Besides, you're leaving in a month. What's the point?"

"The point is that maybe I just want to spend time with you. And if it leads to incredible sex, so be it."

"Pretty sure of yourself, aren't you, cowboy?" She pointed again. "My apartment complex is up here on the right."

"I'm sure the sex would be incredible, and it wouldn't be a one-night stand." I turned into her complex. She led me through the maze of buildings, and I parked in front of hers.

"Thanks for the ride. I'll see you tomorrow." She reached for the door handle.

"Wait." I jumped out of my car and ran around to her side. I opened her door and reached in to lift her out.

"Thanks. I probably would have twisted my ankle jumping out of this thing in my heels."

I reached for her hand and twined her fingers with mine. "I'm not a bad guy, Layla. Let me walk you up."

She tried to pull her hand away, but I held tight. "You don't have to. I walk in by myself every night."

"Not when you're with me. I'd feel better knowing you made it to your door," I insisted.

For once, Layla didn't argue with me. She led the way into her building and up to the second floor. "This is me." When she saw I wasn't leaving yet, she sighed and unlocked not one, but three locks on her door. I was pretty sure that wasn't standard for any apartment. When she finally got the last one open and turned the knob, she leaned against the doorway. "Listen, Draven. I'm not trying to be bitchy here. I just don't see this working. I can't give you what you're looking for."

"Can't or won't?"

"What's the difference? It'll all end the same." Layla stared at her feet uncomfortably.

I lifted her chin, so she had no choice but to look into my eyes. "You don't know that. One date. That's all I'm asking for. We go out and see what happens. You might actually like it."

What the hell was I doing? I didn't date. I fucked. As often as possible. Dating was something other guys did, but Layla had me changing all the rules I'd laid out for myself.

"Fine," she relented. It wasn't the enthusiastic response I had hoped for, but it was something.

"Tomorrow."

Layla shook her head. "My brother is coming into town tomorrow. He'll be here until Monday. I haven't seen him in a long time, so…" She shrugged.

"Monday night then. You and me. No pressure, just two friends spending time together."

She cracked a smile. "So, we're friends?"

"For now." I winked at her. "I'll see you tomorrow." I leaned down and kissed her cheek then backed away.

I jogged down the steps and back out to my Hummer. I was feeling good about the progress I'd made with Layla tonight. She clearly didn't trust me, but I'd work to change that. I had no doubt that with the sparks that flew between us, sex with her would be like fireworks on the Fourth of July. When we got together it would be instantaneous combustion.

I pulled back onto the road and my phone went off. I answered without looking at the caller ID, thinking it was Chase wondering what had happened to me.

I couldn't have been more wrong. The voice on the other end was all business, "I've got a job for you."

Fuck!

Chapter 13
Layla

"Mrs. O'Connor, please tell us how long you've known the defendant," the prosecutor instructed.

"Three years."

"Please describe your relationship with Mr. O'Connor for the court."

"I met Michael, I mean Mr. O'Connor, my junior year of college. We met at a frat party and he swept me off my feet. He was kind and sweet and caring, everything a girl could want in a man. He was a finance major and a year ahead of me. We dated until I finished college. The day of my graduation, he proposed to me. We were married three months later."

"And was it a good marriage?"

I dropped my head, not able to make eye contact. "At first. It was everything I had dreamed of."

"At first? When did it change, Mrs. O'Connor?" the prosecutor prodded.

"Six months into our marriage. He started coming home from work late. He was often drunk or high. I'm pretty sure he was cheating on me."

The high-priced defense attorney practically jumped out of his chair, "Objection! The witness has no proof of that. It's purely speculation!"

The judge hit his gavel on the bench. "Sustained. Mrs. O'Connor, please stick to the facts."

I nodded as silent tears ran down my cheeks.

The prosecutor handed me a tissue. "At any time did the relationship turn violent?"

"Yes," I whispered.

"Please tell the court what happened."

I looked into the first row of the courtroom where my family sat. I didn't want to put them through this, but there was no way I could let Michael get away with *what he had done to me. I locked eyes with my father who gave me a nod of encouragement.*

"I had gotten home from work late and didn't have dinner ready when he got home. That was the first time he hit me, but it wasn't the last." I went on to describe the assaults that followed. My father had his arm wrapped around my mother's shoulders as she sobbed. My brother's eyes were filled with rage as I told about the abuse and rape I endured at my husband's hands. I told the court things I never wanted my family or anyone else to know.

"Did you ever call the police, Mrs. O'Connor?"

"No."

"Why not?"

"I was an elementary art teacher. Things like that don't happen to people like me. I didn't want anyone to know. I thought I could fix it. I just wanted my husband back."

I was ashamed.

Embarrassed.

How could I have been so blind? So stupid? So trusting?

"Tell the court about the night you ended up in the hospital."

I closed my eyes as the memories came flooding back. I remembered the rage. I remembered his dilated pupils. I remembered the whiskey on his breath. I swear I could still smell it lingering in the air around me.

I remembered the way he had screamed in my face and the pain of the first fist that connected with my cheek. I remembered him throwing my keys out the front door onto the lawn. I remembered the arguing and the awful things we said to each other. That was the first and last night I fought back. I kneed him in the balls. The brief reprieve while he clutched his family jewels gave me enough time to run up the stairs to our bedroom. I locked the door and searched for a place to hide. I should have escaped when I had the chance, but I wasn't in my right mind. It was a mistake I'd regret for the rest of my life.

I told my story of the hell I endured that night. At least, everything I remembered. There were parts that were hazy. Like I was watching someone else. The blurry flashes that were my reality were better off left unclear. Because anything else would destroy me.

The prosecutor again approached me. "Tell the court about your injuries."

I wiped at my eyes. "I was in a coma for eight days and for that I'm thankful. I had a concussion, a shattered cheek bone, my right arm was broken in two places and I had four broken ribs." My mom let out a loud sob in the silent court room. I took a deep breath, conjured up my strength, and continued, *"I was stabbed six times in the back and abdomen. One punctured my lung. Another went through my uterus, killing our baby."*

Michael, who had been eerily silent and emotionless during the proceeding, jumped to his feet. *"You cheating whore! That baby wasn't even mine! You got what you deserved!"*

The judge slammed down his gavel several times. *"Control your client or I'll have him removed from the courtroom!"*

The defense attorney pulled his client down and whispered in his ear. Michael's mask of indifference was firmly back in place.

"Miss O'Connor, were you ever unfaithful to your husband?"

I shook my head. "No. I loved him."

"I'd like to present the police report from that night as Exhibit A. I'd also like to enter into evidence Mrs. O'Connor's medical records detailing her injuries as Exhibit B, as well as pictures of those same injuries as Exhibit C."

The prosecutor placed each picture of my shame on a projector for everyone to see. I barely recognized my own face under the bruises that covered it. Each photo was more graphic than the last. The bile rose in my throat and I resisted the urge to throw up. I'd seen the pictures before, but it never got any easier.

"Where was Mr. O'Connor when the police arrived?"

"I don't know. All of that is blurry."

"Do you see your attacker in the courtroom today?"

"Yes."

"Can you identify him for the court?"

"Yes." I pointed to the man sitting at the defense table.

But it wasn't Michael. The man that stared back at me had long dark hair tied in a knot at the back of his head and amber eyes flecked with green. Draven's lips sneered at me, *"You're dead."*

I gasped. I sat straight up in bed, paralyzed by an overwhelming sense of fear. My body was covered in sweat. My eyes darted around the room at the shadows. I slowed my breathing and reached into my nightstand for my gun. I scooted back against the headboard of my bed and rested the gun on my bended knees, ready to take out any threat.

I listened for the telltale signs that someone was in my apartment. All I heard was the neighbor's television. Tires screeched outside, and I swung my gun in the direction of the window. My heart practically jumped out of my chest.

I slowly crept from my bed to the window and peeked out the blinds. Seeing nothing, I started the methodical inspection of my apartment I had mastered. I stole along the walls, staying as silent as possible as I checked out each room. When I reached the apartment door, all the locks were firmly in place and the chair was still under the doorknob.

I let out the breath I'd been holding and slid down against the door. My head dropped between my knees as I tried to gain control over my emotions. *It was just a dream.*

Five years and I was still living in hell. It was never going to end.

I went to work only because I had to. Getting only three hours of sleep wasn't a good enough reason to skip out on my responsibilities. After my dream—no not a dream, it was definitely a nightmare—I couldn't fall back asleep. Seeing Draven sitting at the defense table had rocked me to the core. Maybe it was just because he was the last person I had seen last night. Or maybe my subconscious was trying to warn me he was dangerous.

If I was being honest, I had felt safe in his arms while dancing last night. But I also knew how wrong my instincts could be. I had felt safe once before, and I married a monster.

I realized my biggest problem wasn't trusting someone else. My biggest problem was trusting myself.

It wasn't like Draven was trying to convince me that we could be a couple. He wasn't promising me a happily ever after. What he was offering was a happy-for-now situation. And after a few weeks when it ended, we would go our separate ways.

It wasn't an altogether unattractive proposition. It was something that might ease me back into a real life. One where I wasn't afraid of my own shadow. One where I could let go of the shame of the past and my fear of the future. One where I could be a tigress and not the scared little kitten Draven thought I was.

That's thinking too far ahead. One step at a time. My first decision was whether or not I was actually going to go out on a date with Draven.

I checked the clock in my studio. It was almost four.

James would be here soon. I had offered to pick him up from the airport, but he had insisted on renting a car, not wanting to inconvenience me.

Draven poked his head into my studio. "Hey, *pisoi*. What time are you leaving?"

I looked up from the ink on my client's ribs and glared at him. Some things were not going to change, even if I had kind of, sort of, agreed to go on a date with him. "Are you going to keep calling me that?"

His lips lifted in a half smirk. "Yes."

"You know I hate it, right?" Okay, I didn't totally hate it, but I wouldn't tell him that.

"You don't hate it," he said smugly.

I growled at him. He was making it hard for me to keep up my charade. "Whatever!
My brother should be here soon. I'm going to finish with this client and then we're going to dinner."

"You need me to lock up or is Chase handling it."

I set down my tattoo gun. "Whatever works for you two. It doesn't matter. I won't be in tomorrow either." I hadn't told him, but Chase knew.

He narrowed his eyes. "But we're still on for Monday night, right?"

"About that..." I started.

"Nuh-uh. You're not bailing on me. You promised me a date and I'm holding you to it. Wear jeans and boots. I'm taking you out on my bike."

I rolled my eyes. "You're kind of a pain in the ass. Has anyone ever told you that before?"

He stuck his hands in his pockets. "Maybe once or twice."

"Or a hundred. Tell me again why I should go out with you. We're like oil and water."

"More like a match and gasoline." He held his fists together and moved them apart spreading his fingers wide mimicking an explosion. "And that right there, *pisoi*, is why we should go out."

I shooed him away with my hand. "We'll see." I motioned to my client. "I'm busy right now. We'll talk about this later."

Draven started to back away, "You're not changing your mind. I protected your honor. You owe me."

I got up and shut the door in his face. Sitting back down on my stool, I apologized to Kendra. "Sorry about that. He's…"

"Gorgeous," she supplied. "If you don't go out with him, mind if I do?"

"Sure." *When hell freezes over*, I silently added. I may not have been sure I wanted to date Draven, but I wasn't going to hand him over to someone else either. Not until I knew exactly what this was between us.

I finished the butterfly, one of Kyla's designs, on Kendra's ribs and bandaged her up. I glanced at the clock again. *Where was James?*

The bells over the door jingled and I popped up off my stool to peek out of my studio. "Oh my God! You're here!" I charged toward my brother and jumped into his arms.

He picked me up and swung me around. "God, I've missed you."

Tears pricked my eyes. James was almost six-feet tall, but we shared the same green eyes and honey-colored hair. At least until I dyed mine jet black. Him being here was like having the other half of my soul back.

My brother set me on my feet and held me by the shoulders. "Let me look at you." He ran his hand through my hair and then down over the tattoos on my arm, as if inspecting to make sure it was really me. I could see the questions in his eyes, but he held them back for my sake, knowing now wasn't the time.

"Hold on, let me grab my purse and then we can get out of here." I rushed back to my studio and grabbed my purse from the locked cabinet. In my hurry, I crashed into Draven on the way out.

He grabbed me by the waist to keep me from falling over. "Whoa there. Slow down."

I disentangled myself from his hands. "Sorry. My brother just got here, and I need to go."

"Can I meet him?"

My guard went up. "Why?"

He shrugged. "Why not?"

"It's not necessary," I insisted.

"Sure it is, if I'm going to date his sister." He flashed a smile at me.

It was a smile I was starting to hate. It made me weak. It made me want to say yes to everything he was offering. It made me want things I had no business wanting. "Fine," I huffed.

When I got back up front, my brother was already talking to Chase. I hoped James would remember everything I'd told him. One slip could ruin everything I'd built here. The last thing I wanted to do was move and start over somewhere else.

"It's nice to finally see where my baby sister has been working and living." I watched James as he took in his surroundings. It was a long way from the wholesome upbringing we had. We were raised in a large four-bedroom house in an upper-class neighborhood. White picket fence and all. My mom stayed at home taking care of us and was on the PTA. My dad was a partner in at a prestigious law firm. I was a good girl who got exemplary grades. My parents held the highest expectations for my brother and me. He was a stellar All-American athlete who played football and baseball. I was the captain of the cheerleading squad. Hell, I'd even been the Homecoming Queen. We were the perfect family.

Until we weren't.

Until I fucked it all up.

Until my name ended up in the newspaper along with the tragedy that ripped us at the seams. Our family had always been well-known and admired for our successes, but when people you've known your whole life started whispering behind your back, you found out who your true friends were. Girls like me didn't marry men who beat and raped them, and they sure as hell didn't end up on the front page of the paper. But when your husband was the son of the most successful financial mogul in Oregon, the press nearly trampled each other to get the details.

The story was so juicy that it thrust both our families into the spotlight. We couldn't go anywhere without a camera shoved in our faces. Every bit of the trial was public knowledge. The press had no respect for my privacy or the hell I was going through.

"Baby sister, huh?" Chase questioned, clearly interested in gaining some insight into my life. "Was she a total brat? One of those little sisters that followed you everywhere."

James smiled at me. "Nah. We were actually best friends."

"Not were. Are," I interjected. "He's only older by five minutes. We're twins. Can't you see it?" I sidled up next to James and he wrapped his arm around my shoulder.

Chase studied us carefully. "Are you fucking with me?" His eyes ping-ponged between us. "I don't see it. He's tall and you're short."

It was so typical of Chase to state the obvious. I laughed. "We're not identical, you nitwit."

Draven crossed his arms over his chest. "I see it. It's in the eyes."

"We do have amazing eyes, don't we? People always think they're colored contacts, but they're real," I blinked in quick succession, finishing it off with a wink.

He thrusts his hand forward to James. "I'm Draven. I work with Layla."

James clasped his hand firmly. "Nice to meet you. I'm thinking about getting some ink while I'm here, so maybe I'll see you tomorrow."

What? My clean-cut brother was going to get tatted? That should be interesting. "I'll look forward to it."

Having my brother intermingle with my life here was not what I planned when he said he was coming. Keeping my two lives separate was all I knew. It worked for me. "Let's go. I'm starving and I'm sure you must be too." I tugged on James's hand and led him to the door.

After pizza and a few beers at The Locker, I took James back to my apartment. I felt his eyes bore into the back of my head while he waited patiently for me to key open all the locks on the door. He carried his duffle bag in and set it on the couch. "Jenna, is this not a safe neighborhood?"

"It's super safe," I assured him.

"Then what's with the locks? It's not normal."

"They were already here when I rented this place," I answered nonchalantly. "Do you want a drink?" I wandered to the kitchen and pulled two glasses out of the cupboard.

James stared at me with his hands on his hips. "Part of the condition of me being here was no bullshit, Jenna. You weren't a good liar as a kid and you're not much better now."

"Funny you should say that. I didn't have any problem convincing everyone I had the perfect marriage. And that was a total lie."

"Jenna…"

I held up my hand to stop him. "The last thing I want to do is fight with you. The locks make me feel safe, okay? I know it's weird, but this is me."

"I don't want to fight with you either. It's just a lot to take in. I thought you were okay. You know he's still in prison, right?"

I dropped a few ice cubes in each glass and poured in some Jack. "Logically I know he can't hurt me, but my brain hasn't gotten the message. Trust me, I've tried."

"So, no one here knows about your past? It was so strange hearing everyone call you Layla."

I slid one glass across the counter to James. "My neighbor, Brian, knows most of it. But no one knows who I really am. I don't need anyone poking into my business. I like it here. I like that no one knows my past. They don't look at me like I'm damaged."

"Jenna, you're not damaged."

"The hell I'm not! You saw the locks! I haven't had a relationship with a man in five years. I'm pretty sure my lady parts need dusting."

James cringed. "Please don't talk about your lady parts."

"Oh, grow up! The closest thing I've gotten to cock was groping my gay neighbor the other night. Who, by the way, I would totally fuck given the chance. He's the only one I trust enough not to hurt me."

"Are you serious? You haven't had sex since you got divorced?"

I shook my head and downed my whiskey. Grabbing the bottle by the neck, I poured myself another glass.

"Come here." I walked around the counter and into his arms. James pressed my head into his chest and held me tightly. "I'm so sorry. I didn't realize how much you were still hurting."

I pushed back from his chest. "Most days are good days, but the fear hasn't totally gone away. I don't think it ever will. Which really sucks, because Draven asked me out on a date, but I don't know if I can do it."

"The guy you work with?"

"Yeah, he just started this past week. He thinks we have *amazing chemistry*," I air-quoted.

James smirked at me. "Do you?"

I threw my hands up in the air. "I don't know. Maybe. He hasn't made it a secret that he wants to have sex with me."

"And?"

"What if he hurts me? What if I freeze up? It's been a while."

"Give it a chance. You're not the same girl you were back then. You're so much stronger than you give yourself credit for."

"Am I?"

"Yes, Jenna, you are. You're the strongest person I know. You left everything you knew and started a new life for yourself. That takes a lot of courage."

I tossed back more whiskey. "I ran."

"You started over. The girl I see before me now doesn't take shit from anyone. Mom and dad would be proud of you."

"You think?"

"I know. They miss you, but they understand."

"I'm a long way from our days at the country club. They probably wouldn't even let me in the door looking like this."

"Fuck them! They're a bunch of pretentious snobs. You're beautiful the way you are. I'm so proud of you and I'm honored that you're my sister."

Later that night, James and I laid on the floor underneath a fort made of blankets, just like when we were kids. It was silly, but it was comforting. I held the flashlight while he made the shadow of a rabbit. "Real creative," I said sarcastically. We used to have competitions when we were little as to who could come up with the best shadow.

He grabbed the flashlight from me. "Fine. What've you got?"

I twined my thumbs together and moved my fingers, making a hawk with its wings flapping. "What's that supposed to be? A butterfly?"

"No, you idiot. It's a hawk." I moved my hands side to side, making the hawk soar across the ceiling of our fort.

James pulled my wrist down and inspected it with the flashlight, running his fingers over the scars I had tried to cover. "I'm so sorry, Jenna."

I snatched my hand away. "For what?"

"Not realizing how much you were suffering. Not just during your marriage, but after. The stress you were under must have been debilitating."

I stared at the ceiling. "It wasn't your fault. I was looking for a way out. I was a coward."

"I should have been there for you. I was so wrapped up in my new job. I should have paid more attention. I knew it was hard on you and I wasn't there like I should have been. Part of me wanted to pretend it wasn't real."

My eyes welled with tears remembering. "You don't get to do that," I said softly. "You don't get to take responsibility. It was my fault. I was weak and ashamed. It was my decision to try to make it go away." Neither one of us would say the word.

Suicide.

It wasn't something we discussed.

Ever.

But tonight, apparently, we were breaking the rules.

"I'll never forget that day. Seeing you lying there on the bathroom floor and all the blood. I'm just glad I got to you in time." His voice hitched as he relived the memory.

"Sometimes I think it would have been easier if you hadn't found me," I whispered. "I'm so fucked up," I said honestly.

James pulled me to his chest. "Don't ever say that. I couldn't live without my other half. I may not ever get to see you, but I can feel you. You're part of me. I may not tell you enough, but I love you."

The tears leaked from my eyes. "Do you ever think I'll ever be normal again? Don't bullshit me either."

"Yes. I think you blame yourself for everything, but he fooled us all. We all thought Michael was a great guy. The only one to blame for the abuse he put you through is Michael. Thank God he's paying for it. I hope someone made him their bitch in prison. He deserves that and more."

"You know he's going to get out eventually, right? And he's going to be pissed."

"And that's why you've done what you did. You've moved across the country, changed your name, changed the way you look... there's no way he could find you. You're safe here and that makes me not being able to see you worth it. I'd give up everything just to know you're safe."

"I'm glad you're here now. I've missed you so much."

James kissed my forehead. "I've missed you too. Now, on a different note, about your impending date."

I groaned.

"I think you should do it. You need to get laid, girl. And I'm not saying that as your brother, because that would be gross, but shit... five years?"

"I know. Pathetic, right?" I sat up and crossed my legs.

"Ridiculously so. I mean, don't you have... needs?" he asked.

"Okay, I'm going to preface this with the fact that you and I discussing my sex life is weird. And slightly embarrassing. But, yes, I have needs and I've handled them myself."

James covered his face with his hands. "Okay, now I need to bleach that picture from my mind."

I slapped him on the shoulder. "You asked! And you're not supposed be to picturing it anyways, you pervert!"

"I can't believe I'm going to say this, but... go get yourself some dick." James erupted with a bout of laughter that was contagious.

"Point taken." I laughed back.

Chapter 14
Draven

I thought I was done with this shit, but apparently, I wasn't.

I was strapped to the hilt, two semi-automatics under my jacket and another in my ankle holster. My switchblade laid heavy in my pocket. I had no idea what I was walking into. This city wasn't familiar to me and neither were the people I was meeting. If shit went bad, I didn't have an escape plan. I cursed myself for not coming down here in the daylight to scope things out. But with Layla leaving early tonight, I couldn't very well have left early too.

Detroit had a bad reputation and for a good reason. I was glad I was living forty-five minutes north of it. They'd tried to clean it up with new stadiums and flashy casinos, but beyond the few square miles that drew sports fans and gamblers, was the real heart of the city. Abandoned factories from Detroit's glory days as the automotive capital of the world littered the city. Burned out houses outnumbered the occupied ones. Small time drug dealers did their business right out on the street and prostitutes stood on corners flagging down their next johns. The cops stayed away. They didn't get paid enough to deal with the filthy shit that went down in this city.

The old warehouse I was parked around the back of, was covered in graffiti, windows had been broken out and the lot was overgrown. I was early. No way was I walking into an ambush. I crept inside the warehouse, situated myself out of sight and lit a cigarette. Now the waiting began.

Twenty minutes later, I heard the rumble of a truck pulling up. It backed into the warehouse and I watched as two men jumped out. I caught the profile of my brother, Nico. He put his hands to his mouth, "cacaw." That was my call.

I tossed down my smoke and stepped from the shadows. My hand gripped one of the guns under my jacket. I trusted my brother, my blood, but as for the other guy, not a bit. Trust was how you got killed in this business.

"Just you two?" I asked.

"Besides Mike, I got two more." His fist pounded on the side of the truck. He stepped around back and rolled up the door.

Cyrus and Kane hopped out, strapped with AK47s. *Nice.* My anxiety dropped a couple of notches. "I see Andrei sent the best."

Cyrus clapped me on the shoulder. "The best was already here. Tell me what The Raven is doing in this shithole of a city."

The Raven was the name I'd earned by being dark and dangerous. When I had a job, nothing got in my way. I handled shit even if it meant getting my hands dirty... or bloody as it may be. I'd had blood on my hands since I was sixteen. I was ruthless and cold, black-hearted most would say. The Raven was respected and feared, and I liked it that way. I thrived on it.

"I'm here helping out a friend. Didn't expect to be doing a job."

Nico stepped forward. "You didn't actually think Andrei would let you out, did you?" We always referred to our father by name when in the company of others. He'd earned that respect from us.

"Not out. Just a break." I reached into my pocket and pulled out another cigarette. Cupping my hands around it, I lit it and blew out the smoke. "How long we got?"

"Should be here in the next ten. How's this going down?"

"I'll do the talking. You do the counting. When we're sure they didn't fuck us over we make the trade. Cyrus and Kane can oversee the exchange. We sense anything is off and we take them out. All of them. They may not know us yet, but they'll know not to fuck with us by the night's end."

Kane nodded his agreement to the plan. "That's what I'm talking about. No one fucks with The Raven."

"No one," I confirmed. The sound of tires on the gravel outside alerted us our guests had arrived. This may have been their city, but tonight this was our house. "Showtime, boys."

Car doors slammed, and three guys dressed all in black entered the warehouse. I wasn't foolish enough to think they weren't packing. I took in the way they swaggered with cocky assurance. They were used to being feared. It was ironic that tonight they'd learn what real fear was. And I would be the one to teach them.

"What's up, homies? You got the goods?" their leader asked.

I stepped forward and pressed my semi-automatic to his forehead. Cyrus and Kane flanked the trio from the back, shoving the AKs into their sides. "They call me The Raven and I make my living feeding off shit like you. This is business, don't mistake it for something else. I'm not your homie and I'm not your friend."

Nico and Mike stepped forward and patted the three down, stripping them of all weapons. Nico then grabbed the duffle bag from the gangbanger I had silenced with my gun. He unzipped it on the floor and began counting the money. After a few minutes of tense silence, Nico looked up. "It's all here."

I lowered my gun. "Now we can do business."

"Fuck, man! Was that shit necessary?" the gangbanger asked.

"Fuckin' right it was. I don't know you. I've got zero reasons to trust you."

"I don't exactly trust you either, man."

"You shouldn't. That would be your first mistake. Your next would be fucking me over. We clear?"

"Crystal."

I motioned to the truck. Cyrus, Kane and Mike started unloading the merchandise. The boxes were opened one-by-one to reveal the guns inside. The last thing this city needed was more guns, but if they didn't get them from us it would be someone else. Better the money went in our pockets than anyone else's.

We got the truck unloaded and left the goods on the warehouse floor. We had our money. It was their problem to transport the guns from there.

Cash in hand, the five of us jumped into the truck and vacated the premises. Kane hopped out when we got to my car and rode out of the city with me, as we followed behind the truck. "It was good to have you with us tonight," he said to me, checking the back window to make sure we weren't being followed. Doing a deal like we'd done tonight, we always ran the risk of being followed and hunted down for the money we'd driven away with. Honor among criminals? It didn't exist. "Looks like we're clear."

I breathed a breath of relief. No deal was ever a sure thing. "I'd say it was my pleasure, but that'd be a lie. I didn't come here for this shit. I've got other things that are more important right now." My fingers twitched on the steering wheel.

Kane inspected me from the side. "There's a woman, isn't there?" We'd been friends a long time. He knew my history. Rarely the same girl twice. Definitely no relationships.

I scrubbed a hand over my face. "I didn't mean there to be, but she's different. I've been putting the moves on her from day one and all she does is turn me down."

Kane barely contained the laugh that rumbled his chest. "YOU got shot down? That's got to be a first."

"Yeah," I admitted. "There's just something about her though. She's not like other women. She's sassy and bitchy, but she's sexy as fuck. I can't walk away."

"That's new. You ever had a girl who wouldn't willingly drop to her knees for you?"

Kane was right. I'd never had to work this hard for pussy before. "Nope. It took some prodding, but I finally convinced her to go on a date with me."

Kane crossed his arms over his chest. "Have you ever even been on a date? Ever had to convince a girl to suck your dick or fuck you?"

"No, but I'm willing to try. I'm taking her out on my bike and… well, fuck I don't know what else. It's not just about the sex though." Yeah, dating was not my strong suit. Dinner and romance? I usually had my dessert before we ever got to dinner.

He laughed at me. "You really like her, don't you? What happens if this works? You gonna date her beyond sex? This life isn't conducive to relationships. Plus, there's the little fact that she lives here, and you live in New York."

"What if I decide to stay?" Where that idea came from, I had no idea. New York was my home.

"She gonna be cool with what you do?"

"I'm a tattoo artist." It was what I did. It wasn't who I was.

"You work for Andrei. Don't fool yourself. If you think he's gonna let you out, you're wrong." Kane had known me since I was ten, there was no hiding shit from him.

"First I have to convince her I'm worth taking a chance on. I'll deal with Andrei later."

"Good luck with that, man. Your dad is scary as fuck, but he pays well."

"Yeah, well, she doesn't need to know what I do. No one here does." I'd convinced myself that I could keep my two lives separate. I'd never drag Layla into the darkness of my life. I'd keep her safe. Memories of last night flashed through my mind, remembering the way that piece of shit had touched her. The protectiveness I'd felt toward her had consumed me.

"You're playing with fire, man. You're gonna get burned."

He was right. I knew he was, even if I didn't want to admit it.

I followed Nico's truck to the off-ramp of the expressway and into a parking lot. Kane clapped me on the shoulder. "If you need to talk, I'm just a phone call away. Women are complicated creatures."

"Got you on speed dial, but I can handle my own shit," I assured him.

He quirked an eyebrow at me and opened the door. "See you soon, brother."

Not too soon, was all I could think.

By the time I got back to my apartment, it was well after three in the morning. I threw the envelope containing my night's pay on the bed. Ten grand. That's what The Raven was worth for one night's work. It paid a shit-ton more than tattooing, but it came with a steep price.

Kane was right about so many things.

Things I didn't want to admit were true.

I worked for Andrei.

I was a criminal.

Layla would never be okay with what I did.

It could never work.

I resigned myself to my original plan, before she had gotten under my skin. I'd enjoy her while I was here and then return to the life I knew.

She'd be a good fuck and nothing more.

Chapter 15
Layla

"Are you sure you want to do this?"

"I'm positive."

I held my tattoo gun over James's chest. "It's permanent. There's no going back once I start."

"It's what I want," he assured me. "And there's no one else I trust more than you."

"Okay. It'll sting a little at first, but you'll get used to it." I'd never done a more meaningful tattoo in my entire life.

James cringed when I touched the needle to his chest. I pulled back and let him take a deep breath. "I'm good. Keep going."

I nodded and started tracing over the image I'd put on his skin. It didn't take me long to finish, forty-five minutes tops. When I finished, I cleaned his chest and rubbed a salve over my brother's new tattoo. "I love it," I said through teary eyes. "Go take a look."

James stood and looked in the mirror. "It's perfect." I'd tattooed the astrological sign for twins, Gemini, over his heart, with the word *Forever* above it.

When James told me what he wanted, I couldn't tell him no. It was a tribute to me. To us. To the bond that could never be broken, even with time and distance. It was a promise that we'd never let go of each other. That I'd never be alone. And I was honored that I'd been the one to permanently mark him. It made the tattoo that much more significant.

I pulled off my gloves. "What is Wendy going to think when she sees that?" I pointed at his chest.

"She'll love it. She's the one who suggested it. Wendy knows how much I've missed you and how much I hate that I never get to see my sister."

"Wendy sounds like an amazing woman," I said. I'd only seen her in pictures, but I knew how happy she made James. I loved her for loving him.

"She is. I hope one day you'll get to meet her."

"Me too."

A knock sounded at my closed door. I motioned for James to open it.

Draven poked his head in, and James backed up, so I could see. "I thought you weren't coming in today."

"I wasn't planning on it, but my brother decided he wanted me to take his virginity." I laughed, pointing at James's chest.

"Nice. What are you two up to the rest of the day?" Draven asked.

"My sis is taking me to a baseball game and then we're going back to The Locker afterward for drinks. You and Chase should meet up with us." I glared at my brother. I didn't want them to hang with us. I selfishly wanted to keep James all to myself.

Draven smirked at me, already sensing how I felt. "I might just take you up on that."

"If you already have plans…" I started.

"I don't." He winked at me.

"Fine. Maybe we'll see you later then." I waved my hands at him, shooing him from my studio.

"You can count on it." He turned and left with a promise hanging in the air of seeing me later.

I stood off my stool and shut the door. "Why did you invite him?" I hissed at my brother.

James pulled his shirt over his head and then grabbed me by the cheeks. "I want to know the man who's going to date my sister. I need to know he's good enough for you."

I slapped his hands away. "Maybe date. I haven't decided for sure."

He crossed his arms over his chest. "Yes, you have. You're curious, if nothing else. And… you need it. That guy is smitten with you. I can tell from the way he looks at you. He won't hurt you."

I rolled my eyes. "You've barely met him. How could you know all that?"

"I'm your brother and a man. I know."

"Yeah, well, that's what we thought about Michael too," I challenged.

"Michael always tried too hard. I should have seen it from the beginning, but this guy… I think what you see is what you get. Let's see if he shows tonight. That will tell me a lot."

"What are you, my dating guru now?"

"I'm a man who wants the best for his sister. You deserve that. You deserve to be happy and if I can help, I will."

My heart melted. It had been so long since someone had looked out for me. I felt like I had been alone for the last five years, and I had. But having James being protective over me felt like maybe I wasn't as alone as I thought. It made me yearn for the connection I had been missing. It made me think that maybe I deserved more than I had given myself.

James and I went to the minor league stadium down the street. James loved baseball and I thought this would be the perfect way for us to connect. We sat in the stands eating hotdogs and popcorn. Even though we were pushing thirty, we were just kids as we took in the familiarity of watching a game together. We cheered for the home team and did the wave when it came our way. We were silly and carefree as we sat in the sun enjoying the game.

I yearned for that part of my life to return. Where I was just a girl, and everything was normal. I'd been fooling myself for the last five years. I hadn't been happy... I'd been existing. I was done with that. I didn't want to only exist anymore. I wanted to live and enjoy life.

I wanted to laugh and dance and not worry about monsters or ghosts of the past. My heart cracked open a fraction of an inch. And for the first time in a long time, I saw something besides my past. I saw a future where I could actually be happy. Where I scowled less and smiled more.

James and I exited the stadium arm in arm, laughing as we walked down the street toward The Locker. It was almost seven o'clock by the time we made it through the familiar door of the bar that was my regular hangout. I saluted Lou, the owner and bartender, and dragged James to a table. Although we'd both had hotdogs at the game, I was starving again. We ordered cheeseburgers with bacon and mushrooms, just like we had back in college, when we'd meet up for dinner once a week.

Time ticked by, and I tried to ignore the fact that despite myself, I was waiting for Draven to show up. My eyes kept wandering toward the door, hoping to see him. The shop closed at six on Sundays. Unless he'd gotten caught up in doing a tat, he should have been off work for almost two hours and still he hadn't shown. I guessed he wasn't as serious about going out on a date as he had said.

Fuck him. This was better anyway.

I finished off the last bite of my burger, wiping the grease off my hands on a napkin. I was done waiting on Draven's fine ass. "You ready to get out of here?" I asked, reaching for my purse.

James put his hand on my arm. "What's your hurry? I haven't even finished my beer yet." He quirked an eyebrow at me. "Are you upset he didn't show?"

"Who?" I feigned innocence.

James narrowed his eyes at me, like *fucking really? Who the hell do you think you're fooling?*

Only myself, apparently. James could always read me like a book and right now I assumed the words on my pages were in big, bold print. I sighed. "It was stupid. He made it perfectly clear he wanted to have sex with me. I was the one who thought maybe he wanted more. I should have known better than to get my hopes up. I should have gone with my first instinct. He's an egotistical dickbag."

James suppressed a laugh behind his hand.

"Laugh it up, asshole. If he thinks I'm going to sit around and wait for him, he doesn't know shit about me. I'm not going to ride on the back of his motorcycle and I'm sure as hell not going to ride his dick. He may look like a Greek god, but I'm not some desperate little twit who's going to fall to her knees and worship him." I punctuated my rant by throwing my napkin on the table.

"Actually, I'm Romanian, not Greek," a deep voice sounded behind me.

I closed my eyes in horror. *Fuck! Just kill me now.* Turning my head in his direction, I glared at Draven. "You're late."

"No, I think I'm right on time. Otherwise, I would have missed you saying I was a Greek god."

"Obviously, you missed the part where I called you an egotistical dickbag," I countered.

Draven pulled out a chair and sat down. "No, I heard that too. I just chose to ignore it." He leaned in close to my ear, so James couldn't hear. "But make no mistake, you will be falling to your knees. And trust me, the worshipping will be mutual. I can taste you already." He slowly ran his tongue along the shell of my ear.

Heat crept up my neck and into my cheeks. No one had ever talked to me that way. Michael hadn't been much of a talker before, during, or after sex. It was more of a means to a happy ending for him. And usually only him. When he was finished, he'd roll over and go to sleep, leaving me to finish myself off. Good times.

Sadly, those were the good times. Once Michael decided he didn't need a willing partner and took what he wanted instead, sex became nothing but a torture device for him.

I pushed my chair back from the table. "I need to use the ladies' room." I stumbled my way to the bathroom, feeling a drunkenness that had nothing to do with alcohol. My panties were soaked, and my face was flushed. I leaned on the counter, *Pull yourself together*.

I'd built a wall so tall around my heart, that I'd forgotten what it felt like to be affected. The quickness of my heart, the shallowness of my breath, the flushing of my skin… all of it felt foreign to me. And in that moment, I decided I wanted to remember, if only for a few nights, what it felt like to be desired.

I splashed cold water over my face and neck. I'd made up my mind. I was going out with Draven tomorrow night. And if it led to incredible, life-changing, light-my-body-on-fire sex… so be it.

On Monday morning, I took James to breakfast before he had to leave for his flight. I wished he wasn't going back to Oregon. I wished we had more time together. Part of me wished I had never left in the first place.

But though I longed for home, the memory of why I left was fresh in my mind. James and I had relived my past over the last two days. We talked about all the things I kept deep inside and never shared with anyone. He inspected all my tattoos and assured me I was beautiful. For anyone else, it would have been creepy to have their brother say such things. But, as always, James knew what I needed to move forward.

I stood by his car, his duffle bag in the back seat, and hugged my brother. "Thank you for coming to see me. I'm going to miss you so much." My emotions stuck in my throat, making my voice gritty.

James pressed my head to his chest. "I should have done it a long time ago. I love you, Jenna."

He cupped my face and I stared up at him. "I love you too."

"Go out tonight and have a good time. He's a decent guy. Give yourself a chance to be happy."

"I will. I promise."

"Call me to let me know how it went."

"You want all the gory details?" I teased him.

He scrunched up his face. "None of them, thank you just the same. I need to know you're all right is all."

I let out a sarcastic laugh. "I'm tough. I'm always all right."

James ran his hand down my cheek. "I know you are. Too tough sometimes."

I shrugged, even though it was the truth. "Have a safe flight and tell everyone I said hello." I forced us back on steady ground before things got heavy again.

"I will. And don't forget to call or I'll hound your ass." James opened the door and started his rental. Then he was gone. The only family I'd seen in five years disappeared, leaving behind only his red taillights.

I went inside and got ready for work, showering and shaving myself smooth. Draven and I were going out right after Forever Inked closed and I remembered what he had said. Dressed in dark jeans and combat boots, I braided my long dark hair over one shoulder. I shoved a few things in my bag, so I could touch up later, then headed off to work. Even though I was nervous, I was excited about our date.

I came in the back door and went right to Zack's office. The receipts for the past two nights sat neatly arranged on his desk. It had to have been Draven because Chase's organizational skills severely lacked. I sorted through everything, entering it into the computer.

Chase knocked on the door and poked his head in. "How was your visit with your brother?"

I gave him a genuine smile. "Excellent. Thanks for covering for me the last couple of days."

He leaned against the door. "No problem. You know, I didn't even know you had a brother until this week. That's weird, right? I mean, I've known you for like over four years and I hardly know anything about your family or your past."

I knew this would come up eventually, especially with my brother coming here. "There's not much to know. The past is the past. You know all the important stuff about me. I prefer to live in the present." I tried to give off a *no big deal* attitude.

Chase scratched at his stubbled chin. "Yeah, I gotcha. Don't get defensive, but you've been a little moody this week. Is everything all right?"

I smirked at him. "Since when am I ever not moody?"

"True, but something seems off. Is it Draven? You two are going out tonight, right?"

I set down my pen. "I don't know," I said with a sigh. "You know I never date, but he's a persistent one. Is it going to be weird for you if we go out tonight?"

Chase plopped into the chair across from Zack's desk. "No. You're like my sister. I'm not jealous if that's what you're asking."

"No, I didn't think you would be. He's been here a week. Do you think he's a good guy?"

He shrugged his shoulders. "Seems like it. I know he's got it bad for you. Guy practically lost his mind when Brian came in the other day."

I did an internal fist pump. "You didn't tell him Brian's gay, did you?"

Chase chuckled. "No way. I was too busy watching him lose his shit."

"That good, huh?"

"Yep. Like a volcano exploding."

We both laughed at Draven's expense. Chase started to get up from his spot across from me. I stopped him. "Hey, Chase? I don't know that I've ever said it before... thanks for being a good friend. I'm lucky to have you."

He came around the desk and kissed me on the forehead. "The feeling is mutual. Call me if Draven's a dickhead tonight. I'll come rescue you."

"Thanks, but I think I can handle him."

He shook his head in amusement. "You're right. I should probably be more worried about him. You can be vicious."

I threw a wadded-up piece of paper at his head. "Get the fuck out of here." He was just about to walk out the door. "But seriously, thanks."

"Anything for you, Layla." And I knew he meant it. Chase was one of the few real friends I had.

Chapter 16
Draven

"You ready to ride, *pisoi*?"

Layla crossed her arms over her tits. "Where are we going?"

I tsked her. "Now, what would be the fun if I told you that? Where's your sense of adventure?"

She threw her hands up in the air. "You don't even have a plan, do you?"

God, I loved her feistiness. It was a huge turn on. "Cool your tits woman. I have a plan."

"Care sharing. I'm not going to just ride around aimlessly."

"We have a destination, I assure you."

"What about a helmet? I don't have a helmet and I'm not riding around on a motorcycle without one." She jutted her chin out in defiance.

This woman had more excuses than a pregnant nun and strangely, each one of them turned me the fuck on. I took her hands in mine and I could feel her pulse racing. I ran my fingers over the tops of her hands. "Are you finished? I would never put you in danger. Zack has Rissa's helmet and jacket in the garage out back. Have a little faith in me and just go with it. You might even enjoy yourself."

Her shoulders visibly relaxed. "Why do you want to date me?" At first, I thought it was another act of defiance, but when I looked deeper into her emerald-green eyes, I saw sadness. I didn't know who put it there, but I sure as fuck was going to try to take it away. It became my mission. I didn't know who the fuck I was anymore, because caring about someone else was a foreign concept to me.

I ran my thumb over her cheek. "Why wouldn't I want to date you? You're beautiful and spunky. And if I'm being honest, that sharp tongue of yours gets my dick hard."

Layla swallowed down the lump in her throat. "And I need to be honest with you. I can't promise anything beyond this. A date. Nothing more. I need to know that whatever happens tonight won't make things weird between us."

"Zero weirdness, unless it's in bed and you're into that. Then I'm all over weird and kinky. Only with you."

She slapped me on the chest. "You wish. And if I had to guess, you've had your share of kinky and weird." Layla planted her hands on her hips. "So, are we going out or what?"

She wasn't wrong, but hell if I'd say so. "Right. Let's go." I led her to the garage in back of the shop and lifted the door. I took Rissa's black leather jacket down. "Let's see if this fits you." I slid it over her arms and pulled on the front. "Like a glove. You were made for this." Next, I slid Rissa's helmet over her head and fastened the chinstrap. "So fucking sexy. I could take you right now. Want to just go up to my apartment instead?" Even though I knew she would shoot me down, I was only half joking. I could smell and taste her without even getting into her pants. I already knew she would be delicious.

Layla hopped on the back of my Harley like she was a pro. "I think you promised me a date, Mr. Constantine. No take backs."

I groaned. This woman was going to be the death of me. I straddled my Harley and kick started it. "Hold on, sweetheart. The night awaits us."

Layla's arms loosely held the sides of my jacket. I grabbed her hands and wrapped them around my waist. "Hold on tight. It's going to be a wild ride." I gunned the engine and took off out the gates of Forever Inked. Whatever happened tonight, I wanted to emblazon it in both our memories.

We sailed down M-59, Layla's arms wrapped tight around me. I wanted to push them down a little further. Although we were going east, I wanted her hands moving south. I was shit out of luck, because she had a death-grip around my waist as I cruised in and out of traffic.

Within ten minutes we had arrived at our destination. I turned into the parking lot and backed into a spot.

"Are you fucking kidding me?"

"Nope."

"Miniature golf?"

I unwrapped her hands from my waist. "Not just mini-golf, but go-karts and shit. This bad-ass enough for you?"

Layla laughed. But it wasn't just any laugh, it was almost hysterical. "God, I was so wrong about you. I thought you were going to take me to a strip club or something. This is... fuck, I don't even know."

I loved that I was able to surprise her. In a good way. I knew what she thought of me and I had just knocked down an invisible wall between us. "What? Are you chicken? Afraid I'm going to kick your ass in a game for teenyboppers?"

She climbed off my bike and unfastened her helmet letting her braid free. "Hell no! I rock at this!" The smile on her face was worth every bit of hemming and hawing I'd done. For not being a dating guy, I was already knocking this date out of the park.

I removed my own helmet and grabbed ahold of her hand. "Let's see what you're made of, woman." We walked through a throng of teenage couples toward the mini-golf window.

The girl at the hut took my money and looked bored. "What color balls do you want?"

Layla suppressed another giggle. "I'll take purple and he'll have blue. It's a first date."

The girl at the window definitely got her joke. "Would that be light blue or dark blue?" She smirked.

"Dark blue, for sure. I'm not that easy, despite what he thinks."

The girl put a purple and dark blue ball on the counter. "Have fun!"

"You have no idea," Layla answered.

I smacked her on the ass. "Put your money where your mouth is, sweetheart. Or you can just put your mouth where my money is." I grabbed my crotch in a lude gesture.

Layla pulled back with mock surprise. "You keep your money in your underwear? That's so gross!"

"For that to be true, I'd actually have to be wearing underwear." I wiggled my eyebrows at her.

"Ugh, you're the worst."

"You're the first one to ever say that. Usually it's 'Oh Draven, you're the best. Don't stop! More! Harder!'" I gave her my syrupy sex voice.

"Oh, God!"

"Yep. That's usually screamed too." I had to laugh because she walked right into that one.

Layla couldn't help but giggle at my theatrics. "Okay, enough of your out of control, inflated ego. Are we going to play golf or what?"

I straightened my back and got serious. "Yes, of course. Playing golf is our main priority tonight." We stepped up to the first hole and I motioned with my arm. "Ladies first."

I watched her perfectly round ass as Layla leaned over to place her purple ball on the mat. The things I wanted to do to that ass were almost as criminal as me. She gave it a little wiggle before standing back up. I groaned. "Watch and learn."

"Trust me, I'm watching," I said, not taking my eyes off her ass.

"Eyes on the ball, big guy," she scolded. I refocused my attention on the mat in front of her. Layla pulled the putter back and tapped the ball down the green. It hit the end of the track and ricocheted at the perfect angle, stopping a couple of inches from the hole. She let out a triumphant, "Yes! Your turn."

Layla stepped aside so I could place my ball on the mat. I sized up the hole, trying to figure out exactly where it would have to hit to get as close as hers. Satisfied with my analysis, I pulled the putter back and swung a little too enthusiastically. I watched the dark blue ball fly down the green. It hit the end of the track and flew over the top of the rail, sailed onto the green of another hole, bounced up and hit a teenage girl in the back.

I cringed and rushed forward to claim my runaway ball. Her date gave me a death glare. "Watch it, asshole."

The girl bent to pick up the ball and smiled at me with googly eyes. "It's okay. No harm, no foul, right?"

"I'm so sorry," I apologized. "I was trying to impress my girl and got carried away."

She glanced over my shoulder to where Layla stood holding her stomach, bent over, and laughing her ass off. "Oh, well…better luck next time."

I took the ball from her, getting another nasty look from her boyfriend and jogged back to Layla. She tried, unsuccessfully, to hide her amusement by pressing her lips tight together. "Not so hard next time."

"Again, something I never heard before," I teased, trying to ignore the fact that I had just assaulted a teenage girl with my ball.

Layla rolled her eyes. "Ever hear of a little thing called finesse? Golf is like sex. When you grip the shaft tight and hit it hard, there's the thrill of knowing you're racing toward the finish line, but you might not end up close to the hole. Sometimes she needs a gentle touch and to be rubbed the right way." Layla demonstrated how I should hold the club properly. "Grip it softly and stroke it smooth and you'll sink it right in the hole every time."

I scratched my chin. "Are we still talking about golf?"

She shrugged. "Take it as you like." She nodded to the mat. "Now, try again."

After Layla's very vivid description, all I could think about was sex. Not just sex, but sex with her. Something told me she was speaking from experience. Not saying I wasn't going to stroke her hard, but I'd give her the gentle touch she craved first. I pictured Layla on my bed, legs spread, my face between her thighs. I definitely wanted to hit a hole in one with her.

I shook the fantasy from my mind and placed my ball on the mat. This time I gently pulled the putter back and tapped the ball down the green. It ricocheted off the wall and stopped inches from Layla's ball. I hated to admit it, but she was totally right.

"Better?"

"Better," I confirmed. We walked to the cup and tapped our balls in.

Layla and I spent the next hour going from green to green, hitting our balls through a myriad of obstacles from bridges to windmills to pendulums and finally into the dreaded clown's mouth on the eighteenth hole. Honestly, I was glad the torture was done. If I had to watch her bend over one more time, I was afraid my cock was going to bust right through my zipper.

She sat down at a picnic table and began to tally our scores. I swiped the scorecard out of her hand. "We already know you won. Are you trying to rub it in?"

"Hey, this was your idea. What are you being so crabby about?" she questioned.

I scrubbed a hand over my head. "I don't know." I looked over her shoulder and then back at her pretty face. "Why'd you have to wear those jeans tonight?"

"You told me to wear jeans. I wear these to work all the time."

"I know, and your ass looks phenomenal in them. Every time you bent over I couldn't take my eyes off it." I looked around trying to find something else for us to do. "Want to drive the go-karts? That way you'll be sitting on your ass and I won't be able to stare at it."

"Sure."

I stood and took Layla's small hand in mine, twining our fingers together. The night was perfect, warm but not too hot. We walked to the line for the go-karts. I tugged on her braid. "Are you going to kick my ass at this too? Are you some kind of secret, professional Indy driver?"

She laughed. "No. Actually, I haven't driven one since I was a kid. James and I used to race all the time and he always beat me."

We stepped into the line behind a group of high-schoolers. "You and your brother sound like you were close. How come you hadn't seen him in so long?"

Layla frowned and picked at her nails. "I moved away from home almost five years ago and I haven't been back since." There was no disguising the hint of sadness in her voice.

I tucked a strand of hair that had escaped from her braid over her ear. "Where's home?"

"West coast," she said vaguely.

"A California girl, huh?"

"Something like that." It wasn't a denial, but it wasn't really an admission either.

I didn't push. "So how did you end up as a tattoo artist?"

"I went to Chicago when I was twenty-three and moved in with a friend. She was a tattoo artist and did my first one. After that I was hooked. I was naturally artistic, and she taught me everything I know. Just happened that I was good at it."

"Why'd you leave Chicago? I've been there a few times. It's a cool city, way more exciting than this."

"It was time to move on. I saw Zack's ad online and I've been here ever since. I like it. No one here knows me."

I ran my thumb over her cheek. "Why do I feel like there's a whole lot more to that story?"

Her eyes told me more than her mouth did. Layla shrugged. "There's not."

I nodded. I knew she was lying, but I could tell that she was done with the twenty questions I'd been asking. I wasn't going to get anything else out of her.

"So, what about you? Tell me about your family." It was obvious she was anxious to change the subject.

I quirked an eyebrow. "Not much to tell. My mom died when I was twelve. My dad has his own business. I have a younger brother and sister. My brother, Nico and I work for my dad, but I also tattoo, as you know. My sister, Catina, goes to NYU."

"I'm sorry about your mom. How did she die? Was she sick?"

I shook my head. "Nothing like that. I was young, but my dad said it was a car accident."

"You don't sound convinced," she prodded.

"There were some suspicious circumstances, but nothing ever became of it. My dad buried himself in work and never remarried."

"What kind of business does he have?"

Drugs. Guns. Murder if necessary. "Mostly imports and exports. He's kind of a middleman."

"Not to be critical, but it sounds boring."

"It is," I lied. It hit me right in the chest. What we did was anything but boring. Back home everyone knew who I was, what kind of business my dad ran. He was feared by most and I was following in his footsteps. Kane's words replayed in my head, *She gonna be cool with what you do?* That was a big, fat negative.

I placed my hand on Layla's back and led her forward in line. We were next. "You ready for this?"

Layla bounced on her toes. "Yes. It's going to be fun."

We entered the track and chose cars side by side. I watched as Layla fastened the five-point harness over her breasts. I got caught staring by the teenage attendant. "Sir, strap in." I reluctantly pulled my eyes off Layla and adjusted my own harness.

The lights began to flash, *red, yellow, green.* We eased on to the course waiting for the pack to break. Once it did, Layla hit the accelerator and cruised around the outside of the track, passing the young kids in front of us. I went for the more challenging route, cruising in and out of the cars in front of me. I caught her in no time and gave her a little wave as I passed by. The wind was blowing her hair around and a smile lit up her face as she flipped me the bird. Layla and I jockeyed for position around the track. She looked happy and it was a good look on her. When I saw the checkered flag ahead, I gave it a little more gas and slipped in front of her, crossing the finish line first and winning back my masculinity after the mini-golf debacle.

"Oh my God, my cheeks hurt from smiling!" Layla exclaimed. She undid her harness and I reached for her hand to help her out of the car.

I wrapped my arm around her waist and pulled her into my side. "Are you hungry?"

Layla patted her stomach. "I shouldn't be, but I could eat."

"Let's get you fed." I kissed the top of her head. It seemed so natural, like we were meant to be together. We followed the signs to the bar and grill, finding a high-top table in the corner. The place was busy, but our corner table gave us some privacy.

"So, on a scale from one to ten, how would you rate our date so far?" I asked.

She wobbled her head back and forth. "I'd give it a seven."

I clutched my chest. "A seven? Seriously?"

She shrugged. "Our date isn't over yet. How it ends will determine my final rating."

I took her hand over the table. "What would it take to get a ten?" I knew how I wanted our date to end. With her legs spread and me between them.

"Lean forward."

Like a wounded puppy I did exactly as she said. We both leaned over the table and our lips met, pressing together in a way that was both sinful and sensual. I ran my tongue along her bottom lip, and she eased back from the kiss. "That's a start. You're up to an eight," she teased coyly.

That kiss had caused all my blood to run south, and I discretely adjusted myself. "Call me a perfectionist, but I want a ten. You think I can get there?"

Layla bit her lip. "Maybe. I'm not making any promises, but your prospects are good."

The waitress came over and threw two napkins on the table, breaking the spell. "What can I get you?"

I nodded for Layla to order first. "Can I get a Jack and diet Coke?"

The waitress wrote it down without looking at Layla. "And what can I get you," she asked, tossing her hair over her shoulder, and licking her lips. She told me with her eyes that I could have *anything* I wanted.

"I'll have a Guinness, and can we get the sampler platter?"

"Sure thing. I'll bring your drinks right out." The waitress gave me a big smile and a wink without giving Layla a second glance.

"Flirting with the waitress is not going to score you any points. You're back down to a seven. Maybe a six. What? Am I invisible over here?"

I held my hands up. "I didn't do anything. I'm here with you. You're the only one I'm looking at. Trust me, the last thing I would do is flirt with someone else when I'm sitting with the most beautiful woman in the bar."

Layla rolled her eyes. "I gotta ask you something." She bit her lip again. "Did you sleep with Sydney?"

I shook my head. "I told you I wouldn't." Now that she'd opened that can of worms, I felt justified in asking the questions that had been burning inside me. "What about Brian? You two looked close. And that Sid guy. What about him?"

Layla burst out in laughter. "Sid is a muscle head. He's been after me for years, but he's not exactly my type."

"What about Brian? He seems your type."

Just then the waitress brought over our drinks. She placed Layla's down then angled her body toward me, placing my beer on the napkin. "Can I get you anything else?"

"Nope. I have everything I want sitting right in front of me," I said, not taking my eyes off Layla.

"Okay. I'll just go check on your food." She turned dejectedly and huffed off toward the kitchen.

"Brian?" I asked again.

Layla took a long sip from her straw and smirked. "Oh, I'd totally fuck him."

I narrowed my eyes at her. That was not information I wanted to hear on our first and maybe only date. "But you haven't?"

"Nope. I'm not his type."

"What does that mean? How is that possible?"

"It means I have the wrong equipment. He's my best friend and we bat for the same team. He's gay. I've tried and he's not willing to convert."

I let out a sigh of relief. "Jeez, I thought my gaydar was better than that."

"Yeah, you'd never know unless he wanted you to. I could make a great fireman's calendar with all the guys he parades in and out of his apartment. It's a travesty to women all over the country."

"So... there's nobody else?"

"Nope. I don't really date. This is my first in a long time."

"Why did you agree to go out with me then?"

She shrugged. "For one, you're persistent."

"And two?"

"You did come to my rescue the other night, so there's that."

"So, this is an obligatory date?"

"Not at all. Let's just say, I learned a lot about who you are the other night. And maybe there's more to you than this sex god thing you put off. Maybe I think there might actually be a decent guy inside here." She tapped my chest.

I felt guilty. I wasn't sure she was right. But for Layla I'd try to be the decent guy she wanted me to be.

Our food arrived, and we finished it off in record time, chatting about nothing in particular. "Are you ready to get out of here?" I asked.

"Sure."

We walked out to the parking lot with my arm wrapped around her shoulder. I held her tiny body close to mine and she fit like we were made for each other. On the way back to my apartment, Layla wrapped her arms tightly around me and rested her head on my back. It was perfect.

I pulled into the lot behind Forever Inked and parked in Zack's garage. Layla's car was parked next to the back door. "Are you leaving, or do you want to come up for a while?"

Indecision danced across her face. "Do you want me to come up?"

I ran my fingers down her face. "I think you already know the answer to that." I took both her hands in mine and started walking backward. "Come upstairs with me."

She looked over at her car and then back at me. "I shouldn't, but maybe just for a little bit."

I pulled her in close and wrapped my arms around her waist, then leaned down and kissed her pouty lips. They were stiff at first, then loosened and began to move with mine. Her lips were silky smooth and soft. I could have taken her right there in the parking lot, but that would have proved that I wasn't the decent guy she thought I was. I backed away, still holding her hand, and led us up to my apartment.

I took out my keys to unlock the door. The worry on Layla's face stopped me dead. I didn't know what caused it, but whatever it was ran deep. I lifted her chin with my finger. "Hey, we won't do anything you don't want to do. I'll be a perfect gentleman."

She closed her eyes briefly and let out a sigh. "Okay."

I opened the door wide and led her inside. "Make yourself comfortable."

Layla turned in circles, inspecting the space. "It looks exactly the same as when Zack lived here. The only thing missing is the piano. You haven't changed much."

I quirked an eyebrow. "Did you and Zack date?" It wouldn't be a total deal breaker, but I wasn't crazy about picturing the two of them together.

"Oh, God, no. We've always just been friends. I used to feed his cat when he went out of town and I was friends with Rissa. She lived here before they got married." Then realization hit her face. "Wait. Did you think that Zack and I slept together?"

I rubbed the scruff on my chin. "Just checking."

Layla shook her head. "I told you, I don't sleep around, and I don't date. You're the first in a long time."

"So, you've said." I moved to the kitchen and poured us each a drink. Layla perched on the bar stool and took a sip of hers. "How long has it been?"

"Longer than would be socially acceptable to admit." The answer to every question I asked was like trying to decode a cryptic puzzle. She skirted around each one, her replies only leaving me with more questions. It was frustrating the fuck out of me.

"Let's go sit on the couch," I suggested.

"I'm fine right here."

"Layla, please. I just want to talk, maybe kiss you a little more."

She bit her lip again. "Okay."

I picked up both our drinks and carried them to the coffee table in front of the couch. I sat down and pulled Layla onto my lap, so she was straddling my legs. She was shaking like a leaf. I reached for her braid, pulled the elastic from the end, and started to separate the strands. Her long hair hung down her back and I ran my fingers through the soft waves. "Who is he?"

Layla leaned back. "Who's who?"

"The guy who hurt you."

She turned her head to the side. "What makes you think someone hurt me?"

I turned her face back toward me. "For one, you won't look me in the eye. For two, you're as jittery as a cat on a hot tin roof. And three, a woman as beautiful as you, doesn't just not date unless she has a reason. So, I'll ask you again, who is he?"

Layla swallowed down the lump in her throat. "Someone I loved and trusted."

"Did he cheat on you?"

"Yes."

"What else?"

"I don't want to talk about him. I've been trying to forget him for a long time."

"How long, Layla?"

"Too long. Help me forget him, Draven. You make me feel things I shouldn't be feeling. You make me want to forget, when remembering is what keeps me safe. What keeps me whole."

I ran my hands through her hair again. "I would never hurt you, *pisoi*. I'm not a good man, but you make me want to be better. For you."

"Trust me, you should walk away. We should end this right now," she said quietly.

She was probably right and if I were a better man I would have. I would have set her off my lap, handed her purse to her, and walked her down to her car. I would have heeded the warnings of every red flag she was throwing up.

But I was greedy.

So selfish.

I wanted her like I wanted air.

And because I was a self-serving prick, I needed a taste to be satisfied.

"I can't walk away from you, Layla. I've tried all week, but I can't. From the first moment I met you, I knew I had to have you."

"Kiss me, Draven."

I cupped the back of her head and pulled her close. Our lips touched. Tongues tangled, and she tasted as sweet as I'd predicted. The faint flavor of whiskey mixed with something that was uniquely Layla. One taste would never be enough.

Layla's arms wrapped around my neck and we devoured each other. It became frantic and frenzied, both of us desperately seeking pleasure. My hands gripped her perfect ass, squeezing and kneading her. I pulled her softness to my hardness and she began to rock her hips forward.

Layla's hands crept under my shirt. Her fingers explored my abs and chest. She pinched my pierced nipple and a bolt of electricity shot through me. "I need your shirt off," she gasped, bunching the material in her hands in an impatient plea.

She didn't need to ask me twice. I ripped my shirt off over my head and threw it to the side. Her delicate hands pawed at me, exploring every inch of my hard body. Her fingers traced my tattoos and the barbell that ran through my nipple. "You're perfect, Draven. So damn sexy."

"You're the sexy one, kitten. My own little sex kitten." I snaked my hands under her shirt and rubbed the soft skin of her stomach. My fingers brushed a raised mark on her perfect flesh, and I couldn't help but run my thumb over the top of it. I was drawn to the slight imperfection on her otherwise perfect body.

Layla jerked back, pulling her shirt down and pushing my hands away. "No. You can't touch me there."

I looked deep into her misty, emerald eyes. I wasn't sure what I had done wrong. I kept my voice soft, afraid of scaring her. "Okay, kitten. Whatever you want. I need to feel you though. Where can I touch you?"

Layla closed her eyes as if seeking her courage. Her fingers slowly undid the top buttons of her blouse and pulled the material apart. A black satin bra barely covered her full, round tits. They were more than a handful and I had big hands. "Kiss me here."

It was a contradiction in itself. She wouldn't let me touch her stomach, but she was offering so much more. "Are you sure?"

She gave a small nod. "Yes, I'm sure. Kiss me." Her voice was breathy and full of lust. She may have been scared but there was no denying she needed what I could give her. She craved it as much as I did.

I ran my tongue along her collarbone. Layla moaned and dropped her head back, giving me access to her delicate neck. I peppered soft kisses along the column of her throat, then traced the same path with my tongue. I did the same to the swell of each perfect breast.

Layla rocked against me with need, chasing her own pleasure. "More," she gasped. She dry-humped me like a fifteen-year-old virgin, making me impossibly hard. "Please... suck my tits."

I pulled the cup of her bra down and release one beautiful breast. Her nipple was dark and hard with a small silver ring through the peak. "Fuck, Layla. You're gorgeous." My lips closed over her nipple and my tongue played with the silver hoop. I sucked her hard, bruising her delicate skin, then eased the ache with a gentle swipe of my tongue. Kissing along her breast, I pulled back the other cup exposing both her tits. Both sides were pierced with identical rings. I gave her other tit the same treatment, kissing and sucking and nipping with my teeth. I kneaded them both in my hands, burying my face between them, using my thumbs to play with her nipples.

Layla rocked harder against my cock. "I'm so close, Draven," she panted.

"Come for me, Layla. Rub your pussy all over me." I pushed my hips up into her as she pushed down into my cock. Her head dropped back as she came, moans of pleasure escaping her throat and filling the silence.

Then she collapsed into my chest, her bare skin pressed to mine. She buried her face into my neck in embarrassment. "I can't believe I just did that. That was..."

"Erotic as fuck," I finished for her. "You're so goddamn sexy. I can't wait to get inside you. You've made me so fucking hard I think I'm going to explode."

Layla rubbed my hard cock that was wedged between us. "I can help with that." Her fingers found my zipper and began to pull it down. She reached inside and gripped her fingers around my shaft. It was a tight fit. I started to undo my belt. The buckle clanking was the only sound besides our heavy breathing.

And everything changed in the flash of a second.

Layla froze, then jumped off my lap like I'd burned her. Her big green eyes didn't stare at me, but through me. Her breath quickened, and her chest heaved. Panic consumed her.

I stood and reached out to her. "Layla?"

She held her hands out defensively. "Don't fucking touch me!" As if just realizing her blouse was still open, she quickly tucked herself inside and pulled it closed, frantically trying to button it. Tears streamed down her face. "This was a mistake. I'm so sorry." She grabbed her purse and bolted from my apartment. Her boots echoed on the stairs through the open door.

I made it to the top of the stairs just as she wrenched open the back door to escape. "Layla! Stop!" She didn't. I flew down the steps to the open door. It had started to rain big, angry drops. Lightening flashed across the sky and thunder cracked a deafening boom. "Layla!" I was too late. She was already in her car. Tires squealed on the wet pavement when she sped away.

The rain pelted me in a torrent. "What the fuck!" No way was our date ending this way. I hadn't done anything wrong. I let her lead. I followed her signals. I did what she asked. She wanted what we were doing. I knew she did. But something spooked her, and a switch had been flipped. I wasn't the bad guy here.

I turned my face to the sky and let the rain soak me. I could let her go or I could go after her. It was barely even a choice. Whatever happened tonight, I needed to make sure she got home safe. I needed to know she was all right.

I took the stairs two at a time to throw on my shirt and grab my keys, then went after her. The rain made it almost impossible to see through the windshield of my Hummer. When I got to her apartment complex, my car traversed through the maze of identical buildings. "Fuck!" I should have paid better attention when I dropped her off the other night. Then I saw it. I parked next to her car and headed into her building, taking the stairs to the second floor.

It was easy to remember which apartment was hers. It was the only one with three locks on the door. Angry music played on the other side of it.

I pounded my fist on the door. "Layla, open up!"

Nothing.

She could ignore me all she wanted, but I wasn't going away. My fist hit the door again. "Please, Layla, open the door."

The apartment across the hall opened. No doubt, I'd probably woken up half the building. I didn't give a fuck. I'd wake up the whole damn city if it meant getting to her.

"What the hell, man?" I faced her neighbor, ready to tell him to fuck off. The guy from Forever Inked, Brian, stood there shirtless. He pointed at me in recognition, anger brewing in his eyes. "You! What the fuck did you do to her?" He stepped forward, fists clenched, ready to go toe to toe with me.

I ran my hand over my soaking hair. I didn't feel the need to explain myself to anyone, but this guy was Layla's friend and my best chance at seeing her. "I didn't do anything. We went on a date. Everything was going great. We started making out and she freaked out on me. She bolted from my apartment in tears. I don't even know what happened. I need to know she's all right."

"Oh, fuck! Goddamn it!" He went back into his apartment and returned with a set of keys. He quickly undid all the locks and twisted the doorknob. Brian blocked my entry. "You stay the fuck out here."

"The hell I will. I don't know who you think I am, but I wasn't after a cheap fuck. I care about Layla and I'm not leaving until I see her."

The truth of my words slapped me in the face. Because fucking Layla was exactly what this started as, but somewhere during our date it had turned into more. Much more. He must have sensed my sincerity. "Fine but let me handle her. Stay out of the way."

He pushed the door open and turned down the stereo. A crash sounded from somewhere in the apartment, the sound of glass breaking. Then we heard her. "I fucking hate you! You stupid fucking bitch!" Another crash, more breaking glass. "You fucking knew better! I hate you! I hate you!" Crash. "What the fuck is wrong with you?" Unmistakable sobs and a guttural cry.

I was stunned into silence. I couldn't move. My feet were cemented to the floor.

Brian... not so much. He moved deeper into the apartment. "Baby girl?" Another crash. He moved quicker to the open door and dashed inside. "Stop, baby girl. I got you. You're all right," he cooed as if talking to a child.

She sobbed, "I fucked up. I fucked up big time, Brian."

"What happened?"

I strained to hear their conversation, but their voices were muffled. I forced myself forward and crept toward the open door. Layla was crying. "I should have known better than to try to be normal."

"Did he hurt you?"

"No, he was perfect. I was the one who fucked it up. I had a flashback. I ruined everything. He'll never want to see me again. How will I face him at work? I knew better. I fucking knew it was a bad idea from the start."

I peeked my head around the corner. Brian was holding Layla on the bathroom floor, her head pressed to his chest. The mirror was smashed. It looked like a tornado had ripped through the small space. Brian's eyes met mine and he shook his head.

I backed around the corner, out of sight. "He's here," Brian said.

"What? Why?"

"He was worried about you. I tried to get him to leave, but he won't go. I think you should talk to him."

"I can't. I'm too embarrassed. What would I say?"

"Would it be so bad to tell him the truth?"

"He doesn't need my shit. They're my problems."

"No, he doesn't need your shit. As a matter of fact, he didn't need to make sure you got home safe, and he didn't need to stay. But he did. He might actually care about you. What have you got to lose?"

"My dignity. Although I think I already did that," she sniffed. "What if he's disgusted by me?"

My black heart cracked a little bit at Layla's words. How could I ever be disgusted by her? Whatever she was hiding was destroying her. I had a feeling that no one knew her secrets, except Brian. It must have been exhausting to always put on a front for everyone else.

"Then he wasn't worth it to begin with. He'll leave in three weeks and you'll never have to see him again. But... I think you should give him a chance."

"I'm scared."

"I know you are, but you're strong. If Michael didn't break you, then no one can. You're the bravest person I know."

Michael. I had the name of the fucker that had hurt her.

"Okay," she sniffed again. "I love you, Brian."

"I love you too, baby girl. Now, let's get you out of these wet clothes."

I snuck away and stood in the kitchen. Emotion clogged my chest. It was the most heart wrenching scene I'd ever experienced. The girl I had gotten to know over the last week was not the broken one sitting on the bathroom floor.

I had no business being here. I should have walked out the door. I was the villain, not the hero. I was nobody's savior. For Layla, I would try. But, if I failed, I would only hurt her more.

Brian stumbled into the kitchen, hands deep in his pockets. "She's changing. You better be the real deal, man. That girl's been through enough shit. She doesn't need any more piled on. If you can't handle that, then you need to leave now."

I crossed my arms. "I'm not going anywhere." My decision was made.

"If you hurt her, you'll be dealing with me," he threatened.

"Won't be any need. She's lucky to have you."

"There's nothing I wouldn't do for her." Brian walked to the door. "Lock up behind me. She'll freak if she knows it's not locked."

I nodded and followed him to the door. "Thanks, man."

Brian left and I turned all three locks. It was overkill, but if it made Layla feel safe, I would do it without hesitation. I sat down on her couch, not knowing what to do with myself.

I was a killer. If Layla told me what I thought she was going to tell me, then I'd be handling it personally.

A few minutes later, Layla crept into the room wrapped in a fluffy, purple robe. Her face was washed clean of makeup and her wet hair was combed down her back. She looked so young. Nothing like the hard, take-no-shit girl I worked with. "You're still here." She sat in the chair opposite me.

"I'm still here," I confirmed.

"Why?"

"Why what?"

"Why are you here? Why do you care? Why don't you hate me?"

I leaned forward, my arms resting on my knees. "Layla, I'm not going to lie to you. I don't date. I don't have relationships. I fuck. A lot. I usually don't make it past the bar bathroom or the front seat of my car." She cringed at my honesty. But if she was going to bare her soul, I would too. If for no other reason than to make this a little easier for her. "When I first met you, I wanted to fuck you. There's no way to sugarcoat it. You're so beautiful and sexy, I couldn't wait to bury my dick inside you. But you weren't having any of it." I gave a self-deprecating laugh. "You were tough and sassy and basically one of the biggest bitches I'd ever met. But then, I figured you out. I knew there had to be more than what you were putting off. I knew someone had hurt you. And suddenly, I started caring about you. Not just about getting in your pants, but getting to your heart. This is new territory for me. I don't know that I've ever been in love before, but I know that I feel something for you that's more than just lust. I feel a need to protect you. I don't care very often, but I care about you."

Layla bit her lip. "Do you want to know the truth? Because I'm going to warn you right now, it isn't pretty. And I'm ninety-nine percent sure once you hear it, you'll walk right out that door."

"I want to know why you freaked out on me tonight, because I asked you every step of the way. I let you lead, when I'm used to being the one leading."

"You're right. You deserve that much." She held a picture in her hand. "This is my truth. If I tell you, you'll be the only one besides Brian who knows. I've kept this a secret since I moved here. Chase doesn't know. Rissa doesn't know. Not even Zack knows." She took a deep breath. "And I didn't want you to know."

That she would trust me with something so intimate, humbled me. "Layla…"

"If I trust you with this, you have to promise to keep my secret. It's the only way I can function on a daily basis. You're free to walk away and never look back. We'll be co-workers and nothing else. Just please promise you won't betray me."

"I would never betray your trust. I just want to understand. I need to know what I did wrong."

"You didn't do anything wrong. He did. You asked me who he was. This is him." She passed the framed photo to me.

I stared at the picture, not sure what I was looking at. The girl in the picture was smiling, her blond hair blowing in the breeze. Her skin was flawless, not a mark on it. But what got me were her eyes. The green so vibrant, they didn't look real. The man next to her smiled for the camera. They were obviously in love.

I gulped down the realization. "You're married?"

"Divorced. I keep that picture as a reminder of my mistakes. I met Michael in college. He was a year ahead of me. He proposed the day I graduated, and we were married three months later. I was an elementary school art teacher." She laughed a laugh that held no humor. "Can you imagine that? Me with a bunch of kids?"

I tried to reconcile the woman in front of me with the one she was telling me about. They didn't seem like the same person. I tapped on the picture. "This woman, yes. You… no."

"We're one and the same. I was born into a wealthy family. My dad is an attorney. I had every advantage you could ask for. I was a cheerleader and even the fucking Homecoming Queen. When I graduated from college, I became a teacher. I volunteered to be on every committee and people loved me. I was the darling of our school. I was committed to my job. Too committed for my husband's liking."

I resituated myself on the couch. "The picture you're painting is kind of a turn on. I'm picturing the sexy librarian."

Layla laughed. "Well, I'm a long way from that now." She tucked her feet up underneath her and pulled the robe over her legs.

"So, you were a hot teacher. What happened?" Nothing she had told me so far explained her freak out tonight.

"Six months into my marriage, Michael began to act differently. He would snap at me for every little thing. He became suspicious every time I had a meeting after work. The first time he hit me, he was so apologetic. He promised it wouldn't happen again."

My teeth ground together. I may have been an asshole, but I would never hit a woman. "But it did."

Layla nodded. "It happened more and more frequently. He said it was my duty to please him. And I wanted to. I thought I was doing something wrong. I just wanted to make my husband happy. He began forcing me to have sex with him against my will. He took what he wanted, violating me in every way possible. Pretty soon I was wearing long sleeves and covering the bruises with makeup. Things like that didn't happen to people like me."

My fists clenched. "He raped you and beat you? So, you divorced him?"

"No."

Silence filled the canyon between us, and I knew there was more. I wasn't sure I wanted to hear it. I didn't know if I could handle it.

"I divorced him because he tried to kill me." Tears ran down the sides of her face. How she was telling me this without completely breaking down was a mystery to me.

Rage bubbled up inside me. I was having a hard time keeping it in check. "What. Did. He. Do. To. You?"

"He was high on drugs…"

"Don't make excuses for him," I gritted out.

"I'm not. Nothing can excuse what he did to me. It was the first time I fought back, and I paid for it. I was barely alive when EMS found me. He had beaten and raped me. And when he was finished, he kicked me down the stairs. I had a crushed cheek bone, fractured ribs, a broken arm, and a concussion. I was in a coma for eight days. But what almost did me in was the stab wounds."

My stomach churned and bile filled my throat. I felt like I was going to be sick. How could anyone do something so vile to the beautiful woman in front of me?

Layla stood and dropped her robe. She stood in front of me in only her black bra and matching satin panties. The shape of her body was like a kick to the gut. I sat there feeling unworthy of what she was showing me. "These tattoos are my shame. My penance for trusting someone too much." She turned her back to me. The tattoo that started on her arm and went over her shoulder continued down across her lower back, disappearing beneath her panties. Big colorful flowers covered her skin. The work was intricate and detailed. I ran my hand along her skin. The raised scars were barely visible through the ink. She pointed to one in the middle of her upper back. "This one punctured my lung." Then she turned to the front. She touched the butterfly that sat below her belly button piercing. "This one killed my baby."

She'd been pregnant, and he took that from her. I wanted to kill the bastard for hurting her so completely and deeply. I held it together for the woman in front of me. I ran my finger lightly over the raised bump I felt earlier. It was masked by the body of the butterfly, its delicate wings jutting out on both sides. The emotion that sat in my chest swelled to epic proportions. Tears so foreign to me swam in my eyes. I gripped her hips gently, leaning my head against her stomach. "I'm so sorry, Layla. I didn't know."

She ran her hand through my hair. "I didn't want you to know. I just wanted to be a normal girl, going out on a normal date. I wanted everything we did tonight. It was the belt."

I looked up at her in confusion.

"The clanking of the belt. That's how I always knew he was going to rape me. You didn't do anything wrong. It was me." She fisted her palms and held her tattooed wrists up to me. "This is how I handled it. I was a coward. After the trial, the press wouldn't leave me alone. I wanted to escape, to drift away into nothingness. My brother found me bleeding out on the bathroom floor."

I captured her wrists and brought them to my mouth, kissing the scars there. Tears ran down my cheeks. I didn't even try to wipe them away. I couldn't lessen the pain I felt for her. I wouldn't cheapen it. "You're not a coward."

"So now you know. I'm not some hard-ass bitch. All of this," she motioned to her body, "is a façade. It's the paint I use to cover the ugly. But no matter how much hair dye, eye-liner, and ink I use, it's still there. Underneath it all is still a damaged woman." Layla picked up her robe and slipped back into it. "You should go now." She tied her robe and turned her back on me. "I have nothing to give you. He took every little piece of my soul."

I reached for her hand. "Tell me he's dead. Tell me he paid for what he took from you," I pleaded.

She shook her head. "He's in prison, Pelican Bay State Prison. But one day he'll get paroled, and I have no doubt he'll come after me again."

"That's why you moved." It wasn't a question. It was the pieces coming together. Her vague answers to my every question. The locks on her door. It was all

111

part of the bigger picture I was just beginning to see. This girl trusted no one, but for some reason she was trusting me. "How long since you've been with a man?"

"Five years. Tonight, was the first time I've let anyone touch me in five years. And I failed."

I gulped down her words. *Five years?* "You didn't fail, Layla. You're so fucking brave." She was a complicated mess. She was the last thing I needed, but everything I wanted. I could give her this. "I have three weeks. Let me help you. Let me teach you to trust again. Let me show you that you deserve everything you've denied yourself. You're not a damaged woman. You're strong and sexy and brave. What he did to you doesn't define you."

"I don't want your pity."

"That's good because I don't pity you. I'm in awe of you." I pulled Layla onto my lap and kissed her gently. "You deserve to feel pleasure and I can give it to you."

"I want you to give it to me. I don't want to be afraid anymore," she whispered.

"I promise I will never hurt you."

"You're the only man, besides my brother and Brian, who has ever been in this apartment. Am I wrong to trust you?"

"No. I can give you three weeks of earth-shattering orgasms and the best sex you've ever had. I can show you how a real man treats a woman."

Layla let out a little laugh. "You talk a big game there, Mr. Constantine. Are you sure you can deliver?"

"There's plenty of big, Miss Roberts. And I always deliver," I assured her.

"If we do this, you can't sleep with anyone else," she insisted.

I nuzzled my nose into her neck, taking in the sweet scent of her. "You're the only one I want to be with. I promise you, I'm all yours."

"Okay." She looked at the clock. "It's late. You should go."

"No. I'm staying here with you."

"Why?"

"Because with everything you've shared with me tonight, I need you as much as you need me."

Layla stood and led me by the hand to her bedroom. Funny that all night I had thought about getting her in bed and sliding between her thighs, but now all I wanted to do was keep her safe. Protect her. Take care of her when she'd been taking care of herself for so long.

"I can sleep there," I said, motioning to the chair in the corner. It looked uncomfortable as fuck, but I'd endure it for her.

Layla pulled back the sheets. "Sleep with me."

I'd never actually slept in the same bed as a woman. I'd always left after the main event. "Are you sure?"

"I'm positive." Layla took off her robe and slipped a t-shirt over her head. Then she did that thing girls do, where they covertly remove their bra through the sleeve. She laid on the bed and tapped the space next to her.

I unlaced my boots and slid my jeans and socks off in one motion. I set my phone, wallet, and keys on the nightstand. My shirt came off next. I slid into the bed next to Layla, wearing only my boxer briefs, not knowing what to expect.

She flicked the light off. "Thank you for not running away." Her lips met mine in the darkness. I wrapped one arm around her waist, pulling her close. My other hand cradled her head. Layla let out a contented sigh and rested her head on my chest. She flung one small leg over mine. "I'd give our date an eleven. Good night, Draven."

My heart became a puddle in my chest. I kissed the top of her head. "Good night, *pisoi*."

After a few short minutes, I felt her breath even out. She was sound asleep. I reached over to the nightstand and grabbed my phone to text Kane.

Me: Pelican Bay State Prison. Michael. Attempted murder of his wife. Five years ago.

The fucker wasn't only one of my best friends, but a phenomenal hacker. If anyone could get me the information I wanted, it was him.

Kane: A last name would be helpful.

Me: Try Roberts. It's all I've got.

Kane: Is this about the girl?

Me: Yes

Kane: You're in too deep.

Me: Just work your magic.

Kane: Will do.

I set my phone back on the nightstand. Layla would never have to worry about him coming after her again. That fucker was dead.

Chapter 17
Layla

I woke to the smell of coffee, the bed next to me empty but the sheets ruffled.

Last night. I had hoped it was a nightmare, but the smell of cologne on my sheets told me it wasn't.

What a fucking train wreck. I'd fallen apart like some helpless little girl who needed saving. I'd said too much. Gave too much away. My security and safe haven had been compromised because for one weak moment I trusted someone.

And now I needed to face the man I barely knew and beg him to forget everything. Because if he couldn't keep my secret, my time here was finished. I'd have to move on and start over again.

Wrapping my robe around me, I made the dreaded walk to the kitchen. Apprehension gripped me and clawed at my chest. I felt like I was sixteen again, working up the courage to tell my dad I had smashed his car. The car was fixable.

Me? I was damaged beyond repair. You could shine me up, but the dents and scratches were still there. The worst of them so deep, I would never run right again.

Draven stood with his back leaning against the counter, bare feet crossed at the ankles. Dressed in only his jeans, his body was a work of art. Dark ink covered his arms and chest. I took in the fighting ravens on his chest, the rose over his heart, and the skull on his upper arm. There were too many to catalog, images and words twining together to cover his entire upper body and wind down his arms. He stared off, like he was deep in contemplation.

Stumbling at the sight of him, I tripped into the kitchen and invaded his silence. I crawled up on the barstool across from him. "Hey."

His face was solemn. "Good morning." He poured me a cup of coffee and slid it across the counter.

I took a small sip. Anything to stall the conversation we were about to have. I'd do anything to take last night back. I wanted to pretend it didn't happen. But it did and now I had to face it head on. "About last night…"

114

Draven cocked his head to the side. "What about it?"

He wasn't going to make this easy on me, so I laid everything out there. I set down my cup. "I'll cut right to the chase. No bullshit. I'm sorry about last night. I should have never agreed to go out with you. I knew better and it all turned to shit. To say I'm embarrassed would be putting it mildly. I can't take back what happened. If I could, I would in a heartbeat."

"I wouldn't." His rough timbre caught me off guard. "I had a great time with you last night."

I laughed almost hysterically because he was ridiculous. "Would that be before or after I freaked out on you and had a panic attack?"

"All of it, Layla."

I shook my head in disbelief. "There is something seriously wrong with you. No man in his right mind would stick around for this shit. A smart man would have walked out that door last night and never looked back."

He lifted one eyebrow. "Are you calling me stupid?"

"Not stupid. Foolish. Maybe a little mentally unstable. Or maybe that knot on top of your head is a little too tight."

He chuckled. "There's nothing wrong with my mental health."

I tapped on the edge of my coffee cup. "Good to know. So… if you could pretend that I didn't bare my soul to you last night, I would appreciate it. And I definitely don't need you telling anyone what happened. If I had one of those little gadgets from *Men in Black*, I'd use it on you to erase your memory. But I don't, so all I can do is beg you not to repeat it."

"I'm not going to tell anyone. But I'm curious, why is it such a big secret?" he asked.

I let out an exasperated sigh. "You just don't get it, do you?"

"No, I guess I don't. You didn't do anything wrong."

Frustration built inside me and my words came out harsher than intended. "Because it makes me weak! Because I don't want to be pitied. I don't need people talking about me behind my back. 'Oh, hey, that's the girl whose husband tried to kill her. Why do you think she stayed? She must have been desperate. I heard she's totally deformed underneath those clothes. I heard he was cheating on her. Oh really, I heard she was cheating on him. She's a disgrace to this town. She must have done something wrong, Michael's such a great guy.' Should I go on?"

He let out a huff. "You really think people would say all that?"

"People did say all that. I was a pariah. A blemish on society. They kicked my parents out of the country club, saying they didn't need that type of publicity. My battered face was splashed across the front of every newspaper. This city," I pointed at the counter, "is my safe place. People here don't know who I am. I've gone to extremes to make sure of it. I'm not some princess in a tower who needs saving. I learned a long time ago that the princess has to save herself."

Draven crossed his arms across his wide chest. "So, you're going to hide in a tower with three locks on the door and hope that does the trick?"

"Don't you fucking judge me! You don't know the first thing about what it feels like to be me."

He leaned on the counter in front of me and let out a sigh. "You're right. I don't. But every princess deserves a prince to take care of her."

I dropped my head. "I had a prince once and look where that got me. He turned out to be a monster sleeping in my bed. Thank you for staying last night, but I think you should go. I promise to not make things weird at work for you. You do your job and I'll do mine."

Draven rubbed his fingers along my face in a soothing gesture. "That's not the deal we made last night."

I allowed myself one moment to relish in his touch. "I'm not holding you to anything. You're officially released from all obligations."

"You could never be an obligation, Layla. You can't deny we have a connection. There's something between us. I have three weeks. I think we owe it to ourselves to explore it."

He tugged at my heart. Awakened places that I thought had long since died. I was headed into dangerous territory. "And what if I like it too much? What if three weeks isn't enough?"

"It has to be. It's all the time I have."

"What if I don't want you to leave?"

"You will. I promise you, I'm not worth it."

"Somehow, I don't think that's true." Something told me, I could fall in love with the man in my kitchen. And when he left… it would hurt.

After Draven left, I knocked on Brian's door, hoping to catch him before he went to work. He answered wearing grey suit pants and a black dress shirt, looking good enough to eat. I openly gawked at him.

"Close your mouth, baby girl," he teased.

I snapped my mouth shut, not realizing it had been hanging open and a little bit of drool might have been running down one side. Life was so unfair. "Yeah, ummm, I wanted to thank you for last night. I didn't mean to drag you into my drama again."

He cocked his head to the side. "You all right?" He motioned for me to come inside.

I sat down on his couch. "Yeah. I told him everything and he stayed. There's got to be something wrong with him, right?"

Brian sat next to me. "Maybe he just sees all the things you're too blind to see."

"What do you mean?"

He laughed. "You're a catch, Layla. You're so wrapped up in everything that's wrong with you, that you don't see all the things that are right. Any man would be lucky to have you."

"Except my gay neighbor," I chided.

"Except your very attractive and studly gay neighbor," he agreed.

"Meh. You're all right."

He laughed. "Oh, so Mr. Talk, Dark and Fuckable breezes into town and now I'm just 'all right'? Were you not groping my cock last week?"

I shrugged my shoulders. "It was research. What can I say?"

"And? How did he measure up?"

"Don't know yet, but I'm going to. Seems he thinks it's his mission to show me how a man should treat a woman in bed." I huffed out a breath. "I don't know if it's a good idea. I mean, I want to but I'm not the kind of girl who can sleep with someone and not have feelings for them. How do you keep it separate?"

Brian scratched his chin. "I've never had that problem. Sex is just sex to me. I focus on the pleasure. My head and heart have nothing to do with it. Layla, you deserve this. Go into it with your eyes open and when it's time to let him go… let him go."

I stood up, wiping my sweaty palms on my jeans. "You're right. Easy peasy. No head, no heart. Just tits and dick."

Brian laughed. "You might want to include your hoohaa," he said pointing at my crotch.

117

"Yep. Hoohaa's invited too. It'll be one big naked party minus the balloons and streamers."

"Hey, don't knock balloons and streamers. You can do some creative things with those."

I held my hands over my ears. "La-la-la-la. Too much information." I reached for the door. "And on that note, it's time for me to go."

Brian grasped my shoulder. "Life is about taking risks. I think he's worth the risk and if he breaks your heart, I'll be here. We'll eat ice cream and watch chick flicks together."

I lifted onto my toes and kissed him on the cheek. "One day you're going to make someone very happy. From one commitment-phobe to another, you deserve someone really special."

He swatted me on the ass. "I'm good right now. I like playing the field too much to settle down."

"You'll find him one day," I told him with a wink. "And when you do, there will be no one happier for you than me. You deserve it."

"We both do," he said before shutting the door.

I slipped back into my own apartment, processing everything that had happened in the last twelve hours. I'd popped my own bubble of security by confiding in Draven. My life had taken a turn I never expected.

I always assumed when I finally moved on, my life would be shrouded in secrets and lies. I felt stripped bare. Exposed. I'd revealed everything but my true identity.

It was the one thing I held on to. The last piece of myself that I guarded vehemently. Jenna McNamara didn't exist anymore. Michael couldn't find her if he tried, or so I hoped. She was a wisp in the wind. Jenna was weak, and she had died that night on the bathroom floor.

Layla Roberts was the stone-cold bitch who had taken her place. I needed to remember that. Needed to remember who I was now. Layla was strong, smart, and independent. She didn't have a past because she hadn't existed until five years ago. Her father had helped her create the new identity, complete with paperwork that supported it. Layla was tough and she deserved so much more than I had given her. It was time for her to take everything she was entitled to as a woman, including the pleasure a man could give her.

What Draven was willing to give, despite everything he now knew.

Last night with him was amazing. He had been the perfect gentleman, even though my instincts told me he was usually anything but. Kissing him had awakened something in me I thought was dead. The way he held me with confidence, taking control without being controlling was a total turn on. I had shamelessly rocked against him seeking my own pleasure and he had more than willingly obliged. Encouraging me to come, when he was getting nothing in return.

My panties were wet from thinking about it. I hadn't felt that aroused in years. I took what I wanted, and it felt freeing. I had taken back a little bit of the control I lost with Michael.

Michael made me feel inadequate, less of a woman. I had been convinced there was something wrong with me.

Draven made me feel sexy and wanted. His cock had been rock solid when I ground my hips into him. He wanted me as much as I wanted him. I was ready to give him everything. I wanted him to fuck me last night and there was no doubt he wanted it too.

Then in a flash I destroyed it. I froze. Jenna had returned and all she could see was Michael's face before he forced himself on her. She couldn't get away fast enough.

Never in a million years did I think that Draven would chase me. He had seen me at my weakest and yet he still wanted me. He listened. He accepted. He stayed when he should have left running.

All of it had left me feeling stripped down to my barest elements. With Draven, there was no hiding. He saw the parts of me no one had ever looked deep enough to see.

I stepped into my bathroom, staring at the woman in the mirror. Her reflection was cracked and broken. So symbolic of the woman I had allowed myself to become. I took a deep breath and stripped out of my clothes, leaving only my bra and panties on. I tried to see the woman that Draven saw. He called me beautiful, but all I could see were the scars I kept hidden. Every inch of ink on my skin had a purpose. My ugly, red scars were camouflaged by the vibrant colors that adorned my body. To anyone else it was art. To me, it was a coat of shame.

I'd been hiding for so long and I was done being broken. I'd come a long way in the last five years but failed miserably in the romance department. Last night had been proof. I wasn't sure Draven could fix me, but the way he'd made my body come alive was enough for me to let him try.

I went to the kitchen and rifled around in my junk drawer that contained the few tools my dad insisted I needed. Grabbing the screwdriver, I headed back to the bathroom and hopped up on the counter. With one knee on each side of the sink, I took one last look at the broken woman in the mirror. What was left of Jenna stared back at me. I started removing the four screws that held the reflection in place. I was done with her.

I lugged the mirror down the stairs and hauled it out to the dumpster. Lifting it high above my head, I heaved it into the trash. "Goodbye, Jenna. Stay the fuck out of my life!"

Chapter 18
Draven

Why I stayed with Layla last night, I wasn't sure. It just didn't seem right to leave her after everything she revealed. Truth be told, I liked holding her in my arms with her body wrapped around me. I wanted to hold her close and never let anyone hurt her again.

I needed to check myself. What we agreed to was purely physical. When our time was up, I was going to walk away. Layla didn't belong in my world, and she certainly didn't need me in hers. I couldn't imagine how she would react if she knew she spent the night with a criminal. Someone who'd been trained to pull a trigger with zero remorse. Yeah, she had secrets, but she wasn't the only one. I had plenty.

When I'd come home from Layla's this morning, I took a long hot shower trying to wash the images of her body from my mind. It wasn't the scars that occupied space in my head, it was those damn pierced nipples. They were sexy as fuck and they got my dick hard. I couldn't wait to explore every inch of her body.

I cleared my head and went down to work. I figured Layla would be in late after what happened last night. Surely, she'd need some time to process everything. Lord knew I did.

When I got downstairs, I was surprised to hear classic rock music pumping through the speakers. She was standing on the top rung of a ladder wiping down the blades to one of the three fans that hung from the ceiling. Seeing her balancing precariously on her toes ten feet off the ground made my heart seize in my chest. "What the hell are you doing?" I barked at her.

She wobbled and grabbed onto the top of the ladder. "Jesus, Draven, you scared the shit out of me. Give a girl some warning next time."

I grabbed the ladder to steady it. "Get down. You're going to break your neck if you fall."

She put one hand on her hip pushing her ass out. "I was just fine until you snuck up on me."

"Come down." I motioned to the floor. "I'll do that."

"I'm perfectly capable," she argued.

"I know you are, but this is one of those things a princess shouldn't do. Now, come down."

"Fine," she huffed. Layla started backing down the ladder while I held it steady. When her ass was almost level with my head she peered down over her shoulder. "I'm going to need you to move."

"Actually, I like this view." I smirked at her. "This ass is so perfect I just want to squeeze it." Reaching up with both hands I cupped her luscious ass that peeked out from her shorts. "Mmmm. Perfect."

She rolled her eyes. "All right, that's enough groping of the merchandise. Let me down."

"As you wish." I gripped her by the waist and lifted her off the ladder, setting her down in front of me.

Her hands went to my shoulders, holding a rag in one and a spray bottle in the other. She stared up at me with those big green eyes. "Thank you." Her tongue darted out and licked her bottom lip.

I imagined what those red, pouty lips would look like wrapped around me and my dick automatically strained against my zipper. I put my finger to her lip. "You're teasing me with those lips of yours. You and me tonight. Upstairs. I want you in my bed."

She took a step back. "About that. I have to go to Home Depot tonight. Seems my bathroom needs redecorating. New mirror and all."

I frowned. "Then I'm coming with you. I'm not giving up the night with you. I made you promises I intend to keep."

I finished putting the last screw in Layla's new mirror. She walked in holding a bottle of beer out to me, "Thanks for your help tonight."

I took it from her. gulping down half in one chug. "My pleasure."

She sipped from her own bottle, then tapped her black fingernails on the bathroom counter. "So, how is this going to work? Are you just going to fuck me or what?"

I nearly spit my beer out. She was so bold and direct. This was the sassy woman who first captured my attention. "Is that what you want?" I wiped my mouth with the back of my hand.

She shrugged. "I don't know. It'd kind of be like ripping the band-aid off. You know, get it over with."

I stared at her in disbelief. "Is that what you think you deserve? Just to be fucked?"

She shrugged again. "Isn't that what you want? Isn't that what you've wanted from the beginning?"

Her words ripped me open. "That's not what I want." I sat my beer on the counter and wrapped my arms tightly around her small body, pulling her head to my chest. "You deserve so much more, *pisoi*." I breathed in the sweet smell of her hair and the faint fragrance of her perfume. Everything about her was intoxicating. Addicting.

I turned her toward the mirror. "Look at yourself. Tell me what you see."

Layla stared at her reflection, a myriad of emotions crossing her face. "I'm just me."

I ran my hand through her hair. "You're a beautiful woman, Layla."

She started to turn away from the mirror. I gently turned her back. My hands snaked up under her shirt and lifted it over her head. Her long hair fell over her breasts. I unclasped her bra and slid it down her arms. "Look again." I pulled her hair back over her shoulders so her tits were visible, the small silver rings through her nipples glinted in the light. "You're gorgeous. You deserve so much more than to be just fucked. You deserve to be worshipped."

I yanked my own shirt off and pulled her back against my chest, my arms around her waist. Skin to skin. Flesh to flesh. "Look at us, Layla. Look how sexy we are together."

"You're sexy. Kiss me, Draven," she whispered.

I leaned down and captured her lips with mine. Layla wound her arms back around my neck. Our tongues tangled together in a slow, sensual dance. I couldn't get enough of her mouth. My hands massaged her beautiful tits, running my thumbs over her hard nipples. I watched us in the mirror, moving together as one. "Look at us," I whispered.

"Oh, God," she moaned. "You make me feel so good. Please don't stop."

I turned her body and lifted her onto the counter. She opened her legs and welcomed me into her warmth. I sucked one glorious tit into my mouth, nipping it with my teeth. Layla dropped her head back with a gasp as her hands ran through my hair.

The way she responded to my touch drove me crazy. I continued to worship her tits with every lick, suck, and nip.

I kissed up her neck to her ear. "I'm not going to fuck you with my cock tonight, Layla. But I am going to fuck you. With my mouth. I want to taste you. I want to make you come on my tongue. Would you like that? Do you want me to make you come?"

"Yes."

"Tell me what you want, kitten. I need to hear you say the words. Do you want me to eat your pussy?"

Layla turned her head so she could whisper back in my ear. "Yes, Draven. Fuck my pussy with your tongue. Make me come."

I groaned deep in my chest. "I can't wait to taste you." My fingers worked the button and zipper of her shorts. She lifted her ass so I could slip them down her soft legs and off her bare feet. She was shaved smooth, and I moaned at the sight of her beautiful body.

Layla tensed and locked her knees together. "You don't have to," she said nervously, doing a complete one-eighty and changing her mind.

The last thing I would ever do is force her into something she was uncomfortable with. I stroked the side of her face. "I don't *have* to do anything. It's your call, baby. I know you want it as much as I do. Tell me what's got you tied up inside."

She gulped down her apprehension. "Michael never…"

"Don't say that piece of shit's name," I growled.

She nodded almost imperceptibly. "He wouldn't go down on me. He said it was gross."

I lifted one eyebrow. "And before him?"

She shook her head. "I was a good girl. He was my first and last."

I ran a hand over my face. "Jesus Christ." No wonder she was so fucked up. She was practically a virgin. Her only experience with sex was with someone who abused and belittled her.

Layla reached for her shirt on the counter. "I think you should go."

I grabbed the shirt from her hand and pulled it away. "No. I think I should stay. It's not gross, Layla. Do you know how much I've fantasized about eating you out?"

She shook her head again.

"Since the day I met you. It's part of a normal and healthy sex life. There's not a single part of your body I don't want to explore. Your mouth, your tits, your pussy and your ass. I want it all. I can walk out that door or I can give you one of the best orgasms of your life."

She let out a deep breath. "Can we go in the bedroom with the lights off? I don't want you looking at my scars."

I rubbed my thumb over the butterfly on her abdomen, tracing the raised line. "Your scars make you beautiful. They don't bother me." I took Layla's hand and rubbed it over the serpent inked on my ribs. Her fingers brushed against the four-inch scar hidden underneath. "This was from a knife." I moved her hand to another spot on my chest. "Shrapnel." Then I turned my back to her and touched the puckered skin on my shoulder. "These were bullet wounds." Her fingers lightly ran over the skin.

"We all have scars, Layla. They don't define us; they make us stronger. They remind us that we survived whatever tried to hurt us. They tell a story about where we've been, but they don't determine where we're going. We get to decide that. So, decide right now, are you going to let your scars hold you back or are you going to embrace them as part of what makes you beautiful?" I knew I was pushing her, but she needed it. I wasn't going to let her hide behind her scars anymore.

Her body relaxed and she eased her legs apart. "I want to feel beautiful."

I moved my body between them with my hands on her knees. I gently spread her legs wider revealing her soft, pink pussy. My hands moved up her thighs, my thumbs caressing the faint white lines that crisscrossed the skin at the apex of her legs. That piece of shit had marked her everywhere. "Beautiful." I ran two fingers through her wetness and brought them to my mouth, sucking off her juices. "Delicious. So sweet."

Layla's wide eyes watched me intently. I dipped my fingers back inside her pussy and brought them to her lips. "Suck. Taste how delicious you are." Her lips opened and she sucked my fingers inside, her tongue gliding along the tips.

"You and that fucking mouth." I crashed my lips to hers, our tongues twisting with intensity. Her hands grabbed the sides of my head, pulling me closer. I pushed her back on her elbows, kissing and licking the column of her neck.

"Draven, make me come," she gasped.

I continued down her chest, only stopping to suck on her tits before I continued down her flat stomach. I ran my tongue over the butterfly on her abdomen and trailed it down to her clit.

I sank to my knees, worshiping at the altar of pure perfection. I buried my face between her legs, licking the juices from her wet, warm pussy. I licked up her slickness and flattened my tongue against her clit. Sucking the bundle of nerves between my lips, I let my tongue play.

"Fuck! Oh, God… more," Layla grabbed my head and pulled me to her center, her nails digging into my skull. I couldn't have escaped if I wanted to. But I had no intention of pulling back until she came on my tongue.

I sucked harder at her clit then teased her by licking at her center, wet and delicious. I savored her on my tongue, spearing it inside her. Layla squirmed on the counter, trying to get closer and trying to get away at the same time. I held her still with one hand on her thigh and the other on her hip. I promised her an amazing orgasm and that's what I planned on delivering. My lips returned to her clit, licking and sucking. I slipped two fingers inside her, searching for her G-spot. I wiggled my fingers against the fleshy spot inside her and her hips thrusted erratically, fucking me as much as I was fucking her. Her pussy pulsed around my fingers, telling me she was so damn close. A few more flicks of my tongue and she screamed out my name. The sound was like a choir of filthy angels as curses poured from her lips. My long fingers pumped her through the aftershocks of her orgasm. Then I licked her clean.

Layla slumped back on the counter until her head hit the mirror. Her eyes were glassy. "That was… wow. Just… wow," she panted.

"Worth it?" I asked, wiping my mouth on my shoulders.

"Oh my God, so worth it. I don't think I've ever come so hard." Layla leaned forward and wrapped her arms around my neck. "You deserve a reward."

"For making you come?" I laughed while playing with her hair.

"Absolutely. You're not the only one with a wicked tongue."

"It's not a tit for tat, although I love your tits," I said while palming one. "You don't have to."

Layla rolled her eyes. "I don't *have* to do anything," she said, repeating my own words back to me. She walked her fingers up my chest. "I want to. I've gotten to come twice now. It's your turn."

"I have to come clean. I kind of handled that in the shower this morning."

She mocked gasping. "No! Tell me it isn't true."

"It's true," I admitted.

"Well, that will never do. I can attest, after five years, orgasms are so much better when not self-induced."

"Is that right?"

"It's absolutely right." Layla started carefully undoing my belt, the buckle not making a sound. Her tiny fingers quickly released the button and zipper on my jeans. Her hand snaked down the front of my boxer briefs and grabbed ahold of my hard cock. She rubbed me up and down, her thumb running over my piercing. She pulled down my underwear to get a better look. "Oh my God! You have a frenum piercing?" She ran her fingers over it. "Did it hurt?"

"Only for a quick second. It was the healing that was a bitch."

"I only pierce the girls. Zack does all the guys."

"Oh yeah, who did these?" I flicked the rings on her nipples.

"My girlfriend back in Chicago. It was one of my first acts of defiance. Why'd you get this done?" she asked.

"Got it right after I got out of the Marines. I thought the ladies would like it."

"And did they?"

"I haven't had any complaints, but you'll have to find out for yourself." I smirked.

"Tonight, I owe you a blow job." Layla slipped off the counter and sank to her knees. She peered up at me. "We have a problem. You're really tall and I'm super short. The logistics of this aren't going to work."

I lifted her under the arms, and she wrapped her legs around me. "Then I guess we're going to make it to the bedroom after all."

Chapter 19
Layla

My body still hummed from the intensity of the orgasm that had ripped through every cell of my being. I loved BOB but he couldn't hold a candle to Draven.

He tried to lower me to the bed, and I wrapped myself tighter around him like a monkey. "I kind of don't want to let go. This feels really nice."

He laughed. "Well, it's going to be difficult to suck my cock from this position. Although it is perfect for sucking your tits." He clamped his mouth over one of my nipples and tugged my piercing gently with his teeth.

I leaned back in his arms, basking in the pleasure he brought my body. My back hit the bed and I flopped down like a dead fish. "See what you do to me. I'm pretty sure my body has gone boneless."

Draven lowered his jeans over his hips and pulled them off. "Luckily, I have the only bone we need right now," he said while he stood at the edge of the bed stroking his cock. It was my first view of this gorgeous man in all his glory. He was thick and long and hard as a rock. And pierced. I couldn't forget that little nugget of information. His entire body, from his muscles to his ink, was a work of art. Michelangelo couldn't have sculpted anything better.

I kneeled up on the bed in front of him. I traced the indents of his abs with my fingers, then worked my hands up his chest admiringly. His amber eyes watched me intently as I inspected every inch of his skin. I ran my fingers up the sides of his face and into his hair, pulling the elastic from the top of his head. His dark hair cascaded down to his shoulders. "I've been dying to see your hair. You're beautiful, you know that?"

He scoffed. "Men aren't beautiful."

"In general, I'd agree with you. But you are. You're the most beautiful man I've ever seen." I pushed his hair back over his shoulders. "Lay down on the bed for me."

In one quick motion, he grabbed me around the waist and crash landed on the bed pulling me down on top of him. Our naked bodies pressed together. Our faces inches apart. My hair fell like a curtain over us. "Hi," I whispered.

Draven's hands cupped my face. "Hi."

Our lips collided together again. He was the match to my gasoline, lighting me on fire with every touch. My body burned for him. It was instantaneous combustion.

Reluctantly I pulled back from the kiss and shimmied down his body until my legs straddled his thighs. I lifted his heavy cock from where it laid on his stomach. My fingers didn't touch where they were wrapped around him, stroking his cock from root to tip. He was velvety soft over steel. The most beautiful thing I had ever seen. "I don't think this will fit inside me," I murmured.

"I assure you, it'll fit. When the time comes, we'll fit together like two pieces of the same puzzle."

A drop of precum beaded on his head. I ran my tongue over my lips and then licked it off him, savoring the taste. It had been so long since I'd given a blow job, I prayed my skills were still up to par. My tongue swept along his head, tracing it with the tip and paying special attention to his piercing. I flicked it with my tongue before sinking down deep, taking him to the back of my throat. I was one of those girls who was gifted with no gag reflex, something Draven was sure to appreciate. I eased my mouth back up his shaft, swiping him with my tongue in a back and forth motion.

"Jesus, Layla, that feels so good." He pulled my hair from my face, so he could watch.

My eyes met his and I gave my head a little shake. He had no idea what was coming. I sank back down and opened my throat, swallowing him all the way to the base. I began to bob up and down in shallow thrusts, using one of my free hands to massage the area right behind his balls that allegedly drove men crazy (according to *Cosmo*, the sex bible. Yes, women who weren't having sex, still liked to be well versed in the ways of fellatio and how to pleasure a man).

Draven's hips came up off the mattress. "Jesus fucking Christ! What the hell are you doing to me?" He began fucking my face, my throat getting a workout but more than happy to accommodate. "I'm gonna come. Hard," he panted.

It was a warning I had no intention of heeding. Draven's hands gripped the sides of my head keeping me firmly in place. Hot streams shot down my throat. I swallowed them down, then slowly pulled back, releasing him with a pop of my lips. Just like riding a bike. Michael may have taken my virginity, but I'd popped my blow job cherry long before him. *Thank you, Collin Washby!*

"Fuck, woman! You destroyed me." He pulled me up, so we were face to face again.

"Did I pass the blow job test?" I smirked at him.

"You didn't just pass, you set the curve. I've never been sucked off so good. You've ruined me for all other women."

I hated the implication of his words. We'd only had two nights together and I was already hooked. We had an expiration date. It was agreed upon, but I didn't have to like it. Brian's words rang in my head, *sex is just sex ... leave your head and heart out of it.* Yeah, I was going to focus on that.

I rolled to the side. "So, I guess I'll see you tomorrow then."

Draven pulled back, his face a mask of confusion. "Are you kicking me out?"

Now, I felt bad. "Listen, I know what this is, Draven. I don't have any expectations of you staying the night. Last night was an exception because I was a total train wreck. You already made it perfectly clear you don't do relationships. Spending the night blurs the lines. Sex is sex. I get it."

He propped himself up on one elbow. "Sex with you could never be just sex. I knew we'd be like an explosion. You have to admit tonight was pretty intense."

"It was," I agreed.

"I may not be into relationships but that doesn't mean I want to run away either. We have crazy chemistry. I say we ride this out for the next three weeks and enjoy every minute of it. And, if I'm being honest, I kind of liked spending the night with you last night."

"You did?"

"Yeah, I did. I've never spent the whole night with a woman. Last night was a first for me. I liked having you curled up next to me."

His admission made my heart soar. I cursed the stupid organ that was ready to beat out of my chest. Letting him stay would be dangerous, but how could I resist? "Fine, you can stay." I rolled my eyes. "But only if you give me another orgasm. Otherwise, no deal."

Draven rolled me to my back, pressing me into the mattress. "You drive a *hard* bargain, woman, but I think I can accommodate you." He pressed his cock into my thigh to punctuate his meaning.

"Pun intended?" I laughed.

"Abso-fucking-lutely."

I awoke feeling warm and sated. I stared at the beautiful man in my bed. No way he could be real. I rested my head on his chest. The easy up and down of his breathing assured me he was.

I crawled from under the sheets, threw on his t-shirt and snuck off to the bathroom. After handling my business and brushing my teeth, I tiptoed to the kitchen. With the coffee pot percolating, I pulled out eggs and bacon from the fridge.

I wasn't much of a cook, but breakfast was manageable. I cracked several eggs into a bowl. *What the hell was I doing?* Draven wasn't my boyfriend and I certainly wasn't his girlfriend. Bacon and eggs seemed a little too domestic.

I washed the eggs down the garbage disposal and stuck the bacon back in the fridge. What did you make for the man you were sleeping with for breakfast? Coffee didn't seem like enough, but bacon and eggs were too much. I tapped my fingers on the counter, contemplating the situation.

So, what was I going to do? Cereal? That was lame. Yogurt with granola? Just as lame. I pulled the eggs back out of the fridge. Scrambled eggs were casual. Right? I'd forgo the bacon. Perfect. Eggs. No bacon. It was breakfast without trying too hard.

A half dozen eggs went into the bowl along with a splash of milk to fluff them up. I whipped it into oblivion, added some cheese, then poured the mixture into a hot frying pan. The eggs sizzled, and I stared at the toaster. Toast was totally appropriate with eggs. Still casual.

"Are you making me breakfast?"

I startled. "Jeez, you've got to quit sneaking up on me."

"Sorry. I could smell the eggs cooking." He looked divine in only his boxer briefs and I got a little caught up in staring at him. "Layla?"

"Oh crap!" I grabbed the spatula and pushed the eggs around in the pan. At least I didn't burn them. "Yes. I hope scrambled eggs and toast are okay."

Draven sidled up behind me and wrapped his arms around my waist. He rested his chin on my shoulder. "It sounds perfect. Why didn't you wake me?"

"You looked too peaceful to wake. I was going to wait until breakfast was ready. How did you sleep?"

"Honestly? It was the best sleep I've gotten since I've been here." He nuzzled his face into my neck, placing soft kisses along the length of it.

"Yeah, that bed is really comfortable."

"I don't think it had anything to do with the bed, but the woman who was in it with me."

I squirmed out of his arms and grabbed two coffee mugs from the cupboard. "I'm sure it was the bed," I said while pouring us each a cup. "Do you want cream or sugar?"

He took the cup from my hand, letting his fingers linger on mine longer than necessary. "Just black. I had plenty of sugar last night. It was definitely the woman," he said with a wink.

I popped two pieces of bread in the toaster and pushed the eggs around again. "You wanna grab some plates out of the cupboard." I pointed to my right.

Draven pulled out two plates. "How come there's nothing on the top shelves?"

I cocked a hand on my hip. "Because I can't reach that high without a stool. It's just me, so I don't have that much stuff anyway. Being short you have to make accommodations." I took the plates and started scooping the eggs onto them, giving Draven the majority. I added a piece of toast to each and pulled the butter from the fridge.

"I like that you're short. I think it's adorable. You know what else I like?"

"What?" I scooped a forkful of eggs into my mouth.

"Seeing you in my shirt. Fucking adorable." His eyes stared at me as he inhaled his eggs.

I set my fork down. "Draven, what are we doing?"

"What do you mean?"

I motioned between the two of us. "This. Sleeping together. Having breakfast together. And we work together. You're going to get sick of me. I don't want to ruin it."

"It's not going to ruin it and I won't get sick of you. Are you sick of me?"

I rolled my eyes. "Oh yeah, I'm totally sick of you giving me earth-shattering orgasms. Can you please stop?"

He tapped me on the nose. "Nope. I like spending time with you."

"I like spending time with you, too. So, what do we call this?"

"Why do we have to label it? You're stressing too much about this." He motioned between us. "Relax and roll with it." He finished his last bite of eggs when I'd hardly touched mine. "I'm gonna go take a shower. You don't mind, do you?"

Draven naked and wet in my shower? "No, help yourself. I buy the good conditioner. It'll make your hair soft and shiny."

He kissed me on the head, took his plate to the sink, rinsed it off, and put it in the dishwasher. "Just leave this." He motioned to the bowl and frying pan on the counter. "I'll wash them when I get out of the shower. Thank you for breakfast. The eggs were great. The only thing that would have made it better would have been bacon. I'll pick some up today."

I internally groaned. I should have made the damn bacon.

Draven made his way to the bathroom and started the water. "There's a new toothbrush in the drawer," I shouted.

"No worries. I used yours. I figured we swapped enough germs last night that it didn't matter," he yelled back.

I tromped to the bathroom, only to find a naked Draven about to step into the shower. I'd seen him plenty naked last night, but it still threw me for a loop. I turned away from him and yanked open the vanity drawer. "I have to draw the line here. I'm not into sharing toothbrushes, but you're welcome to this one." I held up a new blue toothbrush. "And don't use all the hot water, I need to shower too."

"You're cute when you're mad, you know that?"

I threw up my hands. "Ugh!" I stomped from the bathroom and shut the door.

"Adorable!" he yelled through the door.

That man was going to drive me crazy. And I already loved it.

I put my plate in the dishwasher and eyed the pan and bowl by the stove. I could wash them or leave them. I decided to leave them to see if Draven would follow through.

Rhythmic knocking alerted me that Brian was at the door. I abandoned the dishes, not even checking the peephole, and undid the locks to let him in.

"Hey, just checking in."

I leaned on the door. "I'm good."

He looked me up and down. "You look happy. Are you wearing a man's shirt?"

"I am happy and yes, this is Draven's shirt. He spent the night."

"Really? Did you guys…?" He wiggled his eyebrows up and down.

I smacked him on the chest. "Not yet." I lowered my voice conspiratorially, "Last night was all oral. He's got a wicked tongue."

Brian smiled. "A risk worth taking?"

"Absolutely."

The bathroom door clicked open, and Draven stepped into the hall with a towel wrapped around his hips, water dripping down his chest. He held up his hand, "Hey, man," then continued into the bedroom.

Brian's jaw dropped open. "That's so not fair."

I laughed. "Ha! Now, you know how I felt. This one's mine." I put both hands on his chest and pushed him backward. "Shoo. Out you go."

"You sure he's not gay?"

"Positive. Now go." Brian reluctantly stepped into the hallway. "I'll talk to you later."

I closed and locked the door behind him, hurrying off to the bedroom. "Did you find everything you needed in the shower?"

"Everything but the naked woman I was hoping would join me. What did Brian want?"

"Just checking on me."

"He's been a good friend to you, hasn't he?" There was no jealousy in his tone. It was refreshing. Michael had been suspicious and jealous of every man I encountered. At first it was endearing that he felt protective of me, but protective turned to possessive and possessive turned to delusional. He'd even accused me of sleeping with his father at one point. Totally delusional.

"The best. He's been like a brother to me. I needed that when I came here. I mean, it was awkward at first, because I didn't know he was gay and I hit on him, but we moved past it."

"I know it might sound weird, but I like that he lives across the hall from you. I know he wouldn't ever let anything happen to you. That guy really cares about you. I saw how much the other night."

"It doesn't bother you?"

Draven whipped the towel off his hips, baring everything. "Why? Should it?" He stepped into yesterday's underwear and pulled his jeans on.

I shrugged. "Just wondered how you felt about it. That's all."

"I'm not the jealous type, especially of a gay guy, no matter how good-looking he is. I'm confident I can give you everything you need." He stepped forward and pulled my shirt—well, his shirt—over my head. "Were you satisfied last night?"

"If you mean, was it toe-curling, spine-tingling, mind-numbingly good?" I wavered my hand back and forth. "Meh, it was all right."

Draven picked me up over his shoulder and swatted my panty clad ass. "It was just all right, huh?"

I couldn't stop laughing. "Okay! Okay! It was better than all right!" He slid me back down the front of him. "It was amazing," I said seriously.

"It was amazing for me too." He rubbed the back of his fingers down my cheek. "I'll see you in a couple of hours?" He pulled his shirt on and laced up his boots.

"Yeah. I'm gonna take a shower." I crossed my arms over my breasts. "I'll meet you at work."

"Okay. I'll do the dishes and lock up on my way out."

I gave him a quick kiss on the cheek and headed to the shower.

When I got out, the kitchen was clean and the locks on the front door had been turned. All three of them.

Chapter 20
Draven

When I left Layla's, I stopped by Brian's to borrow his keys, so her apartment would be locked up tight. He appreciated the gesture but didn't hesitate to give me another warning. The two of us came to an understanding despite our rocky start. We both cared about Layla and only wanted the best for her.

I made one stop on the way home, then texted Kane. These things took time, but it had been over twenty-four hours. If Kane couldn't get me information, no one could.

Me: Talk to me. What did you find?

Kane: About 20 Michaels in for attempted murder. No Roberts. What's the girl's name.

Me: Layla.

Kane: Is Roberts her married name or maiden name?

Fuck! I didn't know. Even with how much she had revealed, I still didn't know shit about her. Asking questions wasn't going to earn me any points. Revisiting her past would only be reopening old wounds and as selfish as it was, I wanted her to stay firmly planted in the present.

Me: I don't know. She said it was a big case. It should be easy to find. Check the California newspapers.

Kane: I'll keep looking. Try to get more info.

Me: Easier said than done.

Kane: You're only there for a few weeks. Cut her loose. You know better.

I typed out a quick response and threw my phone on the kitchen counter next to the bacon and eggs I bought on the way home.

Me: I can't.

That was the truth. From the first moment I met Layla she had gotten under my skin. I had first been obsessed with her tits and ass, then her sassy attitude. Now it was something more.

I couldn't stay away.

As if on cue, my phone buzzed on the counter. Even though I had left her apartment only an hour ago my chest swelled with anticipation.

It quickly deflated when I picked it up and saw the name on the screen.

Andrei. The last person I wanted to talk to.

I reluctantly answered the call. "*Tată.*" *Father.*

"*Fiul meu,*" *my son,* my father addressed me. He continued in Romanian. "Things went well the other night." It was a statement, not a question. No doubt, Nico had filled him in.

"Yes. No problems." I kept it short with him, my own Romanian not quite as fluent as he would have liked. He wasn't calling to congratulate me. I knew my father better than that.

"Good. Seems our clients have a big appetite. They're very happy with the steaks we delivered."

Everything with my father was in code. He'd never risk the feds tapping our phones. "Is that so?"

"Yes. They'd like more for the baseball tournament they're having next week."

I knew what that meant. Guns and drugs. Cocaine to be exact. My stomach sank. The last thing I wanted to do was another deal. "You don't have anyone else who can handle the order?"

"I need the best. You're the only option." His tone left no room for discussion.

"I'll need more servers." No doubt the gangbangers would be ready for us this time.

"You'll have everything you need," he assured me. "Nico will give you the specifics. *Nu mă dezamăgeşti.*" *Don't disappoint me.* He ended the call, giving me nothing else.

I slumped into the couch in frustration. I was living two separate lives. I always had, but here I had a chance to be someone else. No one here knew who Andrei was or cared I was his son. It was liberating. I was starting to understand what Zack meant when he said this city was their safe place. This small town was starting to grow on me. Life here was simple.

The thought of doing this deal, made me sick. How was I supposed to broker a drug deal and then crawl into bed next to Layla like everything was right with the world, when everything was wrong?

I hated having to lie to her. Now that Layla and I were sleeping together, getting away would be more difficult. She had enough trust issues without me adding to them. But, when the time came, I'd have to lie. There were no other choices, because like Kane reminded me, I worked for Andrei.

The day was wrapping up. We'd been crazy busy again. I barely talked to Layla at all, but that was fine because I was spending my night with her.

Chase poked his head in my studio, "Hey, I'm going to The Locker. They've got a band playing. Want to come with?"

I had planned on taking Layla right upstairs. "Ummm…"

Chase let out a chuckle. "I asked Layla too. She's in if you are. I take it your date went well."

"Let's just say we hit it off. She's a mini-golf pro."

"You took her miniature golfing?" he questioned.

I put my hands on my hips. "Yeah. What's wrong with that?"

He shook his head. "Nothing. Just not what I expected from you. So, are you two dating now?"

Why did everyone want to put a label on things? "We're hanging out. It's only been like two days."

"But you like her?" He wiggled his eyebrows.

"Didn't we already establish that? Don't beat it into the ground."

"Yeah, okay. So, are you in?"

"I'm in, a drink sounds good. Give me ten."

I finished cleaning up my work area, locked the back door and headed to the front to meet Chase and Layla. She looked sexy, dressed in a tight concert tee, black skinny jeans, and some amazing shoes. Black strappy heels with silver studs on them, her painted toes peeking out the ends. Visions of fucking her in those shoes, and only those shoes, swam through my head. They would look phenomenal wrapped around my neck, those heels digging into my shoulders.

Suddenly going to the bar didn't sound that appealing. It was too late to back out, so I discreetly adjusted the pressure in my jeans and trudged forward. She was a perpetual walking hard-on.

The three of us entered the neighborhood hotspot. It was super crowded for a weeknight, but Chase nabbed us a high-top toward the back. The waitress was quick with our drinks, setting them on the napkins in front of us.

"Is Becca meeting you tonight?" Layla asked Chase.

"Naw. We're off again. Ask me tomorrow."

She laughed. "You two need to figure your shit out or maybe you need to move on."

"Why do you think we're here? I figured Draven could lure them with his good looks and I could reel them in with my charm." He mimed using a fishing pole to catch a woman.

Layla tapped him on the cheek. "Awww. You don't need Draven. You're cute in your own right. You're a catch, Chase."

"Eh, I do all right. But women seem to only want me for my body. Do you have any idea what it's like to be treated like a piece of meat?" He ran his hand through his shaggy blond hair.

I laughed, disguising it as a cough behind my hand.

Layla dropped her head onto her crossed arms on the table. "And you wonder why you're still single." Then she pierced him with her green eyes. "So why am I here?"

"Duh. You're my wingwoman. You can talk me up to all the lovely ladies. You know, play up my best qualities."

She smiled. "I can do that."

"Besides," he smirked, "Draven wouldn't come without you."

"Is that so?" she asked, turning her attention to me.

I shrugged. "It might have been a consideration."

A tall, attractive, blond-haired older woman squeezed between Chase and Layla, putting her arms over their shoulders. "Two of my favorite people."

Chase gave her a hug and kissed her on the cheek. "Hey."

Layla gave her a tight hug. "Hi, Catherine. Have you heard from Zack?"

She clapped her hands together. "Yes, yesterday. He and Rissa bought a condo in Malibu. Everything is moving really fast for Rissa. They love her."

Layla's eyes got wide, a hint of panic in them. "But they're coming back, right?"

She waved Layla off. "Of course. He can't live in California now that I've moved here. It's just for when they need to spend time there."

Layla clutched her chest. "Oh, thank God. I need him here." Then she turned to me. "I'm sorry. I'm so rude. Draven, this is Catherine, Zack's mom. Draven's helping out while Zack is gone."

Catherine reached her hand across the table. "It's so nice to finally meet you. I know Zack was ecstatic that you could be here."

I gently shook her hand. "It's a pleasure to meet you too. I've heard a lot about you. Zack and I were in the Marines together. I might have partaken in some of your care packages. You successfully made all the other guys jealous."

She winked at me. "It was the least I could do. I'm glad you enjoyed it."

"Last I heard, you lived in New York. Why the move?"

She put her hands on her hips. "I finally divorced Zack's father. After Wes died, I wanted to be closer to my son and his wife. Plus, have you seen Alexandria? How could I possibly resist that beautiful grandbaby of mine?"

I remembered that Zack's dad was a bit of an asshole to put it lightly. He and Zack had never gotten along. After Zack's brother died, it only got worse. It had a little to do with money and a lot to do with power. Not that different than the situation with my own father.

"She's a beauty for sure. His wife's not bad either." I chuckled.

"They're good for each other. I've never seen Zack happier."

Layla leaned over the table. "Catherine's happy too. She's dating Lou." She pointed to the goateed older man who owned the bar.

Catherine nudged Layla. "We're not dating. We're just having fun. Hanging out. It's casual."

Chase smirked. "Sure, it is. That's why you're here all the time. Or is it to see me? Admit it, you have a crush on me."

Catherine tapped Chase's shoulder playfully. "Oh, Chase. You're sweet as can be, but sadly we would never work. You're about twenty years too young."

Chase sat up straight in his seat. "I'm very mature for my age."

"I'm sure you are. Some *young* girl will be very lucky to have you."

"So, you and Lou?" Layla prodded.

Catherine tipped her head side to side. "Okay, maybe it's more, but we're taking it slow. He makes me happy," she conceded.

"He's good in bed, huh?" Layla said smugly.

Catherine started to blush. "That's none of your business, young lady. But... yes. It's a nice change."

"I knew it," she exclaimed. "How's Miss Priss? Is she missing Zack?"

I choked on my vodka. "Miss Priss? Who the hell is Miss Priss?"

"Zack's cat," Catherine explained. "She's been a complete delight. Such a snuggler." The lights started to dim, and the band walked on stage. "I'll leave you kids to it. Have fun tonight."

The band started with an 80's cover. They were good, and the drinks were going down way too easy. Chase scoped out the bar for his next conquest. Layla bobbed her head and swayed to the music while singing along softly.

I leaned closer to Layla. "Are you afraid Zack's not coming back?"

She shrugged. "I wouldn't be happy about it."

"Would you stay if he didn't come back?"

"I don't know. I guess he feels like my safety net. If he closed Forever Inked where would I go?"

"He's not here now and you're fine."

Layla let out a big sigh. "I know, but it's temporary. A lot would change if it were permanent. I'd lose Chase and Zack. All I'd have left would be Brian."

She didn't even factor me into the equation. Why would she? I'd already told her I'd be gone. I would. Wouldn't I? That was my reality. New York was my home. I mulled it around in my brain and it didn't sit well.

Layla looked over my shoulder. "Oh, crap." A tall, leggy brunette approached our table. "Look what the cat dragged in," Layla addressed her.

"A pleasure, as always, Layla. Chase." She winked at him.

Chase perked up. "Oh hey, Gina."

"Who's your new friend?" She held out her hand to me. "I'm Gina."

I reached to shake it, but never made contact. Layla put her hand on mine and pushed it down. "This is Draven and he's not interested. Gina and Zack used to fuck. A lot."

Gina retracted her hand and rolled her eyes. "We're friends."

"They were fuck buddies," Layla reiterated.

"You know, Rissa and I have put it in the past. I don't know why you can't," Gina scoffed.

"Because I don't like you and I don't trust you," Layla said point blank.

"Charming." Gina's voice dripped with sarcasm.

"I like you, Gina," Chase piped in, his tongue practically hanging out of his mouth like an overzealous puppy.

She smiled at Chase. "You're sweet. I like you too. I was just wondering how Zack was doing? That's why I stopped by."

"Zack and his *wife* are doing great. Thanks for stopping by, but there's nothing else here for you. See ya!" Layla waved her fingers at Gina in a dismissive gesture.

"God, you're a bitch," Gina shot back. "See you later, Chase. Draven, nice to meet you. Maybe I'll see ya around."

"You won't. Ba-bye," Layla said as Gina walked away.

Chase slapped Layla on the shoulder. "You kind of suck as a wingwoman. She was totally into me."

"Oh, please! You do not want to stick your dick in that." Then she pointed at me. "And neither do you."

I held up my hands in surrender. "Wasn't even thinking about it." Truth was, before I met Layla, she was exactly the type I would stick my dick in. The fact that it didn't even cross my mind was telling. "What's your beef with her?"

"Long story. She's not a good person."

"But she's hot," Chase stated the obvious.

Layla rolled her eyes and scanned the bar. She pointed to a redhead at another table. "There's your prize, Chase. Go buy her a drink."

Chase craned his neck to see where Layla was pointing. "Yeah, she's hot." He straightened his shirt and ran a hand through his hair. "How do I look?"

"Sexy." She winked at him. "Go get her, boy."

I held my fist up for Chase to bump. "Good luck, man."

"Luck has nothing to do with it. It's all about the body. Girls can't resist all this." He motioned to his body in a sweeping gesture.

"Go." I chuckled.

We watched as Chase swaggered over to her table and leaned down to talk in her ear. She threw her head back and laughed. He pulled up a chair and sat next to her. He was in.

"Looks like Chase has got it covered," I said to Layla.

"For some reason the ladies love him, but he always goes back to Becca. He needs to cut her loose."

I nodded. "Did you really think I would be interested in Gina?"

She shrugged. "Like Chase said, she's hot. Why wouldn't you be interested?"

I took her hand over the table and twined my fingers with hers. "Because I'm interested in you. I meant what I said. You're the only one I plan on fucking. You good with that?"

She swallowed. "Yeah, I'm good with that." She waved her hand in front of her face. "Is it hot in here? I need another drink. You want one?"

She was so damn adorable. "I got it." I went up to the bar and ordered our drinks.

Layla wobbled in her heels as we walked back to my apartment. She held onto my arm with a death grip.

"You drunk?" I asked.

"Not drunk. Pleasantly buzzed. The last two might have tipped me over the edge," she said, holding up three fingers.

I laughed. She was drunk. "Let's get you home."

"Home? But I thought we were going to fuck tonight?"

I leaned her against the building, as I unlocked the door to Forever Inked. Layla slid down the wall and landed on her butt. I looked down at her. "Not tonight, *pisoi.*"

She frowned and stared up at me. "Did you get taller? I think you got taller."

I leaned down, scooped her up in my arms, and carried her into the building. "I'm taking you upstairs and putting you to bed."

She squeezed my bicep. "You're so strong. Do you work out?"

"You're light. What do you weigh? A hundred ten?"

"One twenty. I got a lot of junk in my trunk," she said slapping her ass.

"I like your trunk. It gives me something to grab ahold of."

"I've got big boobs too."

"You don't say." I laughed.

"Wanna see them?"

Drunk Layla was quite entertaining. "I saw them last night, kitten."

"Where's a kitten?" She looked all around as I carried her up the stairs. "Here kitty, kitty." She scrunched up her face. "I don't see a kitten." She pointed to the door. "Is it in there?"

I set her down on her feet to get my key out and unlock my apartment. "The only pussy here is yours."

She shook her finger at me. "You're a dirty boy, Draven."

"Yes. Yes, I am, but not tonight." I picked her up and carried her to the bedroom, setting her down gently on the bed.

She practically melted into it. "This bed is so comfy."

"Let's get you undressed." I took off her shoes, then unbuttoned her jeans and pulled them down her legs. She had red lace panties on. I groaned because I was going to miss out on pulling them off with my teeth tonight. I should have taken her shirt off too, but it would have been testing my own willpower. I pulled the blankets out from under her limp body and tucked her underneath.

"You're a good guy, Draven," she mumbled. "Thank you for taking care of me."

I kissed her head. "Any time, *pisoi*." She was practically unconscious already. I stared down at her and wondered if I should push my luck. Chances were, she wouldn't remember in the morning. "Layla?"

"Yeah?" she whispered, curling up on her side.

"Is Roberts your married name?"

"It's just a name. She's dead. He took her away from me," she mumbled. It made no sense. Another piece of a mismatched puzzle.

I pushed her hair away from her face. "Who's dead?"

"Jenna. He killed her."

Then it clicked. Fuck! She was talking about her baby. I felt like a complete asshole. I should have never pushed. "I'm sorry," I whispered.

"Um hmm." Her breathing evened out and soft snores filled the silence.

I went back to the front door and picked her purse up from the floor where she had dropped it. I carried it to the counter and took out her wallet. Going through a woman's purse was a new low for me, but the chance that it might give me more information was too much of a temptation to pass up.

I opened her wallet. She had a credit card, driver's license, Social Security card. Everything said Layla Lorraine Roberts. Lorraine? I would have never pegged her for a Lorraine. It was cute… Layla Lorraine.

I kept searching for something. Anything. I pulled out a few twenty-dollar bills and some singles. She had some coupons tucked in there too. None of it was useful.

Something poked out from behind her driver's license. I gripped the edge of the card and pulled it from the plastic sleeve that held it in place. Behind it sat a concealed pistol license. *She carried a gun?*

I picked up her purse and dumped the contents on the counter. Sure enough, a sub-compact fell out, along with her phone, keys, a can of mace, some tampons, a tube of lipstick, and a bunch of other girly crap. I picked up the gun and pulled the slide back. Fully loaded. Hollow points. She wasn't messing around.

I swiped my finger across the screen of her phone. It lit up and required a password to gain access. Another dead end.

I stuck everything back in her purse and pulled out my laptop. I typed her name into the search engine. Apparently, there was an actress named Layla Roberts. Never heard of her. I clicked on the link for Facebook profiles. It returned dozens of results. I clicked on each one. None of them were her. It made sense that she wouldn't have an account.

I was going to have to get more specific. I typed *Layla Roberts California* into a new search. Again, dozens of results were returned. Who would have thought it would be such a common name? I tried *Layla Lorraine Roberts California*. It produced several Lorraine Roberts, but no Layla Lorraine Roberts. This was like searching for a needle in a haystack. She was a ghost.

After an hour, I shut my laptop and wandered back to the bedroom. My girl looked so peaceful sleeping. *My girl? When had she become my girl?* It was another unanswered question.

Kicking off my boots, I undressed and crawled into bed with her. My arm reached out and pulled Layla close. She let out a little murmur and snuggled in next to me. I breathed in the sweet scent of her, and all my tension slipped away.

"You're a mystery Layla Lorraine Roberts. What are you hiding?"

What the hell died in my mouth? That was my first thought.

The second was, *Where the fuck am I?*

I pulled back the covers and surveyed my surroundings. There was a pair of black boots by the door, but that was my only clue. The last thing I fully remembered was walking home last night and even that was fuzzy.

I never let myself get that drunk. It wasn't safe. It was reckless and stupid.

I did a quick inventory. I was dressed. Mostly. My pants were gone, but my shirt and bra were still on. Check. I looked down at my waist. Panties? Check. That was good, right?

The door opened, and Draven popped his head in. I let out a breath of relief. "Morning. How do you feel?"

"Better than I should. What the hell happened last night? Did we…?" God, I hoped we didn't have sex.

He walked in and handed me a glass of water and two Motrin. "Give me some credit. You were like a corpse. It's not really my thing. Trust me, when we have sex, it'll be something you won't forget."

I swallowed the pills and gulped down the water greedily. "I'm sorry. I don't know what happened."

He sat down next to me. "You were entertaining. You're a cute drunk."

I dropped my head into my hand. "Oh, God. What did I say?" *What did I say?* That was another reason I didn't get drunk. Loose lips sank ships.

"Nothing bad. But you did tell me you had big boobs." He ran his hand over the front of my shirt. "Good thing you mentioned it, or I might not have noticed."

"Yeah," I rolled my eyes, "they're easy to miss." I looked around the room. "Where's my purse?"

He hiked a thumb toward the door. "Kitchen."

I walked on unsteady feet to the kitchen and grabbed it off the counter. Fishing around inside, I pulled out my phone. I swiped my finger across the screen and entered my code. Shit! I had two missed calls and several text messages from Brian.

Brian: *Where are you?*
Brian: *Are you okay?*
Brian: *Text me! Please!*

I groaned. It wasn't like me to be out all night. He was probably worried sick.

"What's wrong?" Draven asked. I held up my phone, so he could see the messages. "You better call him."

"I know. Can you go down to my car and get my bag from the back seat?" I handed him my keys.

"You packed a bag?"

"Just in case."

"Just in case you wanted to get drunk and pass out in my bed?" He laughed.

"Yeah. That was exactly my plan."

It wasn't my plan at all. I had thought that last night Draven and I would move to the next level. But that didn't happen.

I pulled out the front of my shirt and took a sniff. Ugh! Something hadn't just died in my mouth, it had rubbed its decomposing self all over my body.

I snatched my keys back out of Draven's hand. "You know what? I changed my mind. I'm going to head home and shower."

He raised one eyebrow. "I have a shower here."

"I know, but I didn't bring all my shower stuff and I'm kind of particular. It'll be better."

"Whatever you want, but you're welcome to stay."

I headed to the bedroom and pulled my jeans back on. Looking around, I found my shoes next to his dresser. Putting my feet back into them seemed like torture. I'd just drive home barefoot. I went back to the kitchen and snagged my purse. "I'll see you in a couple of hours. Thanks again for last night."

Suddenly, I couldn't get out of there fast enough. Waking up together two mornings in a row was pushing it. Three was bordering on domestic. Pretty soon we'd be brushing our teeth together in front of the mirror.

It was a routine I didn't want to get used to because, honestly, I liked it too much. And that was dangerous. This was supposed to be about sex. If I let my head and heart get involved, I knew what would happen.

What was already happening.

I was getting in too deep.

He's leaving, I reminded myself.

Don't let yourself fall in love.

After a profuse apology to Brian and a promise to keep in better contact, I showered and felt semi-human again. My teeth were brushed, and my body was scrubbed. After a quick sniff, I deemed myself ready to face the living.

I snuck into Forever Inked and hid in Zack's office. It wasn't like the books were falling behind, but it gave me an excuse to avoid Draven.

I picked up my phone and did something I promised myself I wouldn't do. I called Zack.

"Hey, Layla, what's going on? Is everything okay with the shop?" he said sleepily. I forgot about the three-hour time difference. It was only seven-thirty in the morning in California. My bad.

"Everything is fine, but I talked to your mom last night. Are you coming back?"

I held my breath waiting for him to answer. My future rested on his response. If he wasn't coming back or planned on selling Forever Inked, I was going to need a contingency plan. Better to know ahead of time than be taken by surprise. My mind raced with alternate possibilities. Alabama? Florida? Fucking Puerto Rico? Anywhere that was far from here.

"We're coming back. Utica is our home. LA has glitz and glamour, but our family is there."

"Yeah, your mom would be totally bummed if you moved to California."

He agreed. "She would, but I'm not just talking about my mom. You're our family too. You, Chase, Kyla, all of us. We may not be related by blood, but we take care of each other. That's what families do."

My heart swelled and a sob stuck in my throat. "Thank you."

"For what?"

"Making me part of your family. Please don't change your mind. I really need you two to come home, okay?"

"We are. Hey, are you all right?"

I waved a hand in front of myself. I hadn't planned on breaking down. I took a deep breath. "I'm fine. Everything here is great."

"How's Draven working out? Are you two getting along?" he asked.

Now, that was the question. You could say we were getting along. More like we were getting it on. That was probably too much information to give.

"We're getting along just fine. He's talented and fitting in great here." There. I kept it simple.

"I knew he would. I wish I could convince him to stay."

Me too. "Doesn't sound like he is."

"We'll have to give him a reason. Something he can't get back in New York."

Me! He can have me! "We'll work on it. How's my girl, Rissa?"

"Fabulous! You should see her. She was made for this. She's already done a ton of recording and photo shoots."

I was so happy for her. "She deserves this. I'll be first in line to buy her CD when it comes out."

I could hear Alexandria in the background. "Listen, I gotta go. Alexandria is waking up and she'll be hungry. Call if you need anything."

"I will. Say hi to Rissa for me and give that baby a kiss from her Auntie Layla."

"Will do. And don't worry. We're coming home."

We said our goodbyes and I sat back in Zack's chair thinking.

Home.

For so long I thought of Oregon as my home. The place I grew up. The place I fell in love. The place I ran away from. The place where Jenna died.

But Michigan was my home now. The place where I reinvented myself. The place I worked and lived. The place where my new family was. The place where I was falling in love again.

Give him a reason to stay.

I could be that reason. Couldn't I?

What if he stayed?

For me?

It was a crazy thought. But what if it wasn't?

Chase had the day off, so it was just Draven and me. I peeked my head into his studio and did a double-take. His head was bent over his client's back in deep concentration. His tongue poked out just the tiniest bit, day-old scruff covered his jaw, but what threw me off were the black-framed glasses perched on his face. I felt a stirring down below. If I thought he was sexy before, this kicked it up another notch.

He must have felt my stare because he looked up and gave me his panty-melting smile. "Hey, *pisoi*. Feeling better?"

"I didn't know you wore glasses." The words tumbled out before I could stop them.

"Only when I'm reading or working. Helps me zero in on detail." He pulled them off. "Did you need something?"

I shook myself out of my trance and finally remembered my intentions. "I was going to order lunch from the sub shop down the street. They deliver. Do you want anything?"

"I'm starving. Someone skipped out on breakfast with me this morning." His amber eyes pierced me. They went right to my soul as if he could see deep inside.

My body trembled. "Sorry about that." I shoved the take-out menu at him.

Draven set down his tattoo gun, patting his client on the back. "Take ten. Go have a smoke."

"Thank fuck," he said, stretching out his back. "I'll be out front."

His client left the studio and Draven pulled me inside, shutting the door. He grabbed the sides of my face and kissed me. Hard. I tried to resist, but before I knew it the menu was on the floor, my arms were roped around his neck and I was kissing him back. His hands traveled down my sides to my thighs and in a flash, he lifted me. My legs instinctually wrapped around his waist. Our kiss was fire. An explosion of gasoline set off the minute our lips touched.

He backed us up to the chair that was folded down like a table. Taking me with him, he laid down and pulled me to his chest. "I fucking missed kissing you this morning. Why'd you run away?"

"I didn't run away," I gasped, trying to catch my breath.

He ran his hands through my hair. "You did. What spooked you?"

I sat up, straddling his waist, my hands on his chest. "Nothing," I lied. "I just needed time for myself. A hot shower."

His hands rubbed up and down my thighs. "I want you to stay with me tonight. I want to do bad things to you."

"You do?" I gulped.

"Yes. I need to be inside you. Tasting you the other night was like a tease. I want more of you. All of you."

150

"Okay." I wanted it. Badly. But to say I wasn't nervous would be another lie. I wasn't afraid of him. I was afraid of myself. Afraid I wouldn't be able to go through with it. Afraid I would freak out again and ruin it.

"I looked at the schedule for the night and we don't have any appointments. What do you say about closing early tonight? I'll take you to your place so you can get everything you need, I'll take you to dinner, then we'll come back here so I can take care of all your other needs." His wide hands traveled to the apex of my thighs, his thumbs caressing down my center.

"Like a date?" I asked, unconsciously rocking my hips forward.

"Yes, Layla, like a date. Make no mistake, I want to fuck you so bad it hurts, but I want to spend time with you in other ways too. Will you go out to dinner with me tonight?"

I bit my lip and nodded, "Yes."

It was like déjà vu.

Just like our first date, he'd been a perfect gentleman tonight. He draped his arm over my shoulder as we walked through the outdoor mall at Partridge Creek where we had dinner at an Italian restaurant. He opened the door to his Hummer for me and helped me up inside. He held my hand over the console as we drove back to his apartment.

And just like our first date, Draven unlocked his apartment, and my nerves got the best of me.

The door clicked and he pulled me inside, shutting it behind us. I swallowed down my worry.

Draven led me to his bedroom by the hand. Just outside the door, I stopped, jerking him to a halt. He cocked his head with unasked questions.

"I'm scared," I whispered.

Draven cupped my face with his hands, "I'm not going to hurt you. I only want to bring you pleasure. All you have to do is say no and we stop."

I put my hands over his. "I'm not afraid of you. I'm afraid of myself. What if I freak out? I don't want to do that to you again."

"If you need or want to stop, we stop, but you're not running away again. You're done running."

"I'm done running." I repeated more for myself than for him.

"Good. Now, come here so I can ravage you." Draven pulled my body tight to his, forcing the breath from my lungs and backed me into the bedroom. "I want you so bad. You've been teasing me with this body all night."

"I think it's the other way around." I ran my hands up his chest, feeling the hard muscles under his shirt. "I want this off you." My fingers began undoing the buttons on his shirt and peeling it down his shoulders.

Draven shrugged it off and threw the shirt on a chair. Then he pulled at the hem of my shirt and lifted it over my head. His fingers ran over the tops of my breasts. "God, you're so beautiful." My jeans were next. He shimmied them down my legs. I held onto his shoulders as he kneeled before me. Draven carefully removed my black heels and pulled my legs free of the denim.

I stood before him in only my lacey purple bra and matching thong. He drank me in with his eyes. The desire I saw in them was something I'd never had directed at me before. I'd seen it in Zack, the way he looked at Rissa, but no one had ever looked at me that way. Even my ex-husband. Sure, I believed he loved me, at least in the beginning, but he never desired me.

Not like Draven.

It was there in his eyes.

Pure fire.

For me.

And damn if it didn't get me wet. I could feel it soaking through my thong. I clenched my thighs together for some relief, but it was pointless. He turned me on more than any man should be capable of doing.

Draven started at my ankles and caressed the skin of my calves and behind my knees. He worked his way up my body and effortlessly lifted me into the middle of the bed. "You're perfect. Just like that. In my bed, where I've wanted you since day one."

I raised up on my elbows and bent one leg, so my foot was flat on the comforter, my other stretched out in front of me in what I hoped was a sexy pose. "It would be perfect if you weren't still wearing pants. You need to take them off."

"Your wish is my command." Draven slowly unbuckled his belt, careful not to let the metal clank, and undid the front of his jeans. They were on the floor along with his boots in a matter of seconds.

I crooked my finger at him, beckoning him forward. Draven placed one knee on the bed and crawled toward me like a panther stalking his prey. Me. I was his prey, and I had no desire to escape.

"Kiss me," I said in a breathy whisper.

His lips crashed into mine. My hands ran up the sides of his face and into his hair, my nails digging into his scalp, pulling him closer. Our tongues twisted, our teeth nipped, our bodies pulsed into each other. "Fuck, Layla, I can't get enough of you."

"More, Draven, kiss me everywhere. I want to come so badly," I gasped.

"You will, baby, I promise you that." He rolled slightly to the side, reaching behind me to unclasp my bra. "First, I want to feast on these tits." He pulled my bra away from my body and threw it somewhere into the dark. He licked around my nipple before his lips clamped down over it. I arched toward his mouth urging him to suck harder. He gave both my breasts equal treatment, as he used his teeth to gently tug at my nipple rings. Getting my nipples pierced was an impulse that I'd never reaped the benefits of until Draven.

His hand splayed down my stomach and crept inside my panties. His fingers slid through my wetness and up to my clit, where he rubbed me in slow circles. It was decadent. Devine. Spine-tinglingly pleasing. His thumb continued its slow torture as he slipped two fingers inside me. He fucked me with his fingers while flicking at my hard nipple with his tongue. The sensory overload had me moaning and gasping like a desperate woman.

It wasn't far from the truth. I was desperate. Sex with Michael had been methodical. There was no foreplay. There was no experimentation. There was nothing dirty about it.

It was on my back, except for the few times he forced me over the edge of the bed to take me from behind. I rarely got to come unless it was from my own fingers. My needs were all but ignored.

All this time, I thought it was me. I thought I was doing something wrong. When Michael rolled over and went to sleep, I took it as a sign that I wasn't a good wife who could please her husband. But it was never me, it was him. Realizing the truth gave me an extra boost of confidence.

I'd fantasized about the things I wanted a man to do to me. I'd read about them in the smutty novels I devoured on my Kindle. But I'd never experienced them.

Draven kissed down my body, stopping only to trace the butterfly on my abdomen with his tongue. Kneeling beside me, his fingers gripped the top of my thong and pulled it down my legs. It flew to the side landing somewhere on the floor by the rest of my discarded clothes. "Open for me. I want to eat this pussy."

Well fuck!

Who was I to deny the man what he wanted? My legs opened, and he pushed them wider, setting my feet on the mattress. There was no hiding with this man. I bared everything for him.

He didn't hesitate. He dove in with an eagerness that shook me to the core. His tongue speared up inside me, teasing and tasting. My hands fisted the comforter, my back arching up and my head falling back. "Oh, God. What are you doing to me? Fuck!"

"Only everything you deserve." Draven flattened his tongue and lapped at me, working his way to my clit. He teased it with the tip of his tongue before sucking it between his lips.

Pleasure coursed through my body as he took me higher and higher. Then he inserted a finger inside me and another. God, those magic fingers fucked into me, hitting every pleasure point possible. Between his mouth and his fingers, I wasn't going to last long. My head swam with desire and want. I could feel my orgasm rising to astronomical proportions. The need to come was almost painful as it swelled up inside me. I pushed my hips higher, begging for more, my body winding tighter, my muscles clenching.

Finally… finally, the crest broke, and waves of pleasure washed over me. White spots dotted my vision and my body convulsed out of my control. I thrashed from side to side, a string of filthy words that would have made a sailor blush flew from my mouth. Through it all, Draven never relented. He continued his assault through every wave that rocked my body.

When everything had drained away, I was left gasping for air. "Holy fuck!"

Draven leaned over the bed to the nightstand and pulled out a condom. I was still panting when he stripped his boxer briefs off and kneeled between my legs. He stroked his long, thick cock with one hand giving the head a rough tug. I licked my lips, my teeth biting into the bottom one as I watched his hand stroking up and down. "Are you ready for me to fuck you?"

Despite the euphoria running through my veins, I shivered. "I was serious before. I'm not sure you're going to fit," I whispered. "Maybe we should use some lube."

He ran his fingers through my pussy and painted my lips with my juices. "Trust me, I'll fit. You're plenty wet. We'll save the lube for another time."

I couldn't even comprehend the implication of his words. "Okay. I'm ready."

Draven ripped open the condom with his teeth and sheathed his length. I stiffened my body, ready for the intrusion. "Be gentle with me. It's been a while."

I took a deep breath, grabbed the comforter, and closed my eyes. Fear gripped me and I summoned all my bravery. I could do this. It was normal... and if I was lucky, it would be over fast.

I waited for him to impale me, but it never came.

The seconds ticked by.

I opened my eyes. Draven's face blurred and tears, I hadn't realized I was crying, ran down the sides of my face. A soft sob escaped my throat. I was failing again. I frantically wiped the tears from my face. "I'm so fucking sorry." Another soft sob broke free.

Draven pulled me to his chest and wrapped his arms around me. "My God, you're shaking. You're really scared, aren't you?"

I nodded and blew out a breath. "I'm sorry. Do you want me to leave?"

He held my face in his hands. "No. Do you want to be with me?"

"More than anything." It was the truth. I wanted him so bad, but my head was revolting against my body.

He gently laid me back down. "Then be with me. Keep your eyes open. Focus on me and only me. I won't hurt you. Hold up your hands." I did, and he laced his fingers through mine. "I've got you, Layla. I won't let anything bad happen to you."

"Promise me?"

"I promise you. I'm not him. He can't hurt you anymore." Draven lowered my hands next to my head, never letting go. "I'm gonna push in now, okay?"

"Okay."

Draven's cock nudged at my opening and he slid in barely an inch. I squeezed my eyes shut in anticipation of the pain that never came. "Eyes open, kitten. Focus on me."

My eyes locked with his. They reflected a kindness and tenderness that gave me the strength I needed. They told me everything I needed to know. This was more about me than him. He pushed in a little further. My body stretched to accommodate his width. It was slightly uncomfortable at first, but it didn't hurt. "I'm good. Go all the way."

Draven's lips met mine in a slow seductive kiss. It wasn't frenzied or rough. It was gentle and passionate. I arched up as he slid all the way home. "How do you feel?"

My lips curved upward. "Good. Really good. I feel... full."

He smiled down on me. "Your pussy is so tight. It's like a vice squeezing my cock."

I bit my lip. "Maybe it's just because your cock is so big."

He kissed the tip of my nose. "I'm a big guy. Big hands, big feet, big cock."

I giggled and wiggled my fingers that were twined with his. "I think I love your big hands and big cock." *Did I say love? Like. Like. I meant like.*

Draven didn't react to my faux pas. Instead, he made another joke while buried deep inside me. "What? No love for my big feet?"

"I'm not that well acquainted with them, but if I develop some strange foot fetish, I'll let you know."

"Deal." Draven gripped my hands tighter, and I felt safe. "Are you ready for me to move?"

I took a deep breath. "Yes. Go slow."

Draven slowly pulled out and gently pushed back in. Over and over. I felt his piercing dragging along my inner walls and it was like nothing I had ever experienced before. Pure ecstasy. His body and warmth enveloped me, keeping me safe. I was in the moment. There were no other thoughts than the man who filled me. My body began to move with his. I rose up to meet his every thrust. Our bodies moved together in a dance that was all our own. I never knew it could be so good. I let go of everything but the pleasure he was bringing me. "So good, Draven. More… please don't stop," I gasped.

"I have no intention of stopping. It's too perfect." Draven let go of one hand and grasped my thigh, raising it up so he could go deeper. He swiveled his hips and I damn near lost my mind.

Nothing had ever felt this amazing. I could feel another orgasm bearing down on me. Next thing I knew, Draven scooped me up and pulled me onto his lap, so I was straddling him, my arms wrapped around his shoulders. He pushed up into me as I pushed down. Our bodies moved as one. My breasts rubbed against his hard chest and my clit rubbed against his pelvis on every stroke. His piercing rubbed me on the inside in the most erotic way. He held my body tight to his, as his hands stroked up and down my back and up into my hair. Our lips connected, our tongues twisted. This wasn't fucking. This was so much more and if I didn't know better, I'd swear he was making love to me.

"I can't hold back much longer, kitten. I'm gonna come," he whispered.

"Me too. I'm almost there…" I panted "Oh, God. I'm coming, Draven. I'm coming," I threw my head back and let go of everything. My body convulsed around him and my bones melted into jelly.

He held me tight and roared out his own release. I could feel him pulsing inside me, his hips thrusting madly as he emptied himself inside the condom. I held on tight, afraid he would let me go. But I should have known by now that this man wouldn't let me fall.

Draven pressed his forehead to mine. "That was amazing. Just like I predicted, two pieces of the same puzzle. We fit together perfectly. Our bodies were meant for each other."

No truer words had ever been spoken.

I'd just had the most intimate experience of my entire life.

Chapter 22
Draven

I leaned on the bathroom counter and stared at myself in the mirror after disposing of the condom.

What the hell was that? That's not how you fuck, you idiot!

The problem was, I knew exactly what it was. I may have never done it before, but I recognized it.

I didn't fuck her.

I made love to her.

And worse than that... I wanted to do it again.

I was on dangerous ground. Falling in love with her was not an option. And I certainly couldn't let her fall in love with me.

I remembered our conversation from a few days ago. She'd looked me dead in the eye and asked, *"What if three weeks isn't enough? What if I don't want you to leave?"*

"You will. I promise you, I'm not worth it." I had to stick to what I'd said. My home was in New York.

When we started this, it was supposed to be only about sex. I was supposed to help her get over her fear. When we met, there was something about her that had captured my attention, but I never thought within a few days it would turn into more. It didn't even make logical sense. I was immune to love. *Wasn't I?*

At some point I'd have to show her I wasn't the good guy she imagined. She had no idea who I was. The Raven wasn't someone she could ever love. He was a gunrunner. A drug dealer. A murderer. He lived in the shadows.

She belonged in the light.

Tonight, was not the night for truth, but I needed to pull back a little.

When I returned to the bedroom, Layla was tucked under the sheet, propped up on one arm, a blissed-out expression on her face. "Nothing has ever felt like that before. Thank you."

I crawled into the bed next to her and mirrored her position, so we faced each other. I ran my hand down her cheek. "You don't have to thank me. This is what I agreed to," I said, trying to put us back on even ground.

Disappointment flashed across her face, but it was gone in an instant. If I had blinked, I would have missed it. I immediately felt bad about the words that came out of my mouth.

"Yeah, of course. You're my sex tutor. That's what we agreed to."

"Layla..."

"No, I get it." She rolled to her back. "Do you have any booze? I could really go for a drink." She climbed out of bed and grabbed her shirt from the floor.

"Where are you going? You can't run. You don't have a car here." Knowing her propensity for running, she was liable to call an Uber or walk home if necessary.

She waved me off. "I'm not running. I've got the good stuff down in my studio. I'm going to grab it." She pulled on her thong and headed downstairs.

I dropped back on the bed. "Fuck!" I hurt her feelings with my careless answer. It wasn't my intention, but I'd done it just the same. Her defenses were up, and I put them there.

I scrubbed my hands over my face. I sucked at this. This is what happened when you'd never had a relationship and treated women as disposable. Layla wasn't disposable. Yes, we had an end date, and we could never work, but she wasn't like other women. I had treated her as if what we did meant nothing.

We both knew that was a lie.

After more than a few minutes, Layla hadn't returned. I pulled on my jeans and padded down the stairs. I peeked into her studio.

She sat with her bare foot up on her stool, staring at a bottle of Jack Daniel's. She tapped her fingers on the counter in front of her as if contemplating. Finally, she pushed the bottle away in disgust. "You're so fucking pathetic. How could you think it was something more?" she quietly asked herself.

Because it was. I leaned against her door. "Are you coming back to bed?"

She whipped her head toward me and held a finger up. "In a minute. I'm processing." Her tone was clipped, and her hard demeanor was back.

I stuck my hands in my pockets. "I'm sorry. I shouldn't have said that."

"What? The truth?" She rolled her eyes. "I can handle the truth, Draven. I'm not a child."

"No, you're not. You're a beautiful woman and I treated you as if what we did was just a fuck. And that's not the truth at all."

She threw her hands up in the air. "Then what is the truth?"

I blew out a breath. "I don't know, but that was more than just fucking. It meant something to me." I never intended on telling her, but I couldn't let Layla think I didn't care. Because for the first time in my life, I did. And not only did I care about her, but I cared how she felt.

"Maybe we should just stop now, before this gets complicated. You held up your end of the bargain," she suggested.

"It's already complicated. Truth?"

"I can handle it."

"I don't want to stop."

"I don't want to stop either. I don't have a lot of experience with sex, but I know that" she pointed upstairs, "was more."

I sat down on the other stool in her studio and grabbed the bottle of Jack. Twisting off the cap, I took a sip then passed her the bottle. "It was more, and it scares the shit out of me."

Layla sipped from the bottle. "What? Why?"

"Because I feel things for you that I shouldn't feel."

"I feel it too. It's scary. I haven't let anyone in for five years. Then you came along and turned my whole world upside down and inside out. You think that doesn't scare the crap out of me?"

"I'm not the guy you think I am and that's not changing. You deserve better than me."

"You're wrong. I know who you are. You're the man who protected my honor when you had no reason to. You're the man who chased me when I ran. You're the man who stayed when you should have run. You're the man who cared enough to lock my doors to make sure I was safe. You're the man who tucked me into bed when I had too much to drink. You're the man who made me feel again. So, don't tell me I don't know who you are."

"No, Layla. That's the man I am with you."

"And that's all that matters to me."

I shook my head. "You're looking for a hero. Trust me, I'm not him."

She spun around and poked her finger in my chest. "Fuck you! I don't need a hero or a prince or a fucking white knight. I don't need a man who's perfect because I'm sure as hell not perfect either. I don't want a goddamn fairy tale. I want to go out to dinner and hold your hand. I want to walk through the mall with your arm over my shoulder. I want you to kiss me like there's no tomorrow. I want that..." She pointed back up the stairs. "What we had tonight."

"I want that too, but what happens when Zack comes back? I'm still leaving."

"I know, but you're the one who said we should explore this. And maybe by then, we'll figure it out or we'll be sick of each other."

"Highly doubtful, because all I want right now is to take you back to bed." I pulled Layla onto my lap, "Now that we've done... whatever that was, you wanna fuck now?"

Her lips curled up into a mischievous smirk. "Can I be on top?"

I laughed. "You wanna ride me, kitten?"

Both of us fell to our backs. Rounds two and three had damn near wiped us both out. "Damn, woman! You been storing that up for five years?" She was insatiable and just as wild as I first predicted.

She giggled. "I guess I had a little pent up sexual energy. You think I'm cured?"

"I don't know. It's a good start, but there's so much more I want to do with you," I admitted.

She curled onto her side. "Like what?"

I ran a finger from her shoulder, down her side, and through the seam of her ass. "Everything." I wasn't kidding her when I had said I wanted every part of her—mouth, tits, pussy, and ass. I'd still been gentle with her so far. We were nowhere near the fucking I wanted to do.

She gazed at my hand. "We'll have to work up to that. Or not. Gah! I don't know. I've never done that before. Have you?"

I nodded my head while rubbing my finger over her tightest hole. "I promise you, it's like nothing you've ever felt before." The thought of being the first one to breech that tight little ass of hers was enough to make me hard again.

She clenched her cheeks and set my hand on her hip. "I'll think on it. Can I ask you something?" Layla pulled the black sheet up to cover herself.

I loved having Layla in my bed. It didn't matter if we were fucking or talking, just being with her felt good. "Anything."

"Tell me about your tattoos. You know all about mine and why I have them. Tell me about yours." She pointed to the rose that sat over my heart.

161

"That's for my mom. Her name was Rose. It was my first tattoo. I got it when I was sixteen."

"I'm sorry. It must have been hard to lose her when you were so young."

I crossed my arms behind my head and stared at the ceiling. "It was. My father wasn't really equipped to raise three children on his own. He hired a nanny to take care of us. I was twelve, my brother was ten and my sister was only six. My dad buried himself in work, he wasn't around that much. Thank God we had Danica. When I was fifteen, I started getting into a lot of bad shit. That's when my father took me under his wing, and I began working for him."

"Did that straighten you out?"

I let out a low laugh. "I guess you could say that. He taught me a lot." My father had taken my skills at thieving and sneaking around and used them to his advantage. He groomed me to become part of his inner circle. I had always known my father's job wasn't conventional, but until that time I hadn't known the extent of it. That's also when I became aware of the parade of women he surrounded himself with. I remembered walking into his office, only to find a woman face first in his lap. My father barely flinched when I walked into some bitch sucking him off under his desk. He pointed to the chair across from him and indicated for me to sit as if she wasn't on her knees between his legs. That was my first lesson on how to treat women.

I shook away the memory, embarrassed I wasn't that different from him until I'd met Layla. She was changing me.

Layla pointed to the eagle insignia on my upper right arm. "Marines?"

I nodded. "Zack actually did that one. We served together in the Middle East."

"Is that where you met him?"

"Yeah, we were both from Brooklyn, so we bonded fast. He saved my ass over there. Pulled me from a Humvee before it exploded. Wish I could say I remembered it, but I was pretty out of it."

"Is that why you came when he called? You felt like you owed him?"

"I do owe him. My life. If it weren't for Zack, I'd be another statistic."

"Then I guess I have another reason to owe him," she said tracing my tattoo. "If it weren't for Zack, I'd never have met you."

"And the first reason?" I questioned.

"My job. Taking me in like a lost puppy when I showed up with one suitcase. Giving me a place to start over and feel safe."

"He saved both of us." Too bad he couldn't save me from myself. The only one who could save me from the noose my father had tightened around my neck was me.

"He did. Now tell me about the ravens?"

What the fuck! "Excuse me?"

"The ravens." She tapped my chest. "You've got two fighting here and a huge one on your back, which I love. Its outstretched wings are beautiful. I figured they must have special meaning, so tell me about it."

The tattoos. That's what she was talking about. I chastised myself for jumping to conclusions. There was no way she could know about The Raven.

Layla must have sensed my hesitance because she crinkled up her freckled nose, which I found adorable. "It's okay if you don't want to talk about it."

"No, it's fine. The raven is smart, bold, strong, and unapologetic for who he is. That's how I want to live my life."

"Aren't ravens supposed to be a harbinger for death?"

Yes. That's why they call me The Raven. "Only if you're superstitious." I pinched her cheek playfully. "Are you superstitious, Layla?"

"Maybe a little. I did just break a mirror, so I'll probably have seven years of bad luck. Then again, I broke the mirror and you showed up at my apartment, so maybe not." She gave a little shrug.

I stroked her cheek. "I would have come for you no matter what. There was no way I was letting our night end that way. Luck had nothing to do with it."

"Can I tell you a secret?" she whispered.

Please tell me something that will help me find your piece of shit ex-husband. "Anything."

"I'm glad you came for me. I didn't want to tell you about my past, but I'm glad I did."

"I'll always come for you. Even when I go back to New York. If you need me, all you have to do is call and I'll be here." This woman had gotten to me. There was no denying it anymore. I was making promises, I wasn't sure I'd be able to keep. But one thing I did know for sure was it would take more than my father to keep me from coming if she needed me.

I woke to Layla's naked back pressed to my equally naked front. Despite our activities last night, my body was making it known that it wanted more. I didn't know if I'd ever have enough of her. I pushed my hard-on into her ass.

Layla stretched, arching her glorious body into mine. I massaged her tits and pulled her closer.

"Ummm. What time is it?" she asked sleepily.

I kissed her gently. "Do you really care?"

"Not when you touch me like that," she moaned.

"That's what I thought." I reached down between her legs and fucked her with one finger. "You're already wet for me. Do you want me?"

"You know I do. Don't make me beg."

"I like it when you beg. Do you want to come, kitten?"

"Please, Draven. Don't tease me." She pushed back into me.

"I think you're teasing me with that ass of yours." I rubbed her slickness over her clit and began circling it. Layla squirmed against me, making me even harder. I pulled her leg over my thigh and continued to rub her. "I want you so bad," I whispered in her ear.

"Then take me. I'm yours."

I nudged her pussy with my cock and slid home. Nothing had ever felt so good... except maybe last night. I pushed into her with long, deep strokes. "Fuck, baby, you feel amazing." I continued fucking her slowly, nothing else mattered at the moment. Just Layla and me connecting as one.

"I'm so close," she wrapped her arms back around my neck and our lips connected. Layla pushed back into me as I pushed into her. We moved in perfect sync.

I felt her pussy begin to quiver around me and my balls began to tighten. "I can't hold back any longer, kitten."

Layla fisted the sheets and let go. Pumping into her harder and faster, I released everything and slumped into her back.

"I don't think I can move," she panted.

"Me neither, but it's early so we can go back to sleep." I slipped out of her and cum dripped down her inner thighs. "Shit, fuck, shit, shit, shit..." I murmured. Layla was going to freak the fuck out. I was freaking the fuck out. The last thing I needed was a kid. Kids didn't exactly fit into my lifestyle.

"What's wrong?" She sat up and more cum dripped out of her. Her fingers traced along the insides of her thighs through the mess I left. "You didn't wear a condom?"

I shook my head and started pacing. "I don't know what I was thinking. Apparently, I wasn't thinking at all. I'm so sorry, Layla." I faced her and threw my arms out. "What do you want to do here? I can run down to the pharmacy and get the morning after pill."

"First, I want you to breathe." She was remarkably calm. "Are you clean?"

Breathe in, breathe out. "Yes. I got checked before I came here, and I've always used a condom. I swear."

"Relax. I have an IUD, and even if I didn't the chances of me getting pregnant would be slim. The doctors said after what I endured it was possible, but there are no guarantees."

I let out a breath of relief, sat on the bed and rubbed her leg. "I'm sorry I was thoughtless. When I'm with you I forget everything else. And I'm sorry about what he did to you. One day you'll have babies. Life isn't that cruel. If anyone deserves happiness, it's you."

Layla's eyes began to tear up and she swallowed down the lump in her throat. "Outside of my family, I've never told anyone that before. I'm sorry." She waved her hand in front of her face. "Shit just got real."

I pulled her into my arms and held her tight. "It's okay if you need to let it out." I had a feeling Layla had been burying her emotions for a long time. Over the past week, every barrier she'd built around herself had come crashing down. The flood gates were wide open. I felt humbled that she'd shared so much with me.

"God, I'm such a needy bitch lately." She pulled away, wiping her eyes. "I promise you, I'm not usually like this. I've cried more in the last five days than the last five years."

"Maybe you needed it. You don't have to be tough all the time, it's okay to be scared or sad." I pushed her hair over her shoulder. "I don't think either one of us is going back to sleep. Do you want bacon and eggs for breakfast?"

Her face lit up. "You bought bacon?"

If bacon made her smile, I'd make it every day for her. "Yep. Why don't you go take a shower and I'll start breakfast."

"You don't mind?"

I took her hands and pulled her up off the bed. "The shower is all yours. There are clean towels in the closet."

Layla picked up her bag from the chair and headed off to the shower. "I'll try to be quick." Her heart-shaped ass swayed as she walked away.

"Take your time. Breakfast will be ready when you get out."

I picked up my boxers from the floor and pulled them on. I hadn't cooked breakfast for anyone besides myself in… well, ever. Probably because before Layla, I'd never woken up with a woman wrapped in my arms. It was a feeling I liked way too much. When this ended, I was going to miss having her warm body curled into mine. She was quickly becoming an addiction.

As I entered the kitchen, my phone chirped with an alert. A text message from my brother.

Nico: Tomorrow night. We'll come to you.

Fucking great! It was the last thing I wanted to do. Them coming here wasn't an option. There was no way Layla could find out about this.

Chapter 23
Layla

"Aren't you two the poster children for birth control?"

"Hardy har." Kyla pulled one of her fussing twins from the double stroller. Whether it was Xander or Ryder, I wasn't sure.

Tori balanced her daughter on her hip. "One day you'll want one of these. I didn't think I would be a good mom, but Chris really wanted to start a family. Now, I can hardly wait to give Savannah a brother or sister."

"I can wait," I assured them. "Besides, I have to find a husband first and I don't see that happening anytime soon." I had found the perfect man, but he wasn't sticking around. I never thought I'd want to get married again, but I could see myself with Draven. Unfortunately, he had no intention of making our *relationship* long-term. So yeah, babies were nowhere in my immediate future. If I could even have children. It was something I wouldn't know for sure until I tried. "What are you doing here, anyway? You know we don't tattoo babies, right?"

Kyla gave me the stink eye. "We're here about you."

"We want the dirt on you and Mr. Tall, Dark and Tatted." Tori leaned in close. "Did you two…?"

Heat crept up my neck and into my cheeks. I tried to feign ignorance but failed miserably. "I don't know what you're talking about."

Tori and Kyla smirked at each other. "She totally did."

"I knew when he drove you home from the bar last week something was going to happen." Kyla rocked her son on her hip. "Which brings me to reason number two for us coming by. Girls' night."

I held up my hands. "I don't think so. Last time didn't go so well."

"This time will be different. My house. No boys allowed. Come on, tomorrow night. It'll be fun. You can stay the night if we get shit-faced." Tori shifted a squirmy Savannah to her other side.

It didn't sound so bad, but Draven and I only had a limited amount of time together and the thought of giving up a single night with him wasn't appealing.

"You should go, *pisoi*." Draven sidled up behind me, rubbed my shoulders and kissed the top of my head. "It'll be good for you."

"Interesting," Kyla hummed.

"Ladies," he greeted the girls. "She's in. Layla needs some girl time."

"Don't I get a say?" I protested.

"Nope. I have some work to do for my father I've been putting off. It'll work out for both of us."

I pulled Draven to the side. "But what if I'd rather spend my night with you?"

Draven pressed his lips to mine, forcing his tongue into my mouth for a soul searing kiss that had me leaning back in his arms. He pushed my hair aside and then whispered in my ear. "I'll take care of you before you leave. Trust me, you'll feel me all night. You'll have no choice but to be thinking of me."

Shivers ran down my spine as I let him support my weight. "Are you sure?"

"That you'll still be feeling me hours later? It's a promise."

And now I was soaking wet. It seemed to be a perpetual problem around this man. The way he talked and his promise to do dirty things to me set my core on fire.

"Hello?" Tori waved her arm around. "We're still here."

I reluctantly backed away from Draven and turned my attention to the girls. "I guess it's a yes."

"Perfect. I'll text you my address."

Draven started back for his studio, but Kyla wasn't having it. "Not so fast Mister. Tyler and Chris want you to meet them for a beer. With football season starting soon, Ty won't have many free nights."

"I guess I could meet them for one. Text Layla the when and where." He gave them a wink. "Take good care of my girl."

Once Draven had disappeared into his studio, Tori about burst. "We have so much to talk about. You've been holding out on us."

Kyla strapped her son back into the double stroller. "Tomorrow night. Don't even think about cancelling or we'll come kidnap your ass."

"Fine, fine, I'll be there. Now, shoo. I have work to do." I hustled the girls out the door and let out a sigh. And this was why I didn't have girlfriends. Number one, they were nosy as fuck. Number two, they railroaded you into things like *girls' night*.

I checked the address one more time before knocking on the door. I had shoved a toothbrush in my bag just in case I did spend the night, but if I had my way, I'd be gone by midnight and headed back to Draven. He said he was doing some work for his father tonight, but I couldn't imagine what work he could possibly have to do. More than likely it was an excuse to convince me to spend time with the girls.

It was time to quit stalling. I raised my fist to the door and rapped out my knock.

The door flew open, and Tori pulled me inside, "We were just getting ready to come looking for you."

"I promised I'd be here and I'm here. Relax." Jeez, these two were pushy.

Tori led me through the foyer and into the family room. The coffee table was set with a bottle of tequila, a bowl of lime wedges, and three shot glasses. They weren't messing around.

I set my bag on the couch and was immediately drawn to the photographs on the walls. Beautiful pictures of sunsets and beaches adorned one wall. "These are gorgeous. Where did you get these?"

"I took them. That's what I do. I'm a photographer."

"Wow! They're really great."

"Thanks. My family has a place up by the Sleeping Bear Dunes on Lake Michigan. That's where these were taken. I'd live there for the summer if we could, but unfortunately both Chris and I have to work for a living, so that makes it impossible."

"Must be nice to have a place to get away though."

"It is. You would love it. Maybe you could come up with us sometime."

I pulled back in surprise. "Really? I wouldn't want to intrude."

"Seriously. Kyla and Tyler come all the time. There are five bedrooms, so it's plenty big."

My heart caught in my chest. The only girlfriend I'd had since moving here was Rissa, and she'd been here less than a year. Now, I was having girls' nights and being invited on vacation. "That's really sweet of you. I might take you up on it."

"You should. It'd be a lot of fun. You can bring that hot man of yours too." She nudged me with her shoulder.

"He's leaving in two weeks, so that won't be happening."

"No chance he's staying?"

169

"I don't think so." I sighed. "He said he has to go back to New York where the family business is."

"Hey, you made it." Kyla came from the kitchen carrying bowls of chips and salsa. She sat them on the coffee table and gave me a hug. "Are you ready to tell us all about your new man? Damn that kiss was smokin' hot."

Nothing like getting right to the point. I wasn't sure how much I wanted to tell and how much I wanted to keep to myself. But no matter what, I was going to need a drink before we started. "Not yet. Do you have anything else to drink? I don't want to start with tequila."

"Oh, darling, follow me." Tori led me to the kitchen and opened one of the cabinets. "Pick your poison."

It was stocked full of premium liquors. I took down the bottle of Jack Daniels, poured some in a glass and mixed it with Coke. Kyla and Tori each made themselves a drink before we headed back to the family room. I plopped down on the floor next to the coffee table, while the girls took up similar positions. "So, where are your kids tonight?"

Kyla held her drink up. "I pawned them off on Tyler's parents. Here's to a good night's sleep."

Tori laughed. "Savannah is with my parents and I have no intention of sleeping tonight. Here's to uninterrupted sex!" She held her glass up in salute.

I scrunched up my nose. "Then I guess I'll be heading home tonight."

Tori gave me a light slap on the shoulder. "You're staying if you need to. We're super quiet. You won't hear a thing."

Kyla spit her drink on the table and wiped her mouth. "Oh! My! God! You're such a liar! I lived with them our senior year of college. They're not quiet at all!"

Tori mopped up the mess with a paper towel and scowled at Kyla. "We can totally be quiet."

"Maybe if Chris ball-gags you." Kyla put her hand to her mouth as if telling me a big secret. "They're into some kinky shit."

It was too much information and not enough at the same time. My curiosity was peaked. "What kind of kinky shit?"

"It's not that bad," Tori defended.

"Let's just say Tori took me shopping before our senior prom. She walked out with hand-cuffs, a blindfold, a riding crop, and a butt plug. She nearly killed me with embarrassment," Kyla provided.

"Like you've never been tied up before." Tori scoffed at her best friend.

Kyla blushed. "That, missy, is none of your business."

I pointed between the two of them. "How long have you been friends?"

"Third grade," they said in unison.

"Wow! I can't imagine what it would be like to have a friend that long." I'd had girlfriends back in Oregon, but once I started dating Michael, I lost contact with most of them. That should have been my first clue it was a bad relationship. Isolation, I had learned, was an abusers first act of abuse. "How long have you been with your husbands?"

"Chris and I started dating the summer before our junior year in high school."

"Senior year of high school for Tyler and me. We spent almost a year apart in college, but we found our way back to each other." I remembered when I first met Kyla. She had been single and had some emotionally intense tattoos done. It wasn't long after that she started drawing for Zack. I didn't know her story, but I'd surmised she had been in a dark place. Now, you'd never know it. She was the epitome of happy.

"Enough about us. Tell us about Draven," Tori prodded.

"There's not much to tell." I tried to be coy, but neither one of them was buying it.

"Please, girl. That kiss I saw today says otherwise." Kyla scooped some salsa on a chip and popped it in her mouth. "Spill the details."

"I think I'm in love with him." The words were out of my mouth before my brain had a chance to veto. I slapped my hand over my mouth as if I could pull them back. *Why did I just say that? Because you love him. That's why.*

Kyla's eyes widened to the size of saucers. "You're in love with him?"

I nodded my head.

"And the sex?" Tori questioned.

I let out a huff. "Phenomenal. He's intense. The things he says to me…"

"Chris has a filthy mouth and I love it. He can get me wet without ever touching me."

Kyla threw a chip at Tori's head. "Ewww! Some things are better left unsaid."

"Not when his head is between my legs."

I giggled because I couldn't disagree. Just as he promised, I could still feel the fucking Draven had given me before I left tonight. He hadn't been gentle, but I hadn't wanted him to be. Being with Draven was nothing like being with Michael, everything was so much better. "He's pierced," I blurted. Again, I covered my mouth with my hand. My drink was going to my head way too fast.

171

Immediately they quit their bickering and spun in my direction. Tori's mouth dropped open. "The fuck did you say?"

"He's pierced." I buried my head in my hands at my confession.

"Like..." Kyla motioned between her legs, "down there?"

I nodded.

"Damn, woman! How's that feel?" Tori didn't hide her curiosity.

I gulped down my Jack and Coke and stood up. "I think I need another drink."

Tori grabbed my arm. "Sit your ass back down. You can't drop a bomb like that and not give details."

"Let's just say I would highly recommend it."

"Like through the head?" Kyla questioned, scrunching up her face.

I shook my head. "Barbell. Beneath the head. And it feels... amazing."

Tori tapped her chin. "I wonder if I could talk Chris into that."

"I'm pretty sure you could talk him into piercing his balls if you wanted." Kyla laughed.

"Ewww! Why would I want that? If he gets pierced, I'm going to get some pleasure out of it. Definitely something to think about." She picked up the bottle of tequila and poured three shots. "Time to get down to business, ladies. Never Have I Ever."

"What does that mean?" I asked.

"We each take a turn saying something we've never done. If either of the other two people have done it, they drink. There's only one rule and it's simple. No lying. I'll go first." Tori eyed Kyla with pure evil. "Never have I ever been a cheerleader."

"Seriously?" Kyla picked up her shot and downed it, grabbing a lime as a chaser.

I picked up my tequila and threw it back. The alcohol burned its way down my throat.

Two sets of eyes stared at me. I shrugged my shoulders. "High school and college."

"No way!" Tori exclaimed.

"Way," I confirmed.

Tori rubbed her hands together. "Oh, this is gonna be good!"

Kyla went next. "Never have I ever... had a threesome."

I could rest easy on that one. Having sex with one person was more than enough for me. Tori picked up her shot glass and tilted it side to side. She took a tiny sip.

Kyla eyed her curiously. "What the hell does that mean?"

"It means I'm not sure."

"Come again?" I asked. "How can you not be sure?"

Tori set her glass on the table. "Back in college, Chris and I went to a party and did ecstasy. Things got a little crazy and when we woke up there was another couple in bed with us, but we don't remember any of it. It's not one of our prouder moments, but at least we were together."

"You've done ecstasy?" Clearly this was the bigger issue for Kyla, although I couldn't see how.

"Yeah. We still do on occasion but we're more careful now. Only when we're alone."

Kyla put her fingers to her head and spread them out dramatically. "Mind blown! How did I not know this?"

"We may be best friends, but Chris and I do have some secrets." She stuck her tongue out at Kyla. "Your turn, Layla."

We were each one shot in, and I tried to think of the most innocuous thing possible or we would all be drunky skunks in the next hour. "Never have I ever killed someone." Kyla and Tori both froze. I looked between the two of them. "What?" I asked cautiously.

Tori leaned over and hugged Kyla. "It's okay."

Kyla released herself from Tori's grip. "I'm all right. I had a stalker back in college," she explained. "He broke into my apartment and attacked me. I shot and killed him in my bedroom."

My hands flew up over my mouth. "I'm so sorry! I didn't know. I swear I was trying to keep us all from getting plastered. You don't have to drink."

Kyla put her hand on my leg. "It's fine. I'm not embarrassed, and I'd do it again. It was him or me." She picked up her refilled glass and threw back the shot.

"I'm sorry," I reiterated. "Not just for saying it, but that you had to endure something so awful. Did he hurt you? No, I shouldn't be asking. It's none of my business."

"I don't have anything to hide. I was dating him and when I broke it off, he," she sighed, "... hurt me. He refused to let me go and stalked me for months. Then Tyler and I got back together, and he fell off the deep end. If he couldn't have me, no one could. The law couldn't help me, so I had to protect myself."

Her story sounded suspiciously familiar, and I hoped she hadn't endured the same type of torture I had. "I'm glad Tyler came back into your life. He's a good guy and you deserve it."

Tori tilted her head to the side. "You know, you deserve a good man too. What's it going to take to get Draven to stay."

"More than me," I said dejectedly. "I haven't been with anyone in a long time and then he had to come along. We haven't spent a night apart in nearly a week. I don't even know how I could be in love with him. It's too quick, right? Nobody falls in love that fast. I mean, I hardly know him."

"Sometimes you just know," Kyla said. "I knew right away Tyler was the only one for me."

"Same," Tori added. "Once Chris and I finally went on a date, I was addicted."

I flopped down on my back and stared at the ceiling. "I'm so screwed. I knew this was short-term going into it, but when he leaves it's going to hurt and there's not a damn thing I can do."

Tori laid down resting her head next to mine. "Do you think he loves you back?"

I shrugged. "I don't know. He feels something, but I don't think it's love."

Kyla joined us on the floor, our heads connected like a pinwheel. "Let's come up with a plan. There has to be something you can do to make him stay."

"I don't think there is. He's intent on returning to New York."

"What about moving to New York with him?" Tori asked.

"I can't."

Kyla rolled over on her elbows. "Why not?"

There were so many reasons. "This is my home. Besides, I don't think he would ever ask me to go with him. He told me he doesn't do relationships. He made it clear that what we're doing is temporary."

Kyla gently put her hand on my arm like a true friend. "I'm sorry. We'll be here for you when he leaves."

"Damn right we will be," Tori added her support.

I managed a small smile. "Thank you." I sat up and wiped at the stray tear that ran down my cheek. "I'm not going to cry over him. We gonna finish this bottle of tequila or not?"

Tori sat up and refilled all the shot glasses. "Kyla it's your turn."

She scooted up next to the table. "Never have I ever smoked pot."

Tori rolled her eyes as we both picked up our glasses and downed the tequila. She stood up. "You know what? We're gonna fix that right now." Tori went to her bedroom and returned with a joint.

Kyla held up her hands. "I can't do that, I'm a mom. Of twins!"

174

"Don't be so hoity-toity. I'm a mom too. It won't kill you and the boys will never know. They're not even one yet, for Christ's sake. You used to smoke cigarettes. Same thing."

"It's not the same thing. Cigarettes are legal. I can't be a law-breaker, my husband's a professional athlete."

Tori threw her arms out. "Who's going to tell on you?"

"Not me," I assured her.

"Let's take this to the patio, I don't want to stink up the house."

I grabbed the tequila and the three of us headed out back to sit around the patio table. Tori stuck the joint between her lips and lit the end. She inhaled deeply, keeping the smoke in her lungs, and passed it to me. I took a hit and passed it to Kyla. The pleasant fog that came from smoking weed filled my head and spread through my body. It'd been a while since I smoked, and I savored the buzz. I started smoking weed after my divorce. It helped me escape the nightmares and the fear that clung to me. Alcohol did the same.

Kyla stared at the joint like it was a snake ready to bite.

"Inhale like you would a cigarette but hold the smoke in for a bit before blowing it out. I promise nothing bad will happen to you. Tori and I wouldn't let that happen."

"I can do this." Kyla nodded. She hesitantly brought it to her lips and inhaled like a pro. She closed her eyes and held the smoke in. When she blew it out, Kyla sagged back into the chair. Tori and I watched her intently. The corners of her mouth curved upward. "I like it."

Tori laughed. "I told you. Now pass it over here." We each took one more hit before Tori stubbed it out on the cement and set the roach on the table. "It's my turn. Never have I... or ever will I be... divorced," she said with a satisfied smirk.

Without thinking I picked up my glass and tipped it toward my lips. The burn of the liquor going down my throat cut through the fog. My mistake hit me over the head like a ten-pound weight. I hesitantly set the glass down. Two sets of eyes were focused on me as if I were the starring act in a freak show. "I'm not going to talk about it, so don't ask. He was a mean son of a bitch. End of story."

"Layla..." Kyla started.

I cut her off and went into bitch mode. "It's not public knowledge, so if you want to keep your little pot smoking a secret, I'd keep it to yourself if I were you." I stood abruptly from the table with intent of leaving. I'd had too much to drink and driving wasn't a good idea. I didn't care. I just wanted to get the fuck out of here. "I'm done with this shit!"

Tori grabbed my arm and forced me back into the chair. "You're not driving home. We've all revealed things tonight were not proud of. If you don't want to talk about it, that's fine. We won't push, but we're your friends. Whatever was said tonight stays here. It goes no further."

I analyzed the two women sitting at the table with me. *Were they my friends?* I wasn't sure I could trust them, but at this point I had no other choice. "Fine. I'm serious though. I don't need my business spread around. And I'm done with this fucking game too."

"Agreed," Kyla said. "I only have one question. This is why you don't date, isn't it? You don't trust people." I nodded my response. "What makes Draven so different?"

Now that was a question I could answer without hesitation. "Everything."

Tori rolled her hand. "Elaborate."

I sighed. "He makes me feel safe. He makes me look at myself differently. Makes me feel things I haven't felt in forever. God, the way he kisses me… it melts me from the inside out."

Kyla smirked. "We got that. Shit, my panties almost melted watching him kiss you."

We all burst out laughing.

"That's nothing compared to what he does when nobody's watching." I fanned myself. "That man sets my whole body on fire."

Tori picked up the bottle. "To earth-shattering sex. May the orgasms be strong and plentiful!"

Kyla and I raised our glasses in agreement.

"How do we keep him here, so Layla can keep getting the good dick?" Kyla asked seriously, then she burst out laughing, snorting every time she took a breath. She held her hand over her mouth. "Oh, my God! Did I just say that?"

"Yes. Yes, you did." Tori turned to me. "She's a hoot when she's drunk. But drunk and high? This is priceless."

I poured us each another round and held up my glass. "To pierced penises and the pleasure they deliver." We tossed back our glasses.

Kyla leaned on the table and attempted to whisper but failed on all accounts. "So, what does a pierced penis look like?" She wiggled her eyebrows up and down mischievously.

I pulled out my phone and Googled it. I found a picture of a frenum piercing and held it up to her. "Like that."

Tori and Kyla huddled around my phone, checking out the image. "That's only the third penis I've ever seen in my life. Unless you count the twins, but baby penises don't count, right?"

Tori gave her a playful slap. "No, they don't count! Don't you and Ty watch porn? I've seen so many dicks, I'm like a cock connoisseur."

Laughter erupted again.

"It looks painful." Kyla scrunched up her nose.

"Not when it's inside you." I giggled.

"Wonder what it feels like during anal?" Tori asked.

"Ewww. Just stop."

I pulled my phone back. "Wait. There's more. That's only one kind of piercing." I pulled up images of the Prince Albert, Ampallang, Apadravya, and Frenum Ladder.

The girls flanked me on both sides. We inspected each one, cracking each other up with our ridiculous analysis of pro and cons for the piercings. Basically, we were just looking at dick pics.

Tori pointed to the Frenum Ladder, which was a line of barbells down the entire shaft. "Now that, I would not want in my ass!"

The slider opened, and their husbands stepped outside. "What wouldn't you want in your ass?"

Tori grabbed my phone and shoved it in Chris's face, almost falling over in the process. "This!" She grabbed ahold of his arm to steady herself.

The guys looked at the picture. "What the hell are you girls looking at?" Tyler grabbed the phone and started scrolling through the images. "Who would do this to themselves?"

"Draven has his penis pierced!" Kyla blurted, covering her mouth again.

I pointed at Tori and Kyla. "They're drunky skunks!" I fought to keep it in, but I couldn't hold back my laughter.

"You're all drunky skunks," Tyler stated with a chuckle.

Chris leaned over the table and picked up the roach. "Annnd... they're high."

The three of us started cackling again.

Tyler tilted his head at Kyla. "You high, baby?"

She held a finger up to her lips. "Shhh... don't tell anybody," she whispered.

He tried to hold in his amusement. "I won't tell anyone. And let's not talk about Draven's penis, okay?" He lifted her into his arms. "I think it's time to take you home. Say good night to the girls."

Kyla waved at us. "Good night, girls. This was fun and educational. Thanks for the dick pics." Then she turned to Tyler and started rambling as he carried her away. "I feel really good. Have you ever gotten high…"?

Chris scowled at Tori. "Great! You corrupted our only pure friend. She's gonna kill you in the morning."

Tori waved him off. "Eh, I've been trying to loosen her up for years. It was about time. Plus, it was funny as fuck. And Layla was already corrupted. We had fun. Isn't that what counts?"

I grabbed the roach from the table. "We really did have fun. So, can we finish this bad boy, or what?"

"Let me get a pipe." Chris went in the house and returned with a glass pipe. He unrolled the paper and put the remnants of the joint in the bowl. We passed it around until it was cashed.

Tori stood and stretched. "I'm ready for bed. Let me get you a blanket and pillow."

The three of us went inside and Tori set me up on the couch. "Thanks for inviting me tonight. I know I turned into a bitch, but I really did have a good time." My apology was weak, but it was all I could manage.

"Don't worry about it. But if you ever change your mind and want to talk, I'm your girl. I'm a good listener."

"I'll keep it in mind. Good night." I pulled the blanket up over me and snuggled into the couch.

"Now, I'm off to enjoy my baby-free night. If you don't want to hear us, you might want to turn on the TV." She handed me the remote. "As a matter of fact, I would highly recommend it."

"Have fun." I clicked the TV on and started watching a rom-com I'd seen a million times. Despite my apprehension, I'd had a good time. Maybe I could have girlfriends. And maybe I could confide in them. Or not. Between the booze and the weed, I was exhausted. It didn't take long for me to drift off into a peaceful sleep.

Chapter 24
Draven

I'd done my duty, I met Tyler and Chris for a drink. One. That was my limit. I couldn't get fucked up and still be a ready for the night. When Nico texted and said he was close, I made an excuse and got the hell out of the bar.

I pulled into the back lot of Forever Inked and parked my Harley. Ten minutes. That's all I had. I lit a smoke and waited for them to arrive. I'd hardly smoked at all since Layla and I started dating, but I couldn't break the habit when my father was involved.

A few minutes later a big, white box truck pulled into the back lot with the words *Prime Cuts* printed on the side with the picture of a juicy steak. Nico and Kane hopped out of the truck and met me around the front of it.

"Please tell me there's more than just the two of you." I blew out a puff of smoke.

"No worries, bro. We dropped the others off at a hotel. Got Cyrus and five more prepped and ready to roll at a moment's notice."

That made me feel a little better. "That's good. I don't trust those gangbangers."

"You and me both." Kane pointed to the truck. "Is it secure out here?"

"We've got cameras watching from every angle, as well as motion sensors," I assured him. I just hoped Layla didn't check them from her phone, but by now she should have been too deep into *girls' night* to give two shits about checking security cameras.

Nico nodded. "Let's go inside so Kane can bring you up to speed."

I unlocked the back door and led them right up to my apartment. We went inside and both guys checked out the space. "This is a pretty sweet hook-up. How much you gotta pay for this?" Nico asked.

"Nothing. It was part of the deal for me coming here. Zack moved out a few months ago and bought a house for his new wife and baby." I pulled out a bottle of vodka and three shot glasses. It was tradition before a job. Just enough to take the edge off.

"That's cool." Kane set his duffle on the floor and looked around.

I pointed down the hall. "Bathroom is to the right."

Kane headed off and I eyed Nico. "What the fuck is Andrei thinking? These fuckers are bad news. We don't know shit about them. I don't like this at all."

He patted me on the shoulder. "Don't worry. Kane's got us all set. He's done his homework. We'll be in and out before you know it."

"I fucking hope you're right. I didn't come halfway across the country for this shit. This isn't New York, where we know all the players."

Nico let out a sigh. "I know. This isn't our first rodeo though. Don't forget who you are. If Andrei didn't think The Raven could handle it, he wouldn't have set it up."

I quirked an eyebrow at him. Yeah, I was the best at what I did, but this was different.

Kane came back and unzipped his duffle. He unrolled a schematic on the kitchen island. "This is the old Packard Plant formerly owned by Packard Motor Company. It's been completely abandoned for years. It was recently bought, but renovations haven't started. Right now, it's basically a shithole in the middle of Detroit. It's been vandalized beyond recognition and the outer buildings are falling apart."

"And we're doing the deal there because…?" I wasn't a genius, but it didn't sound safe.

"Despite the wreckage, the main building is structurally sound. It'll provide for good coverage and vantage points for our reinforcements if shit goes south. It also has easy exit routes." He pointed to the schematic, "We place our guys here, here and here. Nobody comes in or out without us knowing."

I crossed my arms over my chest. "And our customer?"

"Same guy as last time," Kane confirmed. "I did a thorough check on him. Name is Vic. He's the leader of a low-level gang trying to increase his street cred through guns and drugs. One arrest for assault and battery and minor drug possession but was released on parole after a year. He's been brought in for questioning for a few other crimes, but nothing has stuck. Seems witnesses didn't see shit."

I shook my head. "How do you even know all this?"

He cocked his head at me. "You really need to ask? I'm the best at what I do."

"True. Yet you haven't found anything on Layla's ex-husband." I was busting his balls, but it was frustrating that he hadn't been able to tell me anything useful.

"Who's Layla?" Nico questioned.

I shot my brother a glare that shut him up and focused back on Kane. I needed answers and I wanted them yesterday.

"That's not totally accurate. You haven't provided me shit to work from. All you gave me was the name Michael, attempted murder, and Pelican Bay." Kane pulled a thick manila envelope from his duffle and threw it on the counter. "In there are the bios of every guy that matched what you told me. None of them had a wife named Layla. I also ran bios on all the Layla Roberts in California. It was a surprisingly common name. You gotta give me more. Go through the bios and see if anything matches what she's told you."

I picked up the envelope. "You think he's in here?"

"If he's in Pelican Bay, yes. If not, then we've got a problem."

"I'll look through it tomorrow and let you know what I find."

Nico picked up the bottle of vodka and poured three shots. "Let's get prepped and ready to roll."

We held up our glasses and tapped them together. *"Noroc!"* The meaning was two-fold, cheers and good luck. Luck was something we were going to need tonight. The three of us threw back the liquor and slammed the glasses back on the counter.

We suited up in body armor and holsters. Each of us wore no less than four fire-arms strapped to our body. Preparing for one of these drops, reminded me of preparing for a mission in the Middle East. Kane had served with me and I trusted him with my life. There was no one else I would want by my side.

Nico made the call to the rest of the team and we rolled out. Forty-five minutes later we pulled onto East Grand Boulevard. Our Escalade and truck pulled into the north entrance of the plant. Our guests would be arriving within the next hour. That gave us plenty of time to scope out and secure the area.

Kane, Nico, Cyrus, and I would handle the transaction. One of the other guys was stationed out front as our eyes. The other four were placed strategically in the abandoned factory at sniper vantage points. We were covered from every angle.

This deal, this place, these gangbangers we were dealing with were all shady as hell. That was saying a lot coming from me. I'd dealt with some fucked up shit before, but nothing felt right about this. I barked orders at everyone. Even I knew I was being an asshole.

Kane placed a hand on my shoulder. "You better cool your shit before our company gets here. We got this. Take a deep breath and put your game face on."

I took his advice and pulled my shit together. It was too late to go back. This was happening. I popped my neck from side to side, working out the kinks. The Raven was ready.

Cyrus listened to something in his earpiece and gave me a nod. "They're here."

The four of us formed an intimidating wall of muscle, as the blacked out SUV rolled in. Nico and I had our Glocks at the ready, while Kane and Cyrus were each armed with an AK47. If shit went south, our guests wouldn't be leaving alive.

Vic popped out of the passenger side, followed by the same two thugs as last time. He sauntered up to us, like we were buddies. We weren't, but I'd give him a false sense of security if that's what it took for this to go smoothly.

"Well, if it isn't The Raven. Figured I'd see you tonight."

"That's right, Vic. You want our merchandise, you deal with me."

He nodded his head up and down. "So, we're on a first name basis now? That's how this is gonna work?"

"I know who you are. I make it my business to know." I crossed my arms over my chest. "Did you bring the cash?"

His lackey on the right pulled his gun, holding it sideways like a punk, and aimed it at my head. "This is bullshit! We see the coke and the guns first, then you'll see the money." Spit flew from his mouth as he spoke, and I caught a flash of silver.

Every instinct told me to pull my gun and put the piece of shit six feet under, but that wouldn't get this deal done. I cracked my neck. Cyrus and Kane had their AKs on Vic and his other crony. Four red dots decorated the gunman's chest and head.

I kept my cool and spoke only to Vic. "That's the way you wanna do business? That shit ain't gonna fly. You better call your dog off, 'cuz if you don't, he's dead. My guys won't hesitate to pull the trigger. He's already been painted."

Vic turned to his guy and saw the red dots from the laser sights that painted his chest and head. He motioned for his lackey to backdown. "Don't be a fucking idiot. You're gonna get us all killed. Let me handle this, or I'll put a bullet in you myself," he threatened.

The guy begrudgingly lowered his gun and stuck it in the back of his pants. He held his hands up in surrender. "Just making sure we don't get fucked." His silver tooth gleamed in the dim light.

"You let me worry about that." Vic turned back to me. "We cool?"

Despite being a gangbanger, Vic handled himself and his guys with authority. I respected his ability to get things back under control. "For now," I answered. "Another stunt like that, and my guys will fire without the courtesy of a warning."

Vic nodded. "Understood, however I'd like to sample the product."

"I got no issues with that." We'd been expecting this and had pulled a brick from the shipment. I held out my hand and Nico placed it in my palm. I pulled out my switchblade and sliced the brown paper packaging, holding it out for Vic to sample.

He licked his finger and ran it through the white powder, then brought it to his mouth and rubbed it on the inside of his lip and gums. He gave me a toothy smile. "Damn! That's good shit."

"We only deal in the best. I promise you won't be disappointed. Are you ready to do business?"

Vic motioned to one of his guys. "Get the cash."

He returned with a black duffle bag and handed it over to Nico. Nico kneeled on the floor and counted out the cash. "We're good."

"Merchandise is in the truck. Same guns as last time, plus the coke."

The seven of us walked toward the truck. Nico rolled up the door and hopped inside with Cyrus. Kane stood guard with me, never taking his eyes or AK off our customers. The crates were unloaded and inspected, then Vic's guys carted them off to his SUV.

When the transaction was complete, I pulled Vic to the side. "I'll admit I wasn't looking forward to doing business with you tonight, but you earned my respect. Word of advice: cut your trigger-happy friend loose. He's a liability. He could have fucked this up for all of us."

Vic reached forward to shake my hand. I tentatively took it. We weren't friends, but business associates. "I would, but he's my cousin. Needs a little more training is all."

"I'd handle that sooner than later. Trust me. I didn't become The Raven on shit instincts."

"I'll take it under advisement. We'll be in touch."

Vic and his guys rolled out of the abandoned factory and we all let out a breath of relief. Nico got in the driver's seat of the Escalade and I took shotgun. Cyrus and Kane hopped in the back. The other guys headed back to their hotel in the truck.

There was a tense silence in the cab of the SUV. Cyrus broke it first. "How the fuck did you stay so cool with that asshole pointing his gun at your head? You didn't even twitch. I thought shit was gonna go bad."

"Only thing that kept me calm was knowing you guys had my back. Soon as I saw those red dots, I knew if I went down, I wouldn't be going alone." It was the truth and a lie mixed together as one. Inside I had been shitting my pants but letting my guys or our customers know that would have been a fatal mistake. Respect was earned, not given, and I had earned it from both sides tonight. Staying calm and seemingly unshaken was the only way to keep my standing in Andrei's organization.

"Let's just hope this was our last dealings with them." Kane cracked his knuckles. "It could have gone the other way. We were lucky tonight."

"Agreed," Nico piped in. "I need a drink and a good night's sleep before we head back in the morning."

"Soon as you drop me off, you can hit last call at a bar and crash." I was ready to call it a night myself. The anxiety leading up to this deal had wiped me out. The only thing that kept me sane was knowing that I'd be with Layla in a few hours.

Nico tapped his fingers on the steering wheel. "About that... we're staying at your place tonight."

I leaned against the door. "Oh hell, no!"

"It's a done deal, brother. We only got one hotel room and it already has five guys in it. We'll be gone first thing in the morning."

"Fuck! And how am I going to explain the three of you? No one here knows my fucking business and I'd like to keep it that way."

"Your girl coming over tonight?" Kane asked.

"No." I sagged back into my seat. "She's at a friend's house. They're having girls' night."

"You've got a girlfriend?" Cyrus asked curiously. My past with women wasn't exactly a secret.

"Yes. No." I fumbled. "It's temporary."

"He's a fucking liar," Kane interjected. "He's head over ass for her."

I gave him a one-finger salute and the smart-ass gave me one back. If we hadn't been friends forever, I would have been annoyed, but he wasn't wrong.

"What's her name again? Layla?" Nico questioned.

I hadn't told Nico a thing about Layla. It wasn't his business, but now Kane had blurted it out. "Yeah. She works with me."

"What's she like?" Cyrus asked.

I sighed. "She's beautiful and tough as nails. She's got a sassy mouth and enough attitude to put all you assholes in your place. She's different than anyone I've ever been with before." Layla was also brave and damaged and sometimes a complete mess. But the way she responded to me when she finally let go drove me insane.

"Oh my, God." Kane shifted in his seat to look me in the eye. "You're in love with her. I knew she had you tangled up, but you've gone and fallen in love with her."

"I'm not in love with her. I like her a lot and we get along great, but I don't love her." It was a lie. A lie I'd been telling myself for days but was having a hard time believing.

"So, you'd be cool with her fucking someone else?" My best friend knew exactly which buttons to push.

My teeth ground together, and my jaw tightened. I clenched my fists. "She's not fucking anyone else, and neither am I. We're exclusive."

He leaned back with a satisfied smirk. "You just told me all I need to know."

"Fine. Maybe it's more than like, but I can't keep her so what's the difference? We all know Andrei won't let me stay. I'll let her go when the time comes and that will be the end of it."

"You think it's gonna be that easy?" Cyrus asked. "I've been with Sara for a while now. Once she gets you here," he pounded on his chest, "it's not that easy to let go. I wish I could because she deserves better than me, but I can't. There's nothing I wouldn't do for her, and that includes taking a bullet. I'd lay my life on the line for her, no questions asked. Would you do the same for Layla?"

I didn't even have to think about it. "I'd protect her at all costs."

"Then you're fucked," He let out a self-depreciating laugh. "The bigger we are, the harder we fall. Sara's changed me in ways I never thought were possible, but I'm a better person with her."

I thought about that. Layla was changing me too. I was undeniably a better person with her, and I was in love with her. Giving her up was going to be one of the hardest things I'd ever done. "All of that may be true, but it doesn't change the reality of the situation."

"Maybe if you talked to Andrei…" Nico started.

I interrupted, "We both know it won't go well. He wants me to take over one day, even if it's not what I want. If you think otherwise, you're delusional."

That shut everyone up. We all had firsthand knowledge of the wrath Andrei could bring down on someone he was displeased with and it wasn't pleasant. The truth was simple. In two weeks, I would return to New York and Layla would be nothing more than a memory.

Chapter 25
Layla

I woke up early, despite our night of drinking. Chris and Tori were still sound asleep, I was sure their night had lasted long past mine. I crept to the bathroom with my purse to freshen up before heading home.

With one eye cracked open, I took inventory of myself. My make-up didn't look half bad, but my hair needed a good brushing. I pulled the band from my ponytail and sleeked it back up, using the hairspray on the counter. Then I brushed my teeth and touched up my eye-liner. Good enough. I'd grab a clean shirt from our stash of merchandise in the stockroom.

I scribbled Tori a quick note, thanking her for last night and promising to catch up with her later. I left it on the kitchen counter and silently snuck out the front door. I stopped and picked up a few breakfast sandwiches from a drive-thru and headed off to see Draven.

It was pathetic that I missed him. I should have just taken the sandwiches home and shared them with Brian. And I almost did, but at the last minute I decided *fuck it* and headed to the tattoo parlor. I only had two weeks left with Draven and I was going to make the most of every minute we had left together.

I parked around back next to a black Escalade. Immediately my hackles rose. There was no reason it should have been parked in our lot, unless Draven lied to me and he had company. If he was with another woman, I was going to lose my shit.

I unlocked the back door and stomped up his stairs. I pounded my fist on the door. I didn't care that it was seven-thirty in the morning. All rational thought left my head the moment I saw the SUV that had no business being there.

I waited impatiently, then pounded on the door again. The lock turned, and the door opened a fraction of an inch. I slammed my hand on it and pushed, smacking the person behind the door in the head. "Damn, woman!"

The voice certainly didn't belong to a girl and it didn't belong to Draven either. My eyes turned to saucers, because an incredibly sexy, tattooed man dressed in only his boxer briefs stood on the other side of the door rubbing his head. "Who the hell are you? And where is Draven?" I demanded. If he was cheating on me, this was not what I expected. Leave it to me to fall for a guy who was bi. What the hell was wrong with my radar? First Brian, now this.

"I'm Kane. Who are you?"

I poked him in the chest. "Don't you worry about who I am. Where the fuck is Draven?" I pushed past him and stormed into the apartment, only to find another half dressed man getting up from the couch, looking just as sexy as the first guy. I threw my arms into the air. "What the hell is going on here? Someone please explain to me before I lose my shit. Is this some kind of gay orgy?"

Kane laughed at me. "No, darling. We're perfectly straight. Draven's still sleeping, or at least he was." He held out his hand to me. "You must be Layla."

I didn't take his hand. Instead, I planted the hand not holding our breakfast on my hip and squinted my eyes at him. "And how do you know that?"

"Because he described you as sassy with a shit ton of attitude. I'd say he was spot on." I wasn't sure if that was meant as a compliment or an insult.

Draven's bedroom door creaked open, and he stumbled out rubbing his eyes. "*Pisoi*, what are you doing here?" He came over and planted a kiss on my cheek.

I pulled away. "The better question is what are they doing here?"

"She thinks we're having a gay orgy." Kane laughed again.

Another guy waltzed out of Draven's room. "Oh my God! How many of you are there?" Now everyone was laughing but me. I was confused as hell.

Draven picked me up and hugged me tight, smashing his lips against mine. "You're so fucking adorable." He set me on my feet. "Everyone, meet Layla." He pointed to the guy coming out of his room. "That's my brother, Nico." Nico gave me a little wave.

Then Draven motioned to the other guys. "Those are my friends Kane and Cyrus. They were driving home from Chicago and paid me a surprise visit last night."

"Oh." I could feel my embarrassment creeping up my cheeks. "So, it's not some kinky guy thing going on?"

"I haven't proved to you I'm not gay? I would think you would have gotten that message loud and clear by now." Draven could barely keep the amusement from his face as he questioned me.

I threw my hands in the air, nearly smacking him in the head with our breakfast. "I don't know. I was wrong about Brian. You could have been bi."

"Not even close, kitten. Do you need me to take you in the bedroom and prove it to you?"

I buried my head in my hand. "No. I'm sorry. It was just a surprise, that's all." I set the sandwiches on the counter. "I brought us breakfast, but it won't be nearly enough." I checked in the fridge and found two dozen eggs. "I can make you all something to eat, but you have to put pants on first. And shirts." I waved my hand around. "There's way too much sexiness in this room. A girl can only take so much."

Cyrus grabbed his pants from the floor. "I'm not gonna say no to food. I'm fucking starving."

Words of agreement were barked throughout the room, as the guys started getting dressed. Draven sidled up behind me and wrapped his arms around my waist. He set his head on my shoulder. "You don't have to cook for us. I can kick them out."

"Don't be silly. It's your brother and your friends. You haven't seen them in a while. Honestly, I think it's kind of cool that they came here."

His hand slid up my stomach and sensuously squeezed my breast. "I missed you last night," he whispered.

My insides turned to goo. His hands felt so good on me. "I missed you too. That's why I came over, but we can catch up later." I gently removed his hand from my boob. "Go get dressed, you're far too tempting."

"Yes, ma'am," he teased and sauntered off to change.

I cracked some eggs in a bowl and began to whip them up. I pulled two frying pans out and started making the guys' omelets, adding shredded cheese and onions. It was the best I could do with the limited contents of Draven's refrigerator. Then I set to making toast. I placed the butter and jelly on the kitchen island for them to spread on the bread.

Kane and Cyrus sat down at the counter first. I plated their omelets, placing a piece of toast on each. "So, how do you know Draven?" I asked while whipping up the next two omelets.

"I met Nico in high school. We played football together," Cyrus shoveled his omelet into his mouth. "Do you have any coffee?"

"Sure. I'll make a pot." I filled the carafe with water and scooped some coffee into the machine. If I wasn't so distracted by all the testosterone in the room, I probably would have made coffee first. The pot began to percolate, and I turned back to the guys sitting at the counter.

"Thanks, sweetness." He gave me a big goofy grin that was endearing on a man his size. I don't know what they put in the water in New York, but these men were all giants. And built. And sexy. *Maybe moving there with Draven wouldn't be such a horrible idea.* I mentally slapped myself for such a ridiculous thought. This was my home. He hadn't exactly offered that up as an option. We were living in the here and now.

"I've known him since we were kids." Kane waved his toast around while he talked. "We were in the Marines together too."

I snapped out of my haze. "Oh, do you know Zack?"

"We were in the same unit, so yeah. He's a cool guy. How long have you known him?"

I tapped my fingers on the counter. "Almost five years. He's been a really good friend to me. Gave me a job and a home."

He quirked his eyebrow up. "Where are you from?"

Crap! Grabbing two mugs, I busied myself by pouring coffee into them. I slid them across the counter, "I moved here from Chicago. That's where I learned to tattoo." It wasn't a lie, just not the whole truth.

"Hmmm. I could have sworn Draven said you were from California."

"West Coast originally. Then I moved to Chicago and now I'm here," I said with a tight smile.

"What made you leave Chicago?"

I was sure it was just small talk, but I didn't like the direction of this conversation. I shrugged my shoulders. "Needed a change is all." I returned to my mission of making omelets and flipped the eggs in the pans.

"Maybe you could tattoo my girl's name on me while we're here," Cyrus suggested.

I breathed a sigh of relief. Tattooing was something I could talk about. "I would strongly advise against it. You have no idea how many cover-ups I've had to do after a relationship goes bad."

Draven and his brother emerged from his room. "She's right. Names are a bad idea."

I cringed a tiny bit. He spoke the truth, but part of me wanted to be etched on his body. Maybe not my name, but something to remind him of our time together.

I hated to think that when he returned to New York, all I would be is a distant memory. *Was I that easy to fuck and forget?*

Temporary, I reminded myself. That's what we were. He was someone to occupy my time and my mind. Anything beyond that was just a dream. A dream that got my panties wet and my heart pumping... but a dream, nonetheless.

I finished making the last two omelets and plated them for Draven and his brother. Nico dug into his with earnest. "She cook for you like this all the time?"

"We take turns," I interjected.

Three sets of eyes focused on Draven. "He's cooked for you?" Nico asked incredulously.

"Yes." I scanned the men in front of me. "What am I missing here?"

Kane dropped his fork on his plate. "Draven's never cooked for anyone."

"Fuck off. I know how to cook," he defended.

"No one said you didn't, but you didn't even cook for me when we were kids." Nico quirked his eye at his brother. His meaning was clear. Draven cooking for me was a big deal.

The tension in the room grew with silence. "Listen, I'm gonna get out of here." I grabbed my bag of breakfast sandwiches and headed out.

"But you haven't eaten yet," Cyrus protested.

I held up the bag. "I'm set. I need a shower before work. It was nice meeting all of you. Have a safe drive back."

A chorus of goodbyes rang out. "Hope to see you again," Kane called.

I pasted on a fake smile. "Maybe." I gave them a little wave and dashed for the door. I would never see any of them again. This was the first and last time I would ever meet Draven's brother or his friends. Of that, I was sure.

My hand was on the door when Draven's covered it. He leaned down and whispered in my ear, "You don't have to go."

This morning hadn't turned out at all the way I had expected. "I do."

He kissed from my ear down to my neck. "You're running."

I pulled back and touched my finger to his lips. "I'm not. I'll see you in a few hours. Take your time." I gave him a quick peck on the lips and left.

I drove home chastising myself the entire way. Instead of going to my apartment, I knocked on Brian's door.

My best friend opened it and welcomed me inside, "To what do I owe the pleasure of this early morning visit?" His hair was ruffled, as if he'd just rolled out of bed.

I held up the bag. "I brought you breakfast."

He took it from my hand. "No coffee?" He opened the bag and pulled out a sausage and egg sandwich. "These are cold."

"Yeah, I know." I plopped on his couch. "Stick them in the microwave, they'll be good as new."

He carried them to the kitchen and popped them in the microwave. "These weren't really for me, were they?"

"No, but I didn't want them to go to waste and I haven't seen you in a few days." I shrugged.

A minute later, the timer dinged. Brian pulled them out, tossing the sandwiches from hand to hand like hot potatoes. "Maybe a few seconds too long." He threw them on a plate and came to sit next to me. "So, how's it going with the new man?"

I sighed. "Well. Too well for my own good."

"What does that mean?"

I leaned forward and grabbed one of the sandwiches, despite the steam coming from them. "He's sweet and considerate and plays my body like a fine-tuned instrument. He makes me feel desired and sexy."

He smiled. "So, the sex is good?"

"Phenomenal. He's so intense in bed. I've let down all my guards with him. He's pushed me to places I never knew existed."

Brian wiped his mouth with a napkin. "I'm not sure I'm seeing the problem here."

I could have hidden the truth from him, but that wasn't the type of relationship we had. "I think I'm in love with him." I shook my head. "No, that's not right. I know I'm in love with him."

He pouted and gave me puppy dog eyes, clearly sympathizing with my situation.

I shrugged my shoulders sadly. "How do I undo it?"

Brian wrapped his arm around my shoulder and kissed the top of my head. "I don't know that you can."

"I knew that's what you would say. So, what happens when he leaves?"

Brian finished off his sandwich with a final bite. "That's easy. We eat ice cream, watch sappy movies, and you cry on my shoulder."

"Sounds like a blast." I rolled my eyes at him. "I can hardly wait."

"It'll suck, but don't waste the time you have left worrying about it. Enjoy every minute while it lasts. Live in the moment, sometimes that's all we have."

He was totally right. I had to embrace what I had now, not worry about the future. Here and now. Draven and I had no future. I kissed him on the cheek. "Thank you, for convincing me to take a chance. I would have really missed out on something good."

"You're welcome." Then he crinkled up his nose. "Were you smoking pot?"

"That's a story for another time. I had a night out with the girls and I actually had fun."

His eyebrows shot up to his forehead.

"I know… shocking, isn't it?"

He gave me a hug and walked me to the door. "I'm proud of you, baby girl."

I held up a finger. "Oh, one more thing. Draven's penis is pierced." I wiggled my eyebrows at him.

Brian groaned. "Okay, now you're just bragging. I get it. He's all that and a bag of chips."

"A really BIG bag of chips." I emphasized moving my hands far apart.

"Get the hell out of here." He laughed, pushing me out the door. "Thanks for the second-hand breakfast."

"Anytime. That's what friends are for."

Brian had a way of always making me feel balanced. I couldn't have asked for a better friend.

Chapter 26
Draven

Layla showing up this morning hadn't been planned, but I should have expected her. It seemed we couldn't stay away from each other. Since we'd started this thing, we'd spent every night together. Sleeping next to Nico last night was a poor replacement for Layla's warm, soft body. I was used to the feeling of her snuggled into my chest and her quiet, little sighs as she slept. She was pure perfection.

Once she'd gotten over the ridiculous notion that I was having a gay orgy in my apartment, she'd calmed down and accepted my story about Nico, Kane and Cyrus visiting on the way home from Chicago. It wasn't that believable, but she had no reason to think I'd lie to her. My chest tightened knowing she trusted me. All I'd done since I'd met her was lie. Layla had created her own image of me based on a fantasy I could never fulfill.

"You're so screwed." Cyrus's voice broke me out of my train of thought.

"What do you mean?" I asked, pretending I had no idea what he was talking about.

"She's pretty great, even if she thought we were all gay." He laughed. "It's going to be nearly impossible to leave her."

"I'll do what I have to," I grumped. "I know what my responsibilities are."

"He's going to be a miserable bastard when he comes home," Kane added. "We'll have to take him out to get laid."

I started shoving the plates in the dishwasher with more force than necessary. "I don't need your help to get laid. I do just fine on my own."

"Yeah," Nico agreed. "But will you?"

I slammed the dishwasher shut. "Why do you guys care about it? Layla's just the chick I'm fucking. Something to occupy my time while I'm here. We're not in a relationship. When this ends I'll go my way and she'll go hers." The lies rolled off my tongue in quick succession.

Kane patted me on the shoulder. "Keep telling yourself that."

I leaned on the counter and let out an exasperated breath. "It's gonna suck. I already know that."

"If I could take your place with Andrei, I would. But he doesn't see me that way. I'll always be in your shadow," Nico admitted.

"That's not a bad thing." I never wanted Nico to think he wasn't enough for our father. "It means that you're not as hard and calloused as me. You still have a chance at a normal life. I'll never be good enough for Layla. She deserves better."

"I thought the same thing when I started dating Sara," Cyrus admitted. "The guy I saw when Layla was here wasn't so hard and calloused. Maybe you should let her decide what she deserves."

"She deserves the truth. My truth is everything she doesn't need. She's been through enough."

"And what happens when her piece of shit ex-husband gets out of prison? You don't think she'll deserve you then? You don't think she'll need you?" Kane asked.

"He'll be dealt with before she ever knows he's out," I growled. "And that's a promise."

"Make sure you go through those bios so we can find out who the fuck he is. I got your back on that."

"Thanks, man. I'll let you know."

I flipped through the pictures and information on every Layla Roberts in the file Kane had given me. None of them were her. Layla Lorraine Roberts didn't exist. How was that even possible? She was a fucking ghost. I saw her social security card and her driver's license, there had to be some record of her. I needed to get ahold of those again and snap a picture to send Kane. She couldn't be completely off the grid. It was almost impossible for someone to hide in this day and age. Everyone left a footprint, but it was like hers had been imprinted in sand and washed away by the ocean.

Next, I looked over the bios of the inmates of Pelican Bay. Some I could eliminate immediately. I narrowed it down to five scumbags. Layla had a picture of him. I had been more focused on her than him when I looked at it. That picture was the key to finding him. *How was I going to get a glimpse of that picture again?* I had to get back in her apartment to do a thorough search. Tonight, we were going back to her place. There weren't any other options.

Frustrated, I went downstairs and peeked into her studio. She was sketching a new design. I stood in the doorway and waited for her to notice me. Suddenly, her head popped up. "Hey. Did your friends leave?"

"Yeah. Shortly after you did. You didn't have to go this morning."

A smile lit up her face. "It was fine. I went home and saw Brian. It's all good."

"How was girls' night?"

She set down her pencil. "Fun, actually. Tori and I got Kyla high, and she was hysterical. I didn't think I would enjoy girls' night, but I did."

"I'm assuming you're talking about pot."

"Yeah. Is that a problem?" She crinkled up her eyebrows.

I shook my head, "Not at all." Just because I dealt cocaine didn't mean I was cool with my girl doing it. Any hardcore drugs were a deal breaker for me. Not that it really mattered. Layla would never really be *my girl*.

"How was guys' night?"

I crossed my arms over my chest defensively. "Uneventful. Mostly drinking and bullshitting," I lied. Looking through all those bios this morning had me on edge. If any of the five I had narrowed it down to were her ex-husband, I had to know. Something inside me told me I was right. One of those slime-balls was the man who had hurt Layla. Prison wasn't enough punishment for the sick fuck. Once I found him, he'd suffer a fate much worse.

Layla stood up and sauntered over to me. She flung her arms around my neck. "Why the serious, grumpy face?" She scrunched up her nose and mouth to imitate me.

"I do not look like that." I wrapped my arms around her waist and pulled her tight against my body. She molded perfectly to me. This is where she belonged. Safe in my arms where no one would ever hurt her again.

"You kind of do," she teased me playfully.

"Maybe I didn't like sleeping alone last night."

"You weren't alone." She smirked. "You had your brother to keep you warm."

"Pfft!" I sputtered. "He snores, and he hogs the covers. Tonight, I plan on being in your bed with your soft tits pushed up against me."

"Well, aren't you presumptuous? What if I want to sleep alone?"

"You don't. I have plans for us tonight."

"You do?" Her eyes widened. "What might those plans be?"

"It's a secret," I whispered. "Do you trust me?"

"Should I?"

"Always." I internally cringed. She could trust me with her body, undoubtably. She could trust me with her secrets, without worry. But there was no way in hell I would be honest with her about who I was. I wouldn't be able to stomach the look on her face if she found out what I really did for a living. I wanted her fantasy of me to continue as long as possible. I couldn't taint it with the truth. Tonight, I would take her out on my bike and let the fantasy live on.

"I trust you. You're part of a small circle of trust. I know you would never hurt me. You know my past and haven't been anything but amazing."

I gulped down my guilt. I ran my hands up her back and into her hair. "Me and you tonight, *pisoi*. No interruptions. I want more from you tonight. Everything about you turns me on."

"Good to know because I feel the same way. I can't seem to get enough of you, so I'll take whatever you give while you're here."

Now, I felt like shit. We were both playing a game of back and forth, knowing it would end in disaster. Layla wasn't naïve about where this was going. It should have made me feel better, but it didn't. At the end of this game, neither one of us would win. I would use her and take her. I was selfish. It proved when all was said and done, she would be better off without me.

I tapped the freckles on her nose. "Tonight, will be amazing. I can promise you that." There was truth in my words. If nothing else, I would make our time together something she would never forget.

The back door opened, and Chase breezed in. He rolled his eyes at us. "You two crack me up. A week ago, you couldn't stand each other, now you can barely stay apart. Must be something in the water. First Zack fell," he shook his head, "and now Layla. Everyone's pairing up around here."

That wasn't true. Layla couldn't be falling for me. She knew better.

Layla untangled herself from me. "Speaking of… what happened with the redhead from the other night?"

Chase let out a self-depreciating laugh. "It got cut short. I took her home and right when we were in the middle of it, she got a call to pick up her six-year-old daughter from a slumber party. I don't need that type of drama. An ex-husband and a kid? No thank you."

Layla put her hands on her hips. "So, because she's divorced, you're writing her off?"

"It's not the ex-husband I'm worried about. I'm more than enough man for any woman," Chase said confidently. "I wouldn't know what to do with a kid, especially a girl. What the hell do I know about being a role model? I'm barely adulting as it is."

I couldn't help but laugh at Chase. "You should give it a chance. You never know what you might be passing up. Maybe the kid's cool."

"Doubtful. Six-year-olds like princesses, fairies and other girlie crap. And to be honest with you, fairies creep me the fuck out. Ever since I watched *Peter Pan* as a kid, the thought of Tinkerbell makes my skin crawl." He shivered dramatically. "She was a crazy bitch."

"Never saw it," I admitted.

"Consider yourself lucky." Chase shivered again. "Fairies are like gremlins on crack only twice as fucked up."

"Then it's a good thing I missed it. My childhood was fucked up enough."

"Men," Layla huffed. "It's about believing in magic. It gives little girls hope that when life is messed up, they can still have a happy ending."

"You believe that shit?" Chase questioned. He didn't know what had happened to Layla, but he knew she'd been hurt.

I waited for her answer. I had accused her of wanting a fairy tale and she assured me she didn't. What she didn't know was that I wanted to be her fairy tale, but I was no prince.

"Not anymore. It's all smoke and mirrors. Lies. Honestly, I think Disney should be sued for every penny. They're nothing but snake oil salesmen." She turned on her heel and walked away. The air around us shifted and got heavy.

Guilt consumed me. She might as well have been wearing a sign that said *Fuck you. I don't need you.* I followed her retreating silhouette into Zack's office. *"Pisoi? We're still on for tonight, right?"* The door shut quietly behind me.

Layla gave me a tight smile as she picked up an invoice off the desk. Pretending it was important, she scanned the pink paper and glanced back up at me. "Of course. Nothing's changed. Two weeks left to fuck and then you're gone."

I pulled the paper from her grip and cradled her face in my hands. "Don't be like that. You knew what this was when we started. It's all I can give you."

She refused to meet my eyes. "All you *want* to give or all you *can* give?"

"What I *want* doesn't matter. Let's not waste the time we have arguing."

The tension released from her body and Layla leaned against me. "You're right. I'm projecting my past on you and it's not fair of me. You didn't deserve it."

I lifted her chin, so she had no choice but to look at me. "You good? Or do I have to take you upstairs and fuck that sass out of you?"

Her lips turned up and her eyes creased mischievously. "I don't know. I'm still feeling a teensy bit sassy."

Wrapping my hands under her ass, I lifted Layla onto the desk. The tension was gone and all that was left was the smoldering embers of desire. Pushing my body over hers, I forced her back on the desk. "Just a teensy bit?"

Papers fluttered, and pens rolled to the floor. I pressed my cock between her spread legs. Layla braced herself with one arm and wrapped the other around my neck. "Maybe a lot a bit," she gasped.

I unbuttoned Layla's jeans and ripped the zipper down. My hand slid inside her panties. She was soaked. "I'd say *a lot* is an understatement."

Layla started breathing heavily. "You might be right."

"I'm definitely right." My thumb began to rub over her clit and Layla moaned softly. "You want me to make you come? Will that help?"

Layla's hips thrust forward into my hand. "No guarantees, but you could give it a try." She dropped her head back, "Oh, god! Yes!" Her teeth sank down into her bottom lip as she sucked in another gasp. She was trying so hard to be silent and it was damn adorable.

I quieted her moans with my mouth. Our tongues twisted in desperation while my fingers worked their magic on her clit. Her body tensed below me, telling me she was close. I pressed harder with my thumb, enough to push her over the edge.

Suddenly her teeth bit my lip. Hard. I hissed at the pain, but it was worth it as her body convulsed and went slack. Her head dropped to the desk, eyes closed and chest heaving. Layla cracked one eye open. "Shit," she whispered, pointing at my face.

I wiped my hand across my mouth. A streak of red covered the back of it. I shrugged. Blood had never bothered me. A split lip was nothing compared to a bullet or a knife, both of which I'd had the pleasure of being on the receiving end of.

"I'm sorry… I didn't mean to…," she started.

I held a finger to her lips. "Hush. Well worth it."

Bang! Bang! Bang! A fist pounded on the door. "You two about done? You've both got clients waiting." Chase sounded irritated, but I knew better. He was so easy going it took a lot to piss him off.

"Were coming!" I yelled back.

"I figured that much. Wrap it up. On second thought, if you're fucking, unwrap it and get out here."

Layla bolted off the desk and jerked open the door. "We weren't fucking," she hissed.

Chase looked down at her waist and quirked an eyebrow. "Your pants say otherwise."

"Oh, crap!" Layla turned her back to him and fastened her pants.

I kissed her cheek gently. "Tonight, *pisoi*." I gave them both a wink and headed out front to find my client.

Chapter 27
Layla

I turned to leave the office, but Chase grabbed my arm and pulled me back inside. "You all right? You got kinda weird earlier."

I sighed. "Yeah, I'm fine."

"You like him a lot, don't you? I've never seen you in love before. It's a good look on you." Chase wasn't being sarcastic or snippy. This was genuine. We had always wanted the best for each other. He had become like a brother to me.

I didn't want to be bitchy with Chase, but it came out anyway. I refused to admit my feelings to him. "Well, don't get used to it. He's leaving." It was the truth I kept repeating to myself, but it didn't make my heart beat any slower. Every time I looked at Draven, that damn organ nearly beat out of my chest.

Chase gave me a look of sympathy I didn't want or need.

"Don't worry about me. I'm a big girl. I can handle it." The lies kept rolling. If I said it enough, maybe it would be true.

I turned to leave, but Chase stopped me. "Hey. If it makes you feel any better, he's in love with you too."

I froze. He couldn't possibly be right. I pushed down my hope before it could float to the surface, "Draven's not in love with me. I'm just something to occupy his time. The truth sucks but it least it's real." I took a deep breath. "And word of advice… give the redhead a chance. Don't judge her on the past. We've all made mistakes, and if I had to guess, her daughter wasn't one of them."

Chase stuck his hands in his pockets. "I don't know if I can handle it. Kids scare the crap out of me."

"Do me a favor. Give yourself a chance. One of us should find a happy ending." I knew it wouldn't be me. And for as crazy as Chase made me, he was a good guy. Any girl would be lucky to have him. Underneath all the bravado he exuded, was a gentle and kind soul.

I headed up front to see my new client. I needed the monotony of tattooing to occupy my mind and make me forget that I was in love with the man in the studio across from mine.

I held on tight to Draven as we flew down Jefferson along the coast of Lake St. Clair. I had never ridden on the back of a motorcycle until I met Draven and I was quickly becoming addicted to the adrenaline rush. Or maybe, it was the man I was holding I was addicted to. My arms tightened around his waist. I couldn't get close enough.

The sun sank low on the horizon, the sky a vibrant mix of pinks and oranges that reflected off the water. Draven made a quick right into a park, driving close to the shoreline. He parked his Harley and I reluctantly released my grip on him. "How did you find this place?"

Draven unfastened the buckle on his helmet, and I did the same. "Tyler. He told me he brings Kyla here when they need to get away from everything else."

I pulled my helmet off and nodded. It made sense. There was no way a boy from New York would have found this place on his own. Draven was trying. Trying to make our time together special. He was creating memories for both of us.

Draven lifted himself off the bike and held out his hand to me. I cautiously took it. He wrapped his arm over my shoulder and walked me to the water's edge. Several large boulders jutted out over the shore. We climbed up one of them and I sat on the ledge, dangling my feet over the water. Draven positioned himself behind me, wrapping me in his warmth. The shore was nowhere to be seen. It was as if we were sitting right in the middle of the lake, floating over the top of it. Draven's arms encircled me. "I love this. Me and you. No interruptions. Just us."

I settled back into his chest. "Me too. Have I told you I hate people? Not you, just people in general."

He let out a low laugh. "I kinda already figured that out. You're not the warm, fuzzy kind of girl, but you're perfect for me."

I choked down my cynicism. How much of this was true, and how much was because he liked having sex with me? I decided I didn't care. I was living in the here and now. Right now, I had a sexy man with his arms wrapped around me. And if I had to read between the lines, I might have thought what Chase said was true.

Draven was falling for me. I didn't want to go there because the alternative sucked. I wanted to believe that he really cared about me. "Why did you bring me here?"

"Because I wanted to make our time together memorable. Bring you someplace special. I hate thinking about when this will end. I've never been with anyone like you before."

"So, you haven't dated a bitch before?" I tried to make light of the situation.

Draven kissed up the side of my neck to my lips. His kisses made my insides flutter with desire. "You're not a bitch. That's just what you want people to think so you can keep them away. I see you, kitten. Everything you try to hide, I see." Draven turned me to face him and braced my back with his strong arms. I was practically leaning over the edge of the rock, but I knew he wouldn't let go. With him, I felt safe. "I've never really dated at all. You're my longest lasting relationship. I fuck, I don't date. You're my exception."

Well, shit! What was I supposed to do with that? "So, we're in a relationship?"

"You're not fucking anyone else, and neither am I. I'd call that a relationship. If I could stay, I would. Picturing you with anyone else kills me."

I let out a low laugh. "You don't have to worry about that. When you leave, I'll go back to being celibate. Brian will be the closest thing I get to being with a man." It was sad, but it was true. The chances of me trusting again were slim.

"That's not what I want for you."

"Then, what do you want?"

"I want you to find happiness. A man who will treat you right. A man who will give you babies and a future. Someone who will take care of you and never leave you alone."

That could be you, I wanted to say. Instead, I deflected. "I'm happy now. That's all that matters."

Draven held me tighter. I could hear the words he wasn't speaking. He was happy too. I held onto that and foolishly let my heart overflow. I was setting myself up for heartbreak, but I couldn't let myself care. Here and now. That's what I focused on. Right now, I was happy. That was all that mattered. I sank deeper into his chest. I let his warmth envelope me. I let him love me in his own way. Because, whether he admitted it or not, he felt something.

And something was better than nothing.

Something was a feeling I could hold on to.

Something was my heart fluttering.

Something was the tingle between my legs.

Something was better than being alone.

Nothing was not an option.

Draven took me home and made love to me. It wasn't fucking. It was love. I would swear on it with my life.

It wasn't fast and furious. It was slow and sensual. He caressed every one of my scars with his lips. He held my hands. He stared into my eyes. He held me close and refused to let me go.

I was in deep.

Too deep.

I laid with my head on his chest, his arms wrapped tightly around my naked body. "Can I tell you a secret," I whispered. Maybe if he knew my truths, maybe if I bared everything, it would show him how much I cared.

Draven ran his hand through my long dark hair, letting it fall through his fingers. "Anything, *pisoi*."

I swallowed down the *I love you* that was on the tip of my tongue. I wouldn't tell him I loved him, because it would hurt too much when he didn't say it back. But this, I could say. "You're the best thing that ever happened to me."

He kissed the top of my head. "Same for me."

It was enough.

For now.

"What the fuck do you think you're wearing?"

I looked down at my outfit. I wore a black pencil skirt and a cream-colored blouse. Yes, the skirt was a little shorter than I usually wore to work, but it was professional. "I have a meeting at the Administration Building today. I had to step it up a bit," I explained.

"And that includes wearing a tight skirt and stripper heels?"

I let out a huff of exasperation as I stepped around him to my vanity. I grabbed an earring and stuck it through my ear. "It's not tight and these are called pumps. They're perfectly acceptable for work." I attached my other earring and wrapped a bracelet around my wrist.

"Who is he?" Michael asked, stepping closer to me so I was trapped between his body and the vanity.

I tried to ignore that he had invaded my space. I didn't want to fear my husband, but I couldn't ignore the way my pulse spiked. "Who's who?"

"The man you're dressing up for. The man who's going to eye-fuck you."

I rolled my eyes and immediately regretted it. He grabbed my jaw in his hand and squeezed. My teeth dug into my cheeks and my eyes began to water. "Nobody."

He squeezed my jaw tighter. The taste of coppery blood filled my mouth. "I don't fucking believe you." Michael yanked me toward the bed and pushed me down on my stomach. He bunched my skirt up around my waist and ripped my panties from my body.

One hand was planted firmly on my back, holding me down, while the other worked open his belt and zipper. I cringed as the metal clanked. "Please don't, Michael," I begged. "Not like this."

"I'm going to make sure you remember who your husband is. Who you belong to. Who owns you." He impaled me with his cock roughly. He thrust into me repeatedly, as I laid helplessly on the bed. All I could do was wait for it to be over. Tears poured from the corners of my eyes, as I cried out.

When Michael finally came, he slumped over my back pushing me deeper into the mattress. "Think about that in your meeting," he growled in my ear.

I sat straight up in bed, my chest heaving. Sweat covered my forehead, as the panic struck. It was pitch black in my room. I blindly felt the bed next to me. It was empty, and the sheets were cool. Draven had left.

Footsteps came from the hall. The sound of cupboards being opened and closed. Someone was out there. My breathing became shallow, as the fear crept through my body. I had locked the door last night, but Draven didn't have a key. He couldn't have locked it on his way out. My hand reached for the nightstand and fumbled to open the drawer. I pulled out my 9mm and released the safety.

I wasn't going down without a fight.

I slunk out of the bed, holding my gun out in front of me. When I made it to the door of my bedroom, I leaned against the wall and peered into the hallway. I couldn't see a damn thing and cursed myself for not leaving a light on. I usually left one on in the kitchen, but Draven had carried me right to bed and I had forgotten about it.

I made it into the hallway and pressed myself against the wall, creeping silently forward. When I reached the end, I scanned my front room. A sliver of light slipped through the blinds but illuminated nothing.

The apartment was eerily quiet. Maybe I imagined the noises. Maybe it was all in my head. I relaxed the grip on my gun and wiped my hand on my shirt. That dream had messed with my head.

My eyes began to adjust to the darkness, but all I could see was shadows. A beam of light hit the wall across from the kitchen and something fell to the floor with a soft thud.

I didn't imagine that!

I brought my gun back up in front of me and padded in my bare feet across the soft rug that covered the floor. I couldn't make a sound. Whoever broke in wasn't going to have any warning before I put a bullet in them. I was done being a victim.

I turned the corner to the kitchen. A dark figure was down on his hands and knees shining his flashlight along the floorboards. I stepped behind him and pressed my gun to the back of his head.

The figure froze.

"Don't fucking move," I gritted out between clenched teeth. Sweat pooled between my shoulder blades and dripped down my back. This is what I'd prepared for. It was why I knew every inch of my apartment in the dark. It was why I went to the gun range regularly. No one would hurt me, especially in my own damn home.

"*Pisoi?*" A deep voice resonated in the silence.

I knew that voice, but it didn't register. It didn't make sense. Draven had left. I stood frozen, still pressing the barrel to his skull.

"Kitten?" the voice said softly. "Can you remove your gun from my head?"

"Dra-a-ven?" I stuttered.

"Yes, kitten, it's just me."

Tears filled my eyes, and I dropped the gun from his head. It hung limply at my side as a sob escaped from my chest. "You scared the shit out of me. What are you doing?"

He stood and wrapped his arms around me, pulling my body to his chest. "I'm so sorry I scared you." He reached for my gun and took it from my hand, setting the 9mm on the counter.

My adrenaline slowly receded. "I had a bad dream about Michael and when I woke, you were gone. I heard noises and I thought someone broke in. What were you doing?" I repeated.

Draven flipped on the light behind me while still cradling me to his chest. "I got hungry, and I didn't want to wake you. I used the flashlight on my phone, so I wouldn't wake you by turning on lights."

It made sense. Kind of. "Why were you on the floor?"

His eyes scanned the kitchen. He reached down and grabbed something from under the cabinets. Draven held up an apple. "I was looking for this." He set it on the counter next to my gun.

I looked up at him with sadness. "I thought you left me."

He caressed the side of my face. "I would never leave in the middle of the night, *pisoi.* Waking up next to you is one of my favorite things."

I let a small smile slip from my lips. "Mine too."

"Let's go back to bed."

"I thought you were hungry?"

"I don't want that apple anymore. I'm hungry for something else. I think eating your pussy will fill me up just fine. I'm going to fuck that bad dream right out of you."

All right, then. I couldn't complain about that.

He picked up the gun, reengaging the safety. The realization of what I had done hit me. "I'm sorry I put a gun to your head," I apologized. "I could have killed you right here in the middle of my kitchen."

"It was my fault. Don't ever apologize for protecting yourself." He took my hand in his, leading me back to the bedroom. He held up the gun. "Where does this go?"

I crawled onto the bed. "Nightstand drawer."

He opened the drawer, placing the gun inside. Then he pulled out my wedding picture and stared at it, examining the photograph. "Why do you keep this? I would have burned it."

That's what any sane person would have done, but I was a glutton for punishment. "It's a reminder. It reminds me that if it seems too good to be true, it probably is. It reminds me why I ran. And mostly, it reminds me that I wasn't always so fucked up. Once upon a time, things were good, and I was normal."

"I hate him," Draven growled. "I hate what he did to you."

"Join the club. I think my family had t-shirts printed up." I tried to force some light into the darkness that had taken over Draven's face.

"You're not fucked up. Yes, bad shit happened to you, but you're an amazing woman. Don't let anyone ever convince you otherwise."

I gently took the picture from his hand and placed it back in the drawer. "I don't want to talk about him. The only man I want to think about is the one standing in my bedroom."

"I can make that happen. Trust me, you'll forget all about that bastard by the time I'm done with you." He stripped off his boxer briefs and laid down on the bed next to me. "Sit on my face, kitten."

I was taken aback by his demand. "Excuse me?"

"You heard me. I want to eat your pussy and make you come on my face. You got a problem with that?"

"Umm... no?" My sexual inexperience made my answer come out more of a question. *Jesus Christ! This man was going to kill me in the very best possible way.*

Draven took my hand and pulled me to his chest. "Then get up here. And lose the shirt, I want to watch your tits bounce when I make you come."

I stripped off my shirt and straddled his chest. "Like this?"

He grabbed my thighs and pulled me up higher. All my girly parts were right in his face. "Right there. Better hold on tight," he warned.

My fingers wrapped around the headboard, preparing for the sweet torture Draven would provide. The first swipe of his tongue made my thighs clench the sides of his head. He let out a growl and pushed my legs wider. Then he feasted.

My hips swiveled and rocked into the warmth of his tongue. It was so good. Every thought of Michael vanished, just like Draven had promised. "Oh, fuck!" I gasped. He licked and sucked and nipped. Every lash of his tongue brought me closer and closer to nirvana. He reached one hand up and pinched my nipple. The quick sensation of pain sent me tumbling over the edge, into the abyss of bliss. My body shattered. I broke into a million pieces, my mind blank of anything except the overwhelming sense of pleasure. When the tingling faded, I was left panting, my head hanging low and my fingers clenching the headboard to keep me upright.

Draven lifted me to straddle his waist. I collapsed onto his chest. Never had I felt anything like that before and Draven had given me some stellar orgasms. "I don't think it can get any better. What are you doing to me?"

He brushed my hair aside and kissed me. "I know how it can get better."

"Not possible," I panted.

"I want you to ride me. Bare."

My head snapped up in surprise. The first time had been a mistake and freaked him out. "Draven?"

"We're protected and we're both clean. You're the only one I've ever done that with, and honestly, since then it's all I can think about. I want to feel you. And only you. Nothing between us."

I wasn't against it. The first time was an accident. We'd been so wrapped up in the moment that neither one of us fully appreciated it. I wanted it as much as he did, but I wasn't going to let him make an impulsive decision. "Are you sure? Nothing's one hundred percent. This isn't a decision you're making spur of the moment and are going to regret later, is it?"

"Layla, look at me."Hhe cupped my face. "I could never regret a single moment I've ever spent with you. I want this."

"You're positive?"

"Absolutely. Are you?"

I nodded my head. "Yes." I lifted up and centered myself over him. Draven gave his cock a rough tug and positioned himself at my entrance. I eased myself onto his long length, feeling his piercing rub me in all the right places. When I was fully seated, we both smiled, soaking in the enormity of the leap we were taking.

Draven ran his fingers from my neck, down between my breasts and to my clit. "God, that feels so good. So much better. Fuck me, kitten."

And I did. Slowly. I braced my hands on his chest and rocked my hips forward, then back. Forward, then back. Repeatedly. It was a painstakingly slow rhythm, dragging out the sensations for both of us. The whole time, Draven's thumb rubbed circles on my clit at an achingly, leisurely pace. My eyes closed, and my head dropped back. I absorbed everything this man was giving me. Everything I was giving him.

I didn't care if he didn't want to call it making love. I knew what it was to me. And for the first time in my life, I took what I deserved. I took what I wanted. I took what I needed to make me feel whole.

And I didn't feel guilty about it.

I thrived on it.

My walls began to flutter, and I squeezed him tighter, consuming him with everything I had. Taking and giving.

"You're about to come, aren't you?"

"Yessss," I hissed. His thumb moved harder and quicker, sending me into a whirlwind of complete and utter bliss. "Oh, god… oh, god!" My walls clenched. I picked up the pace and milked him for all he was worth. And in this moment, the here and now, I knew he was worth everything to me.

Draven bent his knees and pumped into me from below grasping my hips and surely bruising my skin. Evidence that would be left days later as a sweet reminder of our time together.

With one final thrust, Draven released his cum inside me. He held my hips tight against his as he pressed up into me, forcing out every last drop. "Best thing I've ever felt in my life." He relaxed back into the mattress, lacing his fingers with mine. "Nothing has ever compared to you, Layla. Nothing."

I leaned forward and rested my head against his muscular chest. "Same for me. You're everything I've ever dreamed of."

His arms wrapped around my body, holding me like I mattered. After so many years of feeling neglected and abused, I finally felt loved.

Chapter 28
Draven

I did it again. Not once. Not twice. But three times.

I didn't fuck Layla.

I made love to her.

And I liked it more than I would ever admit. There was something seriously wrong with me. I knew better and yet, I let it happen again.

I couldn't regret it.

Everything about her was everything I wanted.

And I was a liar.

I lied to her tonight. Once she fell asleep, I'd set out on my mission. I shamelessly went through her purse in the darkened kitchen to find her driver's license and social security card. I snapped pictures and sent them to Kane. *Nothing you gave me matches. Maybe this will help,* I sent to him.

Why I was so desperate to unveil her secrets, I wasn't sure. None of it made a damn bit of difference. None of it would change who she was to me. I was already in love with her, and nothing would change that.

Thank God I'd dropped that damn apple, otherwise she might have caught me going through her purse. I wouldn't lie. Feeling the cold, hard steel against the back of my head had caught me off-guard.

She was tougher than I'd given her credit for. Layla was nothing but a cold, hard bitch when she wanted to be. I had no doubt she would have put a bullet in my head without a second thought. Fear had a way of changing people, and my girl harbored a shit-ton of it.

It killed me.

Devastated me.

Made me want to never leave her alone again.

Fantasy. All of it was a sick, twisted fantasy. I was leaving, and nothing was going to change that either. I needed to get right with myself. The two of us together was a pleasant interlude in my otherwise dangerous and pre-determined life. Andrei would never allow me to be happy. Of that, I was sure.

But while I was here, he couldn't stop me. I was happy. I was in love. I would live my life like there was no tomorrow.

As Layla rocked into me with nothing between us, I half hoped that I got her pregnant. Maybe Andrei would release me from my obligations if I had a kid on the way.

Doubtful.

After my mom died, he was an absentee father at best. At least until I was old enough to step into The Organization. It was the best and worst day of my life. I finally had my father's respect and attention, but I sacrificed myself for the privilege. Win or lose? There was no definition where Andrei was concerned.

If I could give it up, I would. In a heartbeat.

But I couldn't. My destiny had already been planned for me.

My first two weeks had flown by and spending time with Layla was going to make the rest of my time go by in a flash. We'd say goodbye and that would be the end of it.

If only it were that simple.

I would hate myself when it ended because I had to make her hate me too. There was no other choice.

I'd studied that photograph and committed it to memory. Looking at Layla's ex-husband had made me sick. What killed me most was the smile of the woman next to him. So beautiful, so sweet, so trusting. She had no idea her life was about to become a nightmare.

When I got back to my apartment the next morning, I thumbed back through the five profiles I had narrowed it down to. Bingo! I found the fucker. Michael O'Connor. I texted Kane to let him know what I'd found out.

Now it was a waiting game.

Kane would get every bit of information available on the fucker. I just had to be patient.

Patience wasn't my strong suit. I wasn't even sure what I would do with the information once I had it. All I knew was the better informed I was, the easier it would be to protect her.

Chapter 29
Layla

Another week had flown by and our time together was ticking toward the end. Draven and I had spent every day and every night together. I cherished every moment, knowing that soon the bubble we'd built around us would burst.

Everything would go back to being exactly what it was before he walked into my life.

The lies I told myself were getting out of control. I don't know why I bothered, because I didn't even believe them. Separating fiction from fact had never been a problem before, but lately the lines were blurring.

It would be impossible for everything to go back to the way they were before. Everything had changed.

I had changed.

Draven taught me I deserved more. I deserved a man who would adore me and tell me I was beautiful. A man who could see beyond my past and be my future. A man who would stand up for me instead of pushing me down.

I was still holding on to the shred of hope Draven would be that man. I had a week left to convince the man I loved that I was worth staying for, and that was why I was standing in the middle of a grocery store.

I was out shopping for the dinner I was making him tonight, my mom's veal parmesan. Her cooking was legendary, and I hoped I could replicate her recipe with perfection. In the time Draven and I had been together, the only real meal we'd ever cooked for each other was breakfast. Most of our other meals were takeout.

When I was married to Michael, he'd convinced me I was a bad wife. He'd made me feel like a failure in the bedroom, but Draven had shown me it wasn't true. So, maybe, I wasn't a bad cook either.

I strolled through the aisles collecting the ingredients: tomato sauce, onions, garlic, Italian seasoning, pasta, breadcrumbs, parmesan cheese, and mozzarella. I checked my list again, all I had left was the veal. I made my way to the meat counter and thought about the call to my mom this morning for her recipe. To say she was excited I was cooking for a man would be an understatement. James, my tattle-tale brother, had told her I was dating someone. She was tickled to death that I was finally moving forward. My mom had every reason to be upset with me for leaving Oregon, but she had never been anything but supportive. If I could convince Draven to stay, I might even consider taking him to visit my family. The thought was like a dream. In five years, I'd never had the itch to go home, but with Draven by my side it would be possible.

After getting the veal, I wandered over to the wine. I wasn't really a wine drinker, but something about it felt right. Thanks to Google, I knew exactly what went with veal parmesan. I snatched a bottle of Chianti off the shelf. As a second thought, I placed two bottles in my cart. Better to be overprepared than under.

Excitement rushed through me on the way to the check out. I used to love cooking, until Michael ruined that for me too. In the past five years my cooking had consisted of meals for one, whatever was quick and easy. Now my shopping cart was filled with enough ingredients to make dinner for two.

I was setting myself up for more heartbreak, but I couldn't find it in me to care. Tonight, I was having dinner with a gorgeous man who treated me like a princess and *that* was worth celebrating.

When I got home, I started dipping the pieces of veal in egg and coating them with breadcrumbs. My fingers were a sticky mess from the eggs, when my phone started to ring. It was probably Draven, confirming what time to come over. He should have known by now he didn't need a special invitation.

I quickly rinsed my hands in the sink and wiped them on the towel. I picked up my phone and smiled. It wasn't Draven. It was James. I'd been meaning to call him for the past week, but… "Hey, big brother."

He bypassed my greeting. "Are you alone? Can you talk?"

His tone immediately set me on edge. "I'm at home. What's wrong?"

"I think you should sit down."

"James, what's going on?" It wasn't like my brother to beat around the bush. The last thing I wanted to do was sit if it was bad news. "Are mom and dad all right?"

He sighed into the phone. "Mom and dad are fine. This is about Michael."

"What about him?" I sneered. "He can rot in hell for all I care."

"Jenna, I know. Believe me, I feel the same way." James went silent.

"Just tell me," I urged him.

"You got a letter from the Department of Corrections today." When I left, I had all mail for Jenna O'Connor forwarded to James. He was under strict orders to read and shred every bit of it. Only something important would have him making this call.

"What'd it say?" I whispered.

"I'm so sorry, Jenna."

"What?"

"He's got a parole hearing in six weeks."

Six weeks? That wasn't possible. I stumbled toward the couch and fell into it. "No! That can't be right." I gulped down my disbelief. "His sentence was for ten years. It's only been a little over five. How can that be right? It's got to be a mistake," I insisted.

"I don't think so. This letter looks official, it's signed by the warden of Pelican Bay State Prison."

Tears filled my eyes and rolled down my cheeks. "What am I going to do?"

"He hasn't been released yet. We don't even know if he'll be approved for parole. I don't want you to panic, but you needed to know."

"And what if he does get out?"

"Nothing changes, Jenna. You've prepared yourself for this. There's no way in hell he could find you. Everything you've done has assured it. You're safe where you are. He won't be able to leave the state of Oregon while on parole. He'd be a fool to try."

"The last time I saw him was at the trial. Did he seem sane to you?" I argued.

"Just hold tight. We don't even know what's going to happen yet. With any luck, his parole will be denied, and he'll stay safely behind bars for the next five years."

If he did get out, my days would be numbered. It might not be next month or even a year from now, but he would eventually find me. Everything I'd done was a temporary fix. Michael had promised I'd regret testifying against him. If I learned anything from him, it was to take his threats seriously. "I'm really glad you came to visit me," I started.

"Don't! Don't you do that! Nothing's going to happen to you! Do you hear me? You've got impending auntie duties to attend to."

I wiped the tears from my face. "Okay. I'll try to stay positive," I lied. I didn't believe I'd be safe for long.

"Are you and Draven still dating?"

215

"Yes. Why?"

"Do you love him?"

I nodded my head, even though I knew he couldn't see me. "Yes."

"And does he love you?"

"I'm not sure." Finally, a truth spilled from my lips.

"How much does he know?" James asked.

"Most of it," I admitted. "Why?"

"You should tell him about the letter. He'd want to know. He should know."

"He's not staying. Draven goes back to New York in a week."

"You should still tell him, Jenna. If there's any chance he loves you, you have to tell him."

There was no way in hell I was telling Draven about this. If he wasn't staying, there would be no point. I wouldn't let this be a factor in his decision. "I'll think about it. I still have time." I didn't want to discuss this with my brother, he wouldn't understand. "Thanks for letting me know. I'll talk to you soon."

"Love you, Jenna."

"Love you, too." I disconnected the call and stared at the wall. There was nothing I could do. I'd done a good job at hiding my identity. When Michael found me, and someday he would, all I could hope was that I'd prepared myself enough.

There was no sense dwelling on something that hadn't even happened yet. I wasn't going to waste the time I had worrying about things I couldn't change. I just needed a few minutes to process and then I'd finish dinner.

Wine and a bath would help me process everything perfectly. I started the tub, pouring in an ample amount of lavender bubble bath, then went back to the kitchen. I stuck the veal in the fridge and uncorked a bottle of wine. Pulling down one of the fancy wine glasses my mom insisted I have, I filled it to the rim. I leaned down and slurped the wine into my mouth because I was classy like that. The flavors danced on my tongue. Sweet with just a hint of cinnamon. It was truly delicious. I carried the glass to the bathroom and then doubled back for the bottle. Why not? A little wine before dinner was exactly what I needed.

The tub was full and frothing over with bubbles. I stripped out of my clothes, turned on some soft music and slipped into the tub. This was a luxury I rarely indulged in and I immediately promised myself to do it more often. My first glass of wine went down quickly, so I leaned over the edge of the tub and poured myself another. I drained that one just as fast and set the glass on the floor. My eyes closed, and I leaned back, absorbing the warmth and comfort of the water. The soft music lulled me into a state of semi-consciousness. Just a few minutes was all I needed.

***

I was awakened by soft kisses ghosting over my neck and jaw. "Wake up, kitten."

My eyes fluttered open. "What time is it?" I felt disoriented. I couldn't have been out too long, the water in the tub was still warm and the bubbles still covered me.

"A little after five. The shop was slow, so Chase and I decided to close early." His fingers fluttered along my breasts. "Is there room in there for both of us?"

"Plenty. How did you get in?" I was sure I had locked the door.

Draven stripped his shirt up over his head and pushed down his jeans. "I knocked but you didn't answer, so I had Brian let me in."

I scooted forward, and Draven slipped in behind me. I leaned back into his strong chest, feeling safe and secure, "I didn't mean to fall asleep. I intended to get dinner started."

"I can see how the warm water and wine might have been a distraction." He refilled my empty glass and held it to my lips. I took a small sip and handed it back to him. He took a long drink and set it down on the floor. "I can't say I'm disappointed about dinner." His fingers stroked over my nipples, playing with my piercings. "Finding you like this is even better than dinner.

"Ummm…" I moaned. "You make me feel so good. If you keep that up, I may never get out of this tub."

"Is that right?" he growled in my ear. His hand slid down my stomach to the ache between my legs, "And what if I do this?" Draven slipped one finger inside me and then another. "Your soaking wet. You didn't play with yourself, did you?"

I arched into his hand. "No. I haven't used my vibrator since our first date."

He fingered me with expertise. Wiggling them inside my slick opening while using his thumb to rub my clit. "And before our first date?"

"Yes," I gasped. "Yes, I used it."

"When?" He continued pumping in and out of me.

"The first night I met you," I admitted. I was so close, so fucking close. My body started to constrict around his fingers.

"And did you think about me? What it would feel like for me to fuck you?"

217

His dirty words pushed me closer to the edge. "Yes! I fucked myself and pretended it was you!" Draven pinched my clit, and I came. Hard and long. I slumped back into him, my chest heaving. I would never get enough of the orgasms Draven delivered.

He whispered in my ear. "You want to know a secret?"

"Hmmm."

"I wanted you from the first moment I saw you. I jerked off to you that same night, fantasizing about how you would feel wrapped around my cock. Want to know another secret?"

"Hmmm." I could feel his hardness pressing into my back.

"No fantasy could have compared to the real thing. Fucking you is better than any fantasy I've ever had."

I reached behind my back and wrapped my hand around him. "We are amazing together, aren't we?"

"Like a match and gasoline." Draven let out a deep growl and spun me around. I grasped his shoulders to keep my balance before he sucked one of my nipples into his mouth. His teeth played with the silver ring, tugging it to a sting and then laving it with his tongue to sooth the pain. The combination of pain and pleasure made my head swim in endorphins that had nothing to do with the wine I'd consumed.

"Need to be inside you, *pisoi*."

The feeling was mutual. My legs straddled his and I sank down on his long, thick length, letting him fill me completely. We both moaned out our pleasure. Nothing had ever felt as good as Draven inside of me.

I started to move. Draven's strong hands held my hips tight and guided my motions. We moved together in perfect sync. Water sloshed over the side of the tub, but neither of us cared. We were too lost in the moment to give a fuck about the mess we were making.

"You feel so good, Layla. I'm gonna come. I can't hold back any longer."

"I'm right there with you, Draven." I was already sensitive from my first orgasm and another was crashing down on me.

Draven moved me faster, splashing even more water out of the tub. "Fuck, yes! Yes!" My orgasm shot through my body, shooting electrical pulses from the tips of my toes to the tips of my fingers.

Draven roared out his own release and sagged back into the tub, smacking his head on the tiled wall. I let out a little laugh and rubbed the back of his head. "That good, huh?"

218

"Always is with you, kitten. Always is."

I pulled the elastic band from his hair and let it fall over his shoulders. I ran my fingers through it, caressing his silky locks. I admired his strong jaw that looked as if it were cut from ice, his eyes that were like pools of deep amber flecked with just the tiniest bit of green, and his body that was sculpted from stone. Although those things had been what initially attracted me to Draven, there were parts of him I loved more.

I loved how he saw the real me and not the person I tried to be. I loved the way he made me feel beautiful and brave. I loved how he made me look at myself differently. Even if he left, he wouldn't be able to take those things with him and that made every minute we spent together worth the heartache I would endure.

This was probably our last time making love in a bathtub. It was our first and our last. As a matter of fact, it was the first of many lasts that would come this week. I wasn't going to drown in sadness this week. I was going to revel in the fact that I got to experience this time with Draven at all. He'd given me something I hadn't been able to give myself in five years.

Hope.

For whatever time I had left before Michael found me, I was going to live. I was done hiding in the shadows and being afraid. Because if I did that, I would let Michael win and he'd been winning for too long. It was my turn.

Draven rubbed his fingers down the side of my face. "Why do you look so sad?"

I shook my head. "I'm not sad. I'm actually really fucking happy. How about that dinner I promised?"

He squeezed the sides of my face and kissed my nose. "Only if I can help and I get to have you for dessert."

I tapped my fingers on his chest. "You drive a hard bargain Mr. Constantine, but I think I can oblige you."

"Good, because that's not all that's hard, Miss Roberts."

I playfully swatted at him. "You're insatiable and a very dirty boy."

He grabbed my wrist. "That's what you love most about me, admit it."

Love. He threw the word out carelessly. I knew it meant more to me than to him, but I played along anyway. "You know me so well." But if that's what he really thought, he didn't know me at all.

We eased from the tub, dried off, and got dressed. "What can I do to help?"

"Do you know how to boil water?" I teased.

"Oh, please," he scoffed. "Give me more credit than that."

"Start with filling a pot with water for the pasta. If you master that, I'll think about what else you can do."

"Yes, ma'am." Draven set about finding a pot and filling it with water while I peeled and chopped the garlic. Once the pot was on the stove, he asked, "What's next?"

I let him chop the onion into tiny pieces. He worked slowly and with precision. I could have done it in a quarter of the time, but it gave him something to do, and I liked working side-by-side with Draven in the kitchen.

While he chopped, I got started on the sauce, sautéing the garlic in olive oil. I added the onions as he pushed them my way. When everything was cooked down, I added in the tomato sauce and seasoning. I brought it to a low simmer then pulled the veal from the fridge. Placing it in a baking dish, I poured the sauce over it, topped it off with mozzarella and parmesan cheese, then placed it in the oven.

"You can turn the water for the pasta on now. If I timed this right, everything will be finished at the same time."

Draven turned on the burner. "Where did you learn how to cook?"

I grabbed the open bottle of wine and pulled down another glass, pouring us each some. "My mom. She's a phenomenal cook."

"How long has it been since you've seen her?"

I took a long sip. "Five years. I've never gone home, and she hasn't come here, but we talk on the phone."

The dainty wine glass looked almost comical in Draven's huge hands. "It must be hard having a family and never seeing them."

"It is. I missed my brother's wedding. I've never even met his wife, so yeah, it sucks."

"You should go visit them."

"I can't"

"Why?"

"You know why. Gossip. Rumors. Anonymity. Fear. Take your pick. Besides, I don't fit into that lifestyle anymore. I'd stick out like a sore thumb."

"Your family wouldn't approve of you?" he asked.

"My family could give two shits what everyone else thinks anymore, but I wouldn't do that to them. And I'm not giving any of my ex-husband's family or friends the chance to know who I am, what I do, or where I live. It's better for everyone this way. Safer."

"I'm sorry."

"You have nothing to be sorry about. My life is what it is." I plastered on a smile. "What about your family? Your dad must be happy you're coming home."

He huffed. "Don't mistake my father for being the warm, fuzzy type. He'll be happy I'm home to do business, that's it. After my mom died, he pretty much disengaged from being a dad."

"Do you even want to go home?" I asked, curiously.

"What I want hasn't mattered in a long time." His answer neither confirmed nor denied whether or not he wanted to leave.

"You're a grown man, surely you have a say," I pressed.

"It's complicated," he said gruffly.

"Always is." I found it hard to believe that his life was more complicated than mine. Draven had clammed up and that was my cue the conversation was over. I stepped to the stove and added the dry pasta to the boiling water. Then I poured more wine into my glass and threw it back. "So, tell me about your sister. All I know is her name is Catina and she goes to NYU."

Draven's serious face split into a smile. "She's twenty-four, finishing her masters in fashion design. She has big dreams of taking the fashion world by storm. She's doing an internship with some big designer in Manhattan."

"Wow! That must be cool. How did she get interested in fashion?"

"Danica, our nanny, taught her how to sew. Bought her one of those sewing machines for kids and ever since then she's been hooked. She's good too."

"No interest in working for the family business?" I wondered how she was able to escape the fate that Draven and Nico had been driven to.

"Fuck no! The family business wasn't even an option. There's no place for her in The Organization. The farther away she is from it the better."

The Organization? I thought it was a business. Weird.

"Do you have a picture of her?"

Draven pulled out his phone and scrolled through it. He held up a photo for me to see. It was a picture of Draven, Nico and Catina. Draven's arms were draped over the shoulders of his siblings. All of them had huge smiles. They looked happy and I was jealous that he was so close with them. I was close with James, but I had seen him only once in five years.

Catina had long dark hair and the same amber eyes as Draven. She was young and beautiful. "Does she have a boyfriend?"

He laughed. "Not one that I've met, but if I were her, I wouldn't introduce anyone to my big brothers either."

"No one's good enough?" I teased.

"Not even close. Men are pigs."

"You're not a pig," I pointed out.

"I was until I met you. I told you, I don't do relationships. You've been my exception."

I was his exception. Surely that meant something. I felt that little niggle in the back of my mind that reminded me I had to let him go. My brain was sensible, but my heart was a fool. It was still holding onto that shred of hope that dangled in front of my face on a silk thread.

"Regardless, be nice to the poor guy that captures your sister's heart. Catina may be your baby sister, but she's a grown woman. It will happen." I laughed.

Draven groaned. "Don't remind me. I don't want to think about her having sex."

"Every woman is someone's daughter or sister. We don't stay young and innocent forever." I couldn't help but push his buttons a little more.

"Stop!" He ran his hand over his face. "How do you think your brother would feel knowing all the things I've done to you?"

I pulled his hand away from his face. "You be surprised. My brother is the one who encouraged me to go out with you. Told me to go get some dick."

Draven groaned again. "Fuck, that's just not normal."

I shrugged. "Maybe not, but he was right." I tapped on his nose. "Better get over it, because Catina is a beautiful woman. She's probably already getting the good dick."

He gave me a hard glare. "You're awful, you know that?"

"Truth is the truth. I won't sugarcoat it for you." I turned back to the oven and checked on our dinner. The cheese was bubbling on top. It looked just like my mom's. I pulled it out, strained the pasta and made us each a plate. I set it down in front of Draven. "If this is bad, please don't tell me. I haven't cooked a real meal in a long time."

He gave me a side-eye. "I won't sugarcoat it for you," he said with a smirk.

I handed him a fork and watched eagerly as he took his first bite. Draven closed his eyes and rolled the food around on his tongue for a bit before swallowing. "Oh, my god! I think I've died and gone to heaven. This is the best thing I've had in my mouth in months, except for your pussy. Which I do plan on having tonight for dessert." He shoveled another forkful in and moaned with delight.

222

I gave myself an internal fist pump. Score one for me. "So, it's good?"

"Good would be a major understatement. So good, I might even forgive you for talking about my sister having sex."

Chapter 30
Draven

My stomach was full, but my heart was fuller. Never, in my adult life, had a woman ever cooked for me. Layla was everything I had never known I wanted.

Before her I was content being a bachelor. I was feared by men and loved by women. My dick had seen a rotating door of pussy over the years. And I was fine with that. Actually, I preferred it that way. Zero commitment and zero complications.

Until now.

Going back to the empty existence I led before, didn't seem so appealing. A different woman every night was not what I wanted.

What I wanted was a woman who would cook for me. A woman I could watch a movie and eat popcorn with. A woman I could hold tight every night and wake up with every morning.

What I wanted was Layla.

After we washed the dishes together, I carried her to the bedroom. "What do I want to do with you tonight?"

"Something dirty?" she asked.

"Without a doubt." I tossed her on the bed. "Where's your vibrator?"

She pointed to the nightstand drawer. *How in the hell did I miss that the other night?* I went to the drawer and found some lube and her BOB. It was a good one too, with a studded shaft and rabbit ears. This was going to be fun. I held it up mischievously.

"What are you going to do with that?"

"I haven't decided yet." I smirked at her. "I want you naked on all fours. I'm going to play with you and you're going to love every minute of it."

"If I'm naked, so are you," she said defiantly.

My answer was to rip my shirt up over my head and push my jeans down. I let everything hang out. "This naked enough for you?"

"Come here." She beckoned me with one finger.

I crawled onto the bed like a panther ready to strike. She took ahold of my cock like I might disappear. No chance of that happening. I reluctantly removed her hand. "You're not naked yet."

Layla quickly remedied the situation, her gorgeous curves on full display. "Better?"

"Much." I grabbed a hold of my cock and gave it a hard jerk. "Feel free to continue."

She licked the bead of precum leaking out and wrapped her lips around my dick. I moaned in pleasure. There was really no such thing as a bad blow job, but a truly good one was far and few between. Layla's blow jobs were of another world.

Her tongue rimmed around the head and played with my piercing as her hand stroked me up and down. Sparks of pleasure ran down my spine and up through my balls. "You're teasing me, kitten," I growled.

Layla's lips twitched around my dick, turning up at the corners. She knew exactly what she was doing to me. She moved deeper down my shaft, running her tongue along the underside, and swirling it in spectacular fashion. Layla savored my cock like it was her favorite flavored popsicle, licking and sucking.

I ran my hands through her hair and pulled it away from her face, piling it on top of her head. There was only one thing that could make a blow job better, watching a woman who truly enjoyed giving one. Her eyes glanced up at me. "I like watching you suck me, kitten."

Layla hummed her approval, sending vibrations straight to my balls. She hadn't even taken me all the way yet and I was ready to come in that sassy mouth of hers. Never before had a woman been able to take all of me, but her deep-throating skills put Layla in a class all her own.

As if sensing I needed more, Layla opened her throat and slid her lips all the way to the base of my cock, cupping my ass in her hands and pulling me in deeper. "Jesus Christ, woman!" Her throat gripped me so fucking tight, I'd be lucky to last another minute. Then she started to move, bobbing up and down, the ridges of her throat rubbing along the length of me. I couldn't hold back any longer. "I'm gonna come."

Layla didn't heed my warning, if anything, it made her more voracious. She sucked me with quick shallow strokes that rubbed the head perfectly. My balls tightened, and my cock swelled. "Fuckfuckfuckfuck… holy shit!" I shot my cum down her throat in several long spurts that seemed to go on forever. I slumped back on my heels, letting out a sigh of relief as Layla slipped her lips up my shaft and released them with a pop.

I untangled my hands from her hair, and she pulled it back from her face. "I haven't done that to you nearly enough. I love sucking you off." Her voice was raspy and sexy, turning me on even more.

I couldn't wait to be inside her in a way we hadn't explored yet. Tonight, I was going to make sure that no matter what the future held for us, she wouldn't be forgetting me anytime soon. Despite the spectacular blow job she'd just given me, my dick stirred back to life. My refractory time with Layla was practically non-existent.

I ran my hands from her hips up her soft curves, until I held her face in my hands. "Do you trust me?"

Layla nodded silently.

"I mean completely trust me with your body? Trust that I wouldn't ever do anything to hurt you? Trust that I only want to bring you the greatest pleasure you've ever felt?"

Layla licked her lips and bit down on the bottom one. "You're making me nervous. Should I be afraid?"

"I don't want you to ever be afraid of me, *pisoi*."

She looked up at me with puppy-dog eyes, so full of trust. And something else... bravery? Adoration? Love? Maybe it was a combination of all three. She was no longer the broken woman she'd been on our first date. She was stronger. Her heart wasn't the cold, dark place it had been before. She had opened it and let me in completely. "I'm not. I know with you I'm safe. What are you going to do to me?"

"I want to fill you completely." My fingers skimmed down her back and through the seam of her ass, to the only place I hadn't touched her yet.

Layla swallowed down her nerves. "You want to fuck my ass?" she whispered.

"Yes. I want to be in every part of you, including that gorgeous ass of yours." I gently circled her hole.

"Will it hurt?"

"It may hurt a little at first, but I'll make you forget about it and all you'll feel is pleasure. I'll ask you again, do you trust me?"

"Yes, Draven, I trust you completely." Layla laid down on the bed, her arms raised above her head on the pillow, wrists crossed. She opened her legs for me in invitation. "Fuck me. Any way you like."

226

A growl rose from my chest at seeing her spread out before me. She was perfection in every way imaginable. Layla's full tits rose and fell with her breathing, her dark nipples hardened into sharp points. Her perfect, pink pussy glistened with her arousal. She was a temptress, and I was helpless against her feminine wiles. I wanted to corrupt her in the very best way.

I started with her lips, devouring her mouth with mine. Our tongues lashed and twisted with a desire neither one of us could ever deny. She was the match to my gasoline. We were an explosion of heat and fire. She made me lose all control and I'd barely had any to begin with.

I loved kissing her. I loved sucking on her hard nipples. I loved licking down her stomach and dusting kisses over her tattoo covered scar. I loved nibbling on her clit and feasting on her drenched pussy. I was totally and irrevocably in love with her.

I grabbed her vibrator and ran it over her clit. Layla squirmed and twisted on the bed, moaning out her pleasure. I slipped it inside her. The end was curved, sure to hit her G-spot, while the rabbit ears tickled her clit. "I'm gonna come!" she shouted.

"Come, baby. Take it all. Take all the pleasure I'm giving you." I rubbed my finger through her arousal and rimmed her tightest hole.

"Please... please," she begged, as she neared her climax.

I took my cue and slipped my finger into her ass, easily sliding it in and out. She was soaked everywhere. I slipped in a second finger, stretching her out for the main event. Layla let out a scream of ecstasy as she came hard and long around my fingers. I slid them out, along with the vibrator, and watched as her chest heaved with ragged breaths. "Are you okay?"

"Wow! Ummm... just... give me a minute."

I wiped my fingers on the towel left on the bed from our earlier bath. "How do you feel?"

"Like jelly. I'm officially a jellyfish."

I leaned over her and planted a soft kiss on her lips. "I'm not done with you. Do you think you can take my cock?"

"Yes. I want to try."

"There will be no trying. You'll take every inch I give you and you're going to love it."

"I believe you," she whispered.

I flipped Layla onto her stomach. "On your knees, ass in the air. I'm going to make you come so hard you'll forget everything but the feeling of me deep inside you."

Layla rose to her knees, her elbows on the bed. She looked over her shoulder. "Don't hurt me, okay?"

I ran my fingers between her shoulder blades and down her back. My hands squeezed her perfect ass that was being offered up to me. I wouldn't take her trust for granted. I would worship her in every way she deserved. "I won't hurt you. I promise."

My dick twitched. I still hadn't been inside her. My balls ached, and my cock was like steel, painfully hard. I couldn't wait for her to be wrapped around me. But I had to make sure she was ready for me. Make her forget what I was about to do. Make her so lost in the pleasure that she'd welcome me in freely.

I uncapped the lube and drizzled it between her cheeks. I reached one hand between her legs and began to rub her clit, my fingers sliding in and out of her pussy. My other hand was busy fingering her ass, sliding in and out shallow at first and deepening with every stroke. "I need you to rub yourself, Layla. Use the vibrator on your clit."

Her hand reached blindly for the toy and wrapped around it. She brought it to her clit and let out a moan of pleasure.

I slid my dick into her warm, wet pussy and it was like being home. In the short time I'd known her, Layla had become the only place I wanted to be. The finger in her ass made it even tighter on my cock. "More, Draven.... give me more," she pleaded.

I drizzled more lube on her, pulled out and slipped into her ass one inch at a time. A steady in and out, until I was seated all the way inside her. So tight, so warm, so perfect. I began to fuck her with slow steady strokes. Nothing had ever felt this good.

Layla began pushing back into me, matching me stroke for stroke. Then my greedy girl, filled her pussy with the vibrator, making everything even tighter. She was wild and untamed. I'd awoken something inside her she didn't even know existed. I wasn't going to last long. I gripped her hips and thrust in at a furious pace, groaning and grunting like an animal. We were both lost to the feeling of complete surrender. It was feral. Primal. We were operating on pure sexual instinct.

"I'm coming… I'm coming. Fuck me harder!"

I didn't need to be told twice. I thrusted faster and harder as Layla's body constricted around me. Her orgasm threatened to completely destroy me. I pulled out and jerked my cock furiously. Hot spurts of cum sprayed all over her back and ass. I collapsed over her body, crushing her into the mattress, then rolled to the side bringing her with me, so her back rested against my chest. We were both covered in every bodily fluid possible. I kissed her temple. "Still okay?"

"More than okay. I don't think I'll ever be the same."

"Fucking you like that nearly destroyed me. I don't think I'll ever be the same either."

I helped her up from the bed and into the shower. I shampooed her long, dark hair and gently scrubbed every inch of her beautiful body clean. Layla submissively let me take care of her. Whether she was truly being submissive or just too tired to put up a fight, I wasn't sure. Nor did I care, because taking care of her was exactly what I wanted to do in the brief amount of time we had left.

I took her to bed and wrapped her in my arms. Layla's head rested peacefully on my chest. She was asleep within minutes. I held her close, watched her sleep, and breathed in the sweet scent of her.

Our time was ticking down and moments like this wouldn't exist anymore. I had never been in love before. This feeling in my chest threatened to overwhelm me completely. I could picture moving here permanently. I'd buy a little house for Layla and me, we'd have a couple of kids, maybe a dog. I always wanted a dog, but my father had deprived us of that as kids too.

It would never happen. It would take a miracle for me to leave The Organization. I was the Constantine that was supposed to take over for Andrei. At thirty-years-old, I still feared him. It was pathetic.

The next morning, Layla and I laid in bed drinking coffee, talking about anything and everything except the fact I was leaving. I loved seeing her like this. No makeup, hair wild and messy, and totally relaxed. I didn't think many people ever got to see this side of her. I was getting an inside look at the woman she was before her life had been turned upside-down. Every hard edge she'd carved, had been smoothed away.

I knew it was special for me, because once she walked out of this apartment, her mask would be back in place for the rest of the world to see.

My phone buzzed on the nightstand. I reluctantly picked it up. Generally, when it rang, it was someone from New York; Nico, Kane, or my father. I breathed a sigh of relief when Kane's number flashed on the screen. Him, I would gladly talk to. Hopefully, he had some information for me. The waiting had been killing me.

I let the call go to voicemail.

"Who's calling?" Layla asked.

"It was Kane. Probably work stuff." I climbed out of bed and pulled my jeans on. "How about I go get us some doughnuts for breakfast?"

"If you need privacy to talk to Kane, you could have just said so."

"I do," I admitted. "But I also could really go for a Boston Crème doughnut. What do you want?"

Layla tapped her finger on her lips. "I really shouldn't. It'll go right to my ass and I already have a lot of junk in my trunk."

I leaned over and kissed her, squeezing her luscious ass. "I love the junk in your trunk. A doughnut won't kill you."

She smiled a true smile that lit up her face. "In that case, I'll take a jelly one. Something red. And make sure it has that sinfully sweet glazing on it."

"Red jelly with glaze. Got it."

She grabbed my hand as I pulled away. "Better make it two. I worked up an appetite last night and I need to recharge. Tell Kane I said hello."

I kissed the tip of her nose. "Will do. Don't get out of this bed. I won't be gone long."

"Take my keys and lock the door when you leave. They're on the counter."

I pulled my shirt over my head. "Of course." Layla was obsessive about the door being locked. It killed me, but I'd do whatever she wanted without question.

I made my way out to my Hummer and dialed Kane back. He answered immediately. "Sorry about that, man. I didn't want to be with Layla when I took your call."

"Probably a good idea. This shit is fucked up."

"What do you mean?"

"I know why we couldn't find her. Layla didn't exist until five years ago."

How was that possible? I pulled out of the parking lot and headed toward the nearest Dunkin' Donuts a few blocks over. I didn't like where this conversation was going. "Explain."

"I pulled all the records for the driver's license and social security card you sent me. That social security number didn't exist until five years ago. She changed her identity. Layla Lorraine Roberts isn't her name."

I choked down the revelation. "Who is she?"

"I traced her through Michael O'Connor. Her name was Jenna McNamara until she got married and became Jenna O'Connor. There's been no activity on either of those names for the last five years. She completely went off the grid. New soc number, new birth certificate, new driver's license. Whoever helped her, pulled some major strings."

It made sense. She'd been desperate to get away. I remembered the night she'd been drunk and told me Jenna was dead. I had assumed she was talking about her baby, but she was talking about herself. "Her dad is a lawyer. I'm sure he had something to do with it." *Her name wasn't Layla. What else had she lied about?* "What did you find out about Jenna?"

"A fuck ton. She was born and raised in Sherwood, Oregon. Top-notch, rich neighborhood. Dad is an attorney, mom stayed at home, one brother. She was the darling of her high school, Homecoming Queen and captain of the cheerleading squad. She earned a full academic scholarship to Oregon State University, where she continued cheerleading. She got her degree in elementary education and art."

She'd told me most of her story, except the fact that she'd been a cheerleader. But one thing stood out. "Oregon?"

"Yeah. Didn't she tell you she was from California?"

I thought back over our conversations. *Where's home?... West coast... A California girl, huh?... Something like that.* "Fuck! No, she said West Coast. I just assumed California. What else?"

"Married Michael O'Connor right out of college and got a job at a local elementary school. A year later, he tried to kill her. Ended up in a coma for weeks with a laundry list of injuries. She was lucky to survive. Her face covered every paper and news broadcast in Oregon. It was a huge story."

"Do you have pictures?" I growled.

"Yeah. But it's bad, Draven. Are you sure you want to see them?"

I parked in front of the Dunkin' Donuts. "No, but I need to. Send them."

Kane sighed on the other end of the phone. "Fine. I'm sending them now. Don't say I didn't warn you."

I waited impatiently for the photos to come through. When they loaded I opened them and gasped. What Layla had described didn't come close to what I was looking at. She was practically unrecognizable. It looked as if someone had taken a meat cleaver to her face. My stomach churned, and bile rose in my throat. I was going to be sick. I opened the door of my Hummer and emptied the contents of my stomach onto the pavement. I'd seen some bad shit in my life, but this was beyond my comprehension. I wiped my mouth with the back of my hand. "Tell me about the fucker who did this to her."

"Are you all right?" Kane asked.

"No, but keep going. I need to know everything."

"Michael O'Connor. Fraternity boy born with a silver spoon in his mouth. His drugs of choice were cocaine and heroin. Did a stint in rehab his sophomore year of college, also Oregon State. It was all kept very quiet. His father, Sean O'Connor, is a financial mogul. Owns several huge companies and was able to hide his son's indiscretions by throwing money at them. He hired the best attorneys after the murder attempt, but even daddy's money couldn't protect Michael. Daddy arranged for him to go to Pelican Bay State Prison to keep the media away from his businesses. Michael's been on his best behavior while in prison, looks like he has a parole hearing in six weeks."

"For attempted murder? Five years and he could be out?"

"You know money talks. Daddy's money and hot shot attorneys worked the system."

I scrubbed a hand over my face. *Six weeks?* "What can we do?"

"Nothing until he gets out. But when the time comes, I got no problem helping you bury a body. He's a sick piece of shit. We'd be doing the world a favor."

Kane was a true friend. Not many guys would help you commit a crime and cover it up. "I'll be home in a week. We'll come up with a plan then."

"I'm sorry, Draven. I know you love her, and this was hard to hear. Just know I'm all in, brother."

"Thanks, Kane. I'll talk to you soon." I disconnected the call and sat lifelessly in my car. Layla wasn't Layla, she was Jenna. I let the name roll around in my mind. Jenna fit the girl in the wedding photo, but I could never look at the Layla I knew and call her Jenna. She hadn't just run, she'd totally obliterated her past life. I couldn't blame her. I hated that she felt the need to lie to me, but trust wasn't something that came easily to her. Fuck, if it had been my sister, I would have helped her do the same thing.

I had a new appreciation for the woman I had fallen in love with. She was the bravest, fiercest woman I had ever met. This new information made my chest clench harder. *Six weeks?* It was going to be almost impossible for me to leave her.

But knowing Kane and his twisted mind, he had already started to come up with a plan. We'd take care of Michael O'Connor before he had a chance to stalk my girl. His first day of freedom would be his last. That fucker was as good as dead and my girl, even though I wouldn't be there to protect her, would be safe.

Andrei could go fuck himself, because I would make sure it fit into my schedule. I didn't care what his plans for me were. Layla would be safe no matter what.

I strode into the Dunkin' Donuts and ordered our breakfast. I got three donuts for her. My girl deserved the best and if doughnuts was the way I could prove it, so be it. She could have one for breakfast, lunch, and dinner for all I cared. I loved the junk in her trunk, and I wanted her to be happy. After everything she had gone through, she totally deserved it.

When I got back to her apartment, I looked at my girl in a whole new way. Not only was she beautiful, but she was strong. I already knew that, but she was a fighter. I found that fact more sexy than anything I had known about her before. She could have let Michael get the best of her, but Layla had created a whole new life for herself. I was so proud of her.

And I fell a little bit more in love with the woman who had trusted me with her body and her heart.

Chapter 31
Layla

Something shifted between us. Draven was more attentive than he'd been in the last three weeks. He had always been attentive, but this was different. I couldn't put my finger on it, but something had definitely changed.

Draven bought concert tickets for us. We rode out to DTE Energy Music Theater on his motorcycle, my arms wrapped around his waist. I never wanted to let go. He wouldn't tell me what the concert was. I could have looked it up, but what would have been the fun in that? Instead, I let him surprise me. I hadn't been to a concert since college.

Who would I have gone with?

Nobody.

That was the sad answer to my question. I hadn't had a boyfriend or a real girlfriend in years. Sure, I was down for a night out at the bar with my co-workers. But a concert was like a date and I hadn't been on one of those since before I dated Michael. He hadn't been interested in spending time with our friends. He wanted me all for himself. At the time I thought it was endearing. Michael hadn't wanted to share me with anyone. Now, I knew it was part of his manipulation.

When we arrived at the concert venue, Draven shoved my ticket at me. "I wasn't sure if you would like it, but I took a chance."

I looked down at the ticket. It was for Shinedown and Godsmack. My lips curled into a smile. It was perfect. I loved both bands. Surely Draven knew this from the music I played in my studio, but he seemed unsure.

I held my ticket up. "I love it! You couldn't have done better."

A look of relief flashed across his face. "Are you sure? We don't have to stay."

I grabbed his hand and started dragging him toward the entrance. "I'm positive. I'm so excited, I haven't been to a concert in years. These are two of my favorite bands."

Draven seemed relieved by my reaction. We made our way into the venue and got some drinks. "Where are our seats?" I asked.

He winked at me. "That's another surprise."

I followed him down the stairs of the outside amphitheater. When we were halfway down, I started to get excited. These seats were great, but Draven kept going. He led me down to the front row where a metal barricade separated the audience from the stage. He handed our tickets to the beefy security guy standing guard with his arms crossed over his wide chest. Security examined our tickets and handed them back to Draven, giving him a nod.

"Holy shit! We're sitting front row?"

Draven leaned down and planted a soft kiss on my lips. "Only the best for you."

We found our seats and I looked around. This was amazing. "How much did this cost you?" Draven worked as a tattoo artist. He couldn't make that much money. But then I remembered he also worked for his father. The family business must have been profitable.

Draven wrapped his arm around my shoulder. "I don't want you to worry about that. I can afford it and I wanted to do something special for you."

It'd been a long time since someone did something special for me. "Thank you. This is great."

The lights dimmed and Shinedown came out on stage. The crowd went wild. We got lost in the energy of the show that was playing just a few feet in front of us. We sang and danced to every song. Our bodies bumping and grinding to the beat.

When the band left the stage, I was hot and sweaty from the dancing and the heat of the lights. Draven and I went up top to get another drink and look at merchandise before Godsmack took the stage. We stood at a booth with concert shirts and other mementos. Draven pointed to a black tank top with a cool sun-shaped insignia on the front. "What about that one?"

I gazed from him to the shirt. "Not sure that would look the best on you," I joked.

He bumped me with his hip. "Not for me, you goofball. For you. It would look great on you, show off your rack a little bit."

I cupped my hands under my full breasts and pushed them up. "These things?"

He frowned. "Maybe not."

I playfully slapped his arm. "I'm kidding." I clapped my hands in front of me and bounced on my toes. "I want it. No take backs."

He laughed. "Then you should have it." Draven paid for my shirt and handed it to me.

I slipped it over the spaghetti strap tank I was wearing. I spun in a circle to model it for him. "What do you think?"

Draven groaned. "I think I shouldn't let you out of my sight. You're a sexy little vixen."

"So, I didn't look sexy before?" I teased.

He wrapped his arms around my waist, hooking his fingers in my belt loops, and pulled me close. "You always look sexy, especially when you're wearing nothing. We better head back before the show starts."

We walked down to our seats and waited for the lights to dim again. The stage was shrouded in a huge white drape that hung from the ceiling. I leaned in close to Draven. "I'm so excited! Thank you for this."

"You're very welcome. It makes me happy to see you happy."

My heart overflowed. "You make me happy." It was the truth. I couldn't remember the last time I had been this content with my life.

The amphitheater went black, and the crowd erupted with wild anticipation for Godsmack to take the stage. It started with drums and then an electric guitar. Music blasted from the speakers and the drape fell from the ceiling. Sparks exploded from the stage as they began their opening song.

The energy surrounding us was contagious. Draven and I hooted and hollered along with everyone else. I began moving my body and singing along with everyone else. I was lost in the music and the front-row view we had. Vibrations pulsed through my body.

I looked over and Draven was staring at me with a panty melting smile. "What?"

"Just watching you. I love seeing you like this."

I leaned up on my toes and kissed him. "It's all because of you."

Halfway through the concert, a piano was rolled onto the stage. Sully Erna sat down and began to play "Under Your Scars". It was emotional and beautiful, so different than their normal heavy sound.

Draven pulled me in front of him, wrapping his arms around my waist and resting his head on my shoulder. "I feel like he wrote this just for us. You're my shooting star in the rain. Under your scars, you're the most beautiful woman I've ever been with."

236

I turned my head toward him and brushed my mouth against his. Our lips and tongues moved in a gentle, deep kiss. This, right here, was who we were meant to be. We belonged together. I was sure of it. Tonight, I was going to tell him I loved him. There was no doubt in my mind he felt the same way. If he couldn't stay here with me, I would move to New York with him. We would be happy together. I could make a new life for myself in New York. With Draven by my side, anything was possible.

Draven and I pulled in the back lot on his Harley and parked next to a red '69 Chevelle. "Is that Zack's car?" Draven asked.

My heart plummeted. "They're back."

We went in through the back door, my hand wrapped in his. The light in the office was on. I poked my head inside. Zack was sitting at his desk going over paperwork. "You're back early."

His head popped up and he smiled. "By a few days. Everything with Rissa went better than expected and we were able to head home a few days ahead of schedule."

Zack's eyes focused on our joined hands. Draven quickly pulled his from mine and shoved it in his pocket. My abandoned hand dangled uselessly at my side. *Why wouldn't he want Zack to know we were together?*

"I'm gonna head up." Draven motioned with his thumb and started to walk toward his apartment.

I didn't know how to read his actions. Did he think Zack wouldn't approve? I needed answers. "I'll come with you."

I started to follow when Zack called out. "Layla, can I talk to you for a minute?"

I looked between the two of them, unsure what to do. Draven gave me a nod. I faced Zack. "Sure."

Draven headed up the stairs while I watched him retreat. Zack got up and shut the door, blocking everything else out. "Layla, what's going on? Are you two together?"

I didn't understand why he seemed upset, so I deflected. "I'm doing great, Zack. Thanks for asking. Everything went very well while you were gone. Business as usual." I held my hands to my chest. "Oh, you missed me? I missed you too." I gave him a sickeningly sweet smile.

Zack eyed me from the door. "Of course, I missed you. I never had any doubt that you could handle Forever Inked. If I didn't, I wouldn't have left."

He walked around his desk and sat, motioning for me to do the same. I plopped down in the chair across from him. "I don't understand the problem, Zack. Yes, Draven and I have been dating. Is that an issue for you?"

He shook his head. "No, Draven's a good guy. I'm surprised is all. The entire time I've known you, you've never seriously dated."

I let out a disgusted laugh. "So, what? I'm not good enough for him? Or you just have a problem with us working together and screwing?"

Zack frowned. "That's not it at all. I love you like a sister, Layla. I'm worried about you is all."

"Well, save it. I'm a big girl. I can make my own decisions." I got up and stormed toward the door.

"Does he know?" Zack's voice stopped me in my tracks.

I turned and gave him my best bitch look. "Know what?"

"Please, come sit. I don't want to fight with you, I just got back," Zack pleaded.

"Who's fighting? I don't know what you think you know, but whatever it is, you're wrong." I reached for the doorknob again.

"You're running, Layla. I don't know what happened to you, but you've been hiding here for almost five years."

Ice ran through my veins. I'd never told Zack a damn thing about my past. I slowly turned to face him. "What are you talking about?"

Zack ran his hand through his short hair. "When you first started working here, I did a background check on you. The ink was barely dry on your social security card. I knew you were hiding something, but you were a damn good tattoo artist, so I took a chance. One I've never regretted."

I stomped toward his desk and leaned on the front of it. "You had no right! Who the fuck do you think you are?"

Zack stood and leaned on his side of the desk facing me. "I had every right! You showed up here with a suitcase and nothing else. I knew something was off."

I fell into the chair and the tears started to fall. I quickly wiped them away. "I feel violated."

Zack came around and kneeled before me. He took my hands in his. "I'm sorry. I had no choice. I'm glad I took a chance on you. Whatever your past is, it's never interfered with your work. You've been the best, most dependable employee I could have asked for. But you're more than that. You're one of my best friends. I only want the best for you."

"What makes you think Draven's not the best for me?"

Zack let out a huff. "Draven's a complicated guy. How much do you know about him?"

"I know enough. I know that I love him."

He gave me a tight hug. "Just make sure you're honest with each other. You saw what happened to Rissa and me."

"He knows my story. He knows more about me than anyone else here," I assured Zack.

"But do you know his story?"

"What do you mean?"

"That's for him to tell you. Draven's a great guy and I have no doubt he'd treat you right, but you need to go into this with your eyes wide open."

"My eyes are open. I didn't want to tell you this, but if he's not staying, I'm going to New York with him. Consider this my two-weeks' notice."

Zack stood and angrily crossed his arms over his chest. "You're not leaving. That's not the life for you. It's not safe."

How dare he tell me what I could or couldn't do? I stood and mimicked his stance. "Draven's made me feel safer than I have in five years! You're not my father! You can't tell me what to do!" I spun on my heel and headed for the door.

Zack grabbed my elbow. "You're making a mistake. You don't know what you're getting yourself into."

I removed his hand from my arm. "My whole life has been a series of mistakes. This is the first thing that feels right. I appreciate your concern, but it's my life."

I left him standing in the office while I went after Draven. Tonight, was the night. I was going to lay my heart on the line. Zack was wrong. I knew he was.

Chapter 32
Draven

Layla's knock was soft. If I hadn't been expecting it, I wouldn't have even heard it. I wondered what Zack had told her. Had he warned her away from me? He was the only one here who knew my truth.

I opened the door and pulled her inside. I could tell she'd been crying.

Avoid.

Avoid.

Avoid.

I pushed her against the door, pinning her with my hips and locking her wrists in one hand over her head. "Are you okay?"

"I need you," she panted. "Make love to me."

We'd done it several times, but never said the words. It was always *fucking*, not *making love*. I wouldn't argue with her over semantics. I'd let her have this tonight.

I ripped her tank over her head while her fingers fumbled with the buttons on my shirt. We were a mess of hands and teeth and lips as we stripped each other bare. I worked at the button on her jeans as she clanked the buckle of my belt. I toed off my boots and kicked my jeans aside then pulled off her boots and yanked her jeans down her legs.

My hand slipped inside her panties. "You're soaked, *pisoi*."

She put her fingers over my lips. "Don't talk."

I scooped her up and carried her to the bedroom. There would be no foreplay tonight. I needed her too much and she needed me just as bad. I grabbed her lace panties at the hip and tore them from her body. She already had her bra unclasped and threw it on the floor. My boxer briefs were next.

My lips crashed into hers and then my cock was in her pussy. God, I needed this. Layla wrapped her arms around my shoulders and held on tight, while I thrusted in and out of her. I grabbed her thigh and brought it up around my hip, so I could push in deeper. Every stroke rubbed her clit, bringing her closer to the edge.

I felt her starting to flutter around me. "Don't let go. I'm not even close to being done with you."

If this was our last night together, I didn't want it to be over.

"I can't stop it," she gasped.

"Come, baby, but don't let go." She pulsated around me, coming hard, but I couldn't stop. I wouldn't stop until we were both exhausted. Sweat dripped down my back and covered my forehead. Layla's hands slipped on my shoulders. She locked them around my neck and leaned back, pushing her tits up. I captured one hardened nipple in my mouth and then the other.

"Fuck! I'm gonna come again."

I was right there with her. I thrust in hard and deep, burying myself inside her tight pussy. My balls pulled tight, and electricity shot through my spine. My orgasm seemed to go on forever. I gave her two more deep thrusts and collapsed.

We were both covered in sweat. I pushed up on my forearms. "I don't want to crush you."

She pulled me back down. "I like it." She buried her head in my neck. "I know Zack's back but please don't leave me. I want you to stay."

This was the conversation I had been trying to avoid. The last place I wanted to have it was inside her, with my cum dripping out between her thighs. I was a dick, but I wasn't that big of a dick. I pulled out and went to the bathroom for a towel. I wiped myself clean, then tossed it to her. "I'm not staying."

She grabbed the towel in mid-air. "Then I'm coming with you."

My heart seized, and my jaw clenched. I rested my hands on my hips. "You're not coming with me. You knew what this was when we started it. You knew it was going to end."

She scrambled to the edge of the bed and reached for me. "It doesn't have to end. We're good together. I love you, Draven."

The words I'd been dreading to hear hung in the air. She was going to hate me after tonight, but she left me no choice. I backed away from her. "Well, I don't love you." The lie tore me up inside.

Her eyes welled with tears. "You don't mean it. I love you and I know you love me too."

I shook my head at her. "I don't. Get real, Layla. Don't mistake great sex for love. We fucked. It was phenomenal, but that's all you were... a good fuck. Congrats!"

She pounded on my chest with her fists. "You're a liar! Why can't you admit you feel something for me?"

I grabbed her wrists and pushed her back on the bed. "You're right. I am a liar. I've been lying to you since day one. How can you love me when you don't even know who I am?"

"I know who you are! I know everything that's important! I know how you make me feel in here." She pointed to her chest.

I laughed at her. "Smoke and mirrors, kitten. Do you want to know what I do for my father? I run guns, I sell drugs, and I commit murder. They call me The Raven," I pounded my fist against the tattoos on my chest, "because I'm the best at what I do. I'm the top soldier in my father's organization. He's a mob boss and I'm next in line. I've got so much blood on my hands it would make your stomach curl."

She sat back on her knees with a look of shock. "You lied to me," she whispered. "After everything I shared with you, you still lied to me. I told you all my darkest, deepest secrets and you shit on them."

"Oh, don't act so high and mighty." Then I went for the kill. "You didn't tell me the truth either, did you? I looked through all the California records to try to find you. But that was a waste of time, since you're from Oregon, right? But no Layla Lorraine Roberts ever lived in Oregon. So, who are you really? Jenna McNamara or Jenna O'Connor?"

Her eyes went wide as shock took over her body. All her secrets were out now. She jumped from the bed, collected her clothes furiously and began to get dressed. I grabbed her arm. "What? Nothing to say now?"

"Jenna's dead! She died on the bathroom floor. Layla's who I am now!" She reared her hand back and slapped me across the face. "You have no idea what you've done. Who have you told?"

I rubbed the side of my face. It stung for more reasons than one. I had pushed her too far. I deserved everything she gave me and more. "I haven't told anyone. I wouldn't do that to you."

She stormed toward the door and then turned abruptly. "You know what's so sad? I believe you won't tell anyone. You could have trusted me with the truth, but instead you lied to me." She shook her head in disgust and let out a laugh. "You know what else is sad? I don't care about what you do or who you really are. It doesn't change who you are inside. We could have made it work. I know how you treated me and that's all that mattered. You made me feel brave and beautiful and loved. You made me feel alive for the first time in forever. You can keep lying all you want and say you don't love me, but I know the truth. I love you and you *do* love me. You can't fake what we have together."

What was wrong with her? There was no way she could love the man I really was. "I'm not your fairytale prince, Layla. Quit making me out to be something I'm not."

"Fuck you! I never wanted a prince! All I wanted was you! I'm sorry I lied to you about my name, but everything else I told you was the truth. We both have secrets we're not proud of. You have a choice to make. Are you going to keep lying to yourself or are you going to admit how you feel? My cards are on the table. You know where I stand."

Layla opened the door and left. I didn't chase her this time. I let her go because that was the only way I knew how to protect and love her.

I got dressed and made myself a drink. Nothing would be able to erase the pain in my chest, but vodka was a good start.

Avoidance was becoming my specialty.

It was time to face the fire. I had no doubt Zack was still here, especially after watching the way Layla left.

The light in his office was on, so I sheepishly crept inside. "Hey."

His response was less than enthusiastic. "I'm gonna assume you told her."

"Yeah."

"You're not staying, are you?"

I sat down across from my friend and told him the truth I should have told Layla. "I love her, but I can't. You know how Andrei is. I can't stay and bringing Layla home would be too dangerous for her."

"You have choices, Draven."

I started to make excuses. "It's complicated…"

Zack held up his hand to silence me. "You forget that we're not that much different. My father wanted me to stay in New York and run his Fortune 500 company. I gave him the big ol' middle finger and walked away. My father's a vindictive asshole and he tried to make my life miserable. My relationship with him is done, but I've found the most amazing woman to share my life with. Rissa was engaged to my brother before he died. Did you know that?"

I shook my head and continued to listen.

"Alexandria is my niece, but she's my daughter in every way that matters. Rissa and I practically destroyed each other by denying our feelings for each other. But when push came to shove, I knew I couldn't let her go. I know what complicated is."

"I have to let her go."

"That's your prerogative and I respect your decision, but just know, women like Layla come along once in a blue moon. I appreciate that you stepped up when I needed your help. I wish you were going to be around because Rissa and I will be traveling a lot." He stood and extended his hand to me. "You always have a home here if you want it."

I stood and grasped his hand. "I appreciate that. Maybe one day I'll be back."

I left Zack's office and began packing.

Chapter 33
Layla

I slept restlessly. Draven and I hadn't spent a night apart in the last few weeks and I'd become dependent on him.

I missed his warm body.

I missed his soft kisses.

I missed the safety I felt in his arms.

I missed him.

We weren't over yet. I refused to believe everything we had shared meant nothing to him. We only had two days left and I wasn't going to waste them being mad.

Yes, he'd lied to me but that didn't change the man I knew.

He lied because he didn't think I would accept him. He was so wrong.

Michael had had a respectable job and an impeccable reputation. But behind closed doors he was a monster. He hit me and belittled me and raped me. The fucker had tried to kill me. His vows to cherish and love meant nothing.

Yes, Draven did bad things for a living but that didn't change the way he treated me. He'd never raised his voice to me. He'd never made me feel less than who I was. He'd never raised a hand to me. As a matter of fact, I was sure he would kill *for* me if necessary. If that wasn't love, I didn't know what was.

Draven was wrong. What I had with him wasn't smoke and mirrors. It was the real deal.

I got in my car and drove to talk to him before work. Maybe our night apart had given him time to think. More perspective. I prepared for the worst but hoped for the best.

I rushed in the back door and flew up the stairs to his apartment. I knocked lightly. It was a new day. Our emotions ran high last night. Our heads would be clearer today.

I waited impatiently for him to answer, then knocked again. Harder this time.

Still nothing.

I reached for the doorknob and it turned freely.

Everything was quiet.

NO!

I stepped further into the apartment. The counters were free of clutter. There was no jacket hanging on the hook beside the door.

"NO!"

I ran to his room and pushed open the door. The bed was made neatly. The room was void of any of his belongings.

I rushed to the dresser and opened the drawers.

Empty.

I threw open the closet doors.

Not a thing was left on the hangers.

"NO!" I screamed. "How could you?"

I flopped down in the middle of the bed and began to sob. I pounded the comforter with my fists. It couldn't be true. How could he have left without even saying goodbye?

My hand hit something on the bed. I reached out and pulled the material into my hand. My bra from last night was clutched tightly in my fist. Underneath it was a note.

It was four words. *It's better this way.*

I held the note to my chest, it was all I had left of him.

I don't know how long I sat there in his room crying. Time seemed to stand still. Looking around at all the emptiness, it was as if he had never existed at all. All that was left of him were my memories and four words scribbled on a scrap of paper.

I heard footsteps in the front room. My heart lurched. He had come back for me.

But when the door swung open it wasn't Draven. It was Zack.

"I'm so sorry."

I shrugged my shoulders. "You tried to warn me."

Zack came and sat on the bed next to me. He wrapped his arm around me, and I leaned into his shoulder, "That doesn't make it hurt any less does it?"

"I really love him. How could he do this to me? I thought he loved me too. I'm so stupid."

Zack took my face in his hands. The tears I never let anyone see, fell freely down my cheeks. "You're not stupid, Layla. You're a beautiful, smart woman. If he can't see that, it's his loss."

"If it's his loss, then why does it hurt so bad?"

"Because that's what love does to us. It makes us feel the greatest joy and the deepest despair."

"We had our first real fight last night. He said some awful things, but it was so out of character for him. I think he wanted me to hate him, but I can't. He gave me things that no one has been able to give me." I couldn't give Zack the details without revealing too much. Maybe one day I'd tell him my story, as a matter of fact, I probably owed it to him, but today wasn't that day.

"You've worked crazy hours while I was gone. Do you want to take the day off? Take some time for yourself?"

I wiped at my face. "Thank you, but I think I should work. I need it."

Zack nodded. "I understand more than you know. We're cut from the same cloth, Layla. I've never regretted hiring you."

I smiled at him through my bleary eyes. "I've never regretted answering your ad and showing up with my one suitcase. It was the best decision I've ever made."

"Can I tell you a secret?"

"I'm a good secret keeper."

"You can't tell Chase," he teased.

"I won't."

"You're one of the best decisions I ever made too. Even better than Chase. I love you, sweetheart."

I wrapped my arms around him. "I love you too. Thank you for being my friend and giving me a fresh start."

That night I knocked on Brian's door with a bottle of booze in one hand and a carton of ice cream in the other.

He took one look at me and pulled me into his arms.

"He's gone. He didn't even say goodbye."

"I'm sorry, baby girl." Brian led me to his couch. "What movie are we watching?"

I plopped down and curled my bare feet underneath me. "You pick. I plan on getting so drunk I won't remember anyway."

"Sounds like a plan." Brian went to the kitchen and came back with two spoons and two shot glasses. He held them up. "Booze first or ice cream first?"

I reached for a spoon. "Ice cream." I popped the lid off the carton and dipped my spoon in. I took an oversized scoop and shoved it in my mouth. "No date tonight?"

Brian sat next to me, scooping out his own ice cream. "Nope. I'm taking a break for a while. Remember what I said about keeping your head and heart separate?"

"Yeah."

"The lines started to get blurry, so I broke it off."

I shoved more ice cream in my mouth and swallowed. "Blurry for him or blurry for you?"

"For me. For both of us. I don't know."

I arched an eyebrow at him. "What was his name?" I never asked about names with Brian. I knew they wouldn't be around long enough to bother.

"Patrick."

I turned sideways on the couch and crossed my legs, placing the carton between us. "Tell me about him."

"You don't want to hear this shit."

"Actually, I do." I'd latch on to anything for a distraction right now. I rolled my hand at him. "Start spilling."

Brian dropped his spoon into the carton. "Well, he's good-looking and has the body of an Adonis."

I rolled my eyes. "That describes every guy you've ever dated. What made him different?" I tapped Brian's chest. "What made him get in here?"

"I don't know. He was thoughtful. He would send me texts during the day, just to let me know he was thinking of me. He always asked about my high and my low of the day. He actually cared about how my day was going, not just the hours after work we spent together. Usually when I'm seeing someone, we meet at the bar and head to bed afterwards. Patrick and I went on real dates, movies, dinner, and shit. He even introduced me to his sister and her daughter. He has the cutest little niece."

I couldn't hold back my smile. "You should see your face right now. You really like him. How was the sex?"

Brian groaned. "Phenomenal."

"So why not give it a chance?"

He frowned. "I don't do relationships. It was getting too serious."

I picked up my spoon and took another bite, then pointed it at him. "Well, if you're giving the gay-thing a break, I know a nice girl who's recently become single. No strings attached."

Brian laughed. "First of all, it's not a gay-thing. It's who I am. Secondly, I already told you my P is never going in your V."

"Fine," I huffed. "It was worth a shot. You know what they say: the best way to get over someone is to get under someone else."

"You know what I think you're doing? Avoiding talking about Draven. What happened?"

I sighed. "I'm not even sure. We had a great night together and then I told him I loved him."

"And?"

"He said he didn't love me, but I know it was a lie." I fiddled with the bracelets on my wrist. His words hurt me more than I wanted to admit. I still wasn't sure if I believed him or not. "We had a fight and I left because we were both upset. When I went there this morning, all his shit was packed and gone. He just left." I threw my spoon into the almost empty carton of ice cream. "I think I'm ready for the booze now."

Brian carried the carton into the kitchen and then poured us each a shot. "He didn't say goodbye? No note? No text? Nothing?" He tossed back his shot and I did the same.

"Oh, there was a note. Four words: *It's better this way*." I refilled our glasses.

"That sucks." Brian slammed his second shot back. At this rate he would be drunker than me. I wasn't the only one drowning out my pain. "I hate to say this, but I think Draven and I are a lot alike."

"Besides both being sexy as hell? What do you mean?"

"I think you scared him."

"I scared *him*? How?"

"Well, you said he never had a relationship before, right?"

"Yeah, but I don't follow."

"You made him feel," Brian tapped on my chest, "in here."

"And that scared him?"

He nodded his head. "When you've never been in a serious relationship, feelings are scary. You worry that you're not good enough. You worry that the other person will see the true you and decide they deserve better. Deep down, you know they deserve better. And mostly, you worry about how much it will hurt when it ends, because nothing that good can last."

I remembered Draven's words from the first night we had sex. *It was more, and it scares the shit out of me. Because I feel things for you that I shouldn't feel.* Maybe Brian was on to something. I picked up my shot and tossed it back. Brian had taken to drinking directly from the bottle, not bothering with the glass anymore. "Is that why you broke it off with Patrick?"

Brian held up the bottle and stared at it. "I guess."

I let out an exasperated breath. "God, men are stupid. Patrick would be lucky to have you." I bumped him with my shoulder. "You're a catch."

He smiled at me. "So are you, baby girl. So are you."

Brian and I cuddled up on the couch together, covered by a blanket, and watched a movie. I fell asleep in the arms of my best friend. My heart still hurt, but I didn't feel so lonely anymore.

Chapter 34
Draven

I'd been home for a week and the hole in my chest hadn't healed at all. I figured once I was away from Layla, she'd be like a distant memory. Something you remembered with fondness but moved on from.

I hadn't moved on.

If possible, my chest hurt more than the night I packed up my apartment and left. I was a chickenshit for leaving in the middle of the night like I did, but I couldn't see Layla again. The look on her face when I said I didn't love her, nearly destroyed me. I was an asshole for lying to her. A first-class asshole.

I'd done everything I could to make her hate me. I called her a fuck, like she didn't mean anything to me. I told her my truth. I spewed the secrets she'd been keeping, like they had been a betrayal.

I pushed and I pushed her away from me.

And in the end, she still loved me despite everything I was and everything I had done.

I knew if I saw her again, I would crumble.

I had no business thinking about keeping her. The only thing I kept was the black, lace panties I'd torn from her body our last night together. Everything else was gone.

She deserved better than a criminal.

She deserved a house and a family and a dog.

Definitely a dog.

She deserved to be happy.

I read back through the texts she sent me. They came in rapid-fire two days after I left.

Layla: You're a fucking coward!

Layla: You accused me of being a runner, but that's exactly what you did.

Layla: What are you afraid of?

Layla: Don't answer that. I don't want to hear any more lies. You're a liar.

Layla: You felt something. I know you did!

Layla: We could have made it work. I don't care about what you do. All I ever cared about was you.

Layla: I'm stronger because of you. I'm braver because of you.

Layla: I love you, but I don't need you!

Layla: Don't call. Don't text. Don't respond at all. I won't let you break my heart again.

She was right. Everything she said was right on target. I did as she asked. I didn't call, and I didn't text.

I had a job tonight. I needed to get my head on straight. They were expecting The Raven, not the sad sack of shit I'd become since being home.

Chapter 35
Layla

It'd been over a week. My heart still hurt, but it was healing a little bit more every day. I hadn't heard from Draven, but I didn't expect to. He was gone, and I'd come to terms with that. I didn't like it, but I accepted it.

I'd thrown myself into work. Zack kept urging me to take some time for myself, but that was the last thing I needed. Too much time to think was my biggest enemy.

I stepped out back behind the tattoo shop for a breath of fresh air. I sat down on an overturned crate and hung my head between my knees. I missed Draven desperately.

I missed our banter.

I missed his dirty words.

I missed the way he held me.

But mostly, I missed the way he made me feel alive.

I heard a noise and my head popped up. I looked around but didn't see anything. I was more on edge knowing that Michael might be getting out soon. My imagination was working overtime.

I heard it again. It was soft at first and then a little louder. It was close. I stood up and looked around. Not seeing anything at first, I almost ignored it. But something told me to keep looking.

Hiding behind the bucket Zack had out back for the smokers to put their butts in, was a tiny fluff of black. I kneeled to pet the tiny kitten on the head. "Where did you come from?"

He looked up at me with bright green eyes. "Meow."

"Are you lost? Where is your momma?"

"Meow."

I picked him up and cuddled him to my chest. His sharp, little claws dug into my shirt at first, but when I started to rub his back he relaxed and started purring.

"You don't have a home, do you?"

He looked up at me and purred louder.

I opened the back door. "Come on, baby, you're coming home with me." I took him inside and held him up for Zack and Chase to see. "Look what I found."

"Where did he come from?" Chase asked.

"I don't know. I just found him out back."

Chase petted his head. "Cute little thing." The kitten grabbed ahold of Chase's finger with his paws and started chewing on it. "I think he might be hungry."

Zack took out his phone. "I'll call Rissa and have her bring over some of Miss Priss's food."

I frowned at Zack. "Priss is a grown cat. This little guy needs kitten food. Is it okay if I go to the pet store?"

He put his phone back in his pocket. "You're probably right. Are you going to keep him?"

I snuggled him tight as he chewed on the ends of my hair. "I think I just might."

An hour later, I'd bought a bag of kitten food, bowls, a soft cat bed, a litter box, and an assortment of toys. He sat in the front seat of my car while I drove back to work. "What should I call you?"

He looked up at me. "Meow."

"Hmmm. I'm not sure Meow is a good name for you." I tapped my finger against my chin. "You're strong and smart and bold, plus you have beautiful black fur. Raven. Your new name will be Raven, *pisoi*."

It was probably stupid to name my kitten after Draven, but I couldn't help it. Draven had called me *pisoi* for so long. He had called me his kitten. I hated it at first, but after a while I found it endearing. The name Raven was perfect and although I couldn't have Draven, I would feel like I had a little part of him with me.

Raven and I settled into a good routine. The money I'd spent on a cat bed was a waste, because his favorite place to sleep was curled up on my pillow. Every morning we had breakfast together. At lunch, I went home to check on him. At night we ate dinner together. Him, a bowl of kitten food and me, whatever was quick in the microwave. After dinner, we sat on the couch together and shared a bowl of ice cream. I wasn't sure if ice cream was good for cats, but he liked it and I couldn't tell him no.

Tonight, I was going out with the girls—Rissa, Tori, and Kyla. Since Rissa had been back, she'd been begging me to go out. I didn't feel like it before, but it was time. Some time with the girls might be just what I needed.

Raven sat on the back of the couch and stared at me. I patted him on the head. "Don't look at me like that. I'll be home soon."

A knock on the door pulled me away from Raven. Rissa had offered to drive. She wasn't much of a drinker, so being the designated driver wasn't a hardship for her. I opened the door to my best girlfriend.

She bypassed me completely and went right for Raven. "Oh my god, he's so cute!" She picked him up and cuddled him.

"Hi to you too," I said sarcastically.

Rissa turned to me, her blond curls bouncing, and gave me a hug. "I'm sorry." She pointed to the fluffball in her arms. "But… kitten."

"I know. He's a snuggler." I took Raven from Rissa's arms, much to her dismay, and placed him back on the couch. "Are you ready to go?"

Rissa and I met Tori and Kyla at an upscale bar a few miles away. Rissa wasn't famous yet, but that would change quickly with the time she'd just spent in California. Before we knew it, her face would be everywhere. We were determined to enjoy a night of anonymity before fame hit. When that happened, she'd be lucky if Zack let her go anywhere without a bodyguard.

When the waiter came over, we all ordered drinks except Tori, who opted for an iced tea. Three sets of eyes focused on her.

She threw her arms up in the air. "Fine! I'm pregnant! Chris and I have been trying for a while and I just found out a few days ago."

All three of us shrieked our congratulations, giving Tori hugs. I got my period the day after Draven left, so that was one less thing for me to worry about. At least he hadn't left me *and* a baby behind. It was a relief and a little bit of a disappointment at the same time. I knew the chances of me getting pregnant were slim, but if I had been pregnant, I would have gotten to keep a piece of him.

I got a kitten instead.

Kyla scrunched up her face. "Tyler and I have been trying too, but no luck so far."

Tori winked at her. "Keep at it, it'll happen. Let's just hope Tyler and his super sperm don't knock you up with twins again."

"That would be cruel," Rissa stated. "God wouldn't do that to you twice."

Kyla let out a sigh. "I hope not. Those boys are going to keep me on my toes when they get older. Can you imagine the trouble they'll get into? They already tag team us and they're not even one yet."

All this talk about babies made me sad. All I could think about was the baby I could have had if it weren't for Michael. He or she would have been almost five by now. I tried not to think about it, but it was being thrown in my face. I couldn't blame my friends for their excitement. They had no idea what I'd been through or what I had lost.

I picked up the menu off the table and scanned our options. "I say we order all of the appetizers and splurge in celebration."

Rissa agreed. "Yes! After working hard to lose all my baby weight for the photo shoots, I need food. I swear women in California survive on carrot sticks and celery. I need real food, deep fried and full of fat. I'm an Oklahoma girl, I know how to eat!"

I laughed. "I think we can accommodate you. They have mozzarella sticks, chicken wings, potato skins, mushrooms and fried pickles."

"Pickles?" Tori questioned. "Sign me up for that shit."

"Really? How cliché." Kyla looked over her menu at her best friend.

"Don't judge. I'm starving. I've always had plenty of tits and ass. A little more ass won't hurt me." Tori waggled her eyebrows. "It'll give Chris more to smack."

Our waiter, who obviously heard our conversation, turned bright red as he placed our drinks on the table. Rissa giggled. "Overshare," she said as she sipped her drink.

Tori waved her off. "Speaking of asses being smacked, I want to hear about Layla's man. Is he coming back?"

I saw Rissa out the corner of my eye. She furrowed her eyebrows and shook her head as if it were a taboo topic.

It was, but it wasn't. Maybe talking about it would help me get Draven out of my system. I took a sip of my drink. "He's not coming back."

Kyla pouted her lips. "I'm so sorry."

I waved my hand at her. "Don't be. I knew he wasn't staying from the beginning. I was the one who let myself fall in love with him. It was my own fault."

"Who could blame you?" Tori asked. "When a man kisses a woman like that..." She fanned her face. "...it was hot."

"It was," I agreed. "But he left when I told him I loved him. Packed his shit in the middle of the night and was gone. It was good while it lasted, but I don't need a man like that in my life." I hoped I sounded convincing because the words hurt as they poured from my lips. I'd been foolish enough to think that Draven and I could have a future together.

When I thought about it, I realized I'd built a fantasy around a man I hardly knew. I didn't know his birthday. I didn't know what his middle name was. I didn't know if he was a dog or a cat person, although he did have a penchant for pussy.

Most importantly, I didn't know he was a criminal. It all made sense now. Most tattoo artists wouldn't be able to afford a Hummer and a Harley. No wonder he had been so adamant his sister would never be part of the *family business*. It wasn't a business at all. It was organized crime.

What surprised me the most about these revelations was that I didn't care he was involved in crime. What bothered me was the feeling I'd been played. He pushed me out of my comfort zone. He made me feel like he cared. He was sweet and attentive. He made me feel like he loved me, not just my body but all of me.

I gave him more of myself than I had ever given to anyone else.

But all I was to him… was a fuck.

I was ashamed and embarrassed I fell for his ruse. What made it worse was even though I knew he didn't love me, I still loved him.

My instincts about men were awful and my heart was a traitorous fool.

On the way home, Rissa chatted incessantly while driving. She told me all about the condo they bought in Malibu, the record executives in LA, and the crazy ride she willingly signed on for. I was excited for Rissa and her impending career as a recording artist, but all I could think about was how great her life was going and how mine was standing still. I was a shitty friend.

My phone rang and I held up a finger to pause Rissa. "What's up, James?"

"You have to come home, Jenna."

I looked over at Rissa, even though she couldn't hear my brother. "What's going on?"

"Mom was in a car accident. She got forced off the road and her car rolled down an embankment."

I sat up straighter in my seat. He had my full attention now. "Is she all right?"

James let out a deep sigh and his voice shook. "She's in a coma. They don't know if she's going to make it. I know this is the last place you want to be, but we need you. You need to come home."

My head felt faint and fuzzy. If my mom died and I didn't go I would never forgive myself. I could do this. I wasn't the same scared girl I used to be. I had Draven to thank for that. Michael didn't have his parole hearing for three weeks. By then, I'd be back here safe and sound.

I must have been silent for too long. "Jenna?"

Snapping myself out of it, I found my voice. "I'll be there. I'll get on the first flight out. Can you pick me up at the airport?"

"Of course. I'll see you soon."

I hung up and stared out the front window. It seemed surreal. I was going home.

"Is everything okay?" Rissa asked.

I shook my head and tears filled my eyes. "No. My mom was in a bad car accident. They don't know if she's going to make it. I have to leave for Oregon."

Within an hour, I was packed and booked on a flight from Detroit to Portland. I sat in the front of Zack's Chevelle as he drove me to the airport. I didn't know how long I would be gone and paying for airport parking was expensive.

"Thank you for this. I know driving me to the airport wasn't exactly on your plan for the night."

Zack put his hand on my knee. "You're family, Layla. This is what family does for each other. Are you sure you don't want me to go with you?"

It was so Zack to offer. "No, I'll be fine, but thanks for offering. You just got back, and I don't know how long I'll be gone. I'm sorry for leaving you in a lurch."

"Don't you worry about that. You do what you need to do. Be with your mom, and don't worry about your cat. Rissa was more than willing to do kitten duty while you're gone."

Forty-five minutes later, Zack pulled into the lane designated for dropping people off for departing flights. I leaned over and gave him a kiss on the cheek. "Thank you for this. I'll call when I know more."

"Be safe."

"I will." I pulled my suitcase from the backseat and headed home for the first time in five years.

Chapter 36
Draven

I threw the money from tonight's job on the desk in front of my father. The blond in the short red dress sitting on his lap jumped when it thumped down in front of them. My father whispered something in her ear and she quietly left the room, pulling down her too short dress on the way out.

"What's up your ass? You've been a moody son of a bitch ever since you got back." Andrei steepled his fingers on top of the desk.

I rolled my eyes. "Did you even love mom?"

His eyebrows furrowed together in a look I knew all too well. "I loved her very much. She was everything to me."

I sat down in the chair across from him and laughed. "You have a funny way of showing it. Every young Barbie, Bambi, and Bimbo has been traipsing in and out of this office for the last eighteen years."

"Is there a question in there?" he asked.

"Yeah." I leaned forward resting my elbows on my knees. "What happened to mom?"

"You know what happened. She died in a car accident."

"Fuck you! I want the truth, not what was in the newspaper. What really happened to her?"

Andrei leaned back in his chair and nodded. "It was my fault."

I quirked an eyebrow at him. "What do you mean it was your fault?"

He looked up at the ceiling, then back at me. "She wanted to run to a friend's house who'd had a fight with her husband. It was dark outside, and you kids were ready for bed. I should have driven her, but she didn't want to leave the three of you alone, so she insisted I stay. My car was parked behind hers, so I tossed her the keys and off she went."

"So, she went out alone at dark? How was her accident your fault?" I could understand the guilt, but not the blame.

259

"Because it should have been me in that car!" he roared. "It wasn't an accident. It was a hit, and I was the target. The car was riddled with bullets meant for me." He turned his head and wiped away a tear from the corner of his eye. This was a side of my father I never saw. Maybe he actually had a heart. "It was my fault. I lost the only woman I ever loved because I was a criminal."

I digested this information. My suspicions had been right all along. It wasn't really an accident. "Did mom know what you did for a living?"

He nodded once. "She did, but I tried to keep this shit away from her. She was too good for me and I knew it. I never deserved her, but she loved me anyway."

The comparison between my parents and my own situation was eerily similar. "Do you ever regret being with mom?"

"Never. I regret that she paid for my sins, but I could never regret a day we were together. Your mother was the best thing that ever happened to me."

"If you had to do it over, would you still have married her?"

"I'm too selfish of a bastard not to. Rose was… strong and sassy and so full of love for me." He sighed.

"So why all the other women? What would mom think?"

He crossed himself. "God rest her soul, she'll forgive me. I was lonely after your mom died, but I could never love another woman. After a while they became something to satisfy my needs. I refused to ever fall in love again, but sometimes when it's late at night I can pretend it's my Rose I'm inside. And for a little while I have her back."

"That's fucked up."

He shrugged. "Maybe so." He straightened his suit jacket and pulled himself together. "What's with all the questions? You been thinking about your mom?"

I had expected lies when I came into to his office tonight, but surprisingly he was truthful. After all these years, it felt like I had my father back, even if it was short lived. It gave me the strength to finally be truthful with him.

I looked up at him sheepishly. "I met someone."

"What's she like?"

I chuckled. "Strangely enough, she's a lot like mom. Beautiful. Sassy. Smart. Bold."

He steepled his fingers on the desk again. "Draven, this life… it's not for everyone. It carries risks for everyone you involve in it."

I ran my hand through my hair. "I know the risks. Mom was lesson enough. That's why I left her behind."

"But?"

"I want out," I said, dropping my head.

Andrei pounded his fist on the desk. "No!"

My head snapped up. "What do you mean, no?"

"You heard me! You're not abandoning us for a cheap piece of ass and a good fuck."

I stood up, knocking the chair over. "Don't talk about her like that! I love her. I'm going back! You can't keep me here!"

Andrei threw his hands in the air. "Fine! Go back, but while you're there, you're working. I'm setting up another drop with Vic in Detroit. He's a good client and I'm not losing him because you can't pull your head out of your ass."

I held up my finger. "One job and then I'm out." I could handle one job if it meant I got to stay with Layla.

"One job and we'll talk," he countered. "I'll set it up and let you know when."

I stormed from Andrei's office pissed off. I thought for a brief moment that there was some shadow of my father still alive in there. But I was wrong. Fuck him! I'd do the job, but then I was done. He could disown me. I didn't care anymore.

Now I had to talk Layla into taking me back. I'd apologize and probably lose my man card in the process, but I was miserable without her.

I got in my car and called her. It went directly to voicemail.

I texted her.

Draven: I'm so sorry. You were right... I love you. I'm coming back for you if you'll have me. Please forgive me.

After an hour, I tried calling her again. Layla was ignoring all my attempts to talk to her. I didn't blame her for not answering. I'd broken her trust and hadn't tried to contact her in over two weeks. She was pissed and hurt. I did all of that to her.

I called Kane. "You up for a road trip?"

"Hell, yeah! Where we going?"

"To get my woman back."

"About fucking time! When are we leaving?"

"In an hour?"

"I'll be ready."

I could have gone by myself, but the ten hour drive would give me too much time to think. I could have flown, but I wasn't a fan of boarding a plane without a weapon. The drive would give me a chance to figure out how I was going to win her back.

I picked Kane up at his apartment. He came out with a backpack and a duffle bag. I knew what was in that bag. "Couldn't travel without them, huh?"

"You telling me you're not packing?"

I fist bumped him. "You know I am." I lifted the cover in the back of my Hummer, and he placed his guns next to mine. When you've been friends since grade school, some things didn't need to be discussed. "Good thing you came prepared. Andrei is setting up another drop with Vic."

Kane groaned. "I was hoping we weren't dealing with him anymore."

I clapped him on the shoulder, "One last job and I'm out. That is if I can get Layla to take me back."

"What are we waiting for? Let's go get your woman."

Less than ten hours later, Kane and I pulled up in front of Forever Inked. I tried to call Layla multiple times during our drive, but she refused to answer. I strode in the front door and went right to her studio. It was empty.

Zack came out of his studio and stared at me. "What are you doing here?"

"I came back for her. I can't let Layla go."

He let out a huff. "You're too late, she went home."

I turned on my heel. "Then that's where I'm going." I was almost out the door.

"Draven!" I stopped dead in my tracks. "You hurt her really bad."

"I know and I'm going to fix it."

"Fuck," Zack said quietly.

"What?"

"She went home. Back to Oregon. Her mom was in a car accident."

She was in Oregon? "When?"

"She left in the middle of the night. I took her to the airport."

"Shit!" I opened the door and motioned for Kane to come in. Then I turned the sign on the door to *Closed* and flipped the lock.

Chase poked his head out of his studio. "Hey, Draven. What's going on?"

"Meeting, now!" I barked. "Everyone in Zack's office."

"What the hell is going on? You can't just come in here and close down my business," Zack protested.

I ignored him and kept going. Something was not right. I pointed at Kane. "Check to see if he's out?"

Chase plopped down in one of the chairs. "Someone want to fill me in on what's going on?"

Zack crossed his arms over his chest. "Yeah, I'd like to know too." Anger rolled off him in waves.

I held up a finger and waited while Kane's fingers flew across his keyboard, working his magic on his laptop. After a few minutes Kane lifted his head. "He's out. He was released three days ago."

"Fuck!" I turned to Zack. "You need to tell me everything."

"No," Zack said sternly. "You tell me what the hell is happening."

Layla was going to kill me for this, but I had no choice. "Her ex-husband it is out of prison."

"Layla was married?" Chase asked. "She never told me that."

"Me neither," Zack said.

"How much do you know about Layla's past?" I asked.

Zack scratched at his chin. "Not much. I knew she was running from something, but I never knew what."

Chase held up his hands. "Wait. Did you just say her ex-husband was released from prison? What was he in prison for?"

I placed my hands on my hips. "Attempted murder. He tried to kill her and damn near succeeded too. She moved here to escape."

"That's why she's never gone home." Realization took over Zack's face. "Who is she? I know damn well Layla's not her name, but I never pressed the issue with her."

I looked at Kane. "Just tell him. We don't have time to dick around here. We gotta go."

I prayed that Layla would forgive me. "Her name is Jenna McNamara. Jenna O'Connor after she got married. She changed her name so he could never find her again."

Kane interrupted. "This isn't coincidence. Her going home right after he's been released? She's being set up. We need to get to Oregon fast."

My mind was reeling. "Shit! How are we going to get our guns on board a plane?"

"Wait!" Zack said. "I have an idea." He pulled out his phone and left the room. He returned within a few minutes. "I got us a plane. No security check. Direct flight to Portland. It'll be ready in less than an hour."

Kane ran out to my Hummer and came back with both our duffle bags. He started pulling out the guns and checking the ammo. Zack went to his safe and pulled out three Glocks. He threw them to Kane who placed them in our bags.

"I'm coming with you," Zack stated.

I gave him a nod.

Chase stared at the three of us with wide eyes. "Who are you people?"

Zack, Kane and I all looked at each other. "Marines," we said in unison.

"Well, what about me? Do I get to go?"

Zack put his hand on Chase's shoulder. "No. I need you to go to my house and stay with Rissa and Alexandria. She's going to be freaking out. I don't want you to leave her until we get back. I'll call her on the way."

Chase nodded his head. "I can do that. I'll cancel all our appointments for the next few days and reschedule. I don't want to sound like a pussy, but I'm glad I'm not going. I love Layla, but you guys scare me."

Zack gave Chase an encouraging half-smile. "You'll be helping by holding down the fort while we're gone."

I looked at the men who were going to help me save my girl. "We gotta go!"

In a flurry Zack, Kane and I rushed out to my Hummer and headed to the private airstrip where our plane was waiting.

We had a long flight, and we couldn't have asked for better accommodations. I wish I could have enjoyed them, but I was too wound up to relax. "Who does this plane belong to anyway?"

"One of my clients," Zack offered.

"You must have done a hell of a job on his tats for him to help us like this," Kane said.

Zack twisted his lips to the side. "Actually, I owe him. He helped Rissa get her big break by letting her sing with him at a concert. I'm going to owe him even more after this."

I walked around the cabin of the plane and looked at the pictures on the wall. I pointed to one of them. "Is this who I think it is?"

"The one and only." Zack smirked. "Bobby and Rissa have become good friends and are going on tour together."

"No shit! Ever worry he's going to try to snag your woman?"

Zack shook his head. "Nope. Well, maybe before Rissa and I were married, but not anymore. Besides if you think I'm going to leave my girl alone with a bunch of horny musicians, you're nuts. Everyone will be very clear about who she belongs to."

I stared at the floor and thought back over my time with Layla. "I should have done that with Layla. I should have told her how I felt."

"I think she'll know after this. If flying across the country to save her doesn't scream *I love you,* I don't know what does," Zack reassured me.

"I just hope we're not too late. She got a good head start on us. Every minute she's there alone, is..." I couldn't finish my thought.

Zack clapped me on the shoulder. "We'll get her. She's not totally alone. Her brother was picking her up from the airport. She'll be with family."

Kane had been clicking away on his laptop since we boarded. "Okay. Her mom is at Providence Newburg Medical Center. I got Layla's parents' address and her brother's address. Looks like the ex-husband still owns the house they had when they were married. I have an address for that too. Oh, and I already rented us a car. It'll be waiting for us at the airport."

I let out a deep breath. "Thanks." I started pacing the length of the cabin. "How did that fucker get out early? His parole hearing wasn't supposed to be for another three weeks."

Kane tapped some more on the keyboard. "I don't know. Department of Corrections just amended the records two days ago. It must have been a last minute deal. I should have been monitoring it better, but shit like this never happens." Kane ran his hand through his closely cropped hair.

"Did Layla know he was having a parole hearing?" Zack asked.

I planted my hands on my hips. "I don't think so, she didn't say anything. But I knew. I should have told her. Kane and I were planning on handling him before she ever knew he was out."

Zack gulped down the lump in his throat. "What did he do to her?"

Kane and I filled Zack in on the details of Layla's past. Although it wasn't new information to me, relaying it to Zack brought about a fresh wave of anger and disgust. We had to be in time. Anything else wasn't an option.

When I finished telling the story Layla had told me in confidence, and Kane had shown Zack the pictures, he scrubbed a hand over his face. "Let's bury that piece of shit!"

Chapter 37
Michael

I knew she would come.

She may have changed her look, but I would know my girl anywhere. She was all I had thought about for the last five years.

I snorted a line of coke off the dashboard. "You're mine."

Chapter 38
Layla

James picked me up at the airport as promised. I ran into his arms at baggage claim. "How's mom?"

"She's stable for now. The doctor said the next twenty-four hours are critical. All we can do is pray." He hugged me tight and buried his head in my neck. "I'm so glad you're here."

"Me too." And I was. Being with my brother after all the shit that happened with Draven, was what I needed. I just wished it was under different circumstances.

I pulled the hood of my sweatshirt over my head and put on my aviators. I didn't want to chance that someone would recognize me. We walked to James's car and headed directly to the hospital. It was overcast and dreary out, a light mist hung in the air. That's one thing I didn't miss about Oregon, the constant dampness that seemed to seep right into your bones.

James nodded at me. "I don't think you need the shades."

I pulled them down and peered at him over the top of my lenses. "Humor me. I'm not comfortable here."

"You know the hearing isn't for three weeks. We don't even know if he's going to get parole."

I relaxed back into the passenger seat. "I know, but it's not just him. It's this whole town. I feel like a pariah."

James put his hand on my knee. "People forget. It's old news."

"Old news. New news. It doesn't matter. I wish I was nobody's news, old or new. Once people know I'm in town, the gossip will start again."

"No one even needs to know you're here," James assured me.

"That's the plan."

When I walked into the hospital room, I gasped. Seeing my mom hooked up to so many wires and tubes nearly knocked me off my feet. She looked so thin and frail underneath the flimsy blanket that covered her.

James put his arm around me and walked me further into the room. My dad's head popped up and he smiled a smile that crinkled his eyes. He stood and held his arms out for me. I rushed into them and collapsed into the warm embrace of the only man who had never let me down.

He squeezed me so tight, I thought my ribs would crack. "I've missed you so much, Jenna." He held me out by the arms and looked me over, scrutinizing everything I had done to myself. "You look beautiful. Still my baby girl."

"Thanks, daddy. I missed you too." I ran my hand over his face where his five o'clock shadow was coming in thick. "You need a shave."

He scuffed a hand over his cheek. "And a shower, but I can't leave her."

I sat down in the chair opposite my dad. "How is she?"

"The doctors are optimistic. They said the coma is her body's way of healing. I want to believe them, but I won't be convinced until I see her green eyes flutter open. They're going to try to take the breathing tube out tomorrow."

"That's good." I looked between my brother and my dad. "What happened? Did they get the person who did this to her?"

James cracked his neck. "The police said it was a hit and run. Witnesses saw a non-descript black car side swipe mom's car, but no one got a license plate number. It's still under investigation. Luckily, someone called 911 right away. An off duty fireman witnessed the crash and got to mom fast. He started giving her medical attention before paramedics arrived. He probably saved her life."

"Jesus Christ," I whispered. I carefully picked up my mom's hand and rubbed my thumb across the top of it. "You're going to be okay, mom." I remembered when our roles were reversed. I was laying in that bed five years ago and she was holding my hand. I was sure I was going to die, but she just kept holding my hand, telling me how strong I was and how much she loved me. Tears welled in my eyes. "I love you, mom. You're going to make it. You've always been strong for everybody else. You're the backbone of this family. We need you."

I dropped my head to her bed and let the tears fall from my eyes while my dad rubbed my back. She had to make it. I would never forgive myself for staying away if she didn't. I needed more time with my mom.

I convinced my dad and brother to go home for a quick shower. It was late, and they had been here for over twenty-four hours. I curled up in the corner of the couch in my mom's room. I couldn't leave her. I wouldn't leave until I knew everything was going to be all right.

My eyes were heavy. I took a quick nap on the flight here, but other than that I'd been awake for almost thirty-six hours. I was running on fumes.

I pulled the blanket from the edge of the couch and covered myself with it. I just needed to close my eyes for a few minutes. I drifted in and out of consciousness, never really falling asleep.

I heard the door open and expected either a nurse or doctor. It wasn't either one. A tall, curvy brunette entered the room with a coffee in each hand. "You must be my sister-in-law."

I straightened up and stretched my arms above my head. "Wendy?"

She nodded. "I thought you could use this while the guys were gone." She thrust the coffee into my hand.

I took a small sip from the steaming cup. It tasted divine. "French Vanilla? It's perfect. Thank you."

She sat down on the couch next to me, sipping from her own cup. "This is awkward," Wendy admitted. "I've seen pictures of you from when you were younger and then some from when James came to visit. It's like you're two different people. I don't know if I'm supposed to call you Jenna or Layla."

I gave her a small smile. "Only the outside has changed. I'm still the same person on the inside, mostly. You can call me whichever you prefer. I'll answer to both. My family always calls me Jenna, but my friends don't know she exists, so they call me Layla."

Wendy contemplated this. "Are we going to be family or friends?"

I cocked my head at her. "You're making me an aunt and you brought me my favorite coffee. I hope we can be both."

Wendy's shoulders relaxed. "I'd like that. I'm glad you came home. They really needed you."

I took another sip from my cup. "I feel like I owe you an apology. I didn't want to miss your wedding." I shrugged my shoulders. "I just couldn't make myself come. This town holds a lot of bad memories for me. I don't feel safe here."

She stared into her coffee. "Don't worry about the wedding. James told me what happened, and I understood why you couldn't come."

"I expected he would."

"I'm sorry. No one should have to endure what you did."

I didn't know what to say. She was absolutely right, but I learned something from Draven. He'd taught me one of the most important lessons of my life. I wasn't ashamed anymore. Everything that happened to me laid on Michael's shoulders, not mine.

"Actually," Wendy said hesitantly. "I'm in awe of you. I'm not sure I would have been able to move forward like you did. You're kind of my hero."

I scoffed. "Don't let all this fool you." I motioned to my appearance. "I only recently pulled my shit together. I've been a mess a long time."

"Regardless, I'm happy you're here and I'm happy I'm finally getting to meet you."

I set my coffee on the floor and wrapped my arms around her. "Me too. You must be amazing because you make my brother incredibly happy."

Wendy and I chatted and got to know each other while the guys were away. When they came back, my brother suggested Wendy and I head down to the cafeteria. I wasn't going to argue. I was sure my stomach had started to eat itself I was so hungry.

The two of us moved through the cafeteria line, filling our trays with food that wasn't good for us but comforting, nonetheless. We sat at a table in the corner, and I began to stuff the macaroni and cheese into my mouth.

"So, James said you had a boyfriend," Wendy blurted.

My hand froze halfway to my mouth. I hadn't filled James in on our "breakup", if that's what you wanted to call it. All I had told him was Draven moved back to New York. "That's over. If I'm honest, we weren't even really dating. We were just sleeping together." I internally cringed. I basically told my sister-in-law I was a slut, even though that was the farthest thing from the truth.

Wendy smiled into her meatloaf. "Sounded like more than that to me."

I set my fork down. "Oh, do tell, dear sister-in-law. What did my big-mouth brother say?"

She set her silverware aside and folded her hands. "He said you were in love. He thought this guy, Darren, might be the one."

I laughed. "His name was Draven. I was in love, or so I thought. As Draven so eloquently pointed out, I mistook great sex for love. My mistake."

Wendy crinkled her nose. "That's harsh."

I shrugged. "Maybe he was right."

"Do you think he was right?"

"Pfft! Not at all. I know what love is and I definitely loved him. He just didn't love me. I'm over it," I lied.

"Is there a chance you two will get back together?"

I shook my head. "Not a chance in hell."

Wendy and I finished our late night dinner. It was pushing midnight and I was exhausted. All I could think about was the vinyl couch in my mom's room that had my name written all over it. Comfort be damned, all I needed was sleep.

We headed back up to my mom's room, toting coffee for anyone who wanted it. I walked in the door and dropped mine to the floor, splattering it everywhere.

"What are you doing here?"

Chapter 39
Draven

"Hello, *pisoi*."

"What the fuck are you doing here?" She glared at me.

"Jenna!" her dad scolded.

Layla held out a hand to silence her dad. "You have no right to be here! This is my family!" Then she pointed at Zack. "I thought you were my friend. How could you betray me?"

I stood and wiped my hands on my jeans. "Don't be upset with Zack. You wouldn't answer your phone."

"Yes, well, I turned it off on the plane. The only people I wanted to talk to were already here, and that doesn't include you." She crossed her arms over her chest defensively.

James stood and intervened. "I think you should listen to them, Jenna."

"Why would I do that? That piece of shit," she pointed at me, "left me without even saying goodbye. I have nothing to say to him."

Ouch! She wasn't wrong though. Layla turned her back on me and stormed out of the room. I looked at Kane, who motioned with his head to follow her. She stormed down the corridor like she was on a mission.

I hopped over the puddle of coffee and followed her. "I'm sorry!" I yelled into the quiet.

She turned and glared at me. "You're sorry?" She strode toward me and pushed on my chest. I stumbled back. "You're sorry? That's all you have to say?"

A nurse came around the corner. "Ma'am, you need to quiet down. This is a hospital and it's late. Don't make me call security."

I smiled at the nurse "I'm sorry. That won't be necessary." I grabbed Layla by the arm and dragged her back to the room, shutting the door behind us.

"Let go of me, you asshole." Layla shook free from my grasp. "You need to leave. How dare you come here?"

This wasn't at all the way I planned for this to go. I had been fooling myself thinking she would be happy to see me. Layla was a hot, little fireball of anger and rage. I couldn't blame her. I fucked her and left her.

That was on me, but that little fireball was the sexiest thing I'd seen in weeks. My pulse began to race, and my heart pumped. I grabbed Layla's face in my hands and crashed my lips to hers. Hers hands pushed hard against my shoulders, but I wasn't letting go. I needed her like I need air. With her, I could breathe again.

Finally, she relented, and her lips moved with mine. She was the match to my gasoline. We were fire. I didn't care that we were standing in front of her dad and brother. I wasn't letting her go this time. When we were both out of breath, I released her. "I love you, Layla. I should have never left you. I love you so much."

She blinked up at me. "Is this for real?"

"It doesn't get any more real than this, kitten. I've been a wreck without you." I brushed my thumb against her cheek.

"I love you too," she whispered.

A slow clap started in the room, James's wife leading it. She smacked him on the chest. "That was hot! How come you don't kiss me like that?"

"I kiss you like that," he defended, holding his arms out.

She rolled her eyes. "Hardly."

Layla's dad cleared his throat. "If you two are good, I think we should all sit down and talk. They have something important to tell you."

I led Layla over to the couch, wrapping my arm around her. "Michael's out of prison."

Her face blanched. She shook her head back and forth in denial. "No, no, no, no…. it's three weeks until his hearing."

"You knew?" Kane asked.

She slowly nodded. "James told me about the letter from Pelican Bay."

Her father looked between his children. "You both knew, and you never said anything?"

"We didn't want to overreact before it was official. There was a chance he would be denied."

"Well, that's just fucking great!" Her dad threw his hands in the air in frustration. "You should have said something!"

Layla's lip began to tremble. I turned her chin toward me. "How long have you known?"

She dropped her head. "Three weeks."

"Why didn't you tell me?"

"It wasn't relevant if you weren't staying. You didn't stay."

Guilt seared through me. I should have stayed and kept her safe. Instead, she'd put herself at risk by coming to Oregon alone.

Zack kneeled before Layla, taking her hands in his. "I know you want to stay with your mom, but it's not safe. You need to come home with us."

Layla stuck out her chin defiantly. "I'm not leaving. I'm not letting him run my life anymore. Would you leave if it was your mom?"

Zack contemplated for only a second. "No," he answered honestly.

"I think you should go, honey. Your mom wouldn't want you to stay if it puts you in danger." Her dad tried to reason with her.

"I'm not leaving until I know mom is okay. I want to tell her face to face that I love her. I need this."

I thought about my own mother. I would give anything to have more time with her, to tell her one last time that I loved her. Time had been stolen from me. I couldn't steal it from Layla.

I looked at Zack and Kane for confirmation. They both gave me a nod. "Then we're not leaving either. We'll make sure you're safe and when your mom wakes up, because she will, I'm taking you home with me."

"To New York?"

"No, *pisoi,* to Michigan. I'm moving there with you."

Her eyes got as big as saucers. "But your father…"

I held a finger to her lips, "We'll talk about it later." I didn't think discussing my father and The Organization would make a very good first impression on Layla's father. Actually, I preferred he never knew about my family.

"You can stay at our house, there's plenty of room," Layla's dad offered.

I stood up and shook his hand. "Thank you, sir. We'll be wherever Layla is."

He sighed. "I'm still not used to the name. She'll always be my Jenna."

Kane stood and interjected. "Sir, if I could say something." As hard-ass as Kane was, he could pull out the charm when necessary.

Layla's dad nodded. "I think you've earned it."

"I don't think the accident and Michael's release were coincidental. I think it was a ploy to get Layla here. Michael's not stable and all of you might be in danger. There's no telling the lengths he'd go to to get to her."

"You think Michael caused the accident?" James asked.

"Yeah, I do," Kane answered. He looked around the room at Layla's family. "The three of us are trained Marines. It's my suggestion that no one go anywhere alone until we know if he was involved or not."

Layla's father looked at his son. "You and Wendy are staying at my house until further notice. I'm not letting that asshole harm another member of my family."

"Is that really necessary?" Wendy asked.

Layla's dad gave her a sympathetic look. "You're carrying my grandchild. It's necessary."

Over the next day, Layla's family took turns going to the house to shower and catch some sleep. Kane or Zack always accompanied them. I wasn't letting Layla out of my sight. She was mine and I'd protect her fiercely.

I still had a lot of making up to do with her, but for now she accepted me being there. I hadn't groveled properly. I needed her to know how much she meant to me and I was in this for the long haul. Nothing was going to come between us.

Not my father.

Not her family.

And certainly not the prick she used to be married to.

I loved her, and I wasn't letting her go this time.

Chapter 40
Layla

By the third day, I was exhausted. For two days, Kane, Zack and Draven followed my family around, never letting us out of their sight.

I stood from my place on the couch where I'd dozed on Draven's lap, and stretched. My bladder was going to explode soon and honestly, I just needed to walk around a bit.

Draven grabbed my hand. He'd been like my shadow. I loved him, but I needed some space and a second to breathe. We still had a lot to talk about. Things were better, but I still didn't trust him completely. He'd already burned me once. Before I let my heart fully commit to him, I needed some reassurances. We were going to talk about things he'd rather not talk about, like his father. I refused to be kept in the dark again. I wouldn't do this halfway. It was all or nothing. No more secrets.

"Where are you going?" he asked.

"I need to stretch and pee. That okay with you?"

Draven stood from the couch. "I'm coming with you."

I pushed him back down. "Seriously? I'm going down the hall to pee. I'd hardly consider the ladies' room a dangerous trek. Do I follow you to pee?"

Kane snickered in the corner. Draven shot him a glare.

Kane held up his hands. "It's the bathroom, dude. I think she'll be all right."

Draven relented. "Fine, but come right back."

"Wouldn't dream of going anywhere else." I patted him on the shoulder. "You know, for a guy who insisted he wasn't a white knight, you sure are taking your duties seriously."

"Still not a knight, but I have something very precious and irreplaceable to protect. I'm a greedy bastard and no one is taking what's mine."

Wendy swooned from her seat in the corner.

I laughed. "Okay, Casanova. You might want to work on your pick-up lines. That sounded a little possessive."

277

"When it comes to you, I am." He smacked me on the ass, not helping my bladder situation. "Go pee and hurry back."

I left the room and headed down the hall, relieved to have a moment to myself. I pushed on the ladies' room door, but it didn't budge. There was a sign hung on the door, *Out of Order*.

Shit! I really had to pee bad. I asked the nurse at the desk where the next closest ladies' room was, before I embarrassed myself. She directed me down a long corridor and around the corner.

I saw the sign and hurried my footsteps. If I didn't get there soon, I was going to have a problem. Once inside, I locked myself in a stall and let go. I couldn't remember the last time peeing had felt so good. I may have even let out a moan.

I finished up and washed my hands. I stared at the woman in the mirror. She looked tired and haggard. The last few days had really taken a toll on me. I hoped my mom woke up soon. I was an awful daughter, but I was anxious to get back to normal where Draven wasn't my bodyguard but my boyfriend, if I was going to take him back, which I hadn't decide yet. There were too many factors to be considered. In my current state, I was in no shape to contemplate them all. There would be time for that later.

I pulled the bathroom door open and almost walked right into the orderly on the other side. "Oh! Excuse me."

"Hello, Jenna."

Ice filled my veins. I knew that voice and it was one I'd tried hard to forget. My eyes darted to his, "Michael?"

"Hello, wife."

I barely registered the tiny prick in my neck before my vision went hazy. Everything shifted out of focus and my body became jelly. Michael caught me and sat me down. I was gliding through the hallway before total darkness consumed me.

Chapter 41
Draven

I picked up my phone and checked the time again. Thirteen minutes. She'd been gone thirteen minutes. It didn't take that long to take a fucking piss.

I stood abruptly. "I'm going to check on her."

Zack looked at me over the magazine he was reading. "Maybe she had to go number two."

I flipped him the bird and headed down the hallway. The ladies' room had an *Out of Order* sign on the door. I went to the nurses' station. The blond clicked away on the computer in front of her.

"Excuse me. Is there another restroom around here? My girlfriend said she was using the bathroom, but I can't find her."

The blond chomped on her gum. "Dark hair? Pretty?"

I smiled. "That's her."

"I sent her down the hall. Take a left when you get to the end."

I rapped my knuckles on the desk. "Thank you."

I headed down the hall at a pace that was more than a walk, but not quite a run. When I found it, I knocked on the door. "Layla?"

There was no answer. My nerves were frayed, so I pushed my way inside. It was empty. There was no sign of her. *Fuck!* Where the hell was she?

I exited the bathroom and something shiny on the floor caught my eye. My heart caught in my throat when I picked up a large silver hoop earring exactly like the ones Layla wore religiously.

I'd gladly take the heat if I was wrong, but my instincts told me I wasn't. That fucker had her!

I raced through the halls and back to her mom's room. Layla's purse and phone sat on the table next to where she had been sitting. She wouldn't go anywhere without them. "She's gone," I growled.

Everyone in the room stood, instantly on alert. "Are you sure?" Kane asked.

I held up her earring. "I found this outside the bathroom. It's hers."

"Fucking hell. We're twins, I should have known she was in trouble. Where would he take her?" James asked frantically.

I held my hands out to calm everyone, including myself. "Think. It has to be somewhere that holds meaning for them."

Layla's dad ran his hand through his graying hair. "One of two places. The gazebo where they got married or the house they lived in. I'm betting on the gazebo. The house was sold in the divorce."

Kane cleared his throat. "Actually, it wasn't. According to city records, he still owns it."

Layla's dad shook his head. "No. I was there when she signed the paperwork."

"Well, something's fishy, because the city says he owns it," Kane declared.

Wendy spoke in a timid voice from her place in the corner. "Should we call the police?"

I snapped my head to her. "Michael's not going back to prison. He's going somewhere far worse, where he can never hurt Layla again."

"Where?" she peeped.

Rage for the man who had taken my woman coursed through my veins. I'd kill him. "Hell." I was no saint. I was going there one day too. When we met, I was going to kill him all over again. I looked forward to it.

James yanked his keys out of his pocket. "We'll check both places."

Wendy grabbed his arm. "No! You're going to be a father, you can't go!"

Zack held out his hand. "You're not coming."

"I sure as hell am. She's my sister, plus you don't know where the gazebo is."

Kane grabbed the keys out of James's hand. "Fine. You're with me."

The four of us raced through the hospital and out to the parking lot. We grabbed our guns from the back of the SUV we'd rented and split up.

Zack punched the address for the house into the GPS. It was twenty-five minutes away. Zack saw me staring at the screen. "We'll make it in fifteen."

We sped from the parking lot and onto the main highway. Traffic slowed to a crawl. I banged my hand on the steering wheel. "You've got to be fucking kidding me!"

Zack tapped into an app on his phone. "Four car accident ahead. Pull onto the fucking shoulder. We're gonna get her."

I yanked the wheel to the right and drove along the shoulder, passing cars at a furious pace.

"Take the next exit," Zack instructed.

We'd already been on the road twenty minutes. The GPS said we had ten more to go until we reached our destination.

Zack's phone rang, and he put it on speaker. Kane's voice filled the cab of the SUV. "Gazebo was a dead end. We're heading your way."

Chapter 42
Layla

My eyes were heavy, my brain was foggy, and my body was sluggish. I struggled to open my eyes. *What the fuck had happened to me?* I wracked my brain to figure it out. All I remembered was coming out of the bathroom and seeing...

"Welcome back, Jenna."

Chills ran down my spine. I tried harder and forced my eyes to focus. The flowered wallpaper I'd planned on replacing, filled my vision. I was in our old bedroom. I was going to kill him. I yanked on my arms, only to be met with resistance. I glanced toward my arms and found them tied to the bedposts. Same for my legs. I was tied to the bed in my bra and panties. I pulled on the restraints to no avail, twisting and turning to try to free myself.

Michael laughed as he walked around the bed. "You're feisty now. So different than the little mouse I married. I find it surprisingly erotic. I always knew there was something more to you than the prude I married."

"Fuck you!" I spat.

"Oh, I plan on it. Hell, if you'd been like this when we were married, I never would have had to fuck those whores from the strip club."

I slowed my breathing. "What do you want, Michael?"

He grasped me around the neck, cutting off my air supply. "What do I want? Hmmm... let's see." He let go of my throat and I gasped for air. He walked his fingers down my body, stopping to tweak my nipple, then moved down my stomach to my panties. "I haven't had sex in five years. Did you know that, Jenna? Five years!" he screamed.

I tried to block him out like I did when he'd become abusive in our marriage. I tried to find my happy place. I searched and searched, but all I could think of was Draven. He was my happy place. It turned out he wasn't a white knight after all. Draven was a dark knight, and I was madly in love with him.

"How long has it been since you've had a cock in that tight little pussy of yours?"

I refused to answer him.

"How long!" he screamed in my face.

My body shook, and my eyes filled with tears. "Go to hell!"

Michael laughed maniacally. "Already been there, sweetheart. You should know. You sent me there."

"You sent yourself there," I retorted. "You tried to kill me."

"And you. Just. Wouldn't. Die." He sneered.

"Why? Why did you hate me so much?" I asked the question that I'd never had an answer to.

"Besides the fact that you were a lousy lay? Honey, I pushed that aside. Good pussy can be bought. I was willing to live with it. I never hated you. I loved you!"

He loved me? He was delusional. You didn't abuse and stab the woman you loved. "You're a sick fuck! You never loved me!"

"Such a sassy mouth! I shouldn't be surprised with the trash you've been hanging out with. My, how your standards have dropped. I guess we've both fallen from grace." He walked his fingers down one of my legs and up the other. He dipped his fingers inside my panties. "I did love you. This was supposed to be mine, yet you shared it with everyone."

I twisted on the bed, trying to move away from his probing hands. My skin was crawling with disgust. If Draven knew what Michael was doing to me, he'd kill him.

"I never cheated on you! You were so high on drugs and whores you couldn't see straight!"

"Fuck you, Jenna! I know what I saw! You were mine! You and me, baby. We're going to be together forever, 'til death do us part. You ARE mine!"

He pulled a knife from the back of his pants and waved it around. Then he ran it up between my breasts and sliced the front of my bra in half. He pushed the cups aside and stared at my pierced nipples. "What have you done? You stupid-ass bitch!" He pulled on the rings enough to arch my back off the mattress. Pain seared through me. He released the rings and flicked my nipples with his forefingers. "You really are a little slut, aren't you?"

"Just do it," I cried. I prepared myself for what I was going to endure at Michael's hands as tears leaked from my eyes.

Rape.

Torture.

Death.

This was it. I wouldn't survive it again.

They say your life flashes before your eyes when you're dying.

That's not true.

Your life flashes before your eyes the moment you know you're going to die, not when you're actually dying. I knew this because it was happening to me now.

I thought of all the things I'd done wrong in my life. The people I'd hurt. The regrets I carried.

After that faded, the good things seeped in. The happiest times of my life; birthday parties with balloons, my first love, cheerleading and football games, graduating from high school, the last man who kissed me. That was what stuck in my head now. The man who flew across the country to protect me and kissed me like I was his forever. I remembered what it felt like to have him inside me. I was holding onto that.

I forgave Draven.

I forgave him for the nasty words he'd spewed at me that last night.

I forgave him for lying to me.

I forgave him for leaving me.

I forgave him for all the things that made him my perfect imperfection.

If I had to do it all over again, I wouldn't change a thing. What Draven and I had was true love. I felt fortunate to have experienced it.

I was done fighting. I wasn't going to give Michael the satisfaction.

I only hoped Draven could forgive me for giving up.

On myself.

On him.

On us.

Chapter 43
Draven

We pulled up in front of the house indicated by the GPS. Zack motioned to the empty driveway. "It doesn't look like anyone's here."

The house looked abandoned. The hedges were overgrown, and weeds sprouted from the cracks in the driveway. The blinds were all closed. I pulled on the door handle. "Let's check it out."

"I'll head around back," Zack said as he sprinted around the side of the house.

I approached the garage. Windows ran along the top of the door. I cupped my hands around my eyes to see inside. "Son of a bitch." Inside the garage was a black sedan. The car that caused her mom's accident was black.

I met Zack along the side of the garage and pulled the knife from my pocket. "There's a black car inside."

"You think it's his?"

I jabbed my knife between the door frame and the lock, "Only one way to find out." I jimmied the door open, and we quickly checked out the car. The entire right side was dented and scraped. "It's his."

My eyes scanned the almost empty garage, landing on a door that most likely led into the house. Zack and I pulled our guns and rushed for the door. We immediately slipped into the roles we'd been trained for as Marines. There was no need for talking, we knew what our job was. This was by far the most important mission I'd ever been on.

Zack's hand reached for the knob. It turned freely, and he nudged it open. I silently crept inside, Zack following. We cleared the main floor then headed for the stairs.

We could hear a man's voice. "You know," he said, "if you hadn't called the cops that night, none of this would have happened."

I froze on the steps and motioned for Zack to wait. I needed to hear this. "All you had to do was be a good wife, but you couldn't even manage that. There was

285

no way I was going to jail for domestic abuse. You left me no choice, Jenna. Killing you was my only option. By the time the police got there, I'd be long gone. I'd have been the mourning husband whose wife had been the victim of a home invasion gone wrong. But you had to fuck that up too. Why couldn't you just die?" There was the unmistakable sound of a slap.

I jerked forward, unable to take it anymore. Zack grasped my arm, holding me back until we had a visual. We crept along the hallway wall to the bedroom.

Layla's voice was weak and held no conviction. "I was a good wife. I'm done fighting, Michael. Whatever you're going to do, just do it."

"We're going to have some fun first. It's been five years."

And that was our cue. I didn't need to hear anymore. Zack and I rushed forward, guns at the ready. Layla was tied to the bed in only her panties. Her eyes were closed, and her face turned to the side. Tears leaked from her eyes.

Michael straddled her body, a knife in his hand. He ran the tip of the blade down her stomach.

I grabbed Michael by the shoulders and threw him to the floor. My Glock pressed to his forehead and my knee jabbed into his balls. Fucker wasn't going anywhere.

Michael's eyes were dilated. His skin was ashen and covered in sweat. An awful stench emanated from him. He was high as a kite. "You!" he sneered.

"Yeah, me. They call me The Raven and I'm your worst fucking nightmare, you piece of shit," I growled. "Big fucking mistake going after my woman." It would have been so easy to put a bullet in his head.

"You're going to kill me over a slut like her?" He laughed hysterically.

I pressed the barrel tighter against his head. "I'd kill *for* her a hundred times over. Don't underestimate me." I was in a world all my own. Rage pulsed through my body. This was the man who had tortured Layla and left her to die. The man who would have done it again. Death was too good for him. My finger twitched with the urge to pull the trigger. My body shook with hatred.

"Draven!" Zack's voice got my attention. "Do you really want Layla to see this? Think, man!"

Layla's sobs echoed in the room. No way did I want her to see Michael's brains splattered across the floor. My pulse slowed the tiniest bit. We would take care of Michael, but not in front of Layla. "Call Kane and let him know we've got him. I'm gonna need his help."

Zack made a quick call. "They're just pulling up. They're on their way."

286

Within seconds, Kane and James rushed through the bedroom door.

Kane's gun replaced mine on Michael's head. "Go to your girl," he ordered. "I got him." Kane was one of the few people who could talk me down. I trusted him implicitly.

I reluctantly backed away and went to Layla. Zack had untied her and had her wrapped in a blanket, so she was covered. Layla hung onto him with a death grip, her eyes wide with fear as she watched the scene play out.

I put my hand under her chin and turned her to face me. "Look at me, *pisoi*. You're safe. He can't hurt you anymore."

Her lip trembled, and she let out another sob. "I'm so sorry."

I hugged her tight to my body. "You have nothing to be sorry for. We're going to handle this."

"What are you going to do to him?" she questioned.

"I don't want you to worry about that. You won't ever have to be afraid of him again. I promise you."

"You fucking slut!" Michael screamed. "This isn't over! YOU ARE MINE!"

Kane kneeled into Michael harder, pinning him to the floor with his body.

I wrapped the blanket tighter around her shoulders, pulled Layla from the bed and walked her over to her brother. "Take her downstairs." I reached down and grabbed Layla's clothes where they had been discarded on the floor and handed them to Zack. "Kane and I will handle this. Get Layla out of here." Zack had too much to risk with a wife and a baby. I didn't want him involved in what we were going to do.

Zack nodded. "Be smart. Make it clean. The guy's a drug addict."

I got his message loud and clear.

Chapter 44
Layla

Zack drove, while I sat in the back of my brother's car with his arms wrapped around me. James was talking to my dad on the phone. All I could think about was what could have happened to me if Draven and Zack hadn't shown up.

I would have been raped again. I would have been tortured. I would have never survived it a second time. "What's going to happen now?"

Zack looked at me through the rearview mirror. "The truth?"

I nodded. "Yes." I was tired of being lied to.

"I'm not sure, but Michael will not be a threat to you anymore. I can promise you that. The less we know the better. Draven's protecting us all by sending us away."

"Is he going to kill Michael?" I needed the truth. I needed to know this was truly over.

Zack focused on the road in front of him. "Do you believe Draven loves you? That he would do anything to keep you safe?"

"Yes."

"Then there's your answer."

I should have been repulsed that Draven was capable of murder, but I wasn't. I was relieved. A calmness washed over me that I hadn't felt in years.

The nightmare was finally over.

I could breathe fully.

I would be able to live a normal life without fear as my shadow. Fear and I had become good friends, but I was happy to let her go.

I was cradled in my dad's arms next to my mom's bed, waiting for Draven to return. It was hours before he and Kane came back to the hospital.

Draven's eyes landed on mine with apprehension. They were filled with something I hadn't seen before. Worry.

He didn't need to worry. I was all his. I rushed forward and crashed into his arms. "You're back!"

Draven wrapped one arm around my waist and pressed my head to his chest with the other, "I told you I'm never leaving you again. I'll always come back to you." He kissed the top of my head.

I looked up into his eyes. "Did you...?" I let my question hang in the air.

He held my face in his hands. "It's over. You're finally free." His response was neither an admission nor a denial, but I saw the answer etched in his eyes.

The next day, Zack and Kane went back to Michigan, but Draven stayed with me. He never left my side.

My dad quickly adopted Draven as his own. It was impossible for him not to revere the man who had saved his only daughter. It felt good to be together as a family, even if it was under the worst of circumstances.

On day two, Michael had been found dead in his home. His face was all over the news. I turned up the volume of the television as the story was reported. *"Michael O'Connor, son of Portland's biggest financial mogul, Sean O'Connor, was found dead today in his home from an apparent drug overdose. Michael O'Connor battled drug addiction for years and was recently released from Pelican Bay State Prison for the attempted murder of his wife, Jenna O'Connor. Five years ago, Jenna O'Connor was stabbed repeatedly and left for dead in their marital home. She subsequently left Portland and her location is currently unknown. In a bizarre twist, Michael O'Connor's car has been identified as the vehicle involved in a hit and run accident that only a week ago left Jenna's mother in a coma."* A photo of my old-self appeared on the screen and I flicked the television off. It wouldn't be long before the media connected the dots and found out where I was.

My dad clasped his hands in his lap and sighed. "Do you need to leave?"

I shook my head. "I'm not letting them chase me away again. If they find out who I am, I'll deal with it. I didn't do anything wrong. I'm staying until mom wakes up."

On day three, my mom woke from her coma. She was confused and remembered very little about the accident. We kept her in the dark about everything that had transpired over the last few days. All she needed to focus on was getting better. The doctors gave her a glowing prognosis. If all went well, she'd be going home at the end of the week.

I spent most of the day holding her hand and talking. She smiled when I introduced Draven to her. She thanked him for being there and making her little girl so happy. Draven kissed my mom on the forehead. "It's been my pleasure."

On day four, the media found me. Honestly, it was a relief. I was tired of hiding. Microphones were shoved in my face and cameras flashed all around me as we exited the hospital. I gave my one and only interview with Draven by my side. When asked how I felt about Michael's death I told the truth. *"Michael was a troubled and mentally-ill man. My heart goes out to his family, but I have no sympathy for the man who tried to kill me. He changed my life forever, but I'm a survivor. I've moved on and I've found someone who truly loves me. I just want to live a normal life."* Then I kissed Draven for all the world to see.

On day five, everything changed when Draven got a call from Kane. He looked stressed when he returned from taking the call. He motioned with his head for me to follow him into the hallway.

"I have to leave."

I grabbed his hands. "What? Why?"

Draven ran a hand over his face, "I have one last job to do for my father. That was the deal I made with him. I don't want to, but it's my only way out of The Organization. After this, he promised we'd talk about me leaving it for good."

My heart sank in my chest. With everything that had gone on here, Draven and I hadn't discussed his father or how it was that he was able to move to Michigan with me. I had chosen to ignore the truth that was in front of me.

The man I loved was still a criminal. If everything he told me before was true, whatever this job entailed was very illegal.

Just like killing Michael.

If I gave him shit about this job, I was a hypocrite. I couldn't have it both ways.

But hopefully it was just one more job. I could swallow that, but I couldn't turn a blind-eye toward it. I needed more details. "Where is the job?"

"Detroit."

I thought back to the day I met Nico, Kane, and Cyrus. I remembered how Draven had urged me to go out with the girls the night before. The pieces began to snap together. They hadn't just stopped by on the way home from Chicago. They'd been there for a job.

"And Kane? He's going too?"

Draven nodded. "Kane, Cyrus, and Nico. All four of us. Andrei will send a few more for back up."

I couldn't and wouldn't send Draven back to Michigan alone. Whatever he was doing was dangerous. "I'm going with you."

"*Pisoi*, you should stay here. Your mom's getting better. Spend time with your family."

"I'm coming. You said so yourself, my mom's getting better. When all this is over, we'll come back. Where you go, I go."

He hugged me to his chest. "I would try to change your mind, but you're a stubborn woman. I promise we'll be back."

"I know we will."

I sat in Draven's old apartment over Forever Inked. Nico, Cyrus, Kane and Draven stood around the kitchen island going over their plan for the job. Draven was obviously the leader of this crew and the way he exerted his authority was a bit of a turn on. My man knew how to take charge of a situation. He had shown me this side of him in Oregon, but I felt like I was getting a sneak peek at what made him tick.

Zack wrapped his arm around my shoulder. "You okay with this?"

He had known all along what Draven's job for his father was. That's why Zack wasn't thrilled when he found out the two of us were together. "Not really, but I don't have much of a choice. This is who he is, I won't try to stop him." I took a deep breath. "What about you? You knew who he really was, yet you let him come here for a month. This doesn't bother you?"

Zack sighed. "I've known Draven since he was nineteen. He joined the Marines to get away from his father. He and I had a lot of long talks after he was injured. Working for his father was never the life he wanted, that's why I taught him the art of tattooing. I tried to give him other options for his life. But once he left the Marines, Andrei sucked him back in. It's the only thing Draven's known since he was fifteen. He may be a criminal, but deep down he's a good guy. I thought bringing him here would give him perspective."

I smiled up at Zack. "You tried to save him, just like you saved Rissa and me."

He shrugged. "I just gave him options. As for you and Rissa, what can I say? I'm a sucker for a pretty face."

"Will you stay with me until Draven gets back? I think I might go crazy sitting here by myself knowing what he's doing."

"Of course. I'll call my mom and have her watch Alexandria, so Rissa can be here too."

"Rissa knows about this?" I asked.

"She's my wife. I tell her everything. No secrets, remember?"

I chuckled. "My whole life has been a secret. It's kind of a new concept for me, but I'm getting used to it."

"You could have trusted me. I'm more than your boss, I'm your friend." Zack looked wounded that I hadn't told him about my past.

I put my hand on his chest. "Don't take it personally. I didn't trust anyone except Brian. There's something about a gay guy that makes a girl spill her guts."

He took my hand in his. "Since I'm definitely not gay, I'll accept your almost apology. But seriously, if you ever need anything you can come to me."

"Thank you. What I need most right now, is you being here. I know what they're doing is dangerous and it makes me nervous. I can't lose him now that he's come back to me."

"You don't have to worry. Draven's a professional. This is what he does and he's damn good at it. That's why Andrei doesn't want him to leave The Organization."

I itched to move closer to Draven. I wanted to hear what they were talking about. I wanted details that were none of my business. But most of all, I wanted him to not go on this job.

Kane rolled up the documents that had been spread out in the kitchen. Nico placed four shot glasses on the counter and Cyrus filled them with vodka. The four men picked up the glasses and clinked them together. *"Noroc!"* they shouted in unison. The shots were tossed back in some type of ritual.

Then the real preparation began. Body armor was strapped in place and guns were loaded. These guys were the real deal. They weren't fucking around. Reality slapped me in the face like the cold-hearted bitch she was, and all I could think to do was tell her to shut the fuck up. I was standing in a room full of criminals, yet I had never felt safer in my life. These were not bad men. They did bad things, but I trusted all of them. If this was what my life was going to be like, I could deal with it.

Every single one of them would lay their life on the line for mine. Of that, I was sure.

I hesitantly left Zack and approached Draven as he was sticking his guns into his double shoulder holster. I pulled him to the side, where we had a small semblance of privacy. "Please promise you'll be safe. Come back to me in one piece."

Draven cupped the side of my face. "I've never had a more important reason to come home. I promise you that I'll do everything I can. This is my life. You're the reason I want to change it. You make me want to be a better person. You deserve more than this."

I placed my hand over his. "I deserve you, no matter what that looks like. Just come home to me."

He kissed my forehead. "I'm coming home to you. Wherever you are, that's where I'll be. You're my home. Then we're going back to your place, so I can have you all to myself."

"I'll be waiting." Sex wasn't the first thing on my mind, his safety was, but I craved time alone with him.

"I love you, *pisoi*. I should have told you before…"

I put my finger over his lips. "I already knew, even if you never said the words. I love you too."

Cyrus approached us hesitantly. "I hate to break up this love fest, but we gotta roll."

I saw the darkness take over Draven's features. He left me in that moment and connected with his brothers. "Let's go."

I watched helplessly as the four of them left the apartment. They were strapped to the hilt and looked as if they were going into battle. Maybe they were. My knowledge of what they were doing was extricated from watching hours of Criminal Minds and Sons of Anarchy. These men were an intoxicating contradiction of good and evil. I found it exciting and scary at the same time.

But all I truly cared about was one man. Draven. I prayed to the God I had given up on years ago, for the man I loved to be returned to me safely.

Chapter 45
Draven

We pulled into the Packard Plant just before midnight. It was like a cement cage. Graffiti covered the crumbling walls and weeds grew through the cracks in the floor. A giant hole in the ceiling gave me a perfect view of the starry night. If I tried hard enough, I could almost imagine standing on the rooftop with Layla instead of in an abandoned warehouse. That's where I wished I was.

Something about this job had me feeling uneasy. Maybe it was the shit that went down the last time we were here. Maybe it was because this could be my last job for Andrei. Or maybe it was that I knew Layla was waiting for me at home.

For the first time in my life, I had someone to go home to. Someone who loved me despite who I was. Someone who accepted my flaws because she wasn't perfect either. But we were perfect for each other.

Match.

Gasoline.

Fire.

My brothers approached me while the rest of our guys finished setting up the lights that would illuminate the warehouse. Kane, Cyrus, Nico and me. Together we were a formidable force. Kane cuffed me on the shoulder. "You good?"

I cracked my neck. "Yeah. I don't trust these fuckers. I want every guy covered. Two on the fucker that put a gun to my head last time. If they try to pull anything, we take them out. All of them."

"Fuck yeah," Cyrus agreed. "They pull that shit again, nobody gets out alive."

I pointed at Nico. "Lock the truck down. Nobody gets close to it until we know everything is cool."

"Got it." Nico took off to secure the truck.

I was twitchy. Off-balance. I needed to pull my head out of my ass. If I showed fear, they would smell it on me. That's not who The Raven was. He was bold, unafraid and unapologetic.

I pounded my fist against my chest to remind myself who I was.

When Nico came back, I took him aside. "I don't want you with us. I want you covering us from a safe distance."

Nico balked. "I'm not a child, Draven. I can carry my weight. I always have."

I let out a sigh. I knew he was going to get defensive. That wasn't a surprise. "You're right. I trust you. It's these fuckers I don't trust. I don't have a good feeling about this, Nico. If shit goes sideways, both of us are not going down. One of us needs to be there for Catina. Our sister needs at least one of us."

Nico reached up and grabbed the back of his neck. "I don't like it, but I agree about Catina." He winked at me. "I've always been her favorite anyway."

"You wish," I huffed.

"We got company," Kane alerted.

I gave Nico a shove. "Go."

He backed away. "It's all gonna be good, brother. No worries."

Kane and Cyrus flanked me with the AKs. "Where'd Nico go?" Cyrus asked.

"It's just the three of us," I growled.

"All righty then. Let's get this show on the road." Kane checked his AK one last time.

Two blacked-out SUVs rolled into the abandoned building, parking adjacent to the front of our vehicles. They blocked our only way out.

"What the fuck?" Cyrus whispered.

The hair on the back of my neck stood on end. Something was not right. Vic had never blocked us like that before.

"Looks like they brought extra man-power tonight." Kane nodded to the SUVs.

Four guys got out of one of the vehicles and stood by our cargo truck. Three more exited the other vehicle and huddled together. At this distance I couldn't tell which one was Vic. They all wore ball caps and dark glasses. It reminded me of a shell game. Mix them up and spin them around and no one could sort them out.

There were seven of them and nine of us. Three of us were running the deal. That left six of our guys to cover the seven of them from our vantage points. It left someone uncovered.

Kane and Cyrus had done the math too. They both readjusted their AKs. I reached behind my back and felt the cold, hard steel of the Glock that sat there. My fingers danced on the grip.

Pulling it out early would be like igniting a bomb. Once I drew my weapon it would cause a chain reaction that couldn't be stopped. Bullets would fly, and I'd be putting my whole team at risk.

I took a deep breath and let go of the Glock. I trusted my guys. We had the advantage. They had no idea there were nine of us. From what they could see, it was just Kane, Cyrus, and me.

Vic led his crew our way. He stood center, flanked by one of his guys on each side. My focus was on the one to the right. I remembered Vic's cocky cousin with the silver tooth who'd tried to stir shit up last time. I trusted Vic as much as I trusted any other criminal. His cousin… even less.

He kept his head down as he approached. This was much different than our last two meetings. Vic had always been cocky with a little swagger. Friendly even. I wasn't getting that vibe.

Something had changed.

And that something wasn't good.

Vic stood before me and lifted his head. The dark glasses and cap shielded most of his face. I wasn't even sure it was him. As a matter of fact, I was fairly certain it wasn't. He pulled the glasses from his face, revealing someone I'd never seen before. "Where the fuck is Vic?" I barked.

"Yeah, Vic's not gonna make it tonight."

Cyrus and Kane stiffened next to me. This was a turn of events we hadn't planned on. As far as I was concerned the deal was off unless Vic was part of it. That was the deal that had been negotiated with Andrei.

I straightened my shoulders and clenched my jaw. "Well, you better get him here or no deal. We'll take our shit and go."

"That's gonna be a little difficult," the mystery man chuckled.

I was getting more pissed by the second. I had a truck full of guns and coke that needed to be unloaded. I didn't have time for bullshit games. "Where the fuck could he be that's more important than this right now. Get his ass on the phone. I want to talk to him. Now!"

The guy wobbled his head back and forth. "No can do, Raven," he said, punctuating my name. "Vic don't get good cell service where he is."

Irritation rolled off me. "And where is that?"

The guy swiped his hand across his nose and chuckled. "Six feet under. Like I said, he ain't gonna make it."

Vic was dead and if my instincts were right, we were standing face to face with the guys who did it. This was going downhill fast. Our best option was to get the hell out of here, but it wasn't going to be as easy as just walking away. They came here for what was in our truck and wouldn't be amenable to leaving without it.

"Deals off! We only deal with Vic. That was the arrangement."

The guy on the left lifted his head and smiled, and a flash of silver gleamed in the dim light. "We got a new deal, motherfucker!"

I knew that smile. It was Vic's piece of shit cousin.

Everything that happened next seemed to move in slow motion, although it transpired in no more than a fraction of a second.

I pulled my Glock.

He aimed his weapon at my chest.

Two guns fired. His and mine.

I felt the impact of a direct hit and stumbled back, tripping on my own feet as I fell to the ground. My head bounced on the concrete. I stared up at the graffiti covered ceiling, the colors swirling in front of my eyes.

The warehouse erupted in gunfire and all hell broke loose.

I could hear running and the spray of bullets all around me. Shouting and screams of agony echoed off the walls. Death hung in the air like a physical force I couldn't escape.

I closed my eyes, trying to block out the chaos and the noise.

It was so loud and then all of a sudden it was silent. The only sound was the rushing of blood in my ears. Layla's voice cut through the fog in my mind, *Come back to me.*

Pain seared in my chest and all I could think about was the woman waiting for me at home. She was safe even if I didn't make it back to her. That was all that mattered. I said my goodbyes to her. *I love you, Layla. Every moment we spent together was worth it. Please forgive me for not coming home.* Everything was fading away.

A sharp slap to my face brought me back. I opened my eyes and a blurry Kane stared down at me. "Wake the fuck up, man!"

"My chest fucking hurts," I whispered.

Kane ripped the front of my shirt open and pulled back my protective vest. "Shit! Fuck, fuck, fuck! Armor piercing bullet. It went through the vest." Kane pulled his shirt up over his head and wedged it between my chest and the armor that was supposed to protect me. He began yelling to our guys to clear the blockade the SUVs had formed in front of our vehicles.

This whole night had turned to shit, and I was going to die here laying in the middle of it.

Next thing I knew, Cyrus and Kane were hauling me to our Escalade. They shoved me in the back and Nico jumped into the driver's seat.

"We gotta get him to a hospital," Cyrus insisted.

"No," I growled. "Hospitals mean cops and cops ask questions. No hospital. Get me back to Layla."

"Draven?" Nico questioned.

"Take me home," I ordered. "Did you get the fuckers?"

"Took them all out. Place looks like gangbanger graveyard. We sent our guys back with the truck. Cargo is still intact." Cyrus answered all my questions before I even asked them.

"It wasn't Vic," I mumbled the obvious.

"Yeah, we know. We were set up." Kane checked my chest. "He's bleeding out. Cyrus, give me your shirt." Kane quickly replaced his wadded up shirt against my chest with another. "Drive faster, Nico. Cyrus, call Zack and let him know our ETA and the situation. Tell him it's bad. We're going to need medical help."

I was fading in and out of consciousness. Kane kept talking to me, but I had no idea what he was saying.

I just wanted to see my girl one last time before I left her for good.

No, no, no, no. This couldn't be happening.

Zack got a call from Cyrus. Draven had been shot. The bullet penetrated his vest and caught him in the chest. They were bringing him here.

All the air left my lungs. It wasn't supposed to be this way. Draven was supposed to come back to me. In one piece. Not on the edge of death.

Everything after that was a blur.

Zack was on the phone with Doc Peterson. He was the doctor who helped Rissa through her pregnancy. Doing emergency house calls in the middle of the night wasn't his forte, but Zack made him an offer he couldn't refuse. He agreed to pay Doc Peterson ten grand for helping Draven.

Zack was off to meet the doctor at his office, which was right down the street, to gather supplies and bring him here. Rissa and I gathered clean towels and changed the sheets on the bed. I wished I had something more to do, but right now it was a waiting game.

Wait until Draven got here.

Wait to see how bad it was.

Wait to see what the doctor could do.

Wait.

Time dragged, while Rissa and I sat helplessly awaiting their arrival. Thank God she was here with me or I would have gone out of my mind. I kept fidgeting and pacing the floor. My mind traveled to the worst possible scenario. "How bad do you think it is?"

"It can't be good," Rissa answered honestly. "Zack's a pretty calm guy and he's not calm right now."

She was right. I dropped my head into my hands and began rubbing my temples. "He has to be okay. It can't end like this. It can't."

"Doc Peterson will do everything he can. Don't give up. We're here for you." Rissa wrapped me in a tight hug. I clung to her and gathered my strength. I was going to need it and so was Draven.

The guys made it back to Forever Inked in record time. Cyrus and Kane carried a semi-conscience Draven up to the apartment and laid him on the bed. Kane stripped his shirt and vest off. A dime-sized hole spurted blood from his chest.

I grabbed a towel and pressed it to the opening. "Keep pressure on it," Kane instructed.

"What the fuck happened?" I shouted. "How did this happen?" I put my full body weight on his chest to try to stop the bleeding.

"It was a shit show. Our client wasn't there. His asshole cousin posed as him and took matters into his own hands. It all happened so quick." Kane ran his bloodied hands through his hair. Kane and Cyrus were covered in Draven's blood, their hands, arms, and clothes.

Nico paced the room. "Where is the goddamn doctor? I have to call Andrei. This is bad, really bad!"

Seconds later Zack and Doc Peterson rushed into the apartment, their arms loaded down with supplies.

I was practically pushed out of the way as the doctor took over. I heard words like *no exit wound* and *critical condition*. Cyrus, who had trained to be an EMT before joining The Organization, assisted in getting an IV started. Morphine was pushed into the drip to take the edge off the pain. From the sounds Draven was making, it wasn't working.

"We have to get the bullet out and it's not going to be pleasant," the doctor said. He ordered Kane and Cyrus to hold Draven down. I watched as Doc Peterson used forceps to dig into the wound in search of the bullet. Draven screamed in agony, as his friends held him down on the bed. Blood gushed from the hole at an alarming rate, dripping down his chest and onto the sheets.

I covered my ears to drown out the screaming, but I could still hear him. Draven was in severe distress and pain. It gutted me.

Nico paced back and forth while talking to Andrei, explaining the situation.

After everything that had happened over the past week, I snapped.

I grabbed the phone out of Nico's hand and addressed Andrei, a man I had never met but hated, nonetheless. "You fucking selfish bastard," I screamed. "All he wanted was out and you couldn't give it to him! Your son is dying, and you don't even give a fuck! I hate you!" I ended the call and threw the phone across the room, as tears poured down my face.

Nico chased after the phone and picked it up. The screen was shattered. "Do you have any idea what you just did?" he asked frustratedly.

"I don't give a fuck! He sends you guys on suicide missions. He doesn't care about you or anyone else except for himself! I hate him! I hate what he stands for!"

Nico growled. "You just made things ten times worse! This isn't a fucking joke!"

I pointed to the bedroom where the man I loved, the strongest man I knew, laid in agony, "You don't think I know that? He's fighting for his life and where is your father? In some cushy office calling the shots? He's a fucking asshole! I hope he burns in hell!"

Nico turned his back on me. "He's *my* brother. You don't get a say in how our family works!"

"I'll have my say! I don't give a fuck what any of you think of me! We were going to be happy, and your father couldn't stand to lose his best soldier! That's fucked up!"

"Well, you may have just put yourself on his radar. Nobody talks to Andrei that way!"

"You think I care about that? All I care about is your brother!"

I forced myself back into the room. The screaming had stopped. Draven's skin was pale, and his breathing was shallow. Doc Peterson held up the bullet in his forceps. "I got it!" Blood was still gushing from the hole in his chest.

I couldn't watch anymore, but I couldn't leave Draven either. I grabbed ahold of his hand and squeezed it tightly, as the doctor worked his magic. Leaning close to Draven's ear, I whispered all the reassurances I could. "I love you, Draven. You're going to make it through this. You're the strongest man I know. You fought for me before, fight for me now. I can't lose you."

His hand lightly squeezed mine back. I took it as a sign that he heard me, and he would keep fighting.

When Doc Peterson finished his work, he snapped off his gloves. "He should have been taken to the hospital."

"We know, but it wasn't an option," Nico answered. "Is he going to be okay?"

Doc Peterson looked at all of us and sucked in his cheeks. "I don't want to know how this happened or the circumstances. He was lucky. The bullet didn't hit any organs or vital arteries. He's going to be in a world of pain, but the morphine is keeping him comfortable for now. He shouldn't be moved for a few days. Bathroom and back, that's it."

"He can stay here," Zack assured the doc. "We'll make sure he gets the proper aftercare."

Doc Peterson let out a sigh. "I'm sure you will. I'll come check on him tomorrow. Call me if anything changes."

Zack walked him out. I could see Rissa and Zack talking with the doctor in the front room.

Kane began cleaning up the room. He picked up the bloodied towels and medical supplies, tossing everything into a black garbage bag. Kane's eyes met mine. "I'm so sorry, Layla. I was supposed to protect him, and I didn't. He knew something was going to go wrong. He felt it before they even showed up."

Kane had nothing to be sorry for. This was their life. They'd worked as a team for years. If Draven trusted them, then so did I. "Don't apologize. You're not responsible, his father is. You brought him back to me and for that I can't thank you enough. He's lucky he has such great friends." I swallowed down the lump in my throat. "What happened to the guy who did this to him? Please tell me he's dead."

"Trust me, we handled it. There are no loose ends."

"That's good. I want them all dead!" I had no idea who I'd turned into, but I didn't hate her. I'd do anything to protect Draven, just like he protected me.

"They are," Kane reassured me. "Layla?"

"Hmmm?"

"You're good for him. I've never seen Draven as happy as he is with you. You're a strong woman. You two are the perfect match."

"Thank you. That means a lot."

He cocked his head to the side. "Did you really tell off Andrei?"

"I did. Someone needed to put him in his place."

Kane chuckled and kissed me on the head. "God, you've got bigger balls than all of us."

"Stay away from my woman," Draven growled hoarsely. "She's mine. I'm not gone yet."

"Wouldn't think of trying to steal her." Kane backed away, leaving us alone in the room for privacy.

"How do you feel?" It was a stupid question, but the only thing I could think of saying.

"Like I got shot. I'm glad you're here."

I brushed my lips gently across his. "There's nowhere else I'd be."

"Get up here with me, woman."

I bit my lip. "I'm not sure that's a good idea."

"It's a perfect idea. I need you. I need to feel your soft body next to mine."

Need. He needed me as much as I needed him. I grabbed a blanket off the chair, cautiously climbed into the bed with Draven and covered us both. I curled into his side and carefully rested my hand on his bare chest. His heart beat strong under my palm. "You scared me," I whispered. "I thought I was going to lose you."

"Scared myself. All I could think about was never seeing you again."

I put my finger over his lips. "Shhh… let's get some sleep."

There was a commotion outside the bedroom door. I lifted my head from the pillow and opened my eyes. Sunlight streamed into the room from the cracks in the blinds.

I put my hand on Draven's chest. He was breathing, and his heart was beating. He was sleeping peacefully. I sent up a thank you to the heavens that he'd made it through the night.

I crept from the bed and into the front room to see what all the noise was about. Kane, Cyrus, and Nico stood in a semi-circle arguing with another man I didn't recognize. He was tall and wide with graying dark hair. His angry face was cut from the same stone as Draven's. He wore a dark suit that only managed to make him look more formidable.

There was only one person he could be… Andrei. Draven's father was here.

He must have sensed my presence because his eyes snapped to mine. His eyebrows creased together as he took me in from head to toe. "Is that her?"

Every head turned my way. I wanted to shrink back into the walls with all the testosterone that was filling the room, but I didn't. I straightened to my full height in front of Draven's door. Five-foot three inches wasn't very intimidating, but if he was going to come after me, I was going to stand tall while he did it.

Nico put a hand on the man's chest. "Andrei?"

He removed his son's hand and stalked my way. He didn't stop until we were inches apart, towering over me much like Draven did. I crossed my arms over my chest in defiance and lifted my chin to stare up at him. "I'm Layla."

Andrei ran his hand over his chin as he inspected me with his familiar amber eyes. It was clear where Draven had gotten his good looks from. When he finally spoke, his voice was gruff with a thick accent. "You're a tiny thing, aren't you?" He didn't expect an answer, so I didn't give him one. "Grown men don't speak to me the way you did."

I straightened up even taller. I refused to cower before this man. "I'm not afraid of you. I've already been to hell and back. I've looked the devil in the eyes. He tried to kill me twice and I came out alive. So, if you think I'm going to bow down before you, you're sadly mistaken."

"Jesus Christ," was mumbled from one of the guys. Cyrus maybe, but I wasn't sure.

Andrei held his hand up to silence them, then crossed his arms over his chest to mirror my stance. "You don't disappoint. You're bold, sassy and full of attitude just as Draven described you. Pretty girl too, except you look like you just rolled out of bed, which given the early hour, I assume you did. I only have one question for you Miss Roberts. Do you love my son?"

I should have been surprised that he knew my last name, but I wasn't. I had a feeling he did his research on everyone he dealt with. He probably even knew my real identity.

"I love him more than anything. There isn't anything I wouldn't do for him, including protect him from you. So, if you came here to drag him back to New York, you're out of luck. He's in no condition to leave and I won't allow it."

Andrei's jaw hardened. "Is that so?"

"It is." I was standing my ground. Andrei was going to have to physically remove me if he wanted to get to Draven.

Andrei's face morphed into amusement. "You remind me a lot of my Rose."

He was referring to Draven's mother. I knew very little about her, except she had died when Draven was only twelve. "Well, she must have been one hell of a woman to put up with you." How any woman could have put up with this man, was a mystery to me. He seemed to get his thrills by intimidating everyone around him. The men in this room included. Although my heart was beating out of my chest, I was certain he wouldn't hurt me with so many witnesses. Or at least I hoped.

"She was. I didn't deserve her, but she was mine nonetheless." There was a touch of sadness in his voice as he remembered his wife. In that moment he seemed almost broken.

I recalled how I felt last night when I thought I was going to lose Draven. It was as if my whole world were crashing down on top of me. I couldn't imagine losing him after years of marriage and three children. Maybe Andrei wasn't always this daunting. Maybe losing his wife had hardened him into who he was today.

I eyed him skeptically. "You must have some redeeming qualities if she loved you." I internally cringed because my words came out bitchier than intended. A twinge of empathy twined its way through my heart for the man who stood before me and had lost his wife. "Would you like to see your son now?"

He nodded. "Very much so."

I led him into the bedroom, and we sat in the chairs facing the bed. Draven was still sleeping. I took his hand in mine and ran my thumb over the top of it. "He was lucky. We almost lost him last night."

"I know," Andrei responded quietly. "He's done. I won't let what happened to his mother happen to him or you. I lost the woman I loved because of this life. If I had to do it over again, I would have stood up to my father, like Draven did to me, and left The Organization. He's a stronger man than I ever was."

"You're going to let him out?"

"Yes. I almost lost my son last night. It was a rude awakening."

I breathed a sigh of relief. "Thank you."

Andrei stared out the window. "I saw your story on the news."

"You did?" Part of me was shocked that the story had traveled all the way to New York, yet another part of me wasn't surprised at all. I'd been missing for five years. The media was desperate to force me out of hiding so they could get their headlines. *Where is she now? What happened to poor Jenna O'Connor?* I was the subject of a vicious media frenzy until they moved on to the next big story.

"Yes. Kane filled me in on your past and the abduction in Oregon. You're a strong woman, Layla Roberts. The kind of woman my son needs."

"I need him too. Draven saved me in more ways than one."

He quit looking out the window and focused back on me. "I think you saved each other."

Draven stirred from his sleep and his eyes fluttered open. He looked between his father and me, fixating on Andrei. "What are you doing here?"

Andrei chuckled. "I came to see you and meet the woman who screamed at me last night on the phone, telling me I was a selfish bastard and she hated me."

Draven's head dropped back, and he sighed. "Layla, tell me you didn't."

I shrugged.

"Oh, she did," his father answered. "And she was right. I was a selfish bastard. Your girl's a fiery thing. I can see why you fell in love with her."

Draven's eyes ping-ponged between the two of us. "So, you two are good?"

"We're more than good. He's really not all that scary."

Andrei quirked an eyebrow at me. "I expect that to stay between us."

Draven laughed, shaking his head. "Only you would say that, *pisoi*. Only you."

Chapter 47
Draven

My father, Kane, Cyrus, and Nico stayed for a week. They took care of my every need, while Layla went back to work. If she wasn't working, she was by my side or playing hostess to the guys. Now they were all gone and the two of us finally had some time alone.

I wasn't sure where we would end up living, but for now the upstairs apartment was the most logical place. Zack and Chase could help me when needed, because going up and down the stairs, was out of the question for at least another week. I was going stir crazy cooped up in the apartment, but I'd survive. I was alive and so was Layla. That was all that mattered.

A little, black kitten hopped up on the bed between Layla and me and started purring. I petted his soft, head, "I can't believe you got a kitten and you named him Raven."

"He found me, and I couldn't not keep him. It seemed like fate at the time. He's cute, don't you think?" she asked.

"He is, but I always wanted a dog. Maybe we can have one of each."

She tapped her finger on her lips. "I'd agree to a dog, but he would need a yard. It wouldn't be fair to keep him in an apartment."

"I was thinking a Rottweiler or a German Shephard. Something that would keep you safe when I'm not home. I'll buy us a house. We're going to need more room when we have kids anyway. I want everything with you, Layla."

"In due time." She kissed me softly. "With everything that's happened, I need time for us to just be. I'm not sure I can handle much more right now. I finally feel free, and I want to revel in that for a while."

After all the years of looking over her shoulder and not trusting, I understood where Layla was coming from. Not being a part of The Organization was going to take some getting used to for me. I wouldn't push her if she wasn't ready.

I twined our fingers together. "I just want to be with you. We can get married or not. I don't need a piece of paper to prove to the world that your mine and I'm yours."

"I'm not saying never, I'm just saying not right now. I need to take some time to figure out who I am again. Going home to Oregon got me thinking."

I perked up. "Do you want to move there to be with your family?" Oregon wasn't exactly on my radar, but I'd do it for her.

She shook her head. "No. Did you want us to move to New York?"

"No. I like the pace of life here and it's safer for you."

"Good, then we should stay here. We can always visit our families, they're only a plane ride away. I like the friends I've made here and this small town. This is my home."

I was confused. "So, what were you thinking about in Oregon?"

She hemmed and hawed, fidgeting nervously.

"Spit it out, *pisoi*."

"Fine. What would you think of me going back to working as an art teacher?"

"You want to give up tattooing?"

She shook her head. "Not completely. The building next door is up for lease. I was thinking about starting my own art studio for kids. You know, help foster creativity, but without all the structure of teaching in a school. I was going to ask Zack to partner with me."

I couldn't stop the smile from spreading across my face. "I think it's a great idea, but you don't need Zack. I could be your partner. I have plenty of capital to invest."

Layla let out a breath of relief. "Really? You'd do that for me?"

I grabbed her face in my hands. "Don't you know, Layla? There isn't anything I wouldn't do for you. You are my life and I love you. I want all your dreams to come true."

Layla got tears in her eyes. "I love you too, but what about your dreams?"

"All my dreams already came true the day I met you."

"So, your name isn't Layla?" Tori asked.

"It is, and it isn't." This was part of the new me. I started letting people into my life, knowing I had nothing to be ashamed of.

I was sitting with the girls at The Locker. Rissa was singing tonight, and the guys were meeting us here soon. Rissa had been holding Kyla and Tori at bay for the last two months. It was time to finally come clean.

"My name was Jenna McNamara and I lived in Oregon. I was an art teacher there and I married a very wealthy man who became abusive." Rissa grabbed my hand and squeezed it for support. "He tried to kill me, by stabbing me multiple times. But I survived, and he went to jail. Before I moved here, I changed my identity and became Layla Roberts. That's my legal name now. The tattoos, the hair, the make-up, that's all Layla. I left Jenna behind and spent the next five years running from the stigma of being an abused wife and staying out of the press."

"And when you went home to be with your mom, they found you?" Kyla asked.

"My ex actually caused the accident that put my mom in the hospital. He'd been released from prison early. It was all a ploy to get me back to Oregon."

"Holy shit!" Tori exclaimed. "This doesn't even seem real. It's like watching something on *Dateline*."

"It was very real," I assured her. "If it weren't for Draven, Kane and Zack, I'd be dead. Draven put the pieces together and they flew out to Oregon. They saved my life."

"What happened to your ex? Is he still looking for you?" Kyla asked.

I shook my head, "No. He won't ever bother me again. That's all I'll say." I wasn't going to tell them about me being kidnapped. Less information was better. I would never implicate Draven in what happened to Michael. I'd take that information to the grave.

Tori leaned in close and whispered, "Did Draven kill him?"

Yes. My man committed murder for me, and I love him for it. "He died of a drug overdose while we were there."

"Hmmm." She looked a little disappointed and a lot suspicious. She wasn't buying the story. "And Draven getting shot? How in the hell did that happen?" Tori probed.

She was trying to connect all the dots of a picture I wasn't willing to reveal. Draven and I still had secrets, but they were ours together.

Rissa saved me from the inquisition. "I think that's enough for tonight." She pointed toward the door. "The guys are here and it's almost time for me to sing."

Draven came up behind me and captured my lips with his. My thighs clenched together trying to stave off my desire for him. We hadn't had sex since the night he was shot. Doctor's orders.

He growled in my ear. "Tonight, *pisoi*. We're not waiting any longer. I need to be inside you."

"Tonight," I agreed. Funny how I'd gone five years without sex and now two months was like torture.

Rissa slapped Draven on the shoulder. "Don't even think about leaving early. You two can wait a little bit longer."

Draven held up his hands in surrender. "Wouldn't think about it."

She scrunched up her nose. "Yes, you would, but I love you anyway. I'm really glad you came back."

"So am I. There's no place I'd rather be." His truth made my heart swell with love.

I sat in The Locker with my man, surrounded by friends, old and new. Brian and Patrick (Brian finally came to his senses), Zack and Rissa, Chase and Becca (guess they were on again) Tyler and Kyla, Chris and Tori, even Zack's mom, Catherine, and Lou joined us.

This felt right. They may not have been related by blood, but every one of them held a special place in my heart. We were a family We supported each other and could depend on each other. That's what families did, and I felt fortunate to have them in my life.

Epilogue
Draven
One Year Later

Layla's new business was up and running, Blooming Artists. The first time I watched Layla teach a group of eight-year-olds how to paint, I knew this was what she was born to do. She was great with the kids, and wicked talented in more than just drawing. Chase, Zack, and I all helped out by teaching occasional classes. Forever Inked and Blooming Artists had partnered to bring art and creativity to the community. It was a phenomenal success.

I took over the day to day operations of Forever Inked, so that Zack could travel with Rissa as she pursued her music career. Layla still tattooed, but her new business was her priority. I was in the process of hiring a new artist for Forever Inked. With Zack traveling and Layla working part-time, we needed another pair of hands.

Layla and I had done our fair share of traveling too. We'd flown to Oregon twice, once just to visit and a second time for the birth of her nephew. We'd also gone to New York, where Layla finally got to meet my sister, Catina. My father had fallen in love with Layla from the first time she screamed at him on the phone. My guess was that he saw a lot of my mother in Layla. My father gave us his blessing and kept asking me when I was going to make an honest woman of her.

Three months ago, Layla had agreed to be my wife. I wasn't a flashy guy. My proposal wasn't romantic. I popped the question while thrusting into her from behind in the shower. As she came around my cock, I blurted, "Marry me, Layla." She'd pressed her head against the tiled wall and said, "Yes, Draven. Yes, I want to marry you." We decided that night to start trying on those grandchildren my father wanted.

Today, everyone had flown in to see us. Today, we were getting married. It was a small ceremony with only our closest friends and family. Layla had chosen the Gardens at Meadowbrook. I waited for my bride with Kane by my side.

311

I pulled on the collar of my tuxedo shirt. Kane slapped my hand away. "Stop. Everything is going to be perfect. The two of you are perfect."

"What if she finally realized I'm not good enough for her?"

Kane chuckled. "That might be true, but she doesn't seem to care. That woman is so in love with you."

The music began to play, and I held my breath. Rissa walked down the aisle first. Layla appeared next, holding onto her dad's arm. She was breathtaking in a simple white gown that brushed the cobblestones beneath her feet.

I'd never seen anything so stunning in my entire life. Layla stepped up to me and her father shook my hand. "You're a good man, Draven. Take care of my baby girl."

"I will. With my life if necessary."

"I know you will," he said. "You already have."

"You look beautiful, *pisoi*."

"You look beautiful too." She winked at me. "Every woman here is jealous of me right now."

Layla and I kept the ceremony simple. We said our vows and pronounced our love for each other. At the end, Layla stretched up on her toes and whispered in my ear. "You're going to be a daddy. I'm pregnant."

I bent her backward and kissed the shit out of her in a way that probably wasn't appropriate for our friends or family to witness. When I finally released her, I shouted, "We're pregnant! We're having a baby!"

Applause erupted around us, complete with hoots and hollers.

I wrapped my arm around Layla's waist and kissed her one more time. We'd gone through hell for each other and if I had to do it all again, I would.

Layla was wrong… true love wasn't all smoke and mirrors.

Fairy tales really existed.

Layla was my princess. She'd never have to save herself again, because somewhere along the line I'd turned into a knight. I'd kill every monster and slay every dragon for her. I'd do anything to protect my woman.

This… was our happily ever after.

Bonus Scenes

Life looks a little different for Layla & Draven in the future.
Join them and the whole crew by scanning the QR code for the
Smoke & Mirrors exclusive Bonus Scenes.

**Want more of the Forever Inked crew? Check out the rest of the
Forever Inked Novels.**

Books 1~ Tattooed Hearts: Tattooed Duet #1 (Zack & Rissa)
Book 2~ Tattooed Souls: Tattooed Duet #2 (Zack & Rissa)
Book 3~ Smoke and Mirrors (Draven & Layla)
Book 4~ Regret and Redemption (Chase & Maggie)
Book 5~ Sin and Salvation (Eli & Roxy)

If you have a few moments, I'd love to hear what you thought of *Smoke &
Mirrors*, by leaving a quick review. I am so grateful for your support and that of
the thousands of books available, you chose to read mine.

Keep reading to get a preview of Chase's sexy story in
Regret and Redemption.

Regret and Redemption

Prologue

We stumbled into his apartment, my arms around his neck and his around my waist. Our lips were locked together in a crushing kiss.

I hadn't been on a real date in forever. Not that this qualified as a date. More like a random hook-up with a hot guy from the bar. I'd never done the one-night-stand thing before, but for once I was breaking my own rules. My carefully planned life could use a little shaking up, even if it was only for one night. If I was lucky, two.

He was cute, his blond hair cut short on the sides, with longer strands on top and a dimple on one side of his smile. He won me over with his boyish charm and sense of humor. He was exactly what I needed. Someone who didn't approach life too seriously, but more with a live-in-the moment attitude.

I threw caution to the wind and followed him home like a lost puppy. The two martinis I had at the bar didn't hurt either. I was barely buzzed, but my body hummed from his lips pressed against mine.

He led me to the couch and brought my body down on top of his. My purse fell carelessly to the floor with a thud.

Chase cupped my face in his hands, "You're so goddamn sexy, Maggie. Do you have any idea how bad I want you?"

I shook my head, my curls brushing the sides of my face. "I don't normally do things like this. I don't want you to think I'm easy. I'm not a slut."

He put a finger to my lips, "Shhhh. We're two consenting adults. This is a no judgement zone." His hands ran up under my blouse along my ribs, his fingers brushing lightly along the underside of my breasts.

I wanted him to touch me. I hadn't been touched in so long. My back arched, pushing my breasts forward, "Please."

"Please what?" he teased.

"Touch me. I need it, Chase. Please, touch me," I begged. My voice sounded desperate to my own ears and I cringed. I didn't want him to know how desperate I actually was.

His fingers gently pulled down the cups of my bra under my blouse and ran over my nipples, "Like this?"

My eyes rolled back, and I let out a breathy sigh, "Yes. Exactly like that." There was no hiding the desperation in my voice now. With the way he caressed me, I couldn't have cared less.

Chase wrapped his arms around me and flipped us over. My back crashed against the soft fabric of his couch. He inched my skirt up higher and leaned his strong, lithe body between my legs. His fingers gripped the back of one thigh and brought it up around his waist as he pushed his hardness against my softness. "Do you feel how bad I want you, Maggie?"

I felt the length of him, behind the rough denim of his jeans, pressed against my silky panties. I was defenseless against him. "Yesss," I hissed. I wanted to forget for one night. I wanted to forget who I was. I wanted to forget my responsibilities. I wanted to live life on the edge. I wanted to indulge in this reckless behavior for one reason…. because tonight I could.

My hands ran through his shaggy hair and pulled his lips back to mine. Our tongues twisted together in a slow, seductive dance. When we pulled apart, Chase placed soft kisses on the corners of my mouth. He continued across my jaw, until he nibbled on my earlobe. The sensation sent shivers down my spine. I arched into him and dropped my head back, giving him access to my neck. Neck kisses were the best, especially when delivered by someone so unbelievably sexy. He didn't disappoint. Soft kisses trailed down the column of my neck and along my collarbone.

I grabbed the hem of his shirt and began yanking it up his body. I needed to see more of him. I wanted to run my hands all over him.

The man kneeling between my legs stripped his shirt up over his head, revealing his sculpted chest and washboard abs, inked in intricate designs I couldn't distinguish in the dim light. My fingers traced every indent and crevice along his torso and down to his hips, where the sexy V disappeared beneath the waistband of his jeans. His body was pure perfection, toned and tatted. My hands rubbed over his rock-hard erection straining against his zipper.

I wanted it inside me.

So bad.

I needed it.

Chase lowered down between my legs and kissed the sensitive skin behind my knee. My lady parts clenched in anticipation of what was to come. And if I had to guess, it would be me in the next few minutes. He peppered kisses along the inside of my thigh, as he pushed my skirt even higher, exposing my red, lace panties.

I thanked the sex gods that I had decided to go racier than my usual cotton ones that filled my drawers. My life was practical and red, lace panties weren't. They were one of the few pairs of sexy underwear I had bought on impulse during my latest shopping spree. Victoria Secret and I weren't good friends, but as Chase rubbed his finger over the lacey panel between my legs, I decided she and I should become better acquainted.

"You're soaked for me."

"Yes, and you're teasing me." I wanted nothing more than for his fingers to inch back the fabric and slip inside my panties. My muscles involuntarily clenched and my hips bucked up at the thought of him inside me.

"Not teasing," he growled. "I'm taking my time with you. We'll both get what we want by the end of the night. That's a promise."

God, this man, the way he touched me with a gentle caress, like I was the most precious thing he'd ever had, was killing me. I needed him. Now.

I leaned forward enough to reach the button on his jeans and pushed the metal through the hole. Chase grabbed my wrists and held them above my head, "Nuh-uh. Wait your turn, Red."

"Red?"

"Yes, Red… red hair, red panties. If I were a betting man, I'd wager your bra was red too."

He wasn't wrong. I gave him a seductive smile, "Guess you'll have to find out for yourself."

He shifted my wrists to one hand and trailed the other down my cleavage. He skillfully flicked the buttons open on my blouse one at a time until all of them were undone, then carefully pulled back the sides of my blouse exposing what was underneath. I heard him suck in a breath, "Your beautiful, Maggie."

I knew exactly what he was seeing. I'd examined myself in the mirror before going out tonight, trying to justify the exorbitant amount of money the lingerie set had cost. The matching bra was solid red lace. My nipples were clearly visible through the fabric and with how turned on I was, they were as hard as diamonds. The look on Chase's face told me the lace was worth every penny I'd spent.

He wasted no more time. Chase pulled back the cup of my bra and sucked my nipple into his mouth. His tongue played with the tip, while his teeth gently nipped at me. His hand slid up my thigh to the place I wanted him to touch me most. His fingers slid inside my panties and pushed into my wet heat.

I threw my head back in ecstasy. Soft moans escaped my lips. I was so close to fully losing control. My body hummed and buzzed from his touch.

Buzzzz. Buzzzz.

I was completely under his spell. "More, Chase. More," I pleaded.

Buzzzz. Buzzzz.

Like a splash of cold water, the spell was broken. I gently pushed Chase back and reached for my purse where it had fallen to the floor.

He sat back on his heels, clearly agitated, "You're kidding me, right?"

Buzzzz. Buzzzz.

I fumbled to unzip my bag and reached for my phone, "I wish I was, but I have to get this." Chase got off the couch and headed for the kitchen as I answered, "Hello?"

"Hi, Maggie. I hate to disturb you. I know you don't get much time to yourself."

"It's fine, Jane. Is Ella all right?" I tried hard to hide the tinge of panic in my voice.

"She's fine, Maggie, but she had a nightmare, and I can't seem to console her. She's asking for you."

I stood from the couch and began straightening my skirt, "I'll be there in fifteen minutes. Let Ella know I'm on my way. Thank you for calling."

I started buttoning my blouse as Chase came back with a beer in his hand, "You're leaving?"

I sighed, "I'm so sorry. I have to. My daughter had her first sleep over tonight, and she had a nightmare. I have to go get her." I carefully slipped my feet back into my heels.

Chase's eyebrows narrowed and one lifted high, "You have a kid?"

I'd seen that look before. This was the part where men bowed out. Having a child was a deal breaker for them, but Ella was the whole deal for me. I straightened my spine. "Yes. A six-year-old little girl. Her name is Ella and she's the light of my life."

He nodded. "Well, you better get going then. I'm disappointed, but I understand." Chase came over and kissed me chastely on the cheek, "You're a good mom. Go get your baby."

It was more than I got from most men. "Thank you. I really am sorry."

He walked me to the door and opened it for me to leave, "I'm sorry, too."

I hurried out to my car and headed off to get Ella. Chase hadn't asked for my phone number, but then again, I really hadn't expected him to. It wasn't a big surprise. I pushed down my disappointment and wiped the stray tear that ran down my cheek.

Damn!

I really liked this one. He was sweet and funny and good-looking. I thought for a brief second there were possibilities. But alas, it was the story of my life.

I pulled into the driveway a couple of blocks from my house and hurried up the walk. The door opened, and Jane was holding my daughter on her hip. Ella wiped the tears from her eyes and lit up when she saw me, "Momma!"

"I'm here, baby." Jane passed Ella to me and she clung to my neck. I took her backpack in my other hand, "Thank you for taking care of her. I'm sorry about this."

Jane waved me off, "It was no problem. The girls can try again another night."

I smiled at her, "Thanks again." I carried Ella down the drive and gently buckled her into her booster seat.

"Mommy?"

"Yes, ladybug?"

"You look pretty. Did you go to a party?"

I smiled at her through the rearview mirror, "Kind of."

She kicked her feet back and forth, "Did they have games and balloons?"

"It wasn't that kind of party."

"What kind of party was it?" My baby girl was wide awake now.

I contemplated what to tell her, "The adult kind. It was actually kind of boring." I hated lying to Ella, but it wasn't the first time, and it certainly wouldn't be the last.

We pulled into our driveway, and I carried Ella to her room. "Can I sleep with you tonight, momma?"

I was hoping to be in Chase's bed tonight, but this was probably better in the long run, "Of course you can." I turned around and carried Ella to my bedroom across the hall. Pulling back the covers, I tucked her in. "Give mommy a minute to change her clothes."

I went to the bathroom and took off my blouse and skirt. My red lace bra and panties mocked me in the mirror, as if they were saying *Better luck next time.* I stripped them off, dropped the lingerie in the hamper and grabbed my nightshirt and sleep shorts from the hook on the back of the door. Nothing sexy about them.

After brushing my teeth, I crawled in next to my baby and tugged her close. She curled into my arms and whispered, "I'm sorry I ruined your party."

I stroked her hair and blinked back my tears, "Oh, sweetheart, you're more important than any party. I'll always be here when you need me."

And that was the truth. As much as I would have liked for my night with Chase to have ended differently, nothing was better than holding my baby girl in my arms.

Chapter 1
Chase

Running a hand through my hair, I sat on the edge of my bed and stared at the clock on the nightstand. The red numbers glared at me. Two twelve a.m. I glanced over my shoulder at the dark hair on the pillow and smooth skin that was barely covered by the sheet.

Becca had been a constant in my bed for over three years. We weren't serious. We were on again and off again. There'd been a lot of other women in my bed over the past several years too. I wasn't naïve enough to think the same wasn't true for Becca, but somehow, we always ended up tangled in the sheets again.

She'd become my regular hook up when I wasn't entertaining another one of God's most gorgeous creations. I had a healthy sexual appetite and so did Becca. We satisfied a need for each other. It was zero work, with all the benefits.

I liked her well enough. She was pretty, had big tits, and fucked like a dream… but that was where it ended. We had amazing sexual chemistry but beyond that we didn't have a lot in common. I knew it was a dead-end relationship.

For more years than I was willing to admit, I'd been okay with that. I wasn't ready for anything serious. But now the steady stream of different women was getting old.

I hadn't always been a manwhore. Once upon a time, I was in a serious, committed relationship. Until I fucked it up. Since then I hadn't trusted myself enough, or any woman, truth be told, to go through the heartbreak again. Casual sex kept my dick happy. My heart had nothing to do with it. But now…

Everyone at the tattoo parlor I worked at had coupled up. The owner, Zack, had gone to New York and brought back the beautiful Rissa. Now they were married with a baby. When Draven started to work at *Forever Inked,* I was glad to have another single guy around. Thought we'd hit the bars and seduce all the lovely ladies. That barely lasted a week before he was all over Layla. Now the two of them were shacked up and would likely be together for the long haul.

Something had to change. The problem was I hadn't found anyone who could keep my attention.

I chuckled to myself. That wasn't entirely true. There was the redhead from a few months ago. She was funny and smart and unbelievable sexy. We hadn't even gotten down to the dirty deed before she left in a flurry.

Chick had a kid and there was no way I was ready for that. I barely functioned as an adult as it was. I had no business being with a woman who had a daughter. It was a no brainer.

Then why couldn't I get her out of my head?

She'd been playing on repeat in my fantasies for months. Maybe it was curiosity, the fact that I'd barely gotten a peek at what she hid under her clothes. Maybe it was her eyes, the way they crinkled when she laughed. Maybe it was the freckles that dusted across her cheeks and the impulse I had to run my finger over them. Maybe it was that she was way out of my league, but she didn't seem to care.

Whatever it was, it didn't really matter. I hadn't even gotten her number. The chances of seeing her again were slim at best, but she was there, just under my skin.

The sheets rustled behind me, "Come back to sleep, Chase."

I laid down and stared at the ceiling, "What are we doing, Becca?"

She curled into my side and threw her arm across my chest, "We *were* sleeping, but I'm ready to fuck again if you are."

I wrapped an arm around her back and sighed, "That's not what I was asking. I mean, where is this relationship going? Are we even in a relationship?"

Becca traced the tattoos on my chest, "Ugh! You said the R word. Do you want us to be?"

I shrugged, "I don't know. Don't you ever get tired of it? The bars? The clubs? The one-night stands that never lead to anything?"

She softly kissed my chest, "Yeah, but isn't that why we have each other? Kind of like a back-up plan?"

"I think I want more," I admitted. "This isn't enough for me."

Becca let out a soft giggle, "Are you breaking up with me?"

I ran my hands through her hair, "It's not personal. We were never really together. You've been with other people and so have I. What we have is…" I was lost for words to describe our non-relationship arrangement.

"Comfortable," she supplied.

"Exactly."

"I get it. I really do. I want to get married one day and have kids. I love you, Chase, but I also know that's not us. What we have is different. More of a friends with benefits situation."

My hands palmed her ass and pulled her astride me, "You're going to make someone really happy someday. It's just not how *our* story ends."

Becca kissed my chest, up my neck, and pressed her lips against mine. "Doesn't mean I want to give this up, but your right. We need to. We need to see what else is out there for us."

"Let's make a deal," I suggested. "We need each other, we'll be there, but no sex. We have to do this cold turkey. Let's give it at least a month. Maybe two."

She nodded her head, "Agreed. But… I need to fuck you one more time. Call it a going away present."

I laughed, "I think I can accommodate you. My dick is going to hate me after this. I should make him happy at least one more time before it becomes official."

"You have a relationship with your dick?"

"He's the only one that really understands me," I chuckled.

Becca and I fucked long and hard into the early hours of the morning. And when the sun came up… we went our separate ways.

Song List on Spotify

Smoke & Mirrors

Rock Your Body~ Justin Timberlake
Thinking Out Loud~ Ed Sheeran
Under Your Scars~ Godsmack
Addicted~ Saving Abel
Dirty Deeds Done Dirt Cheap~ AC/DC
Simple Man~ Shinedown
Count On Me~ Default
Feel Like Makin' Love~ Bad Company
Wild Side~ Motley Crüe
Every Part Of Me~ Godsmack

Listen and Enjoy!

Acknowledgments

Thank you for choosing to read ***Smoke and Mirrors***. After writing the "The Tattooed Duet" and developing the characters of *Forever Inked*, I knew there was more story to be told. Layla quickly became one of my favorites. She was dark, mysterious, and feisty. Only someone like Draven would have been able to handle her. My next story will be about the adorable and lovable Chase.

To my husband~ I could have never done this without your love and support. Thank you for putting up with my endless hours of writing, all the take-out dinners, and my hounding of you to read and offer input. I know I've made you crazy, but you were a trooper through it all! Thank you for believing in me!

To Amy, Kristy, Ari, and Denise~ You girls are the best beta readers anyone could ask for! You've supported my journey and spent endless hours reading and rereading. Your suggestions, critiques, and encouragement helped me in ways you'll never understand. Thank you for listening to my obsession day after day!

To Linda~ Thank you for the endless hours you spent proofreading. After reading the book several times myself, I still missed errors. Your expertise and constructive criticism helped me to make this book so much better. I could never thank you enough for all your help!

To Jill~ You've been a great friend! I came to you with a cut and paste version of what I wanted for this cover. It was literally, scraps of paper glued together. You continually rise to the challenge of my ideas even when you don't always see my vision, and again you came up with something amazing. Thank you for the beautiful cover of ***Smoke and Mirrors***… I absolutely love it!

To my readers~ Thank you for supporting me in this journey. There are thousands of books that you could have chosen to read, and I am honored that you chose mine. Please spread the word and leave a quick review on Amazon, if you have enjoyed this book. Without you, writing would still be a dream.

About the Author

Sabrina Wagner lives in Sterling Heights, Michigan. She writes sweet, sassy, sexy romance novels featuring alpha males and the strong women who challenge them.

Sabrina believes that true friends should be treasured, a woman's strength is forged by the fire of affliction, and everyone deserves a happy ending. She enjoys spending time with her family, walking on the beach, cuddling her kittens, and great books. Sabrina is a hopeless romantic and knows all too well that life is full of twists and turns, but the bumpy road is what leads to our true destination.

Want to be the first to learn book news, updates and more?
Sign up for my Newsletter.

https://www.subscribepage.com/sabrinawagnernewsletter

Want to know about my new releases and upcoming sales?
Stay connected on:

Facebook~Instagram~Twitter~TikTok
Goodreads~BookBub~Amazon

I'd love to hear from you.
Visit my website to connect with me.

www.SabrinaWagnerAuthor.com

www.ingramcontent.com/pod-product-compliance
Lightning Source LLC
Chambersburg PA
CBHW051234260626
47162CB00002B/430